I'll *Be* There

SAMANTHA CHASE

sourcebooks
casablanca

Published by Sourcebooks Casablanca, an imprint of Sourcebooks, Inc.
P.O. Box 4410, Naperville, Illinois 60567-4410
(630) 961-3900
Fax: (630) 961-2168
www.sourcebooks.com

Printed and bound in Canada.
MBP 10 9 8 7 6 5 4 3 2 1

Prologue

"THERE IS NO WAY IN THE WORLD YOU'RE GOING TO convince him to do this. No way."

William knew the last two words were added for emphasis, but it still amazed him that people even tried to doubt him. He relaxed in his soft leather desk chair and looked over at his brother, Robert. They'd done this before. And dealt with situations like this before. And not that long ago, either.

"Robert," he began patiently, "we're running out of options. It's obvious that Zach can't go back to the office yet. His rehab isn't going great, he's not focusing, he's mad at the damn world, and if we don't step in, I'm afraid of what's going to happen."

"Don't you think I'm aware of all this? I'm his father, William! You may think you know more than everyone else, but you don't." Robert Montgomery was wearing a pattern into the carpet as he paced back and forth. "He's fired at least six different home health aides already. He doesn't want anybody there."

William waved a dismissing hand at his brother. "Zach doesn't need a nurse. Not really. He's getting more and more mobile each day. On the days he lets the physical therapist come, he shows progress. We just need to get him focused and off the pity party he's having and maybe offer him some…incentive to stop being difficult."

"Zach's middle name is difficult," Robert said wearily. "Honestly, I don't know what kind of incentive we could throw at him that would make him cooperate."

"We strip him of his position in the company."

Robert looked at his brother as if he'd grown a second head. "Don't you think that's a little harsh?"

"Don't you think his behavior is getting a little old?"

Robert took a seat on the couch in William's office and ran a hand over his face. "Look, I'm all for motivating Zach into getting better. Hell, I didn't think this would ever be an issue. I mean, he's a grown man who loves to travel and do all of those extreme sports things. I thought by now he would be champing at the bit to get back to the things he loves." He sighed. "I don't know what's going on with him and I have to be honest, William, it scares me."

Once again, no one understood the power of William's people-watching skills. "I think Zach's had a blow to his ego. He thought he was invincible and this accident proved he's not. He's human, just like the rest of us."

"So maybe we need to get him to a shrink. Maybe that's the solution."

William shook his head. "If he wouldn't tolerate the home health people, I doubt he'll talk to a shrink."

"Apples and oranges. I think the home health people made Zach feel weak. A shrink could almost be like a peer. Just someone to talk to."

"He won't even talk to Ethan and they've been friends since they were kids." William shook his head again. "I'm telling you, we have our ace in the hole. With this plan, we are guaranteed Zach will not only finish his physical therapy, but he'll come out of this funk and be back in the office in…let's say three months, tops."

Robert chuckled at his brother's confidence. "I don't mean to burst your bubble here, Will, but there is no guarantee. First of all, Zach is stubborn."

"That's a given," William agreed.

"Second of all, I don't think threatening him is going to work. And I'm not sure I'm comfortable with doing it."

William leaned forward and placed his elbows on the desk to look at his brother. "Okay, for the record, we won't really follow through on the threat. If there's one thing we all know about your son, it's that he loves a challenge. If we throw it out there that unless he accepts this help, he'll be stripped of his title and we'll give it to…Ethan…or Summer, he's going to fight back. He's going to want to prove us wrong."

"Okay, say he takes the bait. Aren't you forgetting about one very important aspect of the whole thing?"

"I don't think so," William said confidently. "I've thought of this from every angle."

"Gabriella," Robert said with a cocky smile of his own. "You are going to have to convince Gabriella she has to do this. She may very well tell us to take our offer—or request—and shove it. She's not someone who just takes orders lightly. From the looks of things, she and Zach have been butting heads for a while."

William smiled knowingly. He was well aware of the so-called animosity between his nephew and his nephew's assistant. It was almost amusing to him. "Okay, that's what we'll call it—butting heads."

"Oh no…" Robert sighed as he hung his head.

"What? What's the matter?"

"You're doing it again, aren't you? This isn't so much about Zach getting better as it is you playing matchmaker again."

Why argue it? "It's a twofold plan! Zach gets better *and* gets the girl! It's perfect!"

"Has it ever occurred to you that not everyone wants to be married and…and…"

"Happy?" William provided. "No. No, it hasn't. I think Zach has accomplished so many great things in life and yet he's still not happy. Even before the accident, he was…restless. He prowled around here like a caged animal."

"Why Gabriella? If this all blows up in your face, you'll have cost her a job and Zach an assistant. Have you thought of that?"

"Oh, I'm sure it will come to that before all is said and done, but in the end, everything will be as it should."

Robert eyed his brother warily. "I give it a month. And that's only if—and it's a pretty big if—Gabriella agrees. I'd be willing to bet you a month's worth of profits she turns you down."

The grin on William's face widened. "I'll take your wager. And when I win, I'll put the money into a college fund for their first child!"

Robert couldn't help the laugh that escaped. "You're relentless, you know that, right?"

"I am, but I'm also right. I think Gabriella Martine is the answer to all our prayers where Zach is concerned. Mark my words."

"Oh, I will. But I have one stipulation of my own to make."

William's brows rose. "Really?"

"I want to be the one to approach the both of them about this new…situation."

To William, it sounded as if his brother were trying to steal his thunder. "May I ask why?"

"Zach will be suspicious of you. Gabriella will, too. They both know about your antics in the family. They'll see this flimsy plan for exactly what it is—nothing more than a matchmaking scheme."

"You wound me with your words, Robert," William teased, but held out his hand in agreement. "But you have a deal."

They shook on it, but William knew he was going to have to swoop in and smooth things out. His brother was a great businessman, but had little to no finesse with people. Even his own family.

He watched his brother walk out of the office as he relaxed once again in his chair. They'd meet up later and discuss how Robert would approach both Zach and Gabriella with this new arrangement. William strongly suspected Gabriella would put up token resistance, but it was his nephew who was going to be the bigger challenge.

As for William, all he had to think about was what college he hoped their child was going to attend eventually.

Chapter 1

VERY FEW THINGS THREW GABRIELLA MARTINE FOR A loop, but this conversation had done that and more. "I don't think I understand," she said carefully, her blue eyes wide with confusion.

Robert Montgomery smiled serenely at her from behind his desk at the Montgomerys' corporate headquarters. "Zach isn't getting better," he began. "He's fired every home health worker who's shown up, and most days he refuses to work with the physical therapist. Technically, he should still be in the rehab facility, but he pitched such a fit once he was free of the casts, we made arrangements for him to continue his recovery at home."

Gabriella nodded. While she had done her best to stay out of her boss's way during his recovery while still taking care of things for him in the office, she had kept up with his progress through Ethan Reed, the company vice president and her friend. It had been hard to adjust to Zach being absent for so long, but she also knew it was in his best interest for her to stay away. The last time she had seen him, he all but burst a blood vessel.

Not the most glowing recommendation about their work relationship.

"Mr. Montgomery," she began patiently, "you and I both know my presence seemed to…agitate Zach the last time we were together. I don't think I'm the right person for this particular task. Maybe you could ask my assistant, Carolyn. She's very efficient, and she has a good relationship with Zach."

Shaking his head, Robert folded his hands on his desk and leaned forward. "I don't know the cause of all the animosity between you and my son, and I don't want to know. What I do know is that you run this office like a drill sergeant, and that's exactly what Zach needs right now."

"I...I don't know," she said and began to feel a bit panicked. Gabriella cared about Zach—probably more than she should—but that didn't mean she was willing to work so...closely with him. The office was safe; there were other people around to act as buffers. But working from his home? It would just be the two of them. Looking around the office, she was just about to make an excuse to get up when a knock sounded at the door. Both she and Robert turned to see William walk in.

Gabriella just about collapsed from relief. Out of all the Montgomerys—and there were a lot of them—she felt the most at ease with William. She knew all about his matchmaking hobby, but he'd never even hinted at anything along those lines with her so she felt relatively safe with him.

"I'm so sorry to interrupt, Robert, but you left your cell in my office earlier and Zach's doctor is on the phone."

Robert jumped up, took the phone from William, and quickly excused himself. As soon as he was out the door, William pulled up the chair next to Gabriella. "I didn't expect him to leave." He chuckled. "I thought we'd excuse ourselves to give him some privacy."

Gabriella couldn't help but chuckle with him. Although, if she were being honest, she'd say she was relieved to have Robert out of the room. He was making her uncomfortable with all the talk about working from home with Zach. In a perfect world, she would have been able to jump right on board with the idea. But with the way things had been between the two of them in the months leading up to Zach's disastrous climb, it was impossible.

"So tell me," William said, interrupting her thoughts, "how are things going around here without Zach? I know Ethan is doing the best he can and everyone is pitching in to help out, but it can't be easy without Zach's presence."

"Well, we were kind of fortunate in that we were prepared for Zach to be away for the month he was on the climb. We had done a lot of special scheduling with some of our bigger clients, so nothing new was happening for the length of Zach's scheduled vacation time."

"I hate to say it was fortunate, but I suppose it worked out for the best," William said thoughtfully. "And now? It's been quite a while since the accident, surely everything hasn't been in a holding pattern?"

Gabriella shook her head. "Everyone's been great at stepping up and taking on certain aspects of Zach's work. I know Ethan talks to Zach every day and he's been kept up to date with what's happening, but I don't think he's really…engaging. You know what I mean?"

William nodded. "That's what has us all worried. Ethan can't possibly work with Zach as closely as needed to keep him in the loop on everything as it's happening, and I'm afraid it's the only thing that might help him get out of this funk he's in." He smiled at Gabriella. "Although I think 'funk' is too mild a term. He's out-and-out belligerent and completely detaching himself from everything and everyone."

"That's not good," she murmured. "I don't understand why he's not trying harder to get better. Knowing Zach for as long as I have, I would've thought he'd be beyond anxious to get better and get back to his old self."

"We all did." He sighed. "That's why it's going to be devastating to have to remove him from his position in the company."

"*What?*" Gabriella cried out in disbelief. "What do you mean, remove him? He's the president of the company! He started this office, you can't just…just… replace him!"

"We don't have a choice," William said. "We knew he was going to need time to recuperate and get well, but he's not improving. He's not making any effort, and at the end of the day, we still have a business to run. Obviously, we'd rather run it with Zach at the helm, but he's given us no other option. He doesn't want to work and we need someone who does."

"It's going to kill him, Mr. Montgomery," she said imploringly. "You can't do it. This company means the world to him…"

William shook his head. "I used to think so. Maybe there's something more going on with him, I don't know. All I know is it isn't fair to make Ethan take on so much. He and Summer have put their plans on hold for their engagement party and their vacation to see how their house in North Carolina is coming along, all for Zach's sake. How much longer are they supposed to wait?"

"It hasn't been very long, William. Please. Just…give him a little more time," she begged.

If there was one thing William excelled at, it was his ability to observe people and see where they were really coming from. Everything in his gut was telling him what Gabriella was feeling had way more to do with Zach as a person than Zach as her boss. He just needed to be sure.

"Look at it this way—considering the way things went when you were up in Alaska with Zach, you'll get a reprieve from all the stress and his attitude. We'll move Ethan up to president and possibly make Summer the vice president if she's interested, or maybe start interviewing some of the junior executives. I prefer to promote from within. You won't have a big transition to make, and I'm sure you'll want to stay on and help—for Ethan's sake."

Gabriella felt like she was going to be sick. There was no way she could possibly wrap her head around this. How could this family be so cold? Didn't they understand that Zach had nearly died? He was struggling with his recovery for reasons none of them could understand. "Why aren't you encouraging him rather than preparing to pull the rug out from under him?" she asked William.

"Gabriella, we've talked to Zach until we've exhausted ourselves. He's not interested. He needs help. More help than any of us can give him, and he's refusing outside help as well. Until he can get his head back in the game, our hands are tied."

"What if…" She cleared her throat. "What if I went and worked with him? Like you just said, he needs someone who can keep him up to speed with the day-to-day operations of the company."

William's eyebrows rose at the offer. "Really? You'd do that?"

She nodded. "I'm not saying I'll make any more of a difference than the rest of you have, but I can try."

"Oh, I don't know," William said and nearly had to bite his tongue to keep from smirking. "Robert and I talked about asking you, but I don't think it would be a very good idea."

"Why not? Robert and I were talking about it when you came in."

"You were?"

She nodded again. "I didn't think it was the best idea either, but now that I know what you're planning to do to Zach, I have to at least try."

"Well, that's very commendable of you." He squeezed her hand. "Unfortunately, I don't think it's the right thing for you."

"But…but Robert just said…"

"I know, I know. Like I said, we discussed it, but the more I think about it, the more I think it wouldn't be beneficial to anyone."

Her spine stiffened. "I've worked with Zach for many years. I know how to handle him where work is concerned better than anyone. I've been dealing with his moods and his frustrations, and I've broken up my share of fights between him and Ethan. I think I would be the perfect candidate to go in there and help out."

"It's really sweet of you to offer, but I think I know what's best for my nephew," William said as he patted her hand and stood. He cringed at his own intentionally condescending tone, but knew it would galvanize Gabriella's decision. "Tough love. It's time to stop coddling him. If we take his title away from him and let him stew for a while, he'll eventually break out of his pity party and get his head back in the game."

Gabriella stood and faced the man who she had always thought had a soft spot for his family. "That is the coldest thing I have ever heard!" she said with disgust. "You may be willing to throw in the towel but I'm not. Give me a chance to help him."

"We don't have the time…"

"Just a couple of weeks," she begged. "A month, tops. If I haven't made any kind of impact or if Zach hasn't shown any signs of getting better, then I'll step aside." Her eyes pleaded with him just as much as her words. "Please, William. Let me try to help him."

William shrugged, feigning indifference. "I don't see why you'd even want to bother. From what I saw back in Alaska, Zach didn't seem too thrilled with your being there. How do you think he'll react to you practically moving into his house?"

"I…I'm not moving in," she clarified, taking a step back. "I'm going to be there just as I would on a normal workday and try to establish some sort of routine to help Zach get reacquainted with what's going on in the company."

"It may not be that easy, my dear. You may have to take your cues from Zach."

"Meaning?"

"Meaning you may not end up working an eight-to-five shift. He's supposed to have physical therapy twice a day and you'll have to work around their schedule. His physical recovery is first and foremost."

"Of course," she agreed.

"Are you willing to essentially put your life on hold

to work around a man who might not appreciate the effort?" William hated wording it quite so harshly but he had to know with great certainty that Gabriella knew what she was getting into and was committed to it.

Straightening to her full height, she nodded. "I am. I believe Zach deserves a chance."

William couldn't help the smile that spread across his face as he held out a hand to Gabriella. "Then it looks like we have a deal."

―――⁓―――

"What?!"

"You heard me. I know you banged your head pretty hard when you fell off that mountain, but your hearing is just fine."

Zach Montgomery looked at his father and felt nothing but rage. With everything he had been through, this was what he got? "So you're firing me?"

Robert shrugged, trying to seem indifferent to his son and the situation at hand. "I'm not saying fired, it's an ugly word. I'm just saying with everything you have going on, maybe it's best for you to have one fewer responsibility."

"I made this office what it is!" Zach yelled. "You and Uncle William didn't want to branch out to the West Coast. You were more than happy with things as they were. I took the chance and started things out here, and I've made millions for the company! How can you just forget that?"

"I'm not forgetting anything, Zach," Robert said wearily. "We all know what you did and how hard you've worked. But with things the way they are right now, we need someone at the helm and that's not you. We need a full executive staff. I need to get back home and so does William. Ethan can't handle everything by himself, and you're not willing to pitch in and help out."

"So I'm out and Ethan's in?" he sneered. "Who's going to take Ethan's position?"

"We've approached Summer about it."

That felt like a slap in the face. A couple of months ago, Zach had found the idea of his sister working in his office to be laughable. She was more like a damn camp counselor than a business executive and now— after one massive deal—everyone saw her as vice president material? Maybe he had hit his head harder than he thought. "This is the most ridiculous thing I've ever heard. Summer isn't ready to take on that kind of responsibility. Besides, doesn't she have a wedding to plan or something?"

"She did," Robert said, rising to get himself something to drink. There was no way he could look at his son with a straight face right now. The look of sheer shock on Zach's face at the mention of Summer stepping up into his league had been comical. He almost felt bad about it.

"What do you mean, *did*? Has something happened? Is Summer all right?"

"Yes. But you had an accident, Ethan's been running the company, and Summer has really stepped up. They haven't had time to talk about wedding plans or see how their house back east is coming along. You are their main concern right now. Their lives are on hold right now *for you*. I know Summer was hoping to have her engagement party back home, but she won't plan anything until you're better. She wants you there. We all do."

It didn't sound like it to Zach. It sounded like everyone was gearing up to wash their hands of him. "That's not fair, Dad," he said. "There's no timeline for when I'll be better, or even *if* I'll be better."

"There would be if you'd do the therapy your doctor prescribed and make an attempt to help yourself."

"You don't think I've tried?" he snapped. "Do you have any idea how freaking much I've been through already? They tell me I'll walk again and be just like I was before, but I don't see it happening. I still have spells where I can't feel a damn thing, and when I *can* feel, it hurts like hell! So until you've had your entire body broken, don't think you can preach to me about hurrying up and healing. It's not that easy!"

"And when have you ever walked away from a challenge?" Robert yelled back. "For crying out loud, Zach, ever since you were a kid, you've refused to be told you couldn't do something. You challenged your mother and me in every aspect of your damn life! But now? Now that it really counts and it's really hard, you're going to sit here and quit?"

"I'm not quitting! I'm just—"

"I think," Robert interrupted, "that up until now, everything in your life has come easily to you. You were a naturally gifted athlete. School and academics required very little effort from you. Starting this office and getting it off the ground, while challenging, still seemed to go according to your plans. But this injury? This accident? It's messed with your psyche. When you didn't see immediate results, you gave up and quit. It's not happening fast enough for you. Well, news flash, son, no one said it was going to."

"You have no idea how painful it is," Zach said through clenched teeth.

"I don't," Robert said solemnly, "and I hate more than anything that you have to go through it. If I could, Zach, I'd do it for you; I'd take the pain on myself. But I can't. This is something only you can do. You have to decide if you're going to fight for it or if you're going to let it defeat you."

Zach stared defiantly at his father for a solid minute. Seriously, did the old man have any idea the level of pain he was dealing with? Did he even know most days it took a Herculean effort just to get out of bed and move to a chair? Or the humiliation of needing someone to help him get dressed or take a shower?

"I think by taking the responsibility of the company off your shoulders, you can put your focus on your physical therapy," Robert said to break the silence.

"This branch of Montgomerys is *mine*," he growled. "I know Ethan was there with me from the beginning and I appreciate everything he's doing, but you have no right to put him in charge. It wasn't your decision to make."

"What choice did I have?" Robert said with frustration. "We can keep going around and around in circles on this. You can't have your cake and eat it too, Zach! You don't want to work and there's a company to run! Enough now! The decision is made!"

Zach tried to stand up but his legs wouldn't support him and he fell right back down into his seat. He yelled out a curse of frustration and wanted to scream at the unfairness of it all. Thankfully, his father hadn't rushed to his side to offer his help. He hated when people took pity on him and fussed around him like he was an invalid. Taking a minute to calm himself down, he flexed his legs until he had the feeling back in them completely before turning his attention back to his father.

"Please," he said as calmly as possible. "I'm really trying to find a balance here. I don't like asking for help. I don't like *needing* help. What…what can I do to prove to you that I'm trying?"

Robert's expression remained neutral. "For starters, you have to stop firing the therapists. You're not going to get better on your own, Zach. You need them."

"But they're idiots."

"No, they're not. They know what they're doing and you need to listen to them. In this situation, they're the experts, not you."

"Fine," he murmured. "So if I do the therapy you'll back off firing me?"

"No."

"What the *hell*, Dad? I just asked you what I had to do and you said therapy and I agreed!"

"That's only part of it."

If Zach had been able to stand, he would have, and thrown the old man physically out the door. This whole situation was enough to make him crazy and he was tired of being played with. "Lay it all out then, for crying out loud!"

"You do the therapy twice a day as prescribed…"

"Done."

"And you get back to work."

"I'm not going to the office," Zach said quickly, nearly panicking. There was no way he wanted anyone to see him like this. The only way he'd go back to the office was when he was fully recovered and back to the way he'd been before the accident. "It's too soon," he finally said. "I don't need an audience watching me every time I fall on my face or can't get up from my seat."

"I didn't ask you to come back to the office. The office will come to you."

"Excuse me?"

"You're going to get back into the habit of a normal workday—with the exception of taking time to do your therapy sessions. But every day you are going to have some responsibilities pertaining to the business to take care of. You're going to get up to date on new projects and new clients, and then we'll start easing you back via phone conferences."

If Zach had felt defeated before, it was nothing to how he was feeling now. "Why are you doing this?" he asked, his voice cracking on the last word. "Why can't you let me do this at my own pace?"

"Because you're not doing it," Robert said sadly as he came and sat down beside his eldest child. "I can't sit back and watch you give up on life, Zach. You're asking too much. You need to face what's happened to you and move ahead with your life. Sitting here and hiding away from the world is not the way to do it."

"You don't know…"

Robert chuckled. "I do. None of us are guaranteed a perfect life. Some of those patients we saw when you were in the hospital up in Alaska have no hope of recovery. You do. Don't you think those people would give everything to be in your shoes? To know they'd be able to walk again?"

Zach couldn't help but remember the other climbers who had fallen with him, and his gut clenched. One of them was permanently paralyzed from the waist down and the other had lost his leg from the knee down. He knew what his father was saying was right and yet...

"What if I can't?"

"Can't what?"

"Walk again."

Everything in Robert softened. It was the first time Zach had even hinted at his fears. Reaching out, he took his son's hand in his. "You and I both know you will. You've already made great progress."

Zach shook his head. "Some days I can do it, and other days my legs won't cooperate." He looked up at his father. "I don't know what I'll do if I can't walk again, Dad."

"You'll never have to find out," Robert said quietly, "because I have every faith in you that you're going to overcome this and be just fine."

Emotions were clogging Zach's throat so he nodded. They sat quietly, side by side, for several minutes before Zach reached over and hugged his father. "I wish I had your confidence on this one."

"Just give it time. Let me call the therapist in. Let's get started right now."

Panic nearly choked him. It was one thing to say he was going to try with the therapy; it was quite another to be forced to jump right in. "Dad," he began, "you just said to give it time and then you immediately start to cram it down my throat. You need to back off a bit and let me handle this. I'll do the therapy, but you have to... just let me do this my way."

Robert jumped up, the peace from a moment ago completely gone. "No. I knew you agreed too easily to this. You're going to keep jerking me around and I'm like a damn dog chasing his tail. It's now or never, Zach. I'm not waiting on you anymore. Either you're serious about this or you're not."

"I *am* serious, but you show up here today and drop this…this…bombshell on me and just expect everything to change and be all right? Well, it doesn't work that way!" he yelled.

"You have to at least try!" Robert said with frustration. "You have to put in a damn effort! How do you expect to be the man you were before the accident if you don't try? Isn't that your goal? To be that guy?"

"You know what?" Zach said and forced himself to his feet. His crutches were next to the couch and he quickly reached out and planted his hands onto the grips so he could face his father. "No matter how much you push or yell or threaten, I'm not going to be that man ever again. It doesn't matter how much I want it, it doesn't matter how much you want it. Look at me!" he yelled. "I'm never going to climb any more mountains or jump out of any more airplanes. I'm reliant on a pair of damn crutches to get me wherever I need to go and that is not the person I want to be! Maybe it would have been better if the damn fall had killed me!"

Robert was momentarily stunned silent. This was the most they had talked about any of this, and he'd had no idea his son was struggling quite so much. It all made sense and it just frustrated him even more that there wasn't anything he could do to make Zach feel his life wasn't over.

"I'll do your damn therapy and I'll work from home and play at absentee-president, but you don't get to tell me how or where or when. And if that's too much to ask of you then you can have the damn company," he spat. "There isn't a quick fix here and shame on you for trying to force one."

A sigh escaped before Robert could stop it. "I'm not trying to force a quick fix. I'm trying to encourage you not to give up. You're my son and I love you, and I can't bear to sit back any longer and watch you just shut yourself off from everything anymore! I can't do it!"

"Then do us both a favor and don't. Go back east. You've done all you can here and honestly, I don't want to deal with you anymore. I want you to go." His words were calm and did nothing to convey the anger, the hurt, the anxiety coursing through him. He was shaking so hard he feared the crutches wouldn't hold him up but he still held on for dear life.

"Zach…"

"No, I'm serious. We're done."

Robert stood rooted to the spot and stared at his son. Five minutes ago he thought they were fine, and now… He hung his head in defeat. "It doesn't matter to me if you climb a mountain or jump out of a plane, Zach. It never did. Those weren't conditions on my love for you. I just want you to be happy." With that, he grabbed his jacket and walked out.

Zach waited until he heard his father's car pull away before reaching for the glass he'd left sitting on the coffee table and heaving it at the wall. The glass shattering wasn't nearly satisfying enough.

Nothing would ever be enough again.

He slowly made his way across the room and sat down on the chair he had positioned to look out over the West Hills. It was peaceful, it was quiet. It was the only thing he'd had to look at for a long time. Who knew, when he'd purchased this house because of the spectacular view, he'd come to despise it so much? The home that used to be his haven was now a prison.

One of his own making.

Zach growled as he shifted to get more comfortable in the chair. It wasn't as if he had asked to fall off a mountain, but he never expected the recovery process to be like this. The doctors and therapists had all offered him serious pain meds but he had refused them all. He wasn't a weak man and he had a high tolerance for pain.

Or at least he thought he had.

With every little sign of improvement came more pain than Zach thought a human being could bear. He might not even mind it if he felt he was getting somewhere. But along with regaining feeling and range of motion came the uncertainty. There were days he had feeling in all the places he was supposed to, but other days? Nothing. The doctors felt it was nerve related but Zach wasn't so sure. Unfortunately, until the rest of the swelling went down—and God, when was *that* going to happen?—he was stuck.

Everyone thought they understood what he was going through. They felt they had all the answers on what he needed. They didn't know shit. He wouldn't wish this kind of hell on his worst enemy. Turning his head, Zach glanced at the bar in the corner of the room. Two shelves lined with some of the finest liquor money could buy.

Just a drink or two and he might not even care if he felt anything below the waist or not.

He cursed. It was no better than dealing with the pain meds and he knew he was stronger than that.

His head fell back against the chair as he closed his eyes. It wasn't that he didn't want to get better or that he didn't want to go back to work. He wanted all of those things, but he wanted them *now*. Patience had never been his strong suit and with the way things were going now, it would be a freaking lifetime before he felt comfortable being around other people again.

It was bad enough his family had to see him like this. And Ethan. There was no way he wanted to be on display like some sort of curiosity in a freak show. He was the strong one, the athletic one. He knew that was how people thought of him and saw him.

There was no way he wanted anyone to look at him with pity…or worse. It would just about kill him to have people look at him and think how the mighty had fallen. Zach hoped that even if someone dared to think it, they'd have the decency to keep it to themselves. Unfortunately, he *had* been a cocky son of a bitch, and there were undoubtedly hordes of people who would love to see him in this weakened state.

Dammit.

The sun was going down and he'd survived another day. Barely. The housekeeper who came in once a week, Mrs. Graham, also cooked for him and put everything in containers that could be easily microwaved. If it wasn't for her, he'd certainly starve. His stomach growled and he frowned. He was alone and he was hungry, so what was he waiting for?

Someone to share it with might be nice.

Where the hell had *that* thought come from? For far too long he'd had people fluttering around him helping him do even the most basic of functions. It annoyed him. He was a man who enjoyed his independence and his solitude. When he'd started to become mobile, the round-the-clock help was the first thing to go.

Slowly he rose and grabbed the crutches and made his way to the kitchen. He pulled out a meatloaf dinner from the refrigerator, placed it in the microwave, and waited.

Pathetic.

Once upon a time he'd have been dining at some fantastic five-star restaurant with a beautiful woman on his arm or with a group of friends—laughing and having a great time. Now look. His reflection in the microwave glass stared back at him. If any of his friends saw him now, they'd be horrified at his appearance—he looked like a cross between a yeti and Grizzly Adams. Not a look he was ever fond of, and yet lately he had been too depressed to even care. No doubt the first thing one of them would say is "Damn, what the hell happened to you?"

And that would almost be as bad as the pity.

Thank God no one was going to be seeing him any time soon to have the opportunity to make such a statement.

Chapter 2

"OH MY GOD. WHAT HAPPENED TO YOU?"

Those were the first words Gabriella uttered when she stepped into Zach's home the next day. He was covered in sweat and his hand was bleeding, and she noticed a harried-looking woman wearing scrubs scurrying around collecting things.

Zach glared at her and then at the woman in scrubs. "Good riddance!" he yelled as she walked out the door. It slammed behind her but Zach's eyes were instantly back on Gabriella's. "What the hell are you doing here?"

Ignoring his harsh tone, she took off her jacket, hung it on the coatrack by the front door, and placed her leather satchel on the floor beside it. "What did you do to your hand?"

"None of your damn business," he snarled. "You might as well take your coat off the hook because you're not staying."

She rolled her eyes. The man had a nerve. She may be on the thin side but she was tall, and right now—in her less-than-sensible heels—she was eye to eye with him. He looked like hell, like he hadn't slept in weeks, and he was barely steady on his crutches. If she were a mean girl, she'd remind him how she could probably knock him over with a feather.

Or a stiletto.

"The coat stays where it is," she replied coolly.

Stepping around him, she inspected the open floor plan of his home. Her gaze was instantly drawn to the wall of windows at the back of the house with the view of the mountains. She decided to keep her admiration of nature to herself for the time being.

She kept her back to him for two reasons: One, she needed a moment to compose herself. In all the years she had worked for Zach, Gabriella had never seen him look like this—ragged, almost dirty. Defeated. And two, she was waiting him out to see how long it was going to take for him to start throwing his weight around and verbally assaulting her in an attempt to make her leave.

She had the patience of a saint and nothing else to do today. The ball was in his court.

Her confidence was boosted by the mere fact that they had played this game dozens of times in the office, and she was always able to outwait him. Zach hated silence just as much as he hated when people didn't do exactly what he wanted when he wanted it.

She'd missed this. And him.

"You can stand there all day and think you've got the upper hand, but I've got news for you," he taunted. "Your presence here means nothing and once you're done admiring Mother Nature, you're gone. Got it?"

A small smile played at her lips. So cocky. So arrogant. Careful to put on a neutral expression, she turned to him. "You've got an awful lot of attitude for a guy on the verge of losing his job."

Zach paled. *Crap.* He should have known. His old man had mentioned he needed to get back on a regular work schedule, and that would include working with Gabriella. "I guess you haven't talked to my father lately," he said, doing his best to sound calm even though his hand was throbbing and his legs were shaking from standing for too long, but damn, there was no way he was going to collapse in front of her.

"I actually just got off the phone with him," she replied smoothly. "Maybe *you* haven't talked to your father lately."

His gaze narrowed. "Who's covering you at the office?"

"Carolyn."

"She can't possibly handle the workload. You need to go back there. Send Bob or Darren or…anyone else. Or better yet, don't send anyone. Just keep me up to date via email. We can do a phone conference or Skype or something."

Gabriella shook her head. "Nice try, Ace. The only way this is going to work is if you actually buckle down and start to work. I'll be here with you Monday through Friday, eight to five, just like we did at the office. You'll do your therapy twice a day and while you're doing that, I'll take my lunch break or do any personal errands you may need so I'm out of the way."

"Not gonna happen, Gabby." He made sure to use the nickname he knew she hated and almost smiled when her spine stiffened and her face pinched. *Direct hit.*

Stepping away from the windows, Gabriella slowly walked toward him, her eyes never leaving his. She didn't stop until she was practically toe to toe with him. "I know you think if you push the right buttons I'll just up and leave. Well, I hate to break it to you, but it's not going to work. I've worked beside you for too long to fall for any of this name-calling crap, so do us both a favor and skip it." She paused and tried to gauge his reaction. Other than a light tic in his jaw, his expression never changed. "I don't mind working for Ethan, but I'd rather work for you. God only knows why." The last was mumbled under her breath as she stepped away from him and walked toward the kitchen.

"What do you think you're doing?" he yelled after her.

"Clearly you've hurt yourself and you're bleeding all over your crutches and the floor." A minute later she was beside him, putting a wet cloth in his hand and then crouching down with another to clean up the floor. When she stood back up, she met his angry stare. "Now are you going to tell me what you did to your hand?"

Zach carefully made his way over to the sofa and sat down. Without looking at Gabriella, he cleaned up his hand first. When he was done, he leaned back and sighed. "The therapist was pissing me off. We were in the middle of a session and I asked for a drink. She said I had to finish my reps before we could break. I asked her again and she declined." He shrugged. "Finally I walked around her, grabbed a glass of juice, downed it, and told her to leave. She yelled, I yelled, and when she refused to go, I punched a hole in the wall."

So many things whirled through Gabriella's mind. First, what kind of therapist deprived a patient of something to drink? Was Robert aware of the kind of people who were being sent here to help his son? Next was how it must have damaged Zach's pride to lose his cool in front of anyone.

She looked him over and was again taken aback by his appearance—and the fact that he wasn't as far along in his recovery as she had thought. While Ethan and Summer had kept her up to date with Zach's progress, she had thought maybe they were overexaggerating. Clearly they weren't. It was going to make her time with him even more challenging. If he was this angry and had let himself get to this low point, he was going to be nothing short of a nightmare to work with.

Even more so than he usually was.

Oh joy.

"Do you need a Band-Aid?" she asked quietly.

Zach shook his head and sighed again loudly. "Look, I don't need you here playing nurse to me, too. I've got enough of that going on with my family and the steady stream of therapists coming through here. I just need to be left alone for a little while. So go back to the office, where you're actually needed, and let me handle things from here."

A slow smile crossed Gabriella's face. "I'm not going back to the office, Zach, so deal with it. I've got a ton of files in my satchel for us to start going over. We have a phone conference on Friday with the MacMillan people, and it's important for you to be on the line with them."

"Ethan can handle it."

"Actually, he can't."

"Why the hell not? I thought he was some sort of superhero who was ready to jump into my damn spot!"

"Ethan doesn't want your job, Zach. No one does. But if you're not going to do it, then your father is going to make Ethan do it."

"Doesn't answer my question about why he can't handle the call," Zach said defiantly.

Gabriella rolled her eyes and sighed. "He's flying up to Seattle Friday morning to meet with potential clients and then he and Summer are heading back east for the weekend to check on construction of their house."

"So tell him to work in the phone conference. He can do it from a plane."

"Do you even hear yourself? Why can't you do it? There's nothing wrong with your head or your voice. You were the one who set up the contract with MacMillan so it only makes sense for you to talk to him." She stood and walked over to her satchel. "I've got their file here with me. They're interested in branching out…"

"Tell it to Ethan."

Throwing her head back, she growled with frustration. Taking a deep breath, she stomped over to Zach and flung the file in his lap. "No."

Zach glared up at her before flinging the file onto the floor. He crossed his arms over his chest and winced when he tried to close his injured hand into a fist.

Gabriella mimicked his pose. "Did that make you feel better? Because I have to tell you, you're acting like a child." She bent down and picked up the papers and placed them on the coffee table. "Let me ask you something. Do you want Ethan to take over as president?"

"Hell no! This is still my company!" he roared.

"Then act like it!" she yelled back. "There is no reason why you can't be doing the work you did before the accident! You don't want to come into the office? Fine. Don't. But at least be man enough to work from home and save your sorry ass!"

"How dare—" Zach went to stand up and immediately fell back onto the sofa. He cursed violently before turning his anger and frustration back at Gabriella. "Don't try to fool yourself, Gabs," he snarled. "You're not doing this out of the goodness of your own heart. Chances are if I'm gone, you'll soon follow because Ethan will bring his assistant with him and then you'll be out of a job. So save me from your *martyr* routine."

Wow. Everything inside of her simply clenched. How had they gotten to this place? How had they gone from a team who worked so well together to this openly hostile mess? She wanted to cry out that she was concerned about him—and only him. If he wasn't at Montgomerys, she didn't want to be there either. He was the one person who had challenged her, someone whom she had looked up to at one time.

Even when he was acting like a complete jerk.

Her jaw clenched and tears threatened; she willed them not to fall. It wasn't often Gabriella let it show when someone hurt her—she'd learned a long time ago that people often mistook being hurt for weakness. Swallowing the lump in her throat, she did her best to hide the fact that his words had hit their mark and pasted a serene smile on her face.

"Think what you want," she said calmly, smoothly, "but you're wrong. Believe it or not, Zach, I'm not concerned about my job. I already know if Ethan took over as president and brought his assistant with him, I'd have another job within the company waiting for me. Your uncle assured me of that."

Zach's eyes went wide. "What? When?" he demanded. "When did William offer you a job?"

"Back in Alaska. We talked about my job experience and how working as an assistant was really a little beneath my skills. He offered to find me a more challenging position, but I turned him down." Feeling somewhat satisfied that he was momentarily speechless, she took a seat in a chair opposite him. "So you see, my future is fine. No worries in sight. You, however, should be thankful you have someone on your side who is willing to make sure you're not displaced."

"Don't go getting all smug," he grumbled. "I hate this. The whole damn thing. It's not right."

"I agree," she said. "I told both your father and your uncle that I was not on board with their decision to remove you from your position—even temporarily. It's why I'm here, Zach. I'm not the enemy. Let me help you with this. We'll work just as we always have. We'll just be working from here rather than the office." She paused and waited for him to argue with her.

And waited.

And waited.

Zach raked a hand through his hair and was clearly agitated by the situation. He shifted and met her gaze. "We'll try it. For today. If by the end of the day I find it's not working, then that's it. No arguments. No snarky comments. You leave and let me handle things my way."

"No."

He cursed. "What is it with you lately?" he demanded. "Why is this so damn important to you? Why would you want to be here when you're clearly not wanted?"

Gabriella had seen the changes in Zach—particularly in the months before the accident—but in all that time he'd managed to be all bark and no bite. The man sitting opposite her now was just…mean. Deep down she questioned whether he was on to something. What kind of person would purposely open herself up to endless hours of verbal abuse?

Leaning forward in her seat, she made sure her eyes never left his. "You know what? I think you need me. You may not want to admit it and you sure as hell don't like it, but the fact is the only person helping you keep your title, your company, is *me*. You're not used to needing someone to lean on and you don't like it. Just like I'm sure you don't like having to use those crutches to walk. The situation sucks all the way around, Zach, but it is what it is. You can either accept my help and keep what is rightfully yours, or I can walk out of here and you'll have to sit here and stew, knowing Ethan and Summer are calling the shots at the company you started. It's your choice."

"Some choice," he mumbled before reaching for his crutches and standing up.

He was halfway across the room before Gabriella called out to him. "That's it? You're not going to say anything? You're just going to walk away?" She stood up but refused to go after him. "Answer me, damn it!"

Zach stopped but didn't turn around. "I'm going to take a shower. You can set up everything that needs to be looked at. I'll be about thirty minutes." Then he walked into his bedroom and slammed the door.

Zach looked at his reflection in the bathroom mirror and frowned. When had his life gotten so damn out of control? There had been a time when people actually listened to him—damn near hung on his every word!—and now it seemed like everyone felt they had the right to run his life for him.

You've got no one to blame but yourself.

It wasn't the first time that thought had occurred to him. Especially in the last couple of weeks. He knew he was being difficult and was giving everyone a hard time just to prove he could, but it didn't seem to be working in his favor at all.

And now he had Gabriella in his house.

He hung his head and sighed. Clearly he must have died on that mountain because this was hell. There was no other way to describe it. At the office, he was able to keep some distance between the two of them—all it took was closing his office door. But here in his house? There was no place to hide.

Dammit.

Cursing, he looked up at his reflection again. He looked like hell, which was perfect considering he felt like it too. As much as he hated to admit it, both his father and Gabriella were right. He needed to get out of this… whatever it was you'd call it. He was spiraling out of control and if he didn't take some drastic measures soon, Zach was certain he'd never make it all the way back.

It just sucked that he needed help to get moving in the right direction.

And that the help came in the curvy and infuriating form of Gabriella Martine.

Making his way over to the shower, Zach turned the water on and stripped. When the steam began filling the room, he stepped under the spray and moaned with pleasure. The pressure of the water along with the heat went a long way toward making him feel almost human again. That feeling was rare these days. Even though he knew this feeling was waiting for him, some days it was just too damn hard to actually do it.

On the days he made it through a full physical therapy session, taking a hot shower was a necessity. Besides the relief it offered his muscles, the exertion he put forth made him sweat like he'd run a marathon. On the days he half-assed the exercises and threw the therapist out? Well, those days he tended to just sit and wallow in self-pity and sweat.

Something had to change. And soon. The sooner he got a grip on the situation and put enough effort in to prove to his father he was getting better, the sooner he could relax about his position in the company and send Gabriella back to the office where she belonged.

He scrubbed his hair and took a moment to put his irritation with her aside and just…think about her. The day she had walked into his office to interview for the position of his executive assistant, his jaw had practically hit the floor. She was stunning. Normally, he would have counted that against her—there was no way in hell he was going to get caught up in chasing his assistant around a desk or get romantically involved with her—but everything about Gabriella had been perfect. The qualifications listed on her résumé were written almost as if he had put them there himself.

So he'd pushed aside his initial attraction to her and promised himself he was a professional who could control himself around a beautiful woman.

Unfortunately, the longer she worked with him, the more the attraction grew. She was smart and witty, and she anticipated his every thought and need and made his life run seamlessly. She made him laugh and she made him think. He found himself seeking her out when he was on the fence about a client or a contract—sometimes even before he talked to Ethan. Zach knew he could take Gabriella with him to any kind of business function and she would be an asset.

More than once he'd had to stare down the men who lingered with her a little too long in hopes of catching her eye.

She was his…without really being his.

It was a hell of a situation.

Without even realizing it, he had put her up on a pedestal. She was the woman he measured all other women against—and she was a tough act to follow. More than one girlfriend had voiced her annoyance with being constantly compared to Gabriella.

Strange thing about those pedestals: sometimes what you see isn't the real thing. He found that out—quite by accident—and it had forever changed their relationship. No, that wasn't right. The universe seemed to be against him and it was a series of events that had changed everything.

Before, Zach loved interacting with his employees. He enjoyed having a fun work environment—basketball hoops in the conference rooms, Ping-Pong table and dartboard in the break room. He was a cool boss, and everyone loved him.

Or so he'd thought.

Then one Friday night, Zach had left to meet some friends for drinks. Halfway to the bar, he realized he had forgotten his cell phone back at the office. With a quick U-turn, he was back and riding the elevator up to the eleventh floor. Most of the lights were out but he knew a couple of the guys were working late to finalize a contract.

Zach had run to his office, grabbed his phone, and was going to simply head back out, but he wanted to check in and see how his team was doing with finishing up negotiations. He was only a few feet away from the door when he realized they weren't talking about the contract or the client.

They were talking about him.

And Gabriella.

"C'mon," someone said. "You don't think he takes her on those business trips because of her dictation skills, do you?" Everyone laughed. "He's a lucky SOB, I can tell you that. It's amazing he gets any work done."

"Who says he does?" another chimed in. "I mean, we're all here at seven o'clock on a Friday night and he's supposedly out with friends." He snorted with disbelief. "I'd bet good money that by now he's got Gabriella's librarian bun all undone and is stripping her out of that crisp skirt and blouse."

"Oh, but leave on the shoes," another called out with a wolf whistle. "He better let her leave on those shoes. I mean...damn! The woman certainly rocks the hooker heels!" More whistles.

"I'm not going to lie to you," the first guy said. "I actually Googled her."

"Seriously? What did you find? Were there pictures?"

Everyone laughed. "A few, but they were all pretty tame." Then he lowered his voice. "The thing is, before she came here to Montgomerys, it seems Gabriella worked for another high-profile company and rumor has it she was having an affair with a coworker—who just happened to be a top executive and married."

"No way! Dude, how did you find out? It wouldn't have been on Google. She's not that newsworthy."

"I know a guy who works for the company she used to. I asked some questions. And the most intriguing part?"

"What?"

"The guy she was screwing ended up getting divorced and marrying Gabriella's sister!"

"You're kidding me! That's so twisted!"

"So you think she came here prowling for another executive to mess around with?"

More laughter. "She wouldn't have had to look so hard. You see the way Zach practically drools over her whenever they're together. Hell, can you blame him? Like I said, he's a lucky SOB."

Zach had heard enough. He'd stormed into the room like a raging lunatic and threatened each and every one of them with their jobs if he ever heard them talk like that about Gabriella—or him—ever again. He'd put them all on probation and stormed out.

The idea of meeting with his friends no longer appealed to him. He'd gone home and stewed the entire night, guilt eating him up alive. He'd had no idea people looked at them that way. The thought of Gabriella walking into that environment on Monday nearly made him ill. So the next morning he'd called and asked if he could talk to her. In person.

Looking back, he'd heard something in her tone that should have clued him in to the fact that it wasn't a good time. She'd hesitated, made excuses, but in his typical fashion, he had only thought about what he wanted to do, and had gone over to her place. When he'd arrived he'd found she wasn't alone. Her family was in town— her parents, her sister, and her brother-in-law.

If only he had kept his mouth shut and just apologized

and went on his way. But no. He'd stayed and pulled her aside to give her a heads-up on what he had heard. Unfortunately, he wasn't the only one prone to eavesdropping and soon her whole family had joined in. Zach had expected them to come down hard on him and defend Gabriella.

But they hadn't.

Instead they had all shared knowing smirks and commented on how some things never changed. Gabriella's cheeks were flushed but she never met his gaze.

"What is wrong with you?" Zach had said when he confronted her about it. "Why are you letting them say these things to you? They're wrong! The guys at the office are wrong. Dammit, why aren't you defending yourself?"

And then, clear as day, his ever-efficient assistant stunned the hell out of him. "It won't make any difference. Trust me."

"Why?"

"You can't argue the truth," her sister had said, practically salivating at the chance to tell the story. "I mean, she had an affair with her boss. Her *married* boss." Then she shrugged and linked arms with her husband, that damn smirk still on her face. "We had hoped she'd learned her lesson but…guess not." And then she'd laughed. They all had.

Except for him and Gabriella.

He'd looked at her, his eyes imploring her to deny it, to defend herself in some way. But she didn't. All she'd managed was to look at him and say, "You need to go."

"I'm not leaving you here like this. I won't just walk out while these…*people* are talking to you this way!"

"They're my family," she'd stated quietly.

Zach came from a big family and had an even bigger extended family, and not once in his entire life had he witnessed any of his relatives behaving like this. It didn't matter if it was one of his brothers or his sister or any one of his cousins, if someone was being...*bullied* like Gabriella was? He would go to the mat defending them.

"Gabriella, please," he'd begged, leaning in toward her. "Tell them to leave. You don't need to stand here and take this abuse in your own home. Please."

"I want *you* to leave, Zach," she'd finally said. "You're my boss, nothing more. The longer you stay here creating a scene, the worse you're making it."

He'd wanted to stay. He'd wanted to argue with her and then take her with him—anywhere to get her away from these horrible people. "Let's go someplace and talk. I need to understand..."

"If you'd like my resignation, I completely understand," she had said flatly as she stared down at her shoes.

He hadn't wanted her resignation. Zach had known he wasn't going to get anywhere with her now. So he'd left. It had never settled well with him that he'd left her there, but she had made her position clear. And from that moment on, things had never been the same. In a span of twenty-four hours, everything Zach thought he knew about his life had changed.

His employees thought of him as a sleazebag who banged his assistant.

And Gabriella—who behaved chaste as a nun around him—had had an affair with a married man.

And he, Zach, meant nothing to her.

The rest of that weekend was a blur. When they had returned to the office on Monday morning, he had pretty much left his good-guy persona at the bottom of a bottle of Jack Daniel's. The Ping-Pong table was removed, as were the dartboards and basketball hoops. He ran the office like a militant dictator and no one dared to argue with him.

To this day, he and Gabriella never talked about or even made reference to what he had witnessed at her home or how it had changed everything.

Except the fact that he was still attracted to her. Maybe even more now than ever before.

Shit.

The water in the shower was beginning to cool and Zach shut it off and reached for a towel. His left leg was starting to shake, and he knew he would need to sit down as soon as possible and stay off of it for as long as he could today. This was how it started—he pushed himself, then the trembling began, then the tingling, and then…nothing. He'd go numb. Normally, he recognized the signs and always managed to throw out whoever was here. There had only been one therapist to witness it.

He was fired the next day.

Gabriella wasn't an idiot. She was going to know something was wrong. If he could manage to get dressed quickly and get out to the living room and onto the couch, though, he might have a chance of distracting her. There was undoubtedly enough work to keep them going well into the evening.

It was his only hope. He had to keep her attention on whatever work she'd brought with her and nothing else. She'd think he was just being a hard-ass.

She'd never know the truth about what was really going on.

About everything.

Ever.

———~~~———

Hours later Gabriella stood and stretched. They had gone through every file she had brought with her. Twice. She was beginning to see signs of the old Zach emerging but there was still…something. She couldn't put her finger on it but she knew him too well. There was something wrong and she couldn't tell if it was work related or if he wasn't feeling well.

Or if he was still miffed about her being there.

Every once in a while he would grimace, but he hadn't gotten up once since he came out of his bedroom after his shower. In the back of her mind, Gabriella knew it probably had something to do with him just not being as mobile as he used to be—something she wasn't used to just yet.

But she had a feeling it was something more.

"Are you feeling all right?" she finally asked.

Zach's head shot up and he glared at her. "Of course. Why?"

"Well, you just seem a little…tense. You keep making a face. Are you in pain?"

"I fell off a damn mountain, Gabriella. What do you think?"

"If you need to rest…we can take a break. We kind of worked through lunch. Would you like me to pick something up or do you have something here I can get for you?"

"I'm not an invalid!" he snapped. "If I want something to eat, I can damn well get it for myself." He paused and took a deep breath through his nose and released it before speaking to her again. "Why don't you go get something for yourself?"

"Are you sure?" she asked. "I can bring you back a sandwich if you'd like."

"Yeah. Sure. Whatever." He waved her off and then picked up a file and began reading.

Gabriella knew the drill. She was being dismissed. "Okay. Well, I'll probably be gone for about an hour. Are there any errands you need me to run? Groceries? Post office?"

"I'm good," he said without looking up at her.

"Okay," she said again. "I'll...I'll see you in a little bit." She turned and walked to the front door and grabbed her jacket and purse. With one last look over her shoulder to make sure Zach was all right, she opened the door and left.

Once she had driven away, she pulled out her phone and called the office in hopes of getting one of the elder Montgomerys on the line. She couldn't help but smile when William's voice greeted her.

"How's the patient today?" he asked.

"It's been a rough morning."

William laughed. "I'm sure. Did he do his therapy yet today?"

"He fired the therapist who was here this morning. No one else has shown up since. I'm not sure if the agency he's using is even going to send anyone else. Maybe you or Robert can check on it and let me know?"

"I'll get on it. So…how does Zach seem to you? You haven't seen him since Alaska. What are your thoughts?"

"He's…he's very angry," she began cautiously. "I don't think I was expecting… I mean, he's always a little short with me, but this was…different."

William paused. "Are you sure you're all right being there? He's not being abusive, is he?"

She chuckled. "No more than usual. He just… Well, he… I've never seen him…"

"He looks like he's been living in the woods," William finished for her and sighed. "I've known that boy his entire life and he had the natural ability to look good no matter what he was doing. This thing he's doing now? The unshaven, mountain man look? It's a little shocking."

"Exactly," Gabriella said, relieved she wasn't alone in her thoughts. "I wanted to say something to him about it, but…"

"You didn't want to poke the bear?"

Gabriella broke out in a fit of laughter. "Oh, that's awful and yet hysterical," she said when she finally caught her breath. "Thank you."

"For what?" William asked, chuckling along with her.

"I needed to laugh. It's been a tense morning and I really needed a little break."

"Call me anytime, my dear!"

They hung up a few minutes later with William promising to let her know when a new therapist would be arriving, and Gabriella both dreaded and looked forward to the information. She knew Zach was going to be ticked off at having yet another therapist show up, but she also knew it was part of her job to make sure he actually did the therapy.

And it was bound to open the door to another round of arguments.

She nearly groaned at the thought of it.

A little over an hour later, she returned to Zach's with lunch for them both. She let herself in and found Zach sitting in the same spot on the sofa with his head resting on the cushions and his eyes closed. For a minute, she could only stare. He looked so relaxed and peaceful—so different from how he had looked all morning. True, he still needed a good shave and a haircut, but at least he wasn't glaring or snarling. Baby steps.

She walked into the living room and moved some of the files around so she could put the bag of food down on the coffee table. Her intention had been to step around Zach but her heel caught on the carpet and she tripped over his ankles and ended up falling on the couch beside him. "Oh God! Oh, Zach, I'm sorry! Did I hurt you?"

Zach lazily opened his eyes as if just realizing she was there. "That was fast," he said as he sat up and stretched.

Gabriella looked at him as if he were crazy.

"What?" he asked. "What's the matter?"

"I pretty much kicked you in the ankle as I tripped," she said. "I was afraid I hurt you."

Zach's eyes darkened as he looked at her and then his expression went neutral. "No. You didn't hurt me. No big deal." He leaned forward and looked in the bag from his perch on the sofa.

Something wasn't right. Gabriella noticed he was positioned awkwardly. His legs hadn't moved and he was only using his body from the waist up. Come to think of it, he hadn't really moved his legs since he came out from his shower. She stood quickly and began taking their food out—making sure everything Zach needed was easily within his reach. He thanked her without looking at her before taking his sandwich and relaxing back on the sofa to eat it.

Troubled, she excused herself and walked to the kitchen to get them drinks. Her stomach was in knots and she didn't know if she should say anything to him. It had been a solid five minutes of him not barking at her and she didn't want to do anything to rock the boat.

But she had to.

"Um...Zach?" she called out from the kitchen.

"Yeah?"

"Where do you keep the glasses?"

He was silent for a minute. "Top cabinet next to the refrigerator."

The kitchen was huge and there were cabinets on either side of the appliance. "Left side or right?"

"Take your pick."

She rolled her eyes. "Oh, okay. Got 'em." Looking around the kitchen, she tried to think of something else. "Do you want ice for your drink?"

"No."

Good going, she mocked herself. How was putting ice in a glass going to get him to come into the kitchen when she was already there? She needed something bigger, something guaranteed to make him join her. "Oh my God!" she yelled. "I think I just saw a mouse! Zach! Come here!"

Silence.

"Is that a hole in the corner? Oh...no! Do you think there's more than one?"

Silence.

Oh, for the love of it. "Do you have the number for an exterminator anywhere?" When Zach still didn't respond, she walked back into the living room and glared at him. He was happily eating his sandwich as if she hadn't been making a spectacle of herself. She stormed over and put their drinks on the table and sat down.

"Do you feel better now?" He looked at her blandly as he picked up a potato chip.

"What do you mean?" Deciding two could play at this game, she took her salad out and began picking through it.

"What was all that nonsense about?" Zach nodded toward the kitchen. "I don't have mice and you've been here before so you know where the glasses are. What gives?"

She could just play dumb or she could confront him. Looking up, she saw he wasn't quite glaring, but his expression was definitely leaning toward hostile. Putting her salad down, she sighed. "Okay, fine. I wanted to you to walk into the kitchen."

"Why?"

"You haven't gotten up in hours and when I came back and kicked you—accidentally—you didn't even notice. What's going on?"

With a muttered curse, Zach threw his sandwich on the coffee table and raked a hand through his hair. "We need to get back to work."

Gabriella knew she had been right. She also knew pushing him to talk about it—particularly right now— wouldn't accomplish anything. So with a sigh of her own, she pulled out her tablet to get to her agenda. "All right, where were we?"

For the next four hours, they worked. Gabriella went over each file—for a third time for good measure—and then they addressed reassigning some clients Zach had worked with exclusively to some of the junior executives. The time flew by because, when they weren't snapping at one another, they worked beautifully together. Gabriella anticipated Zach's needs where the company was concerned and as they went down the client list, she already had a fairly solid idea of who was going to be assigned to whom.

It was after six when they finally called it quits and she noted they had accomplished everything she had hoped for on their first day. "Tomorrow I'll bring some contracts with me that legal wants you to look over, as well as the résumés for the new division you started planning before the climb. Ethan mentioned the possibility of needing a bigger office space, but I've talked to the building manager and found out there are some offices available on the floor below us. I'll bring the plans for them with me."

"No, you won't."

Not this again. She sighed loudly. "Why not?"

"Look, you came here today, did your time, and I plan on telling my father how much we accomplished. But I don't want someone in my house all day—a subject I thought everyone would have picked up on by now. I mean, I've fired everyone who's been here. I don't like it and I don't want it. Go back to the office tomorrow—where you belong—and we'll work remotely."

"Seriously, we're back to this again?" she snapped with frustration. "You don't get it, do you? You're not calling the shots on this one, Zach. It's out of your hands! Hell, it's out of my hands! We got so much done today, why would you want to sabotage it?"

"I'm not sabotaging anything!" he yelled back. "I said I'd do the work and I did! And I can do everything you mentioned—by myself—here at home. I don't need you here! I don't want you here!"

"Well, too damn bad! Look, I don't know what your problem is with me, but…"

"As you pointed out earlier, there's nothing wrong with my mind. I still hold the majority vote in this company and if anyone wants to argue the point with me, they are more than welcome to." He leaned forward. "Do I make myself clear?"

Gabriella felt ill. This hatred he had for her had festered into something so ugly, so intense, she had no idea what to do about it. All she knew was that she needed to leave. Now. She was either going to get sick or cry.

Neither was something she wanted to do in front of Zach Montgomery.

"Very well," she said primly as she rose and began collecting the files she'd brought with her. "Do you want me to leave these or can I take them back to the office?"

"Take them. We went over them enough times."

All she did was nod. Once all the folders were collected and in her satchel, she cleared up their lunch debris and loaded their glasses into the dishwasher—her head held high the entire time. There was no way she was going to let him see how his words had devastated her.

When she walked back into the living room, she saw him maneuvering his legs around with a pained look on his face. The need to help him even though he had been so cruel was nearly overwhelming. But she didn't. He would only hate her more for it. It still didn't stop her heart from going out to him.

Holding her ground, she walked across the room, picked up her satchel, and then went to the door and put on her coat. She took her time and did her best to look calm. When she could no longer find an excuse to linger and was certain Zach wasn't going to say anything else to her, Gabriella walked out the door and closed it behind her with as much dignity as she could muster.

Zach sat on the sofa and waited. He listened for the sound of her car door and the start of her engine and then even longer to make sure she was gone. When he was certain he was well and truly alone, he tried to flex and stretch his legs. Over the last hour the feeling had started to return and he was anxious to try and get up and move around.

Grabbing his crutches, he stood. It felt good to be off the sofa. He looked around the room and saw it was spotless. It was almost as if Gabriella had never been there at all.

But she had.

And she'd seen more than he wanted her—or anyone—to see.

And that's why she had to go. There was no way he could handle having her see him like this every day. Although, if he were honest, he would admit he had enjoyed the workday. He missed going into the office. Doing what they had done today reminded him he had a life to live and a company to run, and no one was going to take that away from him.

All he needed was to be left to do it his own way. With no help from his father and certainly no help from Gabriella Martine.

Chapter 3

ZACH HAD HIS MORNING CUP OF COFFEE HALFWAY TO his lips when he heard someone coming into the house. *What the hell?* He knew his father and Ethan both had a key, but neither had mentioned they were going to stop by. Sitting on the sofa with his laptop in front of him, he almost dropped the hot liquid on the keyboard when Gabriella walked through the door.

She slammed it shut and stormed across the room and straight for him, her hand held out in front of her to try to stop him from saying a word. "You know what?" she began. "We have worked together far too long for things to keep going the way they did yesterday. I came here and did you a favor, and what did I get for my effort? Nothing. I can understand your anger and frustration at your situation and with your recovery, but none of that is my fault. Now, you can either grow up and face the fact that no matter what kind of weight you think you wield within the company, it's not going to be enough to save your ass and you need to accept my help. Or…I can leave and go and congratulate Ethan on his new position." She crossed her arms over her chest, cocked a hip, and waited.

Zach studied Gabriella for a long moment. Her jet black hair was pulled back in her standard librarian bun, her navy blue pencil skirt hugged her like a second skin, and the plain white blouse—which should have been no big deal—was straining across her breasts with one button looking ready to pop. Maybe it was the way she was standing, but Zach had been studying his assistant's figure for too many years.

He felt himself starting to sweat.

Focus, dammit! Doing his best to remain impassive, Zach tried to ignore her outburst even though he was secretly impressed she had the bravado to show up at his house this morning, right on time. Efficient as usual.

He could go one of two ways here. Option one was throwing something across the room, demanding she leave, making a big show of calling his father and Ethan and anyone else he could get on the phone to have her fired.

Even he was growing bored with option one. Sure, it had felt good the first half dozen times he threw some-one out of the house—or hospital room—because he actually felt like he could still *do* something, but he was beginning to notice a pattern about himself and he didn't like it. Plus, he was beginning to run out of glasses.

Narrowing his eyes slightly, he decided to go about this a little differently while gaining the same results. Option two was skip the temper tantrum and let Gabriella gain a sense of peace and confidence. Then he'd start his campaign to get her to think leaving was her own idea. She'd never see it coming.

Leaning back on the sofa, he crossed his own arms as he continued to stare at her. Actually, he wasn't even sure why he was pushing her so hard. It wasn't that he hated Gabriella—far from it. But she had made her feelings clear a long time ago. Since then, he had done his best to limit the amount of time they spent alone,

one on one. He feared she'd see right through him, and Zach didn't want to come off as being vulnerable. So he needed her to leave. It was his only line of defense. She really was doing him a favor and trying to help him, but it just seemed to irritate him more. How could she possibly want to help him when he'd been such a bastard? Seriously, why didn't she quit?

Her crystal-blue eyes watched him warily and Zach knew his silence was starting to unnerve her. She usually won the battle of wills when it came down to a situation like this. He'd let her have it—her victory—for now.

"Did you bring the plans for the office space that's available?" he asked pleasantly.

Gabriella's jaw nearly hit the floor. "Uh…yes." She quickly put her satchel down on the chair and slipped her jacket off.

Zach watched her hurry across the room to hang it up before she was standing beside him with a folder in her hands that held the floor plans he requested. "How many offices are we talking about? Are they individual spaces or is it a large area like we have with many office spaces inside?"

She opened the folder and pulled out the floor plan. "It's an open space—about a third of what we have on the eleventh floor—but it can be effectively utilized for what you need for the expansion." Sitting down beside him, she pointed to some of the highlights. "It would be self-contained for the sole purpose of this new division. There's a reception area, a waiting area, four private offices, a conference room, and then enough square footage in the main area for ten desks and cubicles." She pulled out a second sheet. "I spoke to the management company and was able to negotiate a better price for the rent. They were looking for a thousand dollars more per month, but I reminded them of our time in the building, our position in the community, and how Montgomerys has worked to maintain the grounds even though we don't own the whole building."

He wasn't surprised by her efficiency and the fact that she took the initiative to negotiate on behalf of the company, but he was impressed. "You've been busy. This all sounds great. Would you be able to do a walk-through and take video of the space so I can see it? It's hard to get a real feel for the space when all I have is a blueprint to use as a reference."

"I don't think it will be a problem." She sounded relieved.

"Is it in good shape? Will we need to do any renovations?"

Gabriella shook her head. "Nothing major. The previous tenants had the entire place painted and cleaned before they moved out. Other than moving in desks and furniture and your standard decorations, you could realistically be set up in about two weeks."

Zach nodded. "We'll need to get in touch with the company we ordered our office furniture from, see if they can match what we already have. Even though we'll be on separate floors, I want the decor to be the same."

"One step ahead of you." She pulled a sheet of paper out of the folder and handed it to him. "They are holding fifteen desks, a dozen bookcases, and chairs for the waiting area for us, pending your approval. I was able to negotiate the price based on our previous relationship with them. We can hire the same design firm we used on the main office to come in and do the decorating—blinds, artwork, and the like—so everything will be cohesive." She pulled out another sheet. "I spoke to them and here's their rate to come in and do what we need."

He chuckled.

"What?"

Unable to help himself, Zach turned toward Gabriella and smiled. "I don't even think I was needed for this deal. You seemed to think of everything."

Her entire face lit up at his praise.

And Zach felt like he had been kicked in the gut. *Damn.* Why did she have to be so beautiful? He immediately sobered and cleared his throat. "Okay, what's next? You mentioned contracts, right? Yesterday you said there were some contracts legal wanted me to look over."

With her smile slowly fading, Gabriella placed the expansion folder on the coffee table and reached for the folder with the contracts. "There are three of them they want your input on. We can go over them out loud—I have two copies of each—and then I can send legal any changes you'd like and pick up the final copies for your signature when I go to lunch."

"Sounds good."

They were midway through the first contract when a knock sounded at the door. Without asking, Gabriella stood and went to answer it. There was a muscular man dressed in athletic wear standing there. "Can I help you?" Gabriella asked.

"I'm Alex Rebat." He held out a business card. "I was sent over by Dr. Webb for Mr. Montgomery's therapy."

Gabriella stepped aside and let him in. Her eyes

immediately went to Zach's for his reaction. Alex walked across the room and held out his hand to Zach for him to shake. Standing by the door, Gabriella breathed a sigh of relief.

"Gabriella," Zach called from the sofa, "I'm going to get set up with Alex for our session. Why don't you see about doing a walk-through of the office space and getting the video while I'm doing this? We'll meet up again after lunch." He almost laughed at the shocked look on her face.

"Oh, okay. I guess I could do that."

"But?" he prompted.

"But we're almost done with the first contract and if Alex could either give us thirty minutes to finish up or I can sit in with you while you start and make the corrections, it would save us a lot of time. I could deliver the marked-up version directly to the legal department and have them work on the revisions."

"No." He was surprised when she didn't argue. With a simple nod of her head, she collected her purse and her folder on the office space and told him she'd be back after lunch.

He breathed a sigh of relief when she was gone.

"I'm not going to lie to you, Mr. Montgomery," Alex said as he began to go through a series of exercises for Zach's legs, "you've got a hell of a reputation in the world of physical therapy."

Lying on his back, Zach chuckled. "I'm not going to lie to you, Mr. Rebat, everything you heard is true."

The two men laughed as Alex held Zach's knee

up to his chest. "Do you want to walk without those crutches?" he asked.

"More than anything." The answer was out before he even had to think about it. What would be the point in lying?

"Then why are you fighting it so hard?"

Good question. "I'm used to doing things my own way," Zach said. "I don't like having people come into my home, ignoring my requests and my questions. Or worse, ignoring the things I say when I try to explain what I'm feeling."

"What are you feeling?"

Zach grimaced as Alex slowly straightened Zach's leg and flexed his foot. "Discouraged."

Alex nodded. "It's not unusual. From what I've read in your file, you were a very physically active guy. Not being able to get up and go is bound to mess with you."

"That's putting it mildly."

"I'll tell you what, why don't you tell me how you see this therapy going? What is it that we can do to make this something you'll commit to?"

"We?" Zach asked incredulously.

"Yeah. We." He released Zach's leg and stood back. "You've been through enough therapists and talked to enough doctors to know what you need to do, and what you don't want to do. You're a businessman; lay out a plan for us that will get you to throw those crutches away."

For a minute, Zach didn't know what to say. Ever since the accident, no one had asked him what *he* wanted; they all told him what he needed. The thought of finally having a say in his own recovery was almost enough to give him hope.

Almost.

"So you're telling me," Zach said as he sat up, "if I told you exactly how I wanted our therapy sessions to go, you'd go along with it."

Alex smirked. "Within reason. If you're going to tell me you only want me to come around a couple of days a week for thirty-minute sessions, I'm going to tell you no. But if you want to actively participate in your recovery and can come up with a plan that is going to motivate you to do the things you know you need to do, then I'm going to promise you that I'll be right by your side when we throw those crutches away."

Zach eyed him warily. "You can't possibly make that kind of promise."

"I believe I can." He took a step away from Zach and began to casually pace the room. "You see, I've thoroughly studied your file. You had a traumatic spinal injury that was compounded by the multiple broken bones and internal injuries. You've already regained an impressive amount of range of motion. The problem is, you've still got some minor swelling, and the muscles are going flaccid because you're not using them. That's why you feel weak. That's why you have so much pain during your sessions—because we are trying to get those muscles to build back up."

"I don't understand why there's so much pain," Zach said. "I was in great physical shape at the time of the accident. It hasn't been that long. Why are my muscles straining so damn hard? You would think this would be no big deal."

"Zach, did you get in great condition overnight?"

"Well…no. I mean, I was always an athletic kid and grew up playing sports. It came natural to me."

"Okay, that's a good thing, but didn't you work out? Didn't you lift weights?"

"Of course."

"You have to think of this as though you're starting over at the beginning. It sucks and it's going to hurt, but you know what the end result will be. Trust me. We'll go over a list of exercises together. If there's something that hurts you or if you don't understand why we're doing something, ask me. I'm not here to torture you. Believe it or not, I want you to get up and walk and jog and…hell, even climb another mountain, just as much as you do."

Somehow Zach doubted it. "I don't think it's going to be possible."

Alex crossed his arms across his chest. "Are you this doubtful and pessimistic in business?"

"Hell no," Zach said adamantly.

"Then why are you being so now?"

"Honestly?"

Alex nodded. "I expect nothing less."

"All my life, things have come easily to me. But this? It isn't." He paused for a moment. "I know the fall wasn't my fault. I know it was a series of unfortunate circumstances that caused it. But having to rely on so many people for my basic everyday functions? I hate it."

"Anyone in your situation would."

Zach shook his head. "It's more than that. I vehemently *hate* anyone seeing me as weak. And whenever someone witnesses it, I need them to leave. I can't bear to look at them and know they're pitying me."

"Hence the revolving door of therapists," Alex stated.

"Yes. On some level, I know it's counterproductive and it's irrational, but I can't seem to let it go. I've held my family at bay because I don't want them seeing me like this. I even threw my own mother out of the hospital." He snorted with disgust. "I mean, who does that?"

"A guy who is struggling to overcome the biggest challenge of his life."

Zach found Alex's direct candor somewhat startling, and yet it put him at ease, somehow. He felt like Alex was actually listening without judging, or worse, pitying.

"Yeah, maybe. But…I think most people would be a little more…receptive to having people around, especially their family. I know they love me and they're concerned for me and even want to help me. It's just too damn hard to accept their help because I've never really needed it before."

"It's a pride thing."

Zach looked up at him. "No…it's…"

"Pride," Alex finished for him. "Normally, I'd say a little pride is a good thing. But right now? In this situation?" He shook his head. "You're only hurting yourself and screwing up your chance for a full recovery."

"So…what am I supposed to do? Open my door and let everyone I know come in here and play nursemaid to me? Let everyone watch me struggle to walk or move or get myself dressed? Why not put some bars on the doors and treat me like a freak in a cage? We can charge admission."

"What's your field of business? Entertainment?"

A frown crossed Zach's face along with confusion. "What? No, why?"

"Because that's a pretty wild imagination you've got there." He chuckled. "Do you think your family and friends are amused by your struggles?"

"I'm sure some of them are."

"There could be a couple of reasons for it," Alex said. "But I think the people who genuinely care about you aren't taking any pleasure in watching you struggle."

Again, Zach wasn't so sure. "So…what do we have to do?"

A wide grin crossed Alex's face. "For starters, I need to know your schedule. I'm guessing that was your assistant here earlier?"

"Gabriella. My father thought it would be helpful for me to start working again and sent her here to help me get back into the swing of things."

"By the lack of enthusiasm in your voice, I'd say you're less than thrilled with the situation."

"That's the understatement of the year."

Alex sighed and thought for a minute. "We can go one of two ways—we can work your sessions into your work day. One session in the morning, one in the afternoon."

"Won't it be inconvenient for you?"

With a shrug, Alex said, "It's my job. I don't mind it at all."

"What's option number two?"

"I speak to your father and tell him you need to focus all of your time and energy on your rehab, and having your assistant here and being forced to work is hindering your progress."

"So you'd lie to him?" Zach asked sarcastically.

"So it *is* a lie?" Alex shot back.

Crap. Zach realized Alex had caught him admitting that having Gabriella around to get him working again wasn't what was hindering his progress.

But, amazingly, Alex didn't push it. "If that's what it would take to get you to commit to your therapy, then I'd do it."

The idea was beyond appealing to Zach. He'd be rid of Gabriella without looking like the bad guy and his family would be off his back because he was finally committing to his therapy. It was a win/win situation for him no matter how he looked at it.

You're a coward.

Oh, yeah, then there was that. Every once in a while, his conscience came out to tell him he was running scared. He'd like to tell it to shove off, but Zach knew better. There was a lot of truth in that statement. Gabriella wasn't the problem, per se, but she was definitely a distraction. A beautiful, sexy distraction. He groaned.

"Are you in pain? Is something starting to bother you?" Alex asked as he stepped forward.

"No. Just thinking about…" He sighed. "Everything."

"Ah. Like I said, we can go either way on this. I want to customize our time together for maximum benefit to you."

It would be so damn easy to tell Alex to call off the hounds and then he'd be left alone to just deal with his physical rehabilitation in his own way and in his own time. Alex seemed like a decent enough guy, and Zach felt they'd be able to work together without too much confrontation, but was that really what he wanted? Working with Gabriella and getting involved with the company again had invigorated him to an extent. Could he really just step back and let Ethan take over and then ask him to step down when Zach was ready to return full time? That just didn't seem fair.

None of this was easy. The only thing that stood out as a necessity was not having Gabriella in close proximity. As much as he knew there was never going to be anything between them—no matter how much he fantasized about it—Zach didn't want her seeing him like this. He had to push her away. For his own sanity.

For his own peace of mind.

Looking over at Alex, Zach studied him for a long moment. "I'm normally a very good judge of character," he began. "Don't make me regret trusting you."

Alex grinned and pulled his iPad out of his bag. "Let's get to work on getting you up your next mountain."

———

Two hours later, Gabriella was back. She saw Alex's car was still in the driveway so she kept herself busy setting up the next round of contracts and files for Zach's approval as well as the video of the proposed new office space. When the task was completed, she did a quick cleanup of the living room and kitchen and even went so far as to take out the trash. When Alex and Zach still didn't emerge, she settled in to answer emails on her laptop.

Alex came into the living room some twenty minutes later. "We had a great session," he said.

"That's wonderful. How do you think he's doing?" she asked, concern lacing her tone.

"I think he still has a long way to go but if he continues on the path we mapped out today, he'll start seeing a big improvement relatively soon."

Gabriella's eyes went wide. "Really? How can you be so sure?"

"I've been doing this for a long time, so I can say that a lot of a patient's recovery has to do with their attitude. Zach and I actually spent a large part of our time today just talking and getting to know one another. I know his expectations and he knows mine. Now we're free to get started."

She almost started to cry with relief—and surprise— and had to wipe away an errant tear. "So…so how is this going to work? How often will you be here? Is there anything I can do to help?"

"Twice a day to start with. Zach requested I come first thing in the morning, so the session shouldn't interfere with your work schedule. Then I'll come back later in the afternoon when you're getting ready to head out. This way each of us can focus on the part we're here for."

"I…I just can't believe he's really agreed to this. Everyone has been hoping and praying he'd engage but…" She couldn't help but let the bubble of excitement come out in the form of a giggle. "You're like some sort of miracle worker!"

"Well…don't go getting all excited yet. I think we're off to a good start but you need to be prepared for good days and bad days. There may be times you show up here after we've done a session and he's going to be too exhausted to work, or I may need to come earlier in the afternoon and interrupt your work day. Are you okay with that?"

"Please, whatever it takes to make sure Zach recovers and is happy again, I'm on board with it. You just need to let me know if there's anything I can do to assist you."

"Just…be patient with him," Alex said and then excused himself to put his equipment in his car.

Gabriella was positively giddy. But as happy as she was, she knew she needed to tone it down once Zach came into the room. She didn't want to overwhelm him or offer him the opportunity to argue with her about being nosy over his time with Alex. She walked into the kitchen and poured herself a glass of water and placed one for Zach on the coffee table.

When she turned around, Alex was right behind her. "Oh! I didn't hear you come back in," she said, her hand over her heart.

"Sorry," he said as he reached into his pocket and pulled out his business card. "Here's my number. If you have any questions or concerns, don't hesitate to call me."

"Thank you." She took the card from him but didn't have a pocket to put it in. "I appreciate you giving me the option. I want to make sure I'm helping in any way I can."

"Zach's lucky to have you." He smiled at her.

"Isn't this cozy," Zach said as he walked into the room slowly, aided by his crutches. "I believe you're being paid to work here, Gabriella, not stand there and flirt with my therapist."

"Zach…seriously, man…" Alex interrupted.

"It's okay," Gabriella said and smiled at Alex. "Thank you for your time." She turned and walked over to her purse, put his business card away, and busied herself until she heard the front door close. Slowly counting to ten, she waited before turning around and facing Zach as if he hadn't just insulted her in front of Alex. "Which would you like to look at first—the video of the office space or the rest of the contracts for legal?"

Zach stared at her as he made his way over to the couch, but once he was settled he looked at everything she had set up and reached for a folder. "Let's do the contracts so you can get the revisions over to legal as soon as possible."

Cautiously, she sat down and they soon fell into the rhythm of their work. Every time Zach quietly read a portion of the contract, she couldn't help but let her mind wander. Why couldn't he be like this all the time? Was there anything she could do to help him…relax? Chill out? Get off her freaking back?

If she could just figure out what was wrong with him or what his issue was with her, she would do everything in her power to fix it so they could go back to the way things once were between them. She missed the old Zach. There was a time when she used to look forward to going into the office, but now it was normally met with a sense of dread. While it was true she loved what she did and was good at it, Zach had a way of sucking all of the joy out of it for her and making her feel like she wasn't good enough.

Sort of like her family did to her all the damn time.

And it was really starting to piss her off.

Gabriella knew she was a good person—a good employee—and she deserved to be recognized as such. This had been brewing inside of her for a long time, and maybe the time wasn't right for her to be pushing the envelope with Zach, but the reality was there was never going to be a good time. It was going to be painful and hurtful and when it was over, one of them was going to be screaming.

And she had a feeling it was going to be her.

"Gabriella?"

She looked up and found Zach looking at her. "I'm sorry…what is it?"

"I was pointing out this clause in article four. I want you to change the terms to net sixty, and then in paragraph C, make a note to change the wording to incorporate all the divisions of Montgomerys."

"Including East Coast?" she asked.

"Yes."

They finished the work on that contract and the other two Gabriella had brought with her, and she quickly put them aside and set up the video for Zach. "If it's all right with you, I'll let you watch this while I call the office and go over the revisions. I took the video myself and narrated it. I think I anticipated all of your questions and concerns so I'm talking throughout the whole thing." She gave a weak smile. "Sorry."

Zach couldn't help but chuckle. "I'm sure I'll live. I'm used to working with you and hearing you talk all the time, Gabriella. It won't be anything new."

It was quite possibly the longest and most pleasant statement he'd made to her since the accident. It warmed her heart but she quickly turned away so he wouldn't notice how much his words pleased her.

They worked separately—she on the phone with the office and he with the video as he made notes. As soon as she was off the phone, Zach called her over.

"I think the space looks good. It's very similar to what we already have upstairs, and hopefully next year we'll be moving to a building of our own."

"Really? So soon?"

He nodded. "It's time." Flipping through the notes he

made, he went over some of his concerns and Gabriella made notes of her own. "If you can get the ball in motion and have management get a contract drawn, then we can start making plans for furniture delivery and for the decorator to go in and do her thing."

"Very good. I'll make the call now and hopefully I'll be able to pick the contract up tomorrow morning on my way here."

"Why don't you take tomorrow to work in the office? Check on Carolyn and make sure everything is going okay."

Here we go again. "I have been checking in with Carolyn. And Ethan. And Summer. Everything is going fine, Zach. My work is with you, not the rest of the company."

"When I'm not there, you need to be," he said with a hint of annoyance.

"Okay, look," she began, her own annoyance more than obvious. "There used to be a time when we actually enjoyed working together. Don't get me wrong, we still work well together, but I have had enough of your...attitude."

"My attitude?" he mimicked.

"And arrogance," she added and took a deep breath, waiting for the fallout.

"Just to be clear," Zach said as he straightened in his seat and rested his elbows on his knees, "I'm the boss and you're the employee, right?"

Gabriella nodded. "Yes, but—"

"Uh-uh. You started this and I think it's only fair I get to have my say."

She rolled her eyes. "I didn't start anything. You did.

Years ago. And I'd finally like to know why! I want to know what it is I've done to make you treat me like… like I'm incompetent!"

"I never said—"

"You didn't have to! It's in your tone, your attitude… every single day!" she cried. "It doesn't matter what I do or how well I do it, you find fault with it. If you think so little of me, why don't you fire me? Why don't you just let me go?"

"Why don't you just quit if you're so damn miserable?" he demanded.

"I asked you first!"

Zach burst out laughing—he couldn't help it. The idea of Gabriella being anything less than a perfectionist was laughable. "You're not incompetent, Gabriella, nor have I ever meant to imply otherwise."

"Well, you have." She stood and began to pace. "Let's just look at the last two days. I've been here, trying very hard to get you up to speed on the things you've missed the last several months and making sure you get to keep your position, but are you thankful? No! You have been trying to get rid of me and treating me like I'm some sort of nuisance who needs to go back and sit at a desk answering phones because I'm not needed here!"

"You're not!" he yelled back. "I was handling things just fine before you showed up, and I'll handle things just fine if you work from the office!"

"Oh, really?" she asked sarcastically. "How would I get contracts to you for your signature?"

"There are plenty of things I do regarding the business without you being right there to hold my hand," he said defensively.

"Could've fooled me," she mumbled.

Zach raked a hand through his hair in frustration. "What is it you want from me?"

"I want to know…what changed? What did I do that was so wrong I have to keep being punished for it?"

You're a distraction. You said I was nothing to you. I was your boss and nothing more. "I didn't like the office gossip," he said belligerently. "We were spending too much time together and I didn't want anyone thinking I was involved with you." It was the truth. Though only a partial one.

"But…but you and I know the difference, Zach. You didn't need to go to such an…extreme with me. I deserve better than that."

"I don't see why," he said blandly. "You're an assistant. You don't deserve any kind of special treatment for doing your job."

If he had kicked her, it would have hurt less. "I give everything I have to this job. I'm not asking for special treatment, I'm asking for a little kindness. A smile. A thank you that isn't grumbled at me like it's killing you."

"I don't see it that way. All I need is for you to do your job. It's exhausting trying to praise you as much as you seem to require." He shrugged. "It's not going to happen. You've seen me around the office, Gabs. I don't go around praising anyone for anything. You're being paid to do a job and that should be enough. So really, the ball's in your court—you can stay and quit bitching to me or you can move on."

Gabriella could barely breathe. Never could she have imagined Zach saying these things to her. He had been short-tempered and out-and-out rude to her. But this?

This was too much. Her throat felt tight and her eyes stung, but this time she would hold on to her composure as much as possible.

"How dare you. I'm not looking for some sort of approval or a pat on the head. I'm talking about simple human decency. It wouldn't kill you to just say thank you once in a while," she said through clenched teeth. Taking a step closer to him, and then another, she stopped when she was a mere three feet away and bent slightly to make sure she could see his eyes. "I used to have respect for you. I used to admire you. But now? Look at yourself. You're a sad, mean mess. Any praise coming from you right now would be pointless."

She quickly spun around, collected her files and tablet, and put them in her satchel. Slinging the strap over her shoulder, she turned to face Zach one more time. "You used to be the kind of man men looked up to and women stopped and stared at. I'll even admit I found you attractive at one time. Not anymore. Take a good look in the mirror at the man you've become. It's pretty damn pathetic."

And then she was gone.

Chapter 4

"I QUIT."

"Why? What's happened?"

Sitting down opposite William, Gabriella ran a shaky hand over her hair. Like she really needed to explain? It should be obvious to anyone and everyone who'd been around Zach since the accident.

"I thought I could do it. But things between us are too…volatile." She looked up at William and willed her heartbeat to calm down. "I won't work for him. I deserve better than to be verbally attacked all day long."

William leaned forward on his desk, his brows furrowed with concern. "Okay, okay," he said soothingly. "Why don't you tell me what happened?"

Where did she even begin? Taking a moment to compose herself—it had only been thirty minutes since she'd left Zach's—she took a deep breath and let it out slowly. In great detail, she shared with William exactly how the day went and all the things they'd said to one another.

"I'm so ashamed of myself," she said when she was done. "I know all he's going through and I…I just snapped."

"I'd say you were well and thoroughly provoked." He sighed. "I really don't want you to quit, Gabriella, but I don't think going back to Zach's is the right thing to do either."

She almost sagged with relief. "I'm not usually a quitter, and I hate that I'm being one now."

"You're not a quitter, my dear. You've put up with Zach more than any of us have. I think you are to be commended."

A weak smile crossed her face. "It's just... We were making such good progress on his workload. Maybe it *would* be best if Carolyn took him his work in the morning and picked it up in the afternoon. That way he could work on his own. Like he wanted."

"It may be what he wants, but it isn't what he needs," William said cautiously as he sat back in his chair. "I honestly didn't think Zach would go this far. It's unacceptable."

"Please, William...Mr. Montgomery, don't do anything drastic. Zach has his reasons for being angry right now. I was just the convenient punching bag."

William vehemently shook his head. "No, I don't accept that. He's a grown man and should know how to control his emotions. We gave him the opportunity to do the right thing, and instead he took that time to be a bully to you. I won't stand for it." Picking up his phone, William called his brother and asked him to join them.

Dread quickly pooled in Gabriella's belly. She didn't really want to cause Zach any trouble. She'd really just needed to vent.

"Is there a problem?" Robert Montgomery strode into the room and looked between William and Gabriella. "What's happened?"

William relayed the entire story as Robert took a seat beside Gabriella. "Robert, I know he's your son, but what he's done is inexcusable. I won't allow him to behave this way with our employees. We gave him a chance and he blew it. Papers need to be drawn up immediately making Ethan CEO until further notice."

Robert sighed loudly and cursed under his breath. "I really hoped it wouldn't come to this."

"Believe me," William said, "I felt the same way. But we cannot condone this kind of behavior. Gabriella was good enough to go in there and try to help him and he blew it."

"He has agreed to a new therapist," Gabriella said, trying to lighten the mood. "His name is Alex and they spent a lot of time together today talking and working on a schedule to keep Zach engaged. Alex seems to think there will be results soon."

"Well, at least that's something," Robert said. "Maybe we pushed him too hard. Maybe we shouldn't have made him take on both things. His health should come first. I know Ethan didn't want to step on Zach's toes, and he's already a little overwhelmed with everything we've thrown at him, but he'll just have to stick it out for a little bit longer."

William nodded. "Do you want to be the one to talk to Zach?" he asked Robert. "I'll handle Ethan and talking to our lawyers to get the papers started."

Gabriella's heart broke. All she'd wanted to do was help Zach. Damn him for being so hateful! "I…I'm so sorry I let the both of you down. I feel awful."

Both men looked at her as if she'd lost her mind. "Let us down?" Robert said. "Gabriella, you seem to be the only one who actually made progress with my son. In the two days you were there, you accomplished more than any of us have in two months! I feel like we let you down."

"How? How is that even possible?"

"We pushed you into going there and rocking the boat. Honestly, we thought it would be a good thing. None of us expected Zach to behave so abhorrently. You never should have had to contend with that," William said as he shook his head. "I hope you can forgive us."

"There's nothing to forgive. If you remember correctly, I really wanted to do it after we discussed it a bit. I thought I could help." She shrugged. "Ultimately I made things worse for him."

"He did it to himself," Robert said sadly as he rose from his seat. "If you'll both excuse me, I need to figure out how I'm going to break this to him."

Gabriella watched as he walked out the door and felt even worse than she had before. Turning back to William, she felt tears form in her eyes. "I did that. It's my fault."

"Gabriella, you have to stop blaming yourself! Zach pushed you to your limits and he knows better than to treat anyone—especially a woman—like that."

"But…the look on Robert's face," she said with a sniffle. "Zach's his son. No matter what, we're still talking about his child. Because of me he has to break this horrible news to Zach."

William shook his head. "Zach knew the score going in. He needed to do the therapy sessions *and* do the work. It should have been a given that verbally abusing his assistant wasn't going to be acceptable."

"It has been in the past," she mumbled.

Reaching across his desk, he held out his hand to her and smiled when she took it. "I don't think any of us knew things had gotten so out of control. If we had known, we would have put a stop to it sooner. I'm sorry. Give me a couple of days and we'll find you another position within the company. Any place you want to go. If you want to leave Portland, we'll pay all of your relocation expenses. You name it, Gabriella, and it's yours."

It was tempting, so tempting to take him up on his offer. But maybe the better option was to step away from Montgomerys completely—branch off on her own. She'd always wanted a business of her own. She'd always imagined running an agency that found positions for administrative assistants like herself. One where she could train her applicants in every aspect of how to be an executive assistant and share the skills she'd honed over the years. It was a small dream but, if she were pushed, it might not be a bad option.

However, without the backing to start her own firm, if she had to make a decision right now, she'd ask to be moved to the other side of the country so she wouldn't have to see Zach ever again.

But the thought of never seeing him again made her heart ache even more.

"I'll think about it, sir," she said quietly. "I've enjoyed working here in this office, but I'm sure Ethan is going to want his assistant with him."

"I'll talk to him about it. Take the next couple of days off to recuperate, if you want. You'll be hearing from me by the end of the week—Monday at the latest."

"Thank you." She squeezed his hand and smiled before leaving his office. It was already late in the day so she didn't feel bad about simply going home. She walked over to her desk, pulled out all of her files, and gave them to Carolyn along with instructions on what she needed to follow up on the next day.

And decided to not mention her situation with Zach or her possible reassignment.

"Hey! Are you heading out?" Ethan asked, as he stepped out of his office with a big smile on his face. "I was hoping to get a chance to talk to you."

So not what she wanted to do, but she asked him to give her a minute to finish up with Carolyn and then she'd join him in his office. Ethan was a good friend and coworker, but he was also Zach's best friend, and right now she wasn't so sure they could have a reasonable conversation. She turned back to Carolyn.

"You'll need to make the bulk of these calls today before you leave to get the ball in motion," Gabriella said to her assistant. "All of the numbers are right here in these files." With a smile and a word of thanks, Gabriella picked up her purse and satchel and walked over to Ethan's office.

"Come on in," he said when she knocked. "Sit down, sit down. Tell me how things are going over at the lair."

"The lair?" she repeated with a chuckle.

"You know, it's like he's living in a cave or something, and now he has the face to go with it. Soon we'll have to make sure he still knows how to eat with utensils." He laughed out loud at his own joke.

Gabriella tried to laugh along with him, but it fell flat.

Ethan instantly sobered. "Uh-oh. Talk to me. What's going on?"

She was really getting tired of talking about it, and each time she did, she felt even guiltier about her parting words to Zach—no matter how much they were deserved. "So now William wants me to take a couple of days off and decide where I want to go and…" She hesitated. "And I think Robert is going to deal with Zach." She put a hand to her mouth. "I probably shouldn't even be talking to you about this because it affects you too."

Ethan waved her off. "Please, I knew this was going to happen. Zach has to hit rock bottom before he can make a comeback. I just seriously thought he'd hit it already." He sighed. "Obviously I was wrong."

"Not possible. You're too handsome to be wrong."

They both turned around to see Ethan's fiancé, Summer Montgomery, walk into the room. There was a big smile on her face and a little bounce in her step, and Gabriella watched as Summer's eyes lit up the moment she looked at Ethan. If she didn't like the two of them so much, she'd hate them right now.

Ethan tugged Summer onto his lap, kissed her soundly, and gave her a quick recap of what they were talking about. "Gabriella's hit her limit and even she only lasted two days with him."

"Oh God. I'm so sorry, Gabriella," Summer said to her friend.

"Me too," said Ethan. "I don't know what we're supposed to do."

"Oh, I just realized," Summer said. "Does this mean we can't go to North Carolina this weekend?"

"Guys," Gabriella interrupted, "you are still going to be able to do everything you wanted to do. We'll just delegate a little more. I know William told me to take a couple of days off, but if my being here will help the two of you finally go out of town with a little less stress, I'll be here."

"No, it sounds like you need the break more than we do, Gabs," Summer said. "Zach's my brother, and remember I had to leave town to get a break from him too. I totally know what you're feeling."

Gabriella remembered. When Summer had first arrived at Montgomerys, Zach had given her a really hard time and they had fought on a daily basis.

"I wouldn't mind a mental health day," Gabriella conceded, "but I can be here Thursday and Friday to help make sure everything is covered." She looked at Ethan. "I'll work with Carolyn and your assistant Dawn. It might be the perfect time for me to give her a little hands-on training on being the assistant to the CEO."

"What? Why?" Summer asked.

With a dramatic sigh, Gabriella looked at her friend. "Summer, we all know Ethan is going to take the helm here—at least temporarily—and that means he'll need Dawn with him. There are some things I've handled that she never has. I'm just saying I'll work with her and hopefully it will make the transition easier."

"Well, actually…" Summer started, and then looked back to Ethan.

Turning to Gabriella, Ethan smiled. "Well, you see… Summer and I ran through pretty much every possible scenario about how this situation could go. As much as I don't want to see Robert and William strip Zach of his title, I think he needs that in order to get his head out of his ass and rejoin the land of the living."

Beside him, Summer barely restrained a chuckle.

"Anyway, we talked about it and decided if it came to this, Dawn would stay on with Summer and you'd stay on with me. That is…if you wanted to."

Gabriella was speechless. She stared at the two of them in disbelief.

"Say something, Gabs," Summer whispered.

"I...I don't know what to say. I never thought it would come to this."

"You and Zach have worked together for a really long time. If you thought he was willing to work from home with you—and play nice—I'd totally step aside and there'd be no hard feelings. I know Dawn would work with me and we have Carolyn and I'm sure we'd be able to get someone else up here without any issues. I don't want you to feel any pressure. Just...think about it, okay?" Ethan asked.

"I will, and...thank you," Gabriella said. "I need to go. It's been a long day." She hurriedly said good-bye to the both of them and made her way out of the office and to the elevator. It wasn't until she was inside that she finally let herself relax.

And let the first tear fall.

~~~

"We can always do rock, paper, scissors," Ethan suggested with a smile—which he instantly regretted when Robert scowled at him. "Or not."

"This isn't a game, Ethan. We're going to have to go in there and take our own share of verbal abuse after we tell Zach what we've done."

"Technically, we haven't *done* anything yet. The papers aren't drawn up or signed, and there's still a hope—"

"No. I'm mortified at the way he treated Gabriella. I have no doubt he was equally abusive to all of those home health aides and physical therapists. He's my son and I love him, but I cannot abide this. I can't let him go on treating people like this and I'm afraid if I don't do something drastic, this is going to be who he is for the rest of his life."

Ethan shook his head. "I don't think so. Zach's frustrated right now and he's angry with the world. Once he starts feeling better and moving around more and starts to feel like his old self again? He's going to go back to being the man we all know."

"But not toward Gabriella," Robert said sadly. "I can't believe he threw away the perfect assistant. Why would he do it?"

"You want my honest opinion or the politically correct one?"

They were sitting in Robert's car in Zach's driveway—neither anxious to get out just yet. "You know I believe in being honest, Ethan."

"I've known Zach for a majority of my life. I know his moods, I know what he likes and what he doesn't like. I know what drives him. He's had a thing for Gabriella since he hired her."

"What?"

Ethan nodded. "It's true. He's never mentioned it, but like I said, I know him. We've gone to clubs and bars together enough times that I know the telltale signs with Zach. I was actually a little surprised he even hired her knowing he was attracted to her. He's against that sort of interoffice dating thing, but he always held himself in check. Nothing inappropriate ever happened but…man, was he smitten."

"I find that hard to believe. Zach's never been smitten with anyone."

"Trust me, we could be arguing about contract negotiations or difficult clients, but once Gabriella walked into the room, I could practically see the stars in his eyes." Ethan chuckled. "For a while there, I thought she was feeling something for him too, but then one day it was like...*wham!* Done. Over. They've been snapping at each other ever since, and Zach has never talked about it, no matter how much I've bugged him."

"I'm stunned," Robert said as his head fell back against the headrest. "So...if they had some sort of falling-out, why did she stay?"

"That's the weird part. I don't think they had a falling-out. At least she didn't. Whatever happened, it was all on Zach's part."

"How can you be sure?"

"Because Gabriella's just as stumped by his behavior as the rest of us. I don't think she knows where it's coming from or even how to stop it. If she did, don't you think she would have tried to fix it by now? The woman's a damn genius in every aspect of her job, and yet she takes Zach's shit and keeps going back for more. It's not right."

"Well, she's taken it before but clearly she's done now."

"I wouldn't be so sure," Ethan said, a hint of a smirk playing at his lips.

"What?" Robert asked. "What are you smirking about?"

"I think if we give them each a couple of days they'll calm down and will be working together again before you know it."

"But...I thought Gabriella was going to work with you?" Robert asked, confusion written all over his face.

"That's the plan for right now, and that's what we're going to be sure to tell Zach." Ethan chuckled and then flat out laughed. "Watch his reaction and then tell me if you notice anything…unusual about it."

"Every reaction from my son has been unusual since the accident. It's like I don't even know him anymore."

Ethan reached out and placed a reassuring hand on Robert's shoulder. "Give him a little more time. I think after today, we're finally going to start moving in the right direction. I just need you to trust me and follow my lead."

"Wait, I'm the one who's telling him about you taking over. How am I following your lead?"

"I meant where Gabriella is concerned. Give your speech, and then I'll sort of chime in and present my plan for the company."

Robert's eyes went wide. "Plans? What plans?"

"Plans guaranteed to get Zach back to leading the company before the ink is dry on my contract as interim CEO."

Robert shook his head and laughed. "You know, you and my brother should go into business together. You're both too sneaky for your own good."

Ethan smiled. "Yeah, but we get results!"

———

Thirty minutes later, Ethan sat back uncomfortably. The room was quiet—too quiet. He and Robert had finally gone to Zach's house, and Robert had done a majority of the talking. He shared his disappointment in Zach's behavior toward Gabriella and the fact Zach would put the company at risk by being so abusive toward an employee.

To his credit, Zach hadn't tried to make excuses or defend himself. If Ethan had to guess, he'd say his friend knew what he'd done and wasn't proud of it. No matter what the reason. He just wished one of them would say something. Anything. The silence was starting to freak him out.

Shifting in his seat, Ethan decided if he wanted conversation, he was going to have to start it. "I'm sorry it worked out this way, Zach," he began sympathetically. "I know this isn't what you want and it wasn't something I was seeking out. Unfortunately, we have a lot going on and there's even more we want to accomplish in the coming year. If we don't get moving, we'll lose momentum and miss out on some great opportunities."

Zach glared at him. "Is Dawn ready to take this on with you? She's not the sharpest tack in the box."

A smirk begged to cross Ethan's face, but he kept his expression neutral. "Dawn is going to stay on with Summer."

"So what are you going to do? Hire a temp? A team of them?"

"Actually…Gabriella's going to work with me. She'll be mine now." He grinned at his choice of words. "I mean…she'll be my assistant now."

Robert coughed beside him.

"What the hell are you talking about?" Zach demanded.

"Well, considering what you did, and the predicament you currently find yourself in, you don't need her. It only makes sense for her to be with me."

Zach's eyes narrowed. "As your assistant," he said through clenched teeth.

"Yeah." Ethan leaned forward, his expression serious. "I'm thinking she'll travel with me this weekend up to Seattle and we'll get...you know, acquainted with one another, and by the time we're back in the office on Monday, it will be like we've worked together forever."

"I thought Summer was going with you?"

Ethan shrugged. "Change of plans."

"And Summer's all right with that?"

"Yes. There's no way we can keep traveling together now that one of us needs to be in the office at all times, so..." He shrugged again.

"What the hell does that mean?"

"This situation isn't anyone's ideal, Zach. I was looking forward to going back east for a couple of days and checking on the house and just having a little time away with Summer. Obviously, that's not going to happen right now. We all have to make sacrifices. Summer will go to North Carolina alone and I'll...go away with Gabriella." Ethan almost laughed at the shocked look on Zach's face.

"For *work*," Zach growled and then cursed. "Whatever."

"Maybe it's all for the best," Robert said. "Now you can focus on getting your strength back. Gab...I mean, I heard your new therapist already has a schedule in place for you. Do you like him?"

Zach shrugged. "If he does what he claims he can do, then yeah. I'm not getting my hopes up."

"Why him then?" Ethan asked.

"He was the first therapist who actually talked with me about what I wanted to accomplish and how I felt about the schedule we were going to need to keep."

He paused. "He talked to me like…a man. Not just a patient."

"It's definitely a step in the right direction," Robert said, a smile crossing his face. "What else can we do for you? Anything?"

Zach opened his mouth and then immediately shut it. He looked over at Ethan with barely concealed rage.

"Robert, why don't you head out?" Ethan finally said, his eyes never leaving Zach's.

"You rode here with me. How are you going to get home?"

"I'll borrow Zach's car. I'll get it back to him tomorrow." He waited for Zach to at least acknowledge what he said and when he saw the slight nod, he turned his attention to Robert. "I just want to stay and hang out for a while."

Robert hesitated a moment, but got up and wished them both a good night on his way out. Both men waited until the door was closed and they heard the car start.

"You don't mind my borrowing the Porsche, do you?"

A mirthless chuckle was Zach's immediate response. "Sure, it's not like I can drive it."

Ethan stood and went to the kitchen to grab them both a beer. He walked back and handed Zach his. "Aren't you tired yet?"

"Of what?"

"Of being a complete tool." He laughed and took a swig from the bottle. "You know, I felt bad for you for a good long while. I was sympathetic and I kept encouraging everyone to just give you time. Well, you know what?"

"No. But I'm sure you're going to tell me."

"This whole 'woe is me' crap you're throwing around

is getting old. I've known you far too long to believe this is the guy you want to be."

"Then you don't know shit."

Ethan sat back down and faced his friend. "What are you afraid of?"

"Me? Nothing. Not a damn thing."

"Don't bullshit me. It's insulting to us both."

Zach sighed loudly. "You want to know what I'm afraid of? How about…losing my job? Getting stabbed in the back by my best friend? Never being able to walk again? I mean, take your freaking pick, Ethan!"

"Okay, now we're getting somewhere," Ethan said, relaxing in his seat with a grin. "Losing your job? Not likely. It's still yours, man. I'm just having to take on some of the tasks you can't—or *won't*—do. I don't like it any more than you do, so you can stop claiming you were betrayed or stabbed anywhere."

"I don't know what to do, Ethan," Zach said wearily after a long moment. "I'm doing exactly what the old man asked—I'm committing to therapy and I'm doing the business stuff. And I still got the shaft."

"You weren't committing to the business stuff and you know it. I don't know what the hell went on here or why, but what you did to Gabriella was not cool. She was a complete mess."

"Oh yeah? Well, she's obviously recovered, since she strutted right over to your camp to work—and travel—with you."

Ethan laughed out loud.

"What? What's so damn funny?"

"What did you expect her to do? Do you realize what could have potentially happened here?" Ethan didn't wait for an answer. "She could have filed all kinds of harassment charges against you and the company! Now, I'm not saying I offered her the position to keep her quiet. Definitely not. Gabriella is freaking fantastic at her job. One in a damn million. I know it. You know it. I'd be an idiot not to keep her on."

"And travel?" Zach sneered.

"Why are you fixating so much on the traveling?"

"You're engaged to my sister! You have no right taking Gabriella with you anywhere. Especially alone!"

Ethan laughed even harder.

"Dammit, I'm serious! You should not be travel-ing alone with Gabriella, and I cannot *believe* Summer would agree to it."

"Summer and I came up with this plan *together*." Putting his beer down, Ethan leaned forward, instantly sobering. "Let me ask you something—did anything ever happen between you and Gabriella on any busi-ness trip?"

A muscle ticked in Zach's jaw. "No."

"Then what is this all about? And you can't say it's about your sister because it's more than that."

"Never mind," Zach grumbled.

"If you can't talk to me, Zach, who can you talk to? I'm your best friend and it's obvious there is so much more going on here. Come on. We've always told each other everything."

"Oh really? Did you tell me everything about you and my sister?"

"Touché," Ethan said and saluted Zach with his beer bottle. "All I'm saying is sometimes it helps to talk about our feelings."

Zach rolled his eyes. "Geez, do you want to braid my hair while we talk about it?"

Ethan chuckled. "If that's what it takes."

"What do you want from me, Ethan? Seriously, what the hell else do you want from me?"

"The truth would be nice." When Zach stayed silent, Ethan figured he'd better go big or go home. "Why are you fighting with her? Really? Hell, why are you fighting what you feel for her? It's been…years, for crying out loud. Why haven't you told her how you feel?"

"What the hell are you talking about?"

Now it was Ethan's turn to sigh. "Remember when we were sophomores in high school and you had a thing for Lisa McCay?"

A slow smile crossed Zach's face. "Head cheerleader? Wore short skirts year-round?"

"Yeah. Her. Do you also remember how long you waited before asking her out?"

"Six months."

Ethan laughed. "You thought nobody knew. You dated other girls and you ignored her, but you couldn't hide it from me. You used to watch that girl all the damn time. And you do the same thing with Gabriella. Since day one. Even when you're bitching at her for something completely ridiculous, you watch her. Hell, you practically drool. What's the holdup?"

"You don't know what you're talking about."

"So enlighten me."

For a minute, Zach looked like he was going to refuse, but then…it all just spilled out. His attraction to her, the conversation he overheard from their employees years ago, and then…Gabriella's family and what she had said to him.

"So…that's why you went a little crazy around the office and got rid of anything even remotely fun?"

Zach scowled, which Ethan took as confirmation.

"And that's when things changed between you and Gabriella."

Zach nodded.

"Dude, you know why she said all that, don't you? Please tell me you're not *that* clueless!"

"What? She told me the truth. I was nothing to her. I'm still not."

Ethan growled as he stood and stalked to the kitchen. He spun around and looked at Zach. "How is it that you are such a freakin' genius and completely stupid at the same time?"

"What the hell are you talking about?"

"Her family was essentially standing there taunting her about some *supposed* previous affair with her boss, right?"

"Yeah."

"So, if you were her, would you admit to having feelings for your boss in front of those people?"

Zach sat there and stared at Ethan for what felt like an eternity. And then Ethan saw the moment he seemed to make the connection.

"*Shit.*"

"Um…yeah." He sat back down. "You completely screwed up, man. You've been crapping on her for years because you didn't pick up on her trying to just get you the hell out of a situation that was embarrassing for her. And worse, you used it against her." He shook his head. "Kind of makes you no better than her family."

Eyes wide with panic, Zach leaned toward Ethan.

"What can I do? How can I possibly make it up to her?" He groaned. "You have no idea the things—"

"Actually, I do," Ethan interrupted. "She told me."

Zach groaned and hung his head in embarrassment. "Seriously, what do I do?"

"I guess it depends," Ethan began cryptically.

"On what?" Zach asked, lifting his head.

"Do you want her back?" Ethan asked as his eyes bore into Zach's. "And I'm not just talking about as your assistant."

"That's all she is, Ethan," Zach said dejectedly. "She's never shown any interest in me at all. Ever."

Ethan stood and took his empty beer bottle to the kitchen. "Okay. I'm done."

"Now what?"

Taking his time, he rinsed the bottle and put it in the recycling bin before washing his hands and strolling back into the living room. He stared down at the man who was like a brother to him and shook his head. "If that's what you believe, then you really are an idiot."

"How can you even say that? When has Gabriella ever shown an interest in me? Don't you think I would have noticed?"

"Dude, why do you think she still works for you?" Ethan asked simply. "She's far too talented to just be an administrative assistant and she could certainly find a job just about anywhere for someone who didn't treat her like a punching bag. Think about it."

Reaching out, he shook Zach's hand, then grabbed the keys to the Porsche from the hook by the front door and was on his way.

His work here was complete.

—~~—

Hours later, Zach's head was still spinning. Ethan was right; he was an idiot.

How could he have possibly misread something so crucial so badly? Looking back—with a little help from Ethan—Zach now saw exactly what Gabriella had been trying to do. And how badly he had screwed up. He'd been riding her hard, punishing her, for years for no reason.

Yeah, he was an idiot.

With that firmly established, Zach had to try to wrap his brain around what he could possibly do to make it right. He'd been a horrible boss, a horrible human being, to Gabriella, and it wouldn't surprise him if she never wanted to see or speak to him ever again.

He just couldn't let it happen.

It was a bitter pill to swallow to think that with all the obstacles he was already facing with his recovery and rehabilitation, he also had to manage a complete per-sonality overhaul. He had gotten so used to being gruff with Gabriella that Zach had no idea how to reverse it and bring them back to where they once were. At least not without losing his mind.

And his heart.

Hell, there weren't any other options. He had to do something—now—if he had any hope of making things right. If he waited too long, Gabriella was going to be working for Ethan, and Zach knew what kind of workload she'd be carrying. There'd be absolutely no time for him. No time for her to come over—since he couldn't physically get to her—and listen to him grovel and beg and plead for her forgiveness. He'd be lucky if she even responded if he did so much as send her a text message.

Unreal.

Zach was normally a better person than this. Or he had been a long time ago. He'd let petty gossip turn his entire world upside down and turn him into a different person. He didn't like it. And it was going to end today.

Looking around the room, he saw his crutches, a cane, and his motorcycle helmet. Dammit. That's what he wanted. He wanted to be able to get up, walk across the room, and take his bike out and ride the mountain roads with the wind in his face until he was exhausted. That wasn't going to happen if he didn't get himself together and make a commitment—here and now—that he was done living in the past. Done letting other people influence who he was and where he was going.

With a nod of his head, Zach slowly pushed to his feet and stood. There was pain. His legs shook. But for the first time in months, Zach opted to push beyond the pain and take the first step.

And then another.

When he made it completely across the room, he was covered in a fine sheen of sweat and nothing had ever felt better. With a flush of victory, Zach braced a hand on the wall in front of him and laughed triumphantly.

"I'm back."

Chapter 5

Sitting around on a paid vacation might be some people's idea of a good time. Not Gabriella's. She paced her living room looking for something to do, and then sat down and channel surfed through all fifteen hundred channels until she threw the remote aside with disgust.

She thought of calling Summer and seeing if she wanted to go for lunch or maybe to get pedicures, but quickly remembered how busy her friend was now that Ethan was moving into the CEO position and Summer was taking on his vice president responsibilities.

Damn Zach Montgomery.

She was bored out of her mind, and the sound of silence was starting to drive her insane. Which was why she screamed when her cell phone rang. With one hand over her heart, she tried to calm herself down, only to feel her heart rate kick up when she read the caller ID.

Zach.

It would have been so easy to just ignore it and send it to voice mail, but her curiosity got the better of her. "Hello." No response. Her immediate thought was he had dialed her number by accident and yet it didn't stop her from repeating a second "Hello?"

"Hey…it's me," he said, and Gabriella could hear something different in his tone.

"Oh," she said quietly. "Hey."

"I, um… I talked to Ethan yesterday. He said you're

going to be working with him now since he's taking over for me."

"I haven't really agreed yet. He mentioned it to me as an option, but…" She sighed and curled up in the corner of her sofa. "Your uncle also made another offer. I'm not sure what I'm doing yet."

"What kind of offer?" His voice was soft, like he used to talk to her so long ago.

"He said I could pretty much write my own ticket and go to any branch of Montgomerys. I'm not sure I'm ready to pack up and move or anything like that, but it's kind of nice that he offered."

"Yeah. He's a prince," he grumbled.

"What do you want, Zach?" she asked as her heart continued to race.

"I just wanted," he began, and then cleared his throat. "I just wanted to say…I'm sorry. I was completely out of line with you. And not just yesterday. I don't have a good excuse and I'm not going to sit here and lie to you. So…I'm sorry."

Gabriella took a steadying breath. She couldn't believe Zach was actually apologizing to her. And he genuinely sounded sincere. It was a little unnerving and she didn't know how to respond to it. "Thank you," she said quietly. "I appreciate that."

"Listen, I know I have no right to interfere or to ask anything of you, but…"

"But you will," she said with a small chuckle.

"You know me too well," he said, his tone matching hers. "Don't work with Ethan. Please."

"Why? It makes perfect sense. I'm familiar with your responsibilities and how to schedule your time. I think it could make the transition go much smoother than if someone else was there with him."

"How does Summer feel about you and Ethan working together?"

It was an odd question, she thought, but kept it to herself for the time being. "She was fine with it when the three of us talked about it. Why?"

Zach hesitated before saying, "You know what, it's nothing. Never mind."

"No, seriously, what is it? Why did you ask that?"

"It's just… You're a single woman. An attractive single woman, and Ethan's engaged to my sister. I don't want him—"

"Oh my gosh. You did *not* just say that," she said.

"Technically, I didn't. You cut me off."

She mentally counted to ten and then sighed loudly. "I'm not doing this with you anymore, Zach. You're not going to get me on some ridiculous technicality. I know what you're implying and it's insulting. Summer is my best friend, and the fact that you would even think…"

"You know what? You're right. You're completely right," he said quickly, wearily. "I'm sorry. It was completely uncalled for. I don't even know why I brought it up."

Because you're a jackass, she was tempted to say, but decided to hold her tongue. They were silent for so long Gabriella started to squirm. "Um…look, Zach, I appreciate you calling and sort of apologizing—"

"I did apologize," he corrected.

"Okay, sure. Whatever," she said. "But I don't think we have anything else to talk about. I hope…I hope you and Alex accomplish what you planned and you get better."

"Gabs," he said softly, "I know I've been a royal jackass, but I really don't want you to work for Ethan because—"

"That's it," she interrupted. "I'm hanging up. Don't call me—"

"No! Wait!" he said loudly. "Please…please just… hear me out." He paused. "I'm totally committed to working with Alex on my physical therapy, but I also need you here with me to get me back on track with the company. I understand why my father put Ethan in charge—I really do—but I want it to be temporary. I need to start pulling my weight. It isn't fair that Ethan's having to do so much and he and Summer have essentially put their lives on hold because of me."

Gabriella found herself cautiously relaxing. He sounded sincere. Nice. Like the Zach she had originally known. "You know they didn't mind doing it, Zach," she said softly. "They're concerned about you. It's just… It would be nice if you actually appreciated what they were doing rather than being so hostile about it."

Silence.

She cursed herself for pushing her luck. They were just starting to gain a little positive ground, and she had to go and put her foot in her mouth. "I mean…"

"I know what you mean," he said quietly and let out a breath. "I've been horrible to everyone. You were all just trying to help me and I was a complete jerk."

There was no point in arguing with him, she thought. He'd know in an instant she was lying.

"I really do appreciate you, Gabriella," Zach continued. "All you do for me…well…I don't know how to tell you how thankful I am for you. You've always taken care of me since day one and for the life of me, I don't know why. You should have kicked my ass to the curb a long time ago."

She chuckled. "Believe me, I was tempted."

"Then why? Why didn't you?"

How could she answer that? How could she possibly tell him she stayed because she longed for the days they used to have? That she loved to be challenged by him? She marveled at his business sense and how exciting it was to watch the business grow with him. But most of all, how could she possibly tell him she stayed because the thought of not seeing him every day, talking to him every day, was more than she could bear?

She couldn't speak. Emotion clogged her throat and it was all she could do to simply keep her heart rate normal. Right now it felt as if it was going to beat right out of her chest.

"Gabs?"

Obviously he wasn't going to simply accept her silence. He wanted an answer. "It doesn't matter. Not anymore," she said.

"It matters to me," he countered softly. "You've always been there for me, even when I didn't deserve it. I want… I *need* things to go back to the way they used to be. If I'm going to recover and get my position back in the company, I'm going to need you by my side. Please, Gabriella. I need you."

She almost groaned out loud. How many times had she dreamed of hearing Zach say that? True, in those dreams they weren't talking about work, but still. It was impossible to know with any great certainty whether he was being genuinely sincere in his request or if he was playing with her to keep her away from Ethan.

It almost made her snort out loud. She had no interest in Ethan. Never had, never would. Besides the fact that he was a friend who happened to be engaged to her best friend, Gabriella had never found Ethan attractive in *that* way.

Not like Zach.

Dammit.

"I don't know, Zach," she began. "I think too much has happened. I can't keep being your punching bag."

"You won't."

"I don't want to hinder your rehab with Alex."

"You won't." He waited. "Come on, Gabs. We make a good team."

A shaky sigh escaped before she could stop it. "I used to think so too."

"Give me another chance. I know I'm asking a lot and I don't deserve it, but I'm asking anyway. I can't do this on my own."

"Oh please. You and I both know you're not on your own. You have Montgomerys from coast to coast anxious to help you out. All you have to do is pick up the phone and any one of them would be willing to come and be there for you."

"I don't want them," he said simply. "I want you."

She ignored the little flutter her heart did at his choice of words. "I could find someone else to work with you. I'd train them in everything I know. You wouldn't be inconvenienced at all, I promise."

"I don't want anybody else. I want…you."

There was that near groan again. Seriously, did he

have any idea how his words were affecting her? That silky tone? She shook her head and did her best to snap out of it. Of course he knew what he was doing. This was Zach Montgomery—the man who always got what he wanted and didn't care how dirty he played to get it. How could she have forgotten so easily?

"I'm sorry, Zach. I really am. But…I can't. I have a little more self-respect than that. I'm not willing to take a chance on coming back to you and having you belittle me again. I'm sorry."

He was silent for so long Gabriella began to wonder if he was even still on the line. She was just about to say his name when she heard him sigh.

"It's for the best," she said with a calmness she didn't feel. "I'll be there for Ethan to keep things on task. I know what you've been working on and I know how to schedule your days. Well…his days now."

"And what happens when I return to the office and Ethan goes back to the VP position?"

"I don't know. I'm going to give some serious thought to the offer your uncle made me. By the time you come back, I'll be ready to move on…someplace."

"I see."

"I'll…I'll make sure someone is trained to take my place. Carolyn would do a great job. She'll need an assistant, but I'll take care of all of it so you won't have to worry."

"I know," he said, his voice sounding small, hopeless.

Gabriella sighed and rested her head on the back of the sofa and closed her eyes and wished things could be different. "I should go," she finally said.

"Yeah, me too."

"Take care of yourself, Zach. Don't worry about

things at the office. Ethan's going to do just fine and anything that needs to get to you, I'll have Carolyn bring it by." She hoped he understood what she was implying.

"It wouldn't be the worst thing in the world for you to come by sometime. You know, just to visit."

Was he crazy? Did he *not* remember how many times he'd thrown her out of his house just in the last several days? This was the longest they had gone without arguing in a long while. "Sure. We'll see."

"Okay."

Was it just her or did Zach seem to not want to hang up either? Maybe it was wishful thinking, but he seemed just as reluctant as she was to get off the phone. Why couldn't it have always been like this?

"So…um…when are you officially starting to work with Ethan?"

"I don't know. I guess I really didn't even realize I was going to accept the position until a few minutes ago. I had talked to him and Summer briefly the other day but I guess it makes sense to just start fresh on Monday."

"Yes, it does." He cleared his throat. "Can you…I mean…will you please do me a favor?"

"What?"

"Will you come by the house this weekend and pick up some paperwork? It's the stuff you and I were working on when you were here. Please."

"I'll call Carolyn and have her stop by," Gabriella said quickly. A clean break. She needed for them to have a clean break and she knew if she went to his house—if she saw him, talked to him—she'd cave.

"So this is it, then?" he asked finally. "I'm trying

to make things right and you're going to keep finding excuses to not see me?"

Basically. "I think it's best for both of us if it's this way. You need to focus on your sessions with Alex and working on the business stuff at your own pace without anyone interfering with you. And I need…" She paused.

"What? What do you need?"

His voice was deep and rich and it washed over her like silk. "I need to…to shift gears and remember I don't work for you anymore."

"You still work for Montgomerys. That hasn't changed."

"No, it hasn't. But I'll be working for Ethan now. Carolyn will take care of getting whatever you need over to you."

"It shouldn't be this way." Gabriella heard the anguish in his voice. "I'm sorry, Gabriella. Honestly and truly sorry. I… If you'll just come by this weekend. I really want to talk to you about…everything. Please."

"We're talking now," she reminded him. "And it's not getting us anywhere."

"Please. Just…just a half hour of your time," he begged.

Inhaling deeply, she felt her resolve weaken. "Okay. I'll stop by at some point."

"When?"

"I don't know. Just…some point over the weekend."

"How about dinner Friday night?" he suggested. "We can get some takeout and kind of hang out and talk."

"I don't think that's a good idea. And besides, you said thirty minutes."

"Right now I'll take what I can get," he said, his

voice sounding a little more hopeful. "But will you at least agree to come by Friday night? Alex will be here until about six. You could come by around seven if it works for you."

Gabriella knew Zach wasn't going to let this go. She'd indulge him this last time. "Fine. Seven on Friday."

"Thank you, Gabriella. You have no idea how much this means to me."

And Zach had no idea just what exactly he was asking of her and what it was costing her. "I'll see you Friday, Zach. Bye."

"Bye."

⁓

Beggars can't be choosers.

It was the first thought that went through Zach's mind after he hung up the phone. He knew it wasn't going to be easy to convince Gabriella to give him a chance, and technically, she wasn't. It was too much to hope she'd simply agree to keep working for him rather than with Ethan. And he could just about kick himself for even putting it out there about his issues with her and Ethan working alone together. What the hell was he thinking?

Still, at least he'd convinced her to come back to the house. She had said she'd give him thirty minutes, but Zach was pretty confident he'd be able to convince her to stay longer. And have dinner. And if all went according to plan, Ethan would be on his own Monday morning because Gabriella would be back to working here at the house with him.

Sure, if the planets aligned while monkeys flew over them.

No. He couldn't think like that. He had to remind himself how he needed to work on changing his negative thoughts around. To stop viewing every situation with doom and disappointment and start finding the positive side of things. Zach wanted to get back to the way things once were between him and Gabriella. It wasn't going to be easy and it meant bringing up a situation he knew— *now*—was painful for her. He planned on apologizing for not realizing how bad the situation was with her parents much sooner and for the way he responded to it all.

And could only pray he wasn't too late.

It was amazing how different he suddenly felt. It was as if a great weight had been lifted off him. Now that Zach had consciously made the decision to actively engage and participate in getting better and getting back to work, he felt a renewed sense of purpose. A sense of hope. Now it was just a matter of getting his body to cooperate.

It occurred to him he had no real reason to trust Alex Rebat any more than he trusted any of the other therapists. He didn't know anything about the guy except what he had stood here and shared. And yet…and yet Zach had a feeling he'd had to go through all of the other therapists in order to get to Alex. If he delivered on what he promised, it wouldn't be long before the crutches were gone.

And then the cane.

Before he knew it, he could quite possibly be out riding on his motorcycle again or going out to eat with friends. He could return to the office full time. Hell, he might even be ready to go out on a date with a beautiful woman—take her dancing.

Take her to bed.

And damn if the only face that came to mind was Gabriella's.

"Are you sure about this, Gabs? You were pretty upset the last time you went over there."

One of the many things Gabriella loved about Summer was the fact that even though they were talking about her brother, Summer had no illusions. She knew Zach for who he truly was and didn't try to make excuses for him. "I'm sure. I guess maybe I need some closure."

"Or you're a glutton for punishment."

Gabriella rolled her eyes. "Look, you know how your brother can be—he's persuasive and relentless when he wants something. Obviously he has something to say to me that he didn't want to say over the phone."

"And that doesn't scare you? Even just a little bit?" Summer asked as she relaxed back in the massive massaging chair. They had made time to go for pedicures before Ethan and Summer left for the weekend.

"I'll admit I'm not looking forward to it, but like I said, he wouldn't let it go. I plan on going over there, hearing him out while holding my ground, and then getting out of there. From now on, I'll be sending Carolyn over to Zach's to pick up and deliver paperwork."

"Why do you hate Carolyn so much?"

"What? I don't! Why would you even suggest such a thing?"

"You're awful quick to toss her into the lion's den, that's all."

Oh. That. "It's not really like that. She gets along fine with Zach. Besides, it's not like she's going to have to actually *work* with him." She shook her head. "She'll merely be acting as a courier. Nothing major. If he's going to require someone to work from home with him, we'll find him a temp."

Now it was Summer's turn to roll her eyes. "I don't know about you, but I find dealing with my brother exhausting. I can't believe how we're all still walking on eggshells around him. I mean, what's the worst he can do right now? He won't even leave the house!"

"He's got a pretty ferocious bark," Gabriella grumbled. "Trust me. You do *not* want to be on the receiving end of one of those nasty tirades."

Summer reached out and took one of Gabriella's hands in hers. "That's why I'm not sure it's a good idea for you to go over there tonight. I think Zach has finally seen the light in a lot of ways since the accident, but it all seems a little too easy. Like he has this massive meltdown and pretty much explodes all over you and now he's begging for forgiveness? I'm not buying it. He's my brother and I love him, but he's never begged anyone for anything in his entire life."

"Great," she sighed. "Just when I was finally starting to relax about the whole thing."

"Look, I'm sorry. I'm just not buying it. The timing is too convenient."

Gabriella thought back to her conversation with Zach and realized something was still bothering her. She glanced over at Summer and then shifted uncomfortably in her chair. "Can I ask you something?"

"Sure."

"Would it bother you if I worked for Ethan?"

Summer laughed. "Why would you even ask such a thing?"

"Well...Zach sort of...*implied*...it wouldn't be appropriate."

Summer looked at her as if she were crazy. "And again...why?"

"He said I was an attractive single woman and Ethan was engaged and—"

"Oh my God. Please tell me you put him in his place? I mean, of course you're an attractive single woman, but his implication is a crappy thing to think, let alone say out loud! Honestly, what is wrong with him?"

Gabriella never shared with anyone the story of her past. The ugly rumors. The lies. Zach had been the only person in her current life to hear about it, and look how *that* had turned out! Rather than getting into it with Summer, she shrugged. "I guess he's just looking out for you."

"Me?" Summer said with an even heartier laugh. "Maybe he was worried about you."

"Don't be ridiculous."

"No, no...hear me out," Summer began.

Gabriella shook her head. "Zach specifically asked if *you* were okay with it. Trust me, his concern was for you."

"He said *you* were attractive," Summer reminded her. "So?"

"I think Zach was jealous of you working with Ethan. I think it bothered him to picture the two of you working together as closely as you used to work with him. And, if we're being honest, I'd say Zach was kicking himself for all the times he wanted to get closer to you and didn't."

"Wow. You should really consider another career change. I think fiction writing is definitely in your future."

"Oh stop." Summer giggled. "Make fun all you want but I'm right."

"No, you're not."

"Yes, I am. Ethan already told me about it."

Gabriella's eyes went wide. "What are you talking about? Told you about what?"

"About his theory of Zach's feelings for you."

"Zach doesn't have feelings for me. Unless you count rage, spite, disdain…"

Summer shook her head. "No. Ethan said Zach's had a thing for you for a while now—maybe even since you started working for the company, but he was too afraid to act on it and ruin your work relationship."

"That's crazy!"

"I know! But completely believable knowing my brother." Before Gabriella could say anything, Summer went on. "Anyway, when Ethan went over to Zach's the other day, he specifically goaded him about you. He made it sound as if he was really looking forward to spending a little…" She cleared her throat. "*Alone time* with you, and Zach just about had a fit. I'm telling you, Gabs, Zach's jealous and it has nothing to do with me."

"No," she said adamantly. "You're wrong. Besides, Ethan would never do something like that. How could Zach be taken in by something so absurd?"

Summer looked at her sympathetically. "Sweetie, trust me. Zach is slow and methodical and he overthinks things. I honestly believe he was overthinking things where you're concerned for years. And now that you've decided to walk away? He wants you back."

"You make it sound like I'm some sort of possession. Like he wants what he can't have and all that crap. It's actually a little insulting."

"Okay, but you and I both know he's not alone in this. You've got feelings for him too."

"What? I don't… I would never… I…"

"Protest much?" Summer smirked. "It's all right, Gabs. I told you in Alaska that I'm cool with the whole thing. Maybe you should go to Zach's tonight as Gabriella Martine, beautiful single woman, instead of Gabriella Martine, executive assistant."

"Um…no. That's not going to happen. I don't really want to go there for any reason. I'm certainly not going to go there with some sort of romantic agenda. That's just wrong."

"Fine. Have it your way, but I'm telling you, my brother did not invite you over to pick up some files. If they were so important, he could give them to me, my dad, or just messenger them over. Tonight isn't about that; he's got something else in mind and you need to be prepared."

"Is this fun for you? Freaking me out?"

Summer chuckled. "Hardly. I'm simply returning the favor."

Gabriella snorted with disgust. "I don't think so. I was not sitting around trying to freak you out where Ethan was concerned. I was supportive."

"Yes, the balloons and the condoms were a nice touch."

"I considered glitter and confetti too, but figured that was overkill."

They both laughed. "Gabs, you are my best friend and I love you. I don't think Ethan and I would have taken that second chance if it weren't for you."

"What does that have to do with me and Zach?"

Sumer sighed loudly. "I don't have balloons or condoms or…glitter, but I want you to know that I'm here for you. I think you and Zach definitely have some unresolved issues with one another, and maybe it's a good thing you're getting together. However," she continued cautiously, "I just want you to be careful. I know how much you care about…everything. I watched you cry for Zach and I remember how hurt you were over and over again because of the things he said to you. You're not the kind of person who can just walk away. You do need closure. And if you need to talk to someone tonight after the smoke clears, I want you to know I'm here for you."

"Thanks, Summer. I'm really hoping this time it's us overthinking things. Maybe he's the one who needs some closure and wants to apologize to my face."

"That would be a quality thing to do."

"But…" Gabriella prompted.

"But," Summer began, "I can't help but think there's more to it."

"What does Ethan think?"

"I don't know. We haven't talked about it."

"What? The two of you talk about everything! I seem to recall having to sit through one riveting conversation on the topic of how you once had to get a poppy seed bagel instead of a sesame seed one and how you found the number of poppy seeds alarming." She rolled her eyes. "My brain went numb from that conversation."

"Okay, so we overshare sometimes, but Ethan's been so bogged down with CEO stuff, and I didn't want to pile on too much. Besides, Zach's been quiet for two whole days. It's been nice."

Gabriella made a noncommital sound.

"Promise you'll call me later if you need me," Summer said as she looked down at the flowers being painted on her toes. "Ooo…pretty!"

"I promise," Gabriella said. "I think we're both blowing this out of proportion. I'm going to go over there, grab the files, make some small talk, and go home. End of story."

Summer gave her the thumbs-up. "Sure. Okay."

A small growl of frustration came out of Gabriella as she twisted in her seat and faced Summer. "Why? Why couldn't you just let me have my moment of ignorant bliss? Just one tiny moment. Was that too much to ask?"

A slow smile crept across Summer's face. "Like I said earlier, just returning the favor for all of the helpful advice you gave me in Alaska."

Slouching down in her seat, Gabriella pouted. "I hate you."

"I know," Summer cooed, "but I'm buying lunch so I'm guessing you'll forgive me." And with a sassy wink, she rose from her chair to put her toes under the dryer.

Gabriella followed her a minute later and now they sat facing one another while their polish set. "There's just one flaw with your logic." Why couldn't she just let this drop?

Summer's brow arched. "I doubt it, but go ahead."

"You had been crushing on Ethan for years. Years! And he was obviously feeling the same way. He wasn't your boss, he wasn't someone who was intentionally mean to you. The only thing the two of you had going against you was your nosy family. I had to nudge you and advise you because you were too scared to take a risk."

"I'm not seeing a difference."

"When was the last time you had your hearing checked?"

"There is nothing wrong with my hearing," Summer said with a serene look on her face. "From what Ethan told me, Zach's been crushing hard on you, and it became pretty obvious while we were in Alaska you were feeling the same way. Now, granted, Ethan wasn't as hard on me as Zach was on you, but he certainly wasn't always nice. Men do stupid things because of their feelings. All I'm saying is give my brother a chance. Maybe he's finally seen the light. Maybe he finally realized no one wants to be around him because he's been a major jerk."

They gave each other mock military salutes. "Major Jerk."

Summer chuckled. "Go there tonight with an open mind." Then she stopped and studied her friend. "And maybe…get a little out of 'work mode.'"

Gabriella frowned. "What does that mean?"

"It means be casual. We're here getting pedicures and going to grab big fat burgers for lunch and you're in a skirt and blouse and your hair's pulled back. You weren't even working today! Seriously, I know you own jeans and sweaters—I saw you wear them in Alaska. You're not going there for work—no matter what excuse Zach used to convince you to stop by. Casual. Jeans. Sweater. And definitely wear your hair down."

Gabriella rolled her eyes. "I never knew you had such a problem with my appearance."

"I don't!" Summer gasped. "I'm sorry! That wasn't what I was trying to say. All I meant was it might be nice for Zach to see another side of you."

"Have you seen the way your brother looks lately?"

"The yeti look?"

"Let's just hope he loses that before I show up there. I've never seen Zach look so…unkempt."

"None of us have. He's like the poster child for looking good in any situation."

One of the nail technicians came by and checked their toes and gave them the thumbs-up that they were good to go. Rising, they walked to the front of the salon, paid, and stepped outside into the cool late September afternoon.

"Okay, no more talk about Zach," Gabriella said as she slid on her sunglasses. "We're going to go enjoy our burgers, complain that our clothes are too tight when we're done, and you're going to tell me all about the progress on the North Carolina house and what you have planned for your weekend there."

"I feel like our lunch will last longer than the actual trip. I wish Ethan and I had more time to get away."

"You will. Soon. I think we're on the upswing here with Zach. I'd say by the time the holidays hit, you and Ethan will have your lives back."

"Ooo…that would be nice." Summer sighed. "I can't wait to have our first Christmas together. I know the house won't be ready by then but I'm secretly fantasizing about it anyway." They walked over to Summer's car. "I think if it's not completely finished, I might still try to convince Ethan we should go there and spend the week anyway. We'll get a tree and decorate and make it our own."

Gabriella smiled and felt a twinge of envy. Summer had hope. She had the love of her life and was planning her future, and it all sounded wonderful. "I think that sounds perfect for the two of you. A little rustic—just like most of your adventures so far. Very fitting."

And then Summer smiled the dazzling smile of a woman in love and climbed into the car.

Chapter 6

ZACH LOOKED AROUND THE ROOM AND FELT THE FIRST pang of uncertainty. What if she didn't show? What if she'd merely told him she'd stop by just to get him off the phone? None of it sat well with him. He knew he wasn't able to do much on his own right now, but he felt like he had made a pretty vast improvement since Gabriella was last here. Running a hand across his jaw, Zach realized the shave had been long overdue. It was good to feel skin again.

He looked at his watch for the tenth time in so many minutes. It wasn't quite seven but Gabriella was always early. Always. His stomach knotted. He hated the feeling. It was vital that she show up. How was he ever going to make things right between them—work-wise—if she didn't give him a chance?

His inner voice snorted with disbelief. *Work-wise? Dude, this has so little to do with work, it's not even funny. You don't want to lose her in any capacity. At least be man enough to admit it.*

While that pretty much was spot-on, Zach knew he had to tread lightly tonight. With his head finally beginning to clear, he realized he'd turned into the type of man he'd always hated—a quitter. Not only that, but a bitter one. Well, he was done with all of that. It was time to prove to himself—and everyone else—he wasn't going to settle for the crappy hand he'd been dealt. He was going to overcome this rehab thing just like he had overcome every other adversity in his life. Zach Montgomery wasn't a man who shied away from a challenge. Any challenge.

As he glanced at his watch again, he vowed he wouldn't let the fact that Gabriella was now a minute late get him all twisted either. She was the top challenge at the moment.

After a couple days of working with Alex, Zach actually felt confident he was going to get better. There were no guarantees he was going to be as strong or in the exact top physical shape he'd been before the climb, but it didn't matter. As long as he could walk again without the use of crutches or canes, he'd be ecstatic.

Now *that* was progress.

Only a week ago, he would have sneered at the thought of being anything less than perfect. It had been what kept him from getting up and trying because his attitude had been "be perfect or why bother." Now he had a little more of a reality check—thanks to his talks with Alex. While it still bothered him that he might not be able to do all the things he'd once enjoyed, Zach was slowly beginning to realize those things weren't important.

His family was important.

His company was important.

And as the doorbell finally rang, he added one more thing to the list: Gabriella was important.

Gabriella had sat in her car for at least fifteen minutes, continually second-guessing if she was doing the right thing. In her mind, she knew she should have stuck to her original plan—stay as far away from Zach Montgomery as humanly possible. It was important to her overall well-being.

Taking the position with Ethan would alleviate all the stress and anxiety she had carefully kept hidden for so long. She had been careful never to show how Zach's brusque treatment had affected her—no use in giving him any more ammunition to use against her. So she'd put a wall around herself for protection.

And she had a feeling tonight was going to play a part in that wall starting to crumble.

Taking Summer's advice, she'd dressed casually. It felt…weird. Sure, she'd dressed casually while they were all in Alaska and, if she were completely honest with herself, she didn't walk around her apartment in a business suit. But those business suits were part of the armor, part of the wall that was there because of Zach.

And maybe because of her family too.

She sighed loudly. "So not the time to let those thoughts in."

Glancing toward Zach's front door, she couldn't help but wonder which scenario was going to unfold here tonight. Maybe Zach really did just want to apologize in person, give her the files, and wish her luck.

"Right," she snorted. "Because my luck is just *that* good."

Then there was the possibility he wanted to try to convince her to stay on as his assistant—working remotely—so his world wouldn't be any more disrupted than it already was.

Somehow she doubted that one too.

Or maybe he'd lured her here under false pretenses and was prepared to fire her, and wanted to make sure he put the final nail in the coffin so she'd leave and want nothing more to do with Montgomerys ever again.

A knot of dread settled in the pit of her stomach. That option didn't sit well with her either. All she'd accomplished with this little exercise was to confuse herself even more. Without her power suit, briefcase, and accessories, she felt a little unprepared, a little naked.

"Why did I listen to Summer?" she groaned. The faded blue jeans, black sweater, and ankle boots—and not to mention the fact her hair was loose—were not enough if she needed confidence to go up against Zach. Reaching for her purse, she pulled out a hair band and pulled the long tresses back into a severe ponytail.

She'd leave that detail out when she relayed the events of the night to Summer.

Knowing she'd wasted enough time, Gabriella checked her reflection in the visor mirror and frowned. For all the effort she put into looking nice and calm and relaxed, she knew it was just a facade. In a matter of minutes, her entire world could be thrown upside down and she didn't like it.

Was dreading it.

She was ready to throw the car in gear and drive away before Zach ever had the chance to make her cry again.

"You are a lot of things, Gabriella," she said as she took a fortifying breath, "but a coward is not one of them. You can face him just as you have hundreds of times before. If he's going to bark at you and be insulting, it's nothing you haven't heard before. Just…get it over with."

And with shaky legs and a racing heart, she climbed from the car and walked casually to the door, took a deep breath, and knocked.

—∿∿—

On the other side of the door, Zach took his own deep breath as he balanced himself on his crutches and pulled open the door. The sight of her momentarily took his breath away. But then again, when had it not? Gabriella Martine was his every fantasy come to life. Seeing her dressed casually, without her usual killer heels on, she was even more so.

"Hey," he said, relieved she was finally here. If he didn't know better, he'd say she was nervous. Her blue eyes looked at him warily and it killed him that he had put that look there.

"Hi," she said quietly, her hands twisting in front of her.

"Come on in." Zach stepped aside carefully and waited for her to enter. He watched as she walked by and stepped into the living room, admiring the way her jeans fit. "You could have used your key," he said with a smile as he slowly followed her into the room.

Gabriella reached into her purse, pulled the key out, and went to hand it to him. With a shake of her head she said, "No. It wouldn't have been right. I don't work for you anymore."

Zach stared at her outstretched hand and frowned. He hadn't expected them to broach this topic quite so quickly. Ignoring the key, he made his way over to the sofa, sat down, and watched Gabriella until she did the same. She put the key down on the coffee table.

"Thank you for coming over."

She shrugged. "You said you had some files for me to take back to the office." She looked around and tried to spot them but gave up after a few minutes. Then she looked at her hands folded primly in her lap.

"Gabs?" Zach began softly. "Come on. I know I've been a real pain in the ass, but can't you at least look at me?"

Big mistake.

Those eyes—those crystal-blue eyes—slowly rose and the way she looked at him nearly brought Zach to his knees.

Hurt.

Uncertainty.

Sadness.

And it was all his fault. Silently cursing himself, Zach knew he had to do something quick to get Gabriella to relax or she'd be running out the door in a matter of minutes. "I really am glad you're here."

"You really didn't give me much of a choice."

He chuckled because she was right. "Well, it was important to me we be able to talk in person." He stopped and took a moment to collect his thoughts. It was funny, he'd been rehearsing in his head all day the things he wanted to say to her, but now that she was here, his mind was practically blank. "I wanted to apologize to you, Gabriella."

She looked at him skeptically. "You did that over the phone already."

Zach shook his head. "That's not how you apologize to someone. I wanted to be able to see you—and have you see me—so you know how truly sorry I am. For everything."

He watched as she took a shaky breath, her gaze never leaving his. "Okay," she said slowly.

"It's not okay," he said with a hint of frustration. "I… dammit…I took things out on you that weren't your fault. I pride myself on being there for the people who mean something to me, and you do, Gabs. You mean something to me. You're more than an assistant to me. There was a time when I thought we were friends."

"I thought so too." Now she looked away. "And then everything changed."

"I wasn't paying attention," he began nervously. "That day. At your house. I…I was so focused on what *I* was feeling and what I wanted to say that I didn't catch on to what was really going on. You were trying to get me out of your house, away from your family, so they wouldn't react the way they did. Because of me, you had to stand there and take their abuse."

She shrugged but kept her gaze averted. "I'm used to it."

She was sitting opposite him, his coffee table between them, and all Zach could think was how he wanted to reach out and touch her.

But he didn't.

"It shouldn't be that way. No one should have to get used to a bunch of people ganging up on them like that. If I had listened to you when I called and just…stayed away, everything would have been different."

She shook her head sadly. "No, it wouldn't. You still heard what the guys at the office said, and even if you hadn't witnessed my family being…my family, things still would have changed between us." She shrugged again. "It's all right, Zach. I understand."

"You're wrong," he said defiantly. "I'm not going to lie to you. I was shocked by what the guys were saying, but I believe in giving someone the benefit of the doubt. I don't put much stock in gossip. I never have. And besides, whatever happened…back then…it had nothing to do with our relationship. Working or otherwise."

Now she did look at him, her gaze even more wary before she shook her head. "I don't think so. Your reaction pretty much said it all. You were disgusted with me and what you heard."

"No!" he shouted, and then he cursed himself for getting loud. Shifting on the sofa, he leaned forward, his elbows resting on his knees. "That wasn't what upset me, Gabriella."

She shifted too, moving to the edge of her seat. "Then what was it, Zach? What in the world did I do to make you treat me the way you have all this time?"

Zach looked away as embarrassment made him flush. "You told me I was nothing to you. Just your boss, nothing more." He lifted his gaze back to hers. "It just about killed me."

Gabriella stared at him with disbelief. "Why? I don't understand."

Zach had really hoped they would have had more time to just sit and get comfortable around one another before he had to make this admission. Goes to show how much he knew about groveling to the people he'd majorly pissed off. "I thought we were friends," he began softly. "I thought we were more than just boss and assistant. I thought…I thought you enjoyed being with me."

She sagged a little bit at his words. "Oh."

Was there a hint of disappointment in that one

quiet word? "Do you have any idea how much I valued our relationship?"

She silently shook her head, her long ponytail swaying behind her back.

"Do you have any idea how much I enjoyed being with you? Talking with you? And it wasn't only about work. It was you, Gabriella. Being with *you* made me…happy."

"But—"

"Maybe I should have said something sooner. Maybe things would have been better if, sometime before that day, I had let you know how much you meant to me. Maybe if I had, I would have known about your family and then I would have done everything humanly possible to protect you from them. Sometimes I forget not all families are like mine."

"You're very fortunate you have them," she said. "I always envied the closeness you had—and not just with your parents and your siblings—but your cousins, your uncle…it must be very nice."

He shrugged. "I'll admit I don't always appreciate it. I've spent the last couple of days thinking about all the ways I've been ungrateful for all the things my family has been doing for me since the accident. I haven't thanked even one of them. Everyone has turned their lives upside down to help me and I've repaid them by being a complete jackass."

Gabriella let out a small laugh. "You're not going to get an argument from me. You've been horrible to be around."

Zach laughed with her for a moment before turning serious. "I want things to go back to the way they were before. I want us to have that kind of relationship again. We're a great team, Gabs. I don't want to lose that."

She stared at him long and hard. "You just don't want me working for Ethan," she said sadly. "It all goes back to that stupid rumor. You think I'm going to—"

"Wait, wait, wait." Zach held up a hand and interrupted. "Rumor? Are you saying the story wasn't even true?"

Gabriella's eyes went wide right before she stood up and began to walk around the room. "You know what? I don't want to talk about this. Where are the files? I really need to go."

Zach did his best to get to his feet, but his progress was still slow and it irritated the hell out of him. "No, please don't," he said with a calmness he didn't feel. "I think it's about time we talked about this. If we don't, things will never go back to—"

"Don't you get it?" she snapped. "We aren't going to go back! We can't! I can't work for you anymore!" She turned her back on him, and if Zach wasn't mistaken, he heard her sniff.

Walking up behind her, he let one crutch fall to the floor before placing a hand on her shoulder. She jumped at his touch before turning her head to look at him. "Let's forget about work for a minute. Talk to me, Gabriella."

"Why? Why does it even matter?"

How could he even describe it? So many of his decisions for the last several years had been based on this one story and now she was telling him it was a rumor? He couldn't let this go. He had to know—once and for all—what was real and what wasn't. And as much as he wanted to pounce on it and demand the story, he knew he needed to tread carefully.

"Come on," he said softly, still unwilling to let her run away. "Sit back down. Can I get you something to drink?"

Gabriella shook her head and took a steadying breath. "I really should go."

"Please. I don't want you to leave while you're upset. I…I feel bad about this. About…everything. I just want to talk to you. It doesn't have to be about this rumor or anything like that. Just stay a little longer."

She pulled out of his grasp and took a few steps away. "I never was one of those girls in high school who was popular or part of the 'in' crowd," she began. "Most of the girls in my class annoyed me and the feeling was mutual. I didn't have a lot of friends and the ones I did have tended to be guys."

"The girls were intimidated by you, I'd imagine."

She gave a mirthless laugh. "They had no reason to be. It would have been nice to be accepted for myself, but girls are catty. They look at you and if you're pretty they automatically assume you're a bitch. Or a slut."

Zach remembered Summer complaining of the same things in her teen years. He nodded and waited for Gabriella to continue.

"I got used to being an outcast. I used the time to study hard and accelerated my grades. I graduated a year ahead of schedule. It was such a relief to be done with the high school environment. College isn't quite so cliquish." Turning, she walked to the other side of the room and rested a hip against the arm of the sofa. "I graduated at the top of my class in college and got a job with a great company based in Seattle. I loved that job," she said wistfully. "I became friends with my boss—Alan. He was a couple of years older than me, married, and basically a nice guy."

Zach hated him already.

"I became friends with his wife, and whenever I was dating someone, the four of us would go out to dinner or to a movie...everyone was just good friends." She sighed. "Then his marriage fell apart—his wife was having an affair with a coworker—and he just sort of drifted for a while. He was always at the office, we were getting things done, but we didn't hang out or anything."

When his leg started to twitch, Zach reached for the chair Gabriella had vacated and sat down. A million questions raced through his mind, but he knew she needed to get this out. He needed her to get this out.

"That Thanksgiving, I felt bad because Alan was going to be alone and so I invited him to come to dinner with me and my family." She looked over at Zach and chuckled. "They were only mildly obnoxious at that point in time. Anyway, he came with me, and my sister just about made an idiot out of herself coming on to him." She rolled her eyes. "In all my life, I had never seen her act that way. So desperate. By the time Alan left that night, I felt like I had to talk to her and sort of give her a heads-up—Alan was going through a divorce, he hadn't dated in a while, blah, blah, blah."

Restless, Gabriella began to pace. "I thought I was doing the right thing. Being a supportive friend and sister. And you know what she said to me? She said I was just jealous. That *clearly* I must have a thing for Alan and that's why I was warning her off! After all, how could I *possibly* work with a man like him for all these years without having slept with him, she said. I was stunned speechless. By that time, my mother wandered into the room, heard us, and put her two cents in, claiming it did seem rather suspicious how I was trying so hard to warn my sister off. Things got heated and loud and finally my dad came in, and once he heard what was going on, he laughed and just jumped on board with the rest of them. Honestly, the man's never had a single opinion of his own in his entire life."

Zach had heard enough. "Why would they just take her word for it? I mean, you're their daughter too, for crying out loud. Why was it so easy for them to believe your sister?"

"Because she's the golden child. I learned a long time ago they aren't the kind of people I would associate with if I weren't related to them. It's not that I think I'm better than them—sort of—it's just that they're very materialistic and judgmental. It was never my thing. They're all cut from the same cloth. I used to joke how I was switched at birth but I look too much like them."

Zach gave her a minute. "So I take it she started dating Alan."

Gabriella nodded. "Oh yeah. I tried to discourage him. We talked the Monday after Thanksgiving, and I told him my sister was probably going to either show up at the office or call him and I didn't want him to be caught off guard."

"That was nice of you."

She snorted. "It came back to bite me in the butt. They went out on a date—because she did call him—and the day after, Alan came in and told me he thought my sister was a petty, shallow, brainless woman with whom he had nothing in common. I was so relieved I thought I would cry."

"But she never forgave you?"

"I'm not sure about that. But when she called him again for a second date and he told her he didn't think it was a good idea, she stalked the hell out of him. Calling. Texting. Showing up at the office. I was so embarrassed. I couldn't believe what a desperate, pathetic person she was." Then she shrugged. "But…she wore him down. They did go out again. And again. And again. Alan would come back to me for advice and I talked to him like I always had. What I didn't know was that he was going back and telling her everything. To this day I swear she was coaching him on what to ask me so she'd have proof of how much I disliked her."

"Geez, Gabs. That's…unreal."

"Isn't it? And yet this is my family."

"How long did they date?"

"They got married a couple of years ago," she said flatly.

"Wait…*what*? You mean, the guy at your apartment…your brother-in-law…?"

She nodded. "Yup. My ex-boss, my ex-friend, is now my brother-in-law."

"But…why…I mean, you never had an affair with the guy. Why didn't he ever set your sister straight?"

"I honestly don't know. I worked for him for another six months after they started dating and she got very jealous of the time we spent together at work. I don't think Alan was really into her in those early months and he used to go out a lot on his own—but would tell her *we* were working late. I caught him more than once talking and flirting with other women. At one point, I actually felt sorry for her and told Alan he either needed to break up with her or quit seeing other women. He didn't take too kindly to the ultimatum and decided it no longer ben-efited us to keep working together. Personally, I don't think he wanted any witnesses to his affairs. Either way, he fired me, and he told my family he did it to keep the peace between him and my sister. After all, it didn't bode well for his 'former mistress' to be working for him."

"*Son of a bitch!*" Zach cursed and in that moment, he wanted to hunt the bastard down and kill him. "What did you do?"

"You've met my family, Zach. There wasn't anything I could do. The more I protested, the guiltier I looked. I stopped spending much time around my family so things could be peaceful and then I got blasted for breaking up the family. I mean, Alan skates along like a prince and I'm looked at like the scarlet woman."

"And then I added to it by barging in and carrying on about our relationship."

She nodded sadly. "But if it wasn't you, something else would have come up for them to dump on me for. I don't see them very often—maybe once a year now—but whenever I do, it takes weeks to get over it."

"Why see them at all?"

"Because they're my family," she said, looking at him as if he were crazy.

"Gabriella, they don't deserve you! You are so much better than they are. They don't want to see you because you're their family. They're looking for a sick form of entertainment. Don't do it to yourself. You deserve better."

"Easy for you to say. You come from the perfect family."

"Believe me, I know I'm lucky," he said, "but it doesn't change anything. Don't let them come around anymore. If that bastard wasn't man enough to own up to the things he did, then he deserves to have your sister as a wife. She sounds like a handful. You should be thankful you don't have to work for him anymore."

She chuckled. "You weren't much better, you know."

He instantly sobered. "Don't compare us, Gabriella. I may have been a bastard in a lot of ways, but I'm trying to make up for it and I certainly would never have allowed you or your reputation to be destroyed to cover up my own indiscretions. Make no mistake there."

"You're right. I'm sorry."

Then he cursed himself yet again. He was supposed to be trying to win her over, not make her feel bad. "No. I'm sorry. I'm making this about me and it's not." He shook his head. "I wish I had known this back then. I would have defended you, Gabriella. I never would have left you alone with them. I would have given them all a piece of my mind and thrown them out. I'm so sorry."

"It wasn't your battle to fight. It still isn't."

"But it is," he said carefully and noted the look of surprise on her face. "I may not have known you when all of it actually happened, but it doesn't mean it's over and done with. It's still with you. It's still affecting you. Affecting us."

She shook her head. "There is no us, Zach." Her voice was a mere whisper.

He wanted to shout out how there could be, how he

wanted there to be, but then he knew he'd be rushing things. And after the way he had majorly messed things up, he knew it was going to take some time to make them right. "Just…promise me you're going to think twice before seeing them again. Or you'll let me know when they're coming around so you don't have to face them alone."

For a minute he thought she was going to pass out— she paled and her eyes went wide. "Why? Why is this so important to you?" she finally asked.

"Because you're important to me."

Gabriella opened her mouth and then shut it. Then without a word, she stood and walked toward the kitchen. Zach watched her and a small smile crossed his lips when he saw her halt in her tracks. "What…what's that I smell?"

Reaching for his crutches, he stood and followed her into the kitchen. "Steamed dumplings from Lin's. I wasn't sure if you'd eaten dinner and I know how much you like them."

She spun around and looked at him. "I…um—" She cleared her throat. "I had a big lunch."

He looked at her doubtfully. "You have a salad every day for lunch and you rarely finish it. Come on, I ordered double and then I got an order of the crispy duck and the lemon chicken." He smiled and shrugged. "I thought I'd cover all the bases."

Gabriella returned his smile. "Zach, you really didn't have to do all of this. Like I said, I had a late lunch and I'm still kind of full."

He looked at her and quirked a brow. "Seriously? On lettuce?"

"Actually, I didn't have a salad. I went to lunch with Summer and she forced me to have a burger."

"Forced?"

"Okay, maybe not forced, but she strongly suggested it."

He smirked. "Strongly?"

"Fine. She mentioned she was having one. There. Happy?"

The smile that spread across his face felt good. "You have no idea." He walked around her. "Come on, let's get some plates, everything's been staying warm in the oven. We can eat here in the kitchen or out in the living room. It's up to you." Looking over his shoulder, Zach could tell she wanted to argue with him, or flat out turn him down, but he knew her weaknesses. And Chinese takeout was at the top of the list.

"Whichever is more comfortable for you," she said as she turned and began gathering plates and utensils.

"Let's sit in here so we can spread everything out on the table and share." It was something they used to do when they were working late. Zach would order the takeout and they'd set up in the conference room back at the office and share their dinners. He didn't realize how much he'd missed that until just this minute.

When he tried to help her, she playfully swatted him away and told him to sit down. In less than two minutes, she had the entire table set and all of the food containers out of the oven with their lids off. "Sometimes I forget how efficient you are with stuff like this. It's like I blink and you've got everything done."

"That's me. Efficient," she mumbled and turned to grab them something to drink from the refrigerator.

"What's wrong with efficient? Did I miss something?"

She shook her head as she placed bottles of water on the table and took her seat. "It's my own mental thing. Forget about it." She looked over all of the food, and Zach sat back and just enjoyed being able to watch her. For far too long he had done his best to hide his feelings for her—his attraction to her—and right now it felt good to just openly look his fill.

When her plate was nearly full, she stopped and looked at him. "Aren't you going to have anything?"

He snapped out of his reverie and immediately began piling food on his plate. They ate in companionable silence for a few minutes and Zach bit back a smile at the look of pure pleasure on Gabriella's face. It was true she normally only ate a salad for lunch, and most of the time he noticed she didn't even finish it. For all he knew, she didn't eat breakfast and probably did very little for herself for dinner. He used to enjoy feeding her when they worked late, just like he was enjoying it now.

"So how is my sister?" he asked, searching for a fairly neutral topic of conversation. "She and Ethan were flying out tonight, weren't they?"

She nodded. "There was a slight change of plans— they were originally going to go to Seattle to meet with a client, but Ethan's going to Skype with them tomorrow morning, so he and Summer are flying directly to North Carolina tonight."

"I'm sure Summer's champing at the bit to get a look at the progress on the house."

Gabriella nodded again. "I think if it had walls, windows, doors, and nothing else, she'd be willing to sleep there all weekend."

"Hopefully Ethan will put his foot down." Zach chuckled. While he knew Ethan was no stranger to roughing it, he had a feeling it didn't include sleeping in the middle of a construction zone.

At least he hoped it didn't.

"She's just super excited about it. I'm sure once she sees it and gets to walk around and touch things and talk with the builder, she'll be fine staying with your parents or at hotel or wherever it is they're planning on spending their time."

"I'm sure my mother guilted them into staying with her and my dad and she'll have everyone over for a big family dinner before Summer and Ethan have to fly back on Monday." He stopped and paused. "Or are they coming back Sunday night?"

"I think Sunday night. Ethan wanted to be in the office Monday morning. He's called a staff meeting."

Zach had to grit his teeth and keep himself from making a snarky comment. Baby steps. He knew this was the way things had to be for the time being. Ethan wasn't going to do anything crazy with the company, and now that Zach had made a commitment to himself to actively participate in life again, he was confident he was going to be getting more and more hands-on very soon.

Gabriella was staring at him as if reading his mind. "You'll be back at the reins before you know it," she said. "Ethan's planning on talking to everyone so they know this is a temporary situation. I think the team deserves to be in the know—especially since Ethan will be assuming all of your responsibilities."

"Well, not all of them. I fully intend to start pulling my weight again." Dammit. He did *not* want to talk about work! "Anyway, back to my sister. Has she talked about any wedding plans yet?"

Now she eyed him suspiciously. "What's up with you?"

"What do you mean?"

"I mean you're being awfully agreeable and doing a whole heck of a lot of changing the subject when we start talking about the office. I thought that was why I was here—to get those files and to talk about work."

Zach pushed his plate away, leaned back in his chair, and sighed. "It's scary how well you know me." He wasn't sure if it pleased him or pissed him off. "What do you want me to say?"

"How about the truth?" she said mildly as she finished off her last dumpling.

The truth? Hell, Zach wasn't even sure *he* was able to handle the truth. What if he laid it all out there and she walked away? What if he told her exactly what he was feeling and she laughed at him? And *then* walked away? He shook his head and remembered his earlier pep talk about not shying away from any challenges.

It was now or never.

Shifting again so he had his arms resting on the table, he looked at Gabriella and studied her face. "The truth?" he asked and waited until she nodded. "Okay, Gabs. But remember, you asked. I invited you here tonight because I need you to realize how sorry I am for the way I've treated you. I've done some serious soul-searching these last few days and I don't like the man I've become. I'm committed to my therapy with Alex and I'm committed to getting back to being the head of Montgomerys. I didn't want you to come in here on the defensive. I wanted us to just have some time to talk and…get to know each other again."

She leaned back in her chair and let out a shaky breath. "Wow. Okay."

That was it? That was all she had to say? "But more than that, Gabriella, I don't want to do any of it without you. I need you. You are the reason I've been able to accomplish all I have with the company. You're the reason I've been successful in just about every aspect of my life for the last five years."

Reaching across the table, Zach took one of Gabriella's hands in his and just marveled at how soft it was. He'd always wondered what her skin felt like and now that he knew, he wanted to feel more. "Don't leave me. Please."

Her blue eyes filled with tears, and she used her free hand to quickly wipe them away before they fell, and then studied their hands on the table. "Zach," she said softly, "we've been over this."

"I know, I know," he replied just as softly. "I need another chance, Gabriella. I need a chance to make things right." He looked up, his gaze meeting hers. "I need you."

Deciding to be bold, he turned her hand over and twined their fingers together and gently squeezed. He was surprised she didn't pull away and thought maybe—just maybe—they were making progress. "I know I can't erase the things I've said and done, but if you'll give me one more chance, Gabs, I promise not to screw up. If I do anything to upset you, you can walk away. Hell, you can slap me in the face, kick me in the shin, or throw something heavy at me and I'll take it. I just… I can't do this without you."

Her eyes never left their joined hands.

"I don't want to do this without you," he said quietly.

"I'm afraid to…believe you." He barely heard her words, they were uttered so softly.

Everything inside of him clenched with pain. His always confident, ever-efficient assistant was now distrusting and uncertain—because of him. "I don't know what to say to make you believe me. Tell me. Tell me what I need to do. Anything. Anything you need from me to gain your confidence, and I'll do it."

She looked up at him. "It's not that easy. Every day I walked into the office, I gave you another chance. Every time you berated me or made me feel like I screwed up and I came back, I gave you another chance. From my standpoint, you've had two years' worth of second chances. I think I've been more than generous."

His other hand reached out to cup her hand in both of his. "I know you have, and you have no idea how much I appreciated it." She looked at him with disbelief. "It's true! I know I never said it but every morning you were there, I was thankful. Every time you walked into my office, I was thankful. Please. I'm begging here, Gabs."

"I…I've already talked with Ethan. I'm supposed to start working with him on Monday. I can't do this, Zach."

He was losing her. He always knew it was a possibility and yet he felt like he was drowning. "Ethan knows I planned on talking to you tonight. If you tell him you've changed your mind, he'll be fine. You can still go in on Monday and help him through the meeting and with getting things set up, but then you can come here and we'll work out a plan on what tasks and responsibilities I can take on to ease Ethan's burden a little bit. I'm hoping I'll start feeling the effects of the therapy soon and I'll be a little more mobile. I'm confident I can be back in the office—at least part time—by early November." He was desperate and there was no room for pride. "With your help, Gabriella, I know I can do it."

Slowly, Gabriella removed her hand from his. "That was low, Zach."

"Do you think I'm enjoying begging? Groveling? Do you think I feel good about myself as I sit here and watch how you're reacting to me? At one time, we were close. And I pissed that all away. I don't know what else to do here. I've pretty much thrown myself at your mercy."

Slowly, Gabriella stood and began clearing the table. Zach had no choice but to sit in silence and watch. This was it. He had nothing else. He'd told her how he felt, shared his feelings with her, and it hadn't mattered. He'd well and truly lost her.

To Ethan.

Well, not *technically* to Ethan, but the end result was the same. Gabriella would be working for Ethan—not for him. And then by the time he was ready to go back to the office, she would leave permanently.

His heart squeezed. It shouldn't have ended like this. He'd been arrogant and self-absorbed for so long he'd lost touch with what was most important. It wasn't about money and power, it was about relationships. It was about the people in his life who mattered most. He'd regain the love and respect of his family. But clearly he wasn't able to make it happen with Gabriella.

The kitchen was spotless and he watched as she stood by the sink and dried her hands. He knew she was leaving. And he knew he wouldn't stop her. What would be the point? He'd laid out his case and begged more than he ever had in his life, and it wasn't enough. It wasn't about coming out the winner here, but he also didn't want to lose. He had hoped they'd come to some sort of compromise and maybe things wouldn't go back to the way they once were, but maybe they'd be better.

One look at the sad expression on her face and he knew it would never be. "You didn't need to clean up," he finally said when he was able to find his voice.

"It wasn't a big deal." She looked around. "Um…I really should be going. Can I get those files?"

Nodding, Zach reached for his crutches and stood. He walked slowly back toward the living room and gathered the folders. When he turned, Gabriella was standing only a few feet away. He smiled sadly and handed them to her. "Thank you for being willing to come by and get them."

"Thank you for dinner. It's been a long time since I had Lin's dumplings. I'd forgotten how much I like them."

They were polite strangers and it made him want to scream. With nothing left to say, he watched Gabriella turn toward the door, where she placed the files in her purse before hooking it over her shoulder. Zach walked over to her and moved in a little closer than was considered polite. His eyes scanned her face.

Gabriella was tall, not as tall as Zach—especially without the stilettos—but he was still able to look down into her face. Her eyes were a little wide as she looked at him and she took a small step back. He followed. When her back hit the wall, Zach knew she'd have to stand still for at least a minute. "If you change your mind…" he began.

"I don't think I will," she said and fidgeted with her purse strap.

Zach's mind rioted with more arguments to convince her to stay and decided he had nothing else to lose. "I understand." He released one crutch and leaned it against the wall. "I guess there's some good coming out of you no longer working for me."

Those wide blue eyes narrowed, and a smile tugged at his lips at the look. She thought he was going to insult her. Hell, she was probably bracing herself for one last verbal onslaught.

Not. Gonna. Happen.

Reaching up, he cupped her cheek in his hand and marveled at how much softer it felt than her hand had earlier. "If you no longer work for me, then it's totally not inappropriate for me to do this."

And he lowered his lips to hers.

Chapter 7

SHOCK.

Then more shock.

And then…*aah*… Gabriella melted into Zach. After all they had been through together, after everything they had talked about tonight, this was so not the way she'd envisioned their time together ending.

But she was completely on board with it.

For years she had dreamed about what it would be like for Zach Montgomery to kiss her, and now that he was, she needed to stop talking to herself and start enjoying it!

Zach must have realized she was on board because his second crutch fell to the floor as his arms banded around her waist. Everything inside Gabriella melted at the heated contact. He was hard where she was soft and they just…fit. Her hands tentatively stroked their way up his muscular arms and then paused on his shoulders. It felt…naughty…to be touching her boss like this.

Wait…not her boss. Zach. She was touching Zach. *Get your head out of the office, girl!*

A low hum emanated from Zach and she let her hands slowly glide up the strong column of his throat—lingering on his now clean-shaven jaw—and up into his hair. It was longer than he'd ever worn it but it was thick and silky and her fingers just sort of gently grasped and tugged to hold him to her.

If possible, Zach moved in even closer and Gabriella was thoroughly pressed from head to toe between him and the wall. His lips were devouring her but his arms stayed as they were—tightly banded and holding her close as if he was afraid she'd get away.

Not likely.

Right now, there wasn't another place on the planet she wanted to be. Which was a bit ironic considering that less than a minute ago she wanted to be anyplace but here! Funny how fast things could change.

She struggled between needing to take a breath and never letting Zach's lips leave hers again. As if reading her mind, he began to trail kisses along her cheek and her jaw. He nipped at her earlobe and then stopped to simply inhale her scent.

"Do you have any idea how long I've wanted to do this?" he growled low against her ear.

"Hopefully as long as I've wanted you to," she openly admitted as she rubbed herself against him.

He chuckled softly. "The first time you walked through my door, I wanted to touch you. Kiss you." His tongue lightly traveled down the side of her neck to her collarbone. "Make love to you."

Gabriella trembled at his words. How was it possible she hadn't noticed that? How had he kept it a secret for so long? And why? It was on the tip of her tongue to ask him, but he raised his head and gave her a very sexy grin before reclaiming her lips. There was no shock this time, just anticipation. Zach's admission had pretty much done it all for her. She was putty in his hands.

She wanted to move, to get to a place where her back wasn't pressed against a wall. But again, she didn't want to stop what Zach was doing long enough to even say anything. Her nails raked his scalp and she felt the growl vibrate through him. She pushed her breasts more firmly against him, and felt his erection nudge her belly.

The wall was just fine.

Now it was his turn to rub against her and Gabriella was shocked to hear herself purr. It had been so long since a man had touched her like this—and never had one made her purr. Slowly, she lifted one denim-clad leg and let it move up the back of Zach's calf. If all went as planned, she'd hook it around him and pull him closer—if it was even possible. But just as she started to move, Zach pulled back and cursed.

"What? What is it?" she asked nervously. "Are you all right?"

Zach's eyes were squeezed shut as he blindly reached for one of the crutches. "I need…I need to sit down."

Gabriella sprang into action as she quickly thrust both of his crutches into his hands before guiding him over to the sofa. Awkwardly, they got him seated and she took a step back, uncertain of what she should do. Zach was rubbing his thigh and his knee, and his face was twisted in pain.

She kneeled down in front of him. "What can I do?" she asked softly. "What can I get you?"

Zach looked up at her. "Nothing," he said darkly. "Just…you should go."

Rising, Gabriella stood, hands on hips, and stared down at him. "No."

His head snapped up. "Excuse me?"

"You heard me. I said no."

"Gabs, this really isn't the time—"

She held up a hand to stop him. "Yeah, yeah, yeah. Save it. We've been here before. You've spent the entire night trying to convince me to stay and come back to work for you, then you kiss me senseless by the door, and now you're throwing me out? Make up your mind, Zach, because if that's what you're doing, I'm staying gone."

He looked like he was about to say something, but nothing came out.

"If you want me to come back and work for you here in your house, you're going to have to deal with the fact that I'm going to see you in pain. You're going to have to face the fact that these things are going to happen and you aren't going to be able to hide it. Now you can either accept my help, or I'm leaving. For good."

She could see the indecision on his face for a split second before resignation set in. "Fine." He leaned back against the cushions, eyes closed, and continued to rub at his thigh.

"Okay," she said softly and knelt back down in front of him. "Tell me what's going on."

"Sometimes…my leg just gives out. One minute it's fine, and then it starts to twitch and tingle and then it goes numb."

Because she had known Zach for so long, she knew how much it cost him to share that information with her. She nodded and placed her hand over his. "All right. What do we need to do? Heating pad? Ice? Massage? What does Alex suggest?"

"It's part of the healing process—or so he tells me. There's still some swelling, and the fact that I haven't been consistent in my therapy has kind of worked against me. He hasn't been here when this has happened."

"Do you want me to call him? Ask him to come over right now so he can see what you're dealing with?" It was the first thing that came to her mind, but she wouldn't make the call unless Zach agreed. They had made great strides tonight in mending their relationship. She didn't want to do anything to ruin it right now.

"No," he said quietly, opening his eyes and meeting Gabriella's gaze. "It's not so bad this time. But...would you...stay? Stay with me for a little while longer?"

"Of course." Rising, Gabriella sat beside him on the sofa. "Can I get you something?"

In a surprising move, Zach took one of her hands in his and tugged her close. They were shoulder to shoulder, thigh to thigh. Gabriella sighed and rested her head on his shoulder and smiled when Zach rested his head close to hers.

It was a good feeling.

Zach was more than a little unnerved.

To the casual onlooker, this should be no big deal. He'd been in an accident, he was recovering and was still having some setbacks. The only problem was the fact that, for the better part of three months, he hadn't allowed anyone to simply sit with him while he rode the wave of pain and disappointment.

Until now.

As if knowing he simply needed the silence, Gabriella sat beside him, her soft, delicate hand in his, and let him be. It almost made him chuckle. He knew if she had her way, she'd be bustling around the house getting the heating pad, ice pack, and ibuprofen while propping him up on pillows and calling Alex at the same time. Zach took a minute to evaluate how he was feeling and found...he was feeling. The tingling and the twitching had simply gone away. Slowly, he tested his leg—bending it, stretching it—and found it felt...normal.

What the...?

Without conscious thought, he turned his head and placed a gentle kiss on top of Gabriella's head. "Thank you."

She didn't move or do anything to disrupt their position. "How are you feeling?"

"Better," he replied. "It...it just sort of fixed itself."

"Has it ever done that before?"

Zach shook his head. "Remember the first day you came here? It lasted hours."

She chuckled. "I knew something was wrong. I wish you would have just told me. I know there isn't anything I can do about it, but I would have felt better just knowing what you were going through." She paused. "Why didn't you?"

He gave a slight shrug. "This whole thing—the accident, the recovery—it's been...hard."

"Well...yeah," she said. "You fell off a mountain, Zach. What did you think it was going to be like?"

"It's not just the physical aspect of it." Releasing her hand, he wrapped his arm around her shoulders, careful to keep her head close to his. "The mental part has been brutal. It's amazing what happens when you're forced to spend so much time in your head. I spent so many weeks hardly being able to move and there was nothing to do but think. There were times when the pain was so bad it made me want to cry out, but it was my mind that was really doing a number on me."

"What do you mean?"

"Every fear, every form of self-doubt I ever had seemed to plant itself firmly in the forefront of my mind. And I couldn't get around it. Whenever I made progress, there was a dark inner voice telling me how I'd probably never walk again or I'd never be a real man again."

Holy crap. Was he really sitting here spilling his guts to her? Ethan, his father, his brothers…hell, even the doctors and therapists had been after him for months to open up, and he decided to let it all come tumbling out now? Not the most romantic follow-up to the kiss they'd shared. The old Zach would have maneuvered them so Gabriella was lying underneath him on the sofa, picking up where they'd left off at the door.

Clearly the new Zach needed to get in touch with his feelings first.

Fan-freaking-tastic.

"It's amazing what our subconscious can do to us," she said quietly. "But you've come so far, Zach. You have to realize you've made great strides. I know it hasn't happened as fast as you'd probably like, but you're doing really well."

"I thought I'd be back at work by now. I thought I'd be walking without using crutches," he said. "I know I did a lot of things to hinder my recovery, but I'm over it now. I know what I want and it's not being stuck in this house cut off from the rest of the world. I want to get up and get out."

"So what's stopping you?"

Zach raised his head and waited until Gabriella did the same and met his gaze. "Other than the obvious?"

"Zach, people with worse disabilities than yours

leave their houses and go out into the world every day."
Her eyes lit up. "Let's go someplace!"

"Now?" he asked incredulously. "It's late. Where
would we even go?"

She rolled her eyes. "How about tomorrow? I'll come
by and pick you up and we'll go someplace."

And just like that, Zach felt himself shut down. *What
if you fall? What if your leg gives out? What if people
take pity on you?* "I don't think so. But thanks."

Her eyes narrowed. "You're doing it again."

"Doing what?"

She stood and walked over to the front door. "You
say you're in, that you're committed, but you're not. Not
really. You're committed as long as things go according
to your plan with no surprises. Well, news flash, things
don't always go according to plan!"

"You think I don't know that?" he yelled, grabbing a
crutch and standing. "Look at me! This is the result of
things not going according to plan!"

"I get it," she countered, calming down. "I really do.
But you've talked all night about all this soul-searching
and wanting to reengage in your life, but as soon as an
opportunity presents itself, you're still choosing to sit out."

He raked a hand through his hair. "It's not as easy as
you think."

Slowly, Gabriella walked over to him. "I'm sorry."
Reaching out, she placed a hand on his forearm. "I really
am just trying to help."

And he knew she was telling the truth. She wasn't
pushing or trying to manipulate him. Gabriella was honestly and truly trying to help him do what he claimed he
wanted to do. "Where would we even go?"

Taking a minute to think, she tapped one perfectly manicured finger against her lips and then it came to her. "We'll start small. And private. I know you're not going to want an audience around you—even if they're complete strangers."

"You've got that right. So? What are you thinking?"

"We'll go out to eat."

He looked at her like she was crazy. "Too many people."

"Okay, how about we go to a movie?"

The idea actually didn't sound so bad to him. "It's a lot of sitting. I don't see where it's going to help."

"It's not really about getting you to walk," she began diplomatically. "It's about getting you out of the house and out into the world again." Taking a step away, she walked around the room. "We won't go to the multiplex by the mall. We'll hit one of the smaller theaters on the outskirts of town. We'll grab lunch someplace small and then see a matinee. By the time the movie's over, I'm sure you'll be ready to come back home, and you'll have the rest of the night to relax and think about how it felt to be out and where you'd like to go next."

"What if I like it and want to go out again on Sunday? Would you go with me?"

"Absolutely." Her answer was immediate. It was a no-brainer.

Zach studied her. "What if…what if while we're out, something happens? What if something like what just happened here happens at the theater?"

"We'll be sitting in a dark theater with a very loud movie playing. No one will be paying any attention to you."

"Not even you?" he asked quietly.

A small smile crossed Gabriella's face. "Only me. I'll be right there with you. If you want to leave, we'll leave. If you want to stay, we'll stay. If you're committed to doing this, Zach, then I'm committed to being there with you. What do you say?"

He took a minute and just stared in wonder at her. Was it really this easy? Was it really just a matter of sharing his fears and she was going to be there with him no matter what? He thought about it and then shook his head. Either way, she was staying and he was thrilled.

"I say, what's playing?"

Gabriella drove back to Zach's late the following morning and felt a sense of anticipation she'd never felt before. The sudden turn in their relationship should have felt weird, but it didn't. If anything, it seemed to make everything fall into place. She was happy. She was content.

She was hopeful.

Zach had kissed her breathless when she'd left the night before, and there was a small part of her that wanted him to ask her to stay. It was too soon, she knew it was too soon, but she couldn't help but feel a little disappointed when she drove home. Soon, she told herself. When Zach was feeling more like his old self, maybe they'd transition into a more physical relationship, but for now she would need to be patient and supportive and be there for him however he needed.

Even though she still had the key to his house, she knocked. Then she felt guilty because it meant he had to struggle with his crutches to answer the door. Fishing through her purse, she had her fingers on the key when Zach suddenly appeared.

"Hey," he said, a little breathless.

"Hey, yourself." Gabriella held up the key with a lopsided grin. "I wasn't sure if I should use it or not."

Zach took a step back and motioned for her to come in. "Always use it. I gave it back to you because you're always welcome here."

"You weren't saying that a few days ago," she muttered and was surprised when Zach's arm quickly banded around her waist and he pulled her in close.

"I thought we were moving forward." His eyes scanned her face, his expression serious. "I know I can't erase all the things I said, but I also don't want to keep rehashing them."

"You're right," Gabriella conceded. "I shouldn't have brought it up. I'm sorry."

Now it was Zach's turn to grin. His head bent toward hers. "You're forgiven." And then his lips touched hers, tentative at first, and then with more urgency. He sighed with pleasure when Gabriella instantly responded to him.

She couldn't help herself—he was quickly becoming addictive. The man certainly knew how to kiss and if she wasn't careful, they wouldn't be leaving the house any time soon. Her tongue gently traced Zach's lips, and Gabriella couldn't help but smile when she heard him growl. She felt empowered—and turned on—but quickly did her best to take it down a notch and put a little space between them.

"I bought tickets to the one o'clock movie. We need to get going if we're going to stop for lunch and get to the theater in time. It's about forty-five minutes away."

"Seriously? You can think of a movie right now?" he asked breathlessly, his forehead resting against hers.

Gabriella sighed and leaned in closer to him. "Crazy, right? I guess I'm just good at multitasking," she said teasingly and giggled when he groaned. "Come on," she finally said and forced herself to move away again. "This is a big day and I'd think you'd be excited to get out of the house for something other than a doctor's appointment."

"I am," he said, but Gabriella knew he wasn't.

"Did you tell anyone what we were doing today?"

He shook his head. "I wanted to wait and see how it went. I don't want to jinx it."

She could understand that but wished he was a bit more enthusiastic.

Unable to help herself, she busied herself around the living room, straightening stacks of papers, fluffing pillows, and putting dirty glasses in the dishwasher while Zach was getting ready to go.

"You're not on the clock, Gabs," Zach said as he took a look around the room and slid a jacket on. "I don't expect you to clean up the place every time you're here."

"Sorry," she said as she walked back into the room. "It's just habit, I guess. I'll stop."

There was an awkward silence as they made their way out of the house and out to Gabriella's car. She drove a fairly sensible sedan, but Zach was so big that she suddenly worried about his comfort.

"Um…Zach?"

"Yeah?"

"Would it be better if we took your car? I mean, it's

bigger…more leg room and whatnot. If you're okay with me driving it…?"

"Thank God," he said with a chuckle. "I didn't want you to think I was ungrateful but as soon as we stepped out here and I got a good look at your car, I began to second-guess this whole plan." They both seemed to relax as they shared a laugh. "The keys are back in the house. If you don't mind running back in to get them, I'll wait here."

"No problem." Gabriella quickly spun around and went back into the house and found the keys on the shelf next to the front door. Locking the house back up, she met Zach over by his SUV. His face was turned up, his eyes closed, and from what she could tell, he was simply enjoying the feel of the sun on his face.

Halting in her steps, she could only smile and stare. Gabriella was certain that being forced to be inside for so many months was just another disappointment for someone as active as Zach. Gabriella made a mental note to find some outdoor activities for them once he was stronger. Nothing dangerous or even remotely tricky— maybe a picnic or a walk in the park—someplace where Zach could simply enjoy the fresh air.

Gabriella closed the gap between them and walked over to the car. "Got them," she said and jingled the keys in her hands. She'd never driven such a big SUV before, but figured they'd be fine. "Do you need any help?"

Zach shook his head. "This is actually the easy part. Because the car is up a little higher, I can get in much easier than if I had to lower myself into your car." He grinned at her as they both took their seats. "Sorry."

"For what?"

"I'm sure you had everything all worked out and I threw a monkey wrench into your plans. I know you don't like that."

Normally she didn't, but there were extenuating circumstances here. "It's fine. Really. I just hope you realize I'm used to driving something much smaller. This is…um…well, this is a little intimidating."

"I think you can handle it," he said with a wink.

Fortunately, they made the drive without any issues, talking the entire time. Gabriella had forgotten how well they used to get along and how they never seemed to run out of things to talk about. From news, to sports, movies, books…there was never a lull in the conversation. She parked the car in front of a small mom-and-pop diner and looked over at Zach.

"I thought someplace remote might make you feel more comfortable. I've eaten here before and the food is really good, but there's never a crowd."

His smile conveyed his gratitude. They went inside and sat in a corner booth. It took Zach a little longer to get situated, and by the time he was ready to look at a menu, there was a light sheen of sweat on his brow.

"Are you all right?" Gabriella asked quietly.

"I guess I didn't think it would be so much work."

She looked around. "Maybe we should have sat at a table," she said nervously.

Zach reached across the table and took one of her hands in his. "Hey, it's all right. How were we going to know unless we tried, right?"

Visibly relaxing, Gabriella smiled at him. "I just don't want you to get discouraged."

"It's amazing the things we take for granted," he

said, pulling his hand back. "A few months ago, I never would have given sliding in and out of a booth a second thought. But now? Now I have to think about leg room and where to put the crutches and using my upper body more than my lower." He sighed. "I never thought it would be this hard."

"It's going to get easier, Zach. You and Alex are going to work together and figure everything out and before you know it, you won't have to be thinking about these things. Everything will be back to normal."

"I wish I had your optimism," he said as he opened his menu.

Gabriella took it as her cue to do the same and let the subject drop. Before the waitress could come over, Zach took the menu from her hands.

"Promise me something," he said, with a smirk and a hint of a challenge.

"What?"

"Please don't get a salad. I know it's your go-to lunch, but just for today, please get something else. A sandwich, a burger, just…not a salad."

She chuckled. "I had no idea my choice of lunch food caused you such distress."

"It's not that," he said and then couldn't help but laugh with her. "I just enjoy sharing a meal with you—a real meal."

Gabriella sighed dramatically. "Fine. If it's that important to you, then I'll get a BLT. But that means I'm skipping the popcorn at the movie theater."

"You can't skip the popcorn. It's the best part of going to the movies!"

"Shouldn't the movie be the best part of going to the

movies?" she asked, trying to wrap her brain around this ridiculous conversation.

Now it was Zach's turn to sigh dramatically. "Okay, let's just say it's a tie. Movies and popcorn go hand in hand. It's the total experience. You can't have one without the other, in my opinion."

She shrugged. "Take your pick. Either I get a BLT or the popcorn. I'm not doing both. I don't think we'll have to worry about whether you can handle this outing if I'm sick from overeating."

"Seriously? You're going to compare me not being able to walk to you having a snack?"

A light blush crept up her cheeks. "I don't expect you to understand, but…I eat the way I do for a reason. I'm not big on junk food and I enjoy my salads."

"Fine. But this time, get the BLT and skip the popcorn." He grinned broadly. "More for me."

She laughed. "That's fine with me. Have at it."

—◠◠◠—

An hour later, it was all Zach could do to keep from laughing out loud. It wasn't that the movie was funny. Far from it. It was a serious action drama. Right now, two people were plunging to their potential demise on the screen, but his focus was on Gabriella. She kept reaching for the popcorn and then pulling her hand back—while thinking Zach wasn't paying attention.

Oh, he was paying attention. How could he not when they were sitting so close together and she smelled like heaven? Her signature scent was clean and floral and it drove him wild. Plus they were shoulder to shoulder and her hand kept creeping closer to him.

Without a word, he took her wayward hand in his and planted it firmly on his thigh and held it there. She shot a quick look at him but Zach pretended to be interested in the whole plunging-to-their-death scene playing out on the screen.

Bad idea.

Not pretending to watch the movie, but putting her hand on him. Now all he could do was imagine what it would feel like on other parts of his body—sans clothes. Dammit. When they'd made these plans yesterday, his biggest fear was being able to walk in and out of the damn movie theater without his leg giving out. Now he had to worry about getting in and out of the movie theater while sporting a major hard-on.

Normally not a bad problem to have but right now it was pretty awkward.

Carefully, he placed the large bucket of popcorn strategically over his lap and prayed Gabriella wasn't going to cave in and have any. If she did, he'd have to distract her. Maybe feed the popcorn to her.

Watch her tongue slowly dart out of those perfectly glossed lips.

He groaned at the image.

"Are you all right?" she whispered in his ear and suddenly Zach didn't care about his legs, the movie, the popcorn, or his own arousal.

Reaching over, he cupped a hand behind her nape and drew her in for a kiss. Gabriella didn't even resist, and that was hotter to Zach than anything else she ever could have done. Her hands reached up and cupped his face as his tongue pressed through the seam of her lips to mate with hers.

At this rate, he might have to dump the popcorn out on the ground and turn the bucket upside down on his lap to hide his growing erection. Zach couldn't remember the last time he had been so overwhelmed, so consumed with need for a woman.

Far. Too. Long.

He couldn't believe he was sitting here making out with Gabriella in a movie theater. He hadn't done anything like this since he was about sixteen and yet…and yet it just seemed to fit for them. Nothing about their relationship was normal. Nothing about it was rational. And if he was honest with himself, he liked that about them. He liked that they were being unconventional. That they were behaving a little like teenagers who were both so into each other they couldn't wait another minute to act on their attraction.

Gabriella purred into his mouth and Zach was lost. If they were anyplace else but here, he'd have her sprawled out beneath him while he touched her from head to toe. It was going to happen.

Soon.

Not here, but soon.

Beside him, Gabriella shifted and he'd swear she was trying to keep herself from crawling into his lap. Something he would definitely be on board with if they were alone, but here and now, it just couldn't be.

Reluctantly, he ended the kiss and pulled back slightly. "You're killing me, Gabs," he said quietly.

Her eyes were closed, her breathing ragged, her hands still cupped his jaw. "I'd apologize but you're killing me too." Her eyes slowly opened and scanned his face. "How did this happen? How did we get here?"

The thought of making a joke briefly crossed his mind, but it was quickly forgotten. All he could think of was how thankful he was she'd come over the night before and he'd finally been brave enough to share his feelings with her. Had he known how she was going to respond, he would have acted on those feelings sooner.

Much sooner.

Like years ago.

"I've got to be honest with you," he murmured, his lips gently caressing her ear. "I don't give a damn about this movie or about anything else right now except leaving here with you and going back to my place. I want to be alone with you, without an audience, and that has nothing to do with being self-conscious about my injury." He pulled back so she could see his face. "I want us to be alone together, Gabriella, like I've fanta-sized about countless times."

She took a shaky breath as her gaze met his. "This is all happening so fast."

"It's been years," he fairly growled. "If anything, we're really behind."

"Zach—" She sighed. "I don't know. I just…"

He pressed a finger to her lips. "Shh…it's all right." He removed his finger and placed a gentle kiss on her lips. "I don't want to rush you or make you uncomfort-able. I'm sorry." Pulling back and settling back into his seat, Zach reached over and put his arm around Gabriella's shoulder and smiled when she rested her head there. He liked that a lot.

Unable to help himself, he reached into the bucket of popcorn and pulled out a couple of pieces and held them up to her lips. Beside him, Gabriella hesitated for a moment before accepting them. It certainly wasn't helping the situation when her tongue gently grazed his finger, but he managed to stay in control.

A minute later he heard her whisper, "Thank you."

He kissed the top of her head and relaxed.

It had been a long time since Zach had gone out on a date and even longer since he'd gone out on one where he'd enjoyed himself so much. For all the years he spent wining and dining beautiful women, who knew it would be *this* beautiful woman in an out-of-the-way movie theater who would turn his life upside down?

And make his body react like a horny teenager.

It was almost enough to make him laugh. But at that moment, Gabriella lifted her head and kissed him gently on the cheek.

"I think this is the best date ever," she whispered before resting her head back on his shoulder.

It was as if she'd read his mind. And wasn't that the basis of it all—they were one. He'd known it since the beginning. They understood one another and worked well together, and he had no doubt they were going to continue to work well together—even when work wasn't involved.

A smile played across his lips as he put his focus back on the big screen.

Yeah, life was pretty damn good.

Chapter 8

A MONTH LATER, ZACH WAS LYING DOWN ON THE massage table Alex had brought with him, grimacing in pain.

"We are definitely making progress," Alex said as he worked on Zach's calf muscles. "I can feel and see a difference. What about you?"

Zach shrugged and grunted. Alex immediately released him and stepped back. Lifting his head, Zach looked over his shoulder. "What?"

"Seriously? That's all I get out of you? A few weeks ago you couldn't do half the reps we're doing now. You're able to move around without the use of the crutches for longer amounts of time. I thought you'd be happier about it."

The sigh came out before he could help it. "I am happier. Honest." Zach sat up. "I know I'm the main reason I'm not further along in my recovery. I get it. But now I'm committed and I'm doing the work, I was hoping—"

"For what? A miracle?" Alex interrupted. "It doesn't work like that, Zach. You're still going to have to put in the time."

That did little to make Zach feel better. Ever since he and Gabriella had gone to lunch and the movies, he was even more anxious to make progress with his therapy. He enjoyed kissing her and touching her, but he was way too wary to go any further than that until he knew for certain his body wasn't going to throw him for a loop in the middle of an intimate moment with Gabriella.

It wasn't something they had discussed, but Zach knew Gabriella understood. They spent every day together—working and just hanging out—but Zach always managed to put on the brakes before they got too carried away.

Something that was becoming more and more difficult with every passing day. The woman personified temptation.

They'd started to settle into a routine—she arrived at his house every morning just as he and Alex were finishing up their session. While Zach showered and Alex packed up, Gabriella got their work laid out for the day along with whatever breakfast she had picked up on the way to his place.

Zach and Gabriella worked at a fairly slow pace, getting Zach back up to speed on all the company business he'd missed since the Denali climb. They videoconferenced with Ethan, and Zach spoke on the phone every day with his father. Zach knew his father and Ethan were both relieved that he was finally engaging in running the company again. So was he. He hadn't realized how much he truly missed it until he pulled his head out of his ass and actually took the initiative.

Twice during the past week, he and Gabriella had left the house under the pretense of going to lunch. They'd picnicked in the park and then would take short walks on some of the paved trails just so he could be outside. It was amazing how much he had missed just being out in the fresh air.

Alex was right—his mobility had improved, and that,

combined with getting out of the house, had made an incredible difference in just about every aspect of his life. He was sleeping better, his appetite was better, and his overall outlook on life was better. If he was an optimistic person, he'd say he was starting to feel like his old self.

Light at the end of the tunnel.

"You've gone quiet again," Alex said, interrupting Zach's thoughts.

"I'm impatient. Now that I'm finally doing the work, I expect my body to catch up. Excel. Be done with all of this."

Alex chuckled. "Yeah, athletic guys like you are usually the worst. No patience. You'll get there. I promise. You keep doing what you've been doing and you'll be back on your feet—literally—in no time."

"God, I hope so. I'm losing my mind."

"Nah. I think you hit that point a couple of weeks ago. Your head is finally on straight." He motioned for Zach to lie back down. "You have a doctor's appointment on Monday, don't you?"

Zach nodded.

"I'd like to go with you if it's all right."

"Why?"

Alex started massaging Zach's calf again. "I think if the three of us sit down together and we hear what your scans are showing, we can personalize your sessions even more. I'd like to know where the swelling is—if there still is any—and I find it helpful to get the doctor's input on how your recovery is going." He stopped and made eye contact with Zach. "But it's completely up to you. If you'd rather go without me and fill me in on the details later, I'm cool with that too."

Zach shook his head. "I just don't expect you to give up any more of your time for me. You're already here twice a day, five days a week. Don't you have other clients?"

"I sure do," Alex said good-naturedly. "But just like you would understand if I told you one of them needed me, they'll understand if I need to spend a little extra time with you."

Zach couldn't argue that logic. "I had planned on asking Gabriella to take me, but it's not a big deal."

Alex smiled. "She's a great lady. I can see she's just as invested in your recovery as you and I are. It's important to surround yourself with people who are supportive. You wouldn't believe how difficult it can be when you have friends and family interfering with therapy sessions because they think I'm being too hard on a patient. Or when the patient is lazy and complains. You've got an amazing support group in your family, Zach. You're lucky."

"Don't I know it." He paused and just let Alex do his thing for a few minutes. Questions about his recovery and what he should—and shouldn't—be doing began to form in his mind, but pride kept him from voicing them. What was happening between him and Gabriella was private, but he wouldn't mind some input on when it might be…safe…for him to initiate taking things to the next level with her.

"I can hear you thinking from here," Alex said. "What's on your mind?"

Zach considered asking the question, just to get it out in the open, but he couldn't make himself form the words. "It's…it's nothing. Really."

Alex continued with the massage. "Fine. Have it your way."

Zach lay there in silence for a solid five minutes before his inner dialogue could no longer be contained. "Okay. Here's the thing." He cleared his throat. "I know I'm getting better, stronger. But there's kind of a difference between being able to walk without crutches and...other things. You know what I mean?" God, did he sound as lame as he felt?

For a minute, Alex didn't say anything. "Are you asking me about when you'll be free to resume other...activities?"

By the way Alex said the word "activities," Zach figured they were on the same page. Still...just in case. "I'm not talking about basketball or...riding a bike. You know?"

Alex chuckled. "Ah...riding a bike. Good one." He switched to Zach's other leg. "How does it feel?"

They went through this after every session. They worked Zach's muscles until he didn't think he could take any more, and then at the end, Alex took the time to massage them and make sure the muscles were in good shape. "It feels fine. They don't hurt like they did a week ago or even a few days ago."

"Good. That's a good thing. It means they're getting used to the activity and not fighting it so much. Or you're not fighting it so much."

Zach gave a muffled snort. "Anyway...we were saying..."

"Right. Riding a bike. I can't give you a definitive time line, Zach. You know your body better than I do. Off the record, I don't see why you couldn't resume...activities."

"Okay, now I feel like we're a couple of kids in

church. Sex. We're talking about sex!" It felt so much better to finally just say it out loud.

Alex burst out laughing. "Oh thank God! I wasn't sure if I could come up with any other euphemisms for the whole damn thing." They both laughed. "But seriously, Zach, I don't see why you couldn't or shouldn't be able to have sex."

"I'm kind of...well...what if, you know, like my leg, things just...don't work?"

Luckily Alex didn't laugh. "That would be more of a psychological thing than anything else, man. From everything I read in your reports, there wasn't any damage to your—"

"Yeah, yeah...I know."

"Have you experienced any...issues with...?"

Zach wished the floor would open up and swallow him. This was way more embarrassing than he ever could have imagined. "You know what? Let's just forget I even mentioned this, okay?"

"No, no, come on," Alex said and came to stand in front of him. "Look, Zach, I'm honored you feel comfortable enough to talk to me about this kind of thing. From everything you've told me and what I knew of you before I took you on, you weren't comfortable with any of your doctors or therapists. I want to help you. I know it's not the most...comfortable...conversation to have, but I think it's an important one."

"But it has nothing to do with my recovery," Zach said quickly, averting his eyes and moving to get off the table. "I never should have brought it up."

Before Zach could get down, Alex blocked him. "Actually, it's a big part of your recovery. I mean, yeah, it's not like that was part of your injury, but you've struggled with a major physical trauma. You're easing back into what your life was like before the accident, and sex is a natural part of it."

In his entire life, Zach couldn't remember ever talking to his brothers or Ethan about issues like this. It was embarrassing. It was humbling. He was a healthy, virile guy who had always enjoyed a normal, healthy sex life. There had never been a reason to discuss it.

He wished there wasn't a reason right now.

"It just feels…weird," Zach mumbled. "I'm not the kind of guy who—"

"Yeah. I got that." Alex moved away from the table and began putting towels and weights away. "There's nothing to be embarrassed about. If you feel you're ready, then you should. Unless you're one of those guys who likes his sex full of props and acrobatics," he said with a laugh. "Then maybe you shouldn't. But if you're looking to just sort of…ease back into things, I think you'll be fine."

Zach wanted to believe him. There had been times over the last week when he'd had Gabriella in his arms and he'd thought, "Yes! I can totally do this!" and then that little voice of doubt crept up and planted the idea of him getting a cramp or a pain or just…not being able to finish what they'd started. It had never been an issue for Zach—ever—and he wasn't prepared to take a chance on it happening now.

He could sit here and talk to Alex for hours, but the bottom line was there were no guarantees. "Do you… do you think it's something we could address Monday at the doctor, or should I just not bring it up?"

By now Alex had the room back in order and his

supplies stacked by the door. "This is clearly something important to you, Zach. You know no one is going to be able to give you a promise that everything is going to be what you're hoping it's going to be. We can talk about it. You can talk about it with your doctor. You can talk about it with Gabriella if you—"

"Wait," Zach interrupted. "Why would you say that? Why would you bring Gabriella into this?"

Alex's eyebrows rose before he crossed his arms and chuckled. "Seriously? She's who you're talking about, right? I mean, I know she's your assistant but it's pretty obvious she means more to you than that. Come on. I'm not blind."

Zach muttered a curse.

"What's the big deal? I think it's great, and like I said earlier, Gabriella is clearly on board with helping you with your rehab. You're a lucky guy. All the way around."

"Yeah, I'm living the dream," he mumbled. "I'm weaker than a preteen and I still need crutches to walk most of the time. Remind me again where the luck is?" he asked.

Shaking his head, Alex walked over and gave Zach a quick and friendly pat on the back. "I'm not going to do that. You know damn well all the reasons why you're lucky. It's late and I've got to go." He walked over to the door and began collecting his bags and supplies. "Have a good weekend and try to relax. We'll skip our session Monday morning and I'll just plan on picking you up at ten to take you to your appointment. Is that all right?"

Zach nodded. "Sure. Whatever."

Alex's shoulders slumped. "Really? That's how we're going to end this successful session? Here I was feeling really good about all we accomplished and you're going to get all sad and dejected on me? And on a Friday?" He chuckled. "Come on. What do you have planned for the weekend? You told me about the movies and getting out last weekend. I'm sure you've got something on the calendar."

A small smile crept across Zach's face.

"I knew it! I knew you had something going on. Now, promise me you'll get out of your damn head and allow yourself to enjoy it."

The smile grew.

Alex looked at his watch and then put his stuff down. "Out with it, Montgomery. What are you going to be doing?"

"Actually, it's not really a big deal. I'm just looking forward to spending the weekend with Gabriella without having to deal with work and contracts and video conferences. To have it just be the two of us."

"I can see that." He stared at Zach in contemplative silence for a moment. "I know you're not ready to go out to some of the places you used to just yet, but you might want to consider the Chinese gardens."

Zach shrugged. "We've gone to a couple of parks that have paved trails to make walking easier. I feel bad that she has to walk so slowly because of me."

"How about checking out one of the movie brew-pubs? They're actually kind of cool. They have couches instead of typical movie seats and you get to eat a casual dinner and taste some in-house brewed beers. Even if you're not a beer drinker, the whole scene is really laid-back. Perfect for a casual night out."

"Maybe," Zach said, and then held out his hand to Alex to shake it. "Thanks, man. Seriously. I appreciate all you're doing here with me and for taking the time to talk with me."

"I'd like to think that even if you weren't a patient or a client, we'd be friends," Alex said, shaking Zach's hand. "I'm looking forward to playing racquetball with you when you're better or doing one of those bike tours you were talking about the other day."

Zach laughed. "That would be cool. Definitely." He pulled his hand back, his expression a little more serious. "Thanks, Alex."

"Have a good weekend, and tell Gabriella I said hello."

It was after nine when Zach finally sat down on the sofa and was able to relax. After Alex had left, Zach had taken the time to shower and shave and even made himself something to eat. Well, he had reheated some chili his housekeeper had made and left for him, but it still required a little effort on his part.

Now he had nothing left to do. He wasn't particularly tired but he was restless. With no one around, he decided to do something he had tried a couple of nights ago: seeing how long he could move around without his crutches.

Most of the time he didn't feel as if he really needed them, but because his legs were still weak, it was smarter to use them and prevent any further injuries. Taking a deep breath, he rose from the sofa and took a minute to just confirm he was steady on his feet. Once he felt confident, he began to walk around the room. His pace was slow—slower than he would have ever walked before the accident—but it was a pace he was comfortable with, and he reminded himself of the importance of taking things slow.

After three laps around the living room, he walked into the kitchen. Looking around, he decided to load his dinner dishes in the dishwasher and even took the trash out.

"Not too shabby," he said as he shut the back door to the house. Normally he would have left the bag by the door and asked Gabriella or Alex or whoever happened to stop by to take it out for him. But he'd done it on his own—maneuvering up and down the two outdoor steps to get to the pails. He figuratively high-fived himself.

Next, he walked out of the kitchen and across the house to his bedroom. He had spent a majority of his recovery time in this room and the sight of it was starting to depress him. Looking around the room, it felt more like a glorified hospital room rather than the retreat it once was.

A wheelchair was folded up in the corner from his early days at home. There was a weight bench in another corner that he and Alex used for therapy sessions, along with mats for floor exercises. Bars had been attached to strategic spots along the walls to help him get around.

He wanted it all gone.

This wasn't the room of a man who was recovered. It was the room of a man still struggling, and Zach no longer wanted to be that man. It was time to take away all of the crutches—literally and figuratively—and do something about making his surroundings something that inspired him, rather than enabled him to stay in recovery mode.

Inspiration hit.

Walking back out to the living room, he found his cell phone and pulled up Gabriella's number. It might be too late to call, but she was the only person he wanted to talk to.

"Zach?" she said as she answered the phone. "Is everything okay? Are you all right?"

He longed for the day when her immediate reaction to him wasn't to inquire about his health. "Yeah, everything's fine. Great, actually. I was just walking around the house and decided I need to do something with it."

She was silent for a moment. "Wait…what? The house?"

"Yes," he said with a nod. "I want to start with a makeover on the bedroom. It reminds me too much of a hospital room. I want to get rid of the equipment and move it to one of the guest rooms. I'm going to talk to Alex on Monday about doing our sessions someplace else."

"Okay. Wow," she said. "I don't think it should be a problem. Maybe we can call Ethan and ask him to come over and help move the furniture. I'm sure Summer will come with him and between the three of us, we can get it done. You can tell us where to set everything up."

"That won't be necessary. I'll call professionals to do the heavy lifting. Ethan has enough to do without having to come here and do manual labor. But it's more than that, Gabs."

"What do you mean?"

"I want to get rid of all the hospital equipment. The wheelchair can definitely go. Donate it to the hospital or maybe I'll give it to Alex to use at the rehab facility, but I want it gone. Then I want all the bars removed from the walls."

"Hmm…that will require the walls being patched up. I can find a contractor to come in and do it."

"Good, good," he said. "And while he's at it, I'm going to want the entire room repainted in a new color."

"What's going on, Zach?" she asked suspiciously.

"Fresh start," he said simply. "I look around here and I see something that reminds me of my limitations. Or I see things I'm tired of seeing because I've been stuck in this house for so long. In all the years I've owned this house, I've never spent this much time confined to it. I'm just ready to freshen the place up. Will you help me?"

"Me? Wouldn't you prefer to hire a decorator? We can call the firm who does the offices if you'd like. I know she does residential design along with commercial."

He shook his head even though he knew she couldn't see him. "No. I hired a damn decorator when I bought the place and now that I've been stuck here, I realize nothing here really reflects the person I am. I want to pick the colors. I want to choose what goes on the walls. I don't need three guest rooms. I want to convert one to a home gym to use not only for my sessions with Alex but for when I'm better. And I want a home office."

She chuckled. "Why? I would imagine once you're comfortable with coming back to work, you'll never use it."

"That was my logic when I moved in here and how I ended up with so many damn guest rooms." He paused and finally allowed himself to sit down. It wasn't that he needed to sit—he wanted to. And it was a pretty awesome feeling. "With so much time to sit and think about my life, I realized I was only doing two things—working at the office or going on those adventures with Ethan."

"You weren't that bad, Zach. You went out and socialized. You dated. Spent time with your family."

"Those things were fairly minute in comparison to the amount of time I spent at the office. From now on, I want to make sure I leave the office at a reasonable time. I want to…I don't know…go see a movie or go to a museum or walk in the park…"

"We did some of those things just this week," she reminded him, though her tone was light and playful. "I think right now you're excited because you're making progress, but I don't want you to get too far ahead of yourself."

"Gabs, you know the biggest thing that's been missing from my life?"

Silence.

"Gabs?" he repeated softly.

She quietly cleared her throat. "Um…no. What?"

"A life."

"Oh."

"That's going to change."

"Okay."

He almost chuckled at the wonder in her voice. "What do you think? Are you up for the challenge?"

"What challenge?"

"Helping me freshen this place up, for starters."

"Starters?"

"Um…Gabs?"

"Yeah?"

"Are you okay? You're sort of floundering on your

end of the conversation," he teased. "We usually have a lot more banter going on when we talk."

"Oh, sorry," she said with a hint of a giggle. "You took me by surprise."

"Good. That's good." His voice turned slightly husky. "I plan on doing a lot more of that, too."

"Oh."

It would have been so easy to start seducing her over the phone, but he cared for her more than that. When he did finally seduce her, they would be face to face. It wouldn't be a game. She'd know he was serious. Clearing his head of any sexy images of her, he got back to his plan. "So what do you say we start working on it this weekend? We can maybe spend some time online looking at some design and decorating ideas."

"Or…"

"Or what?"

"Or we can actually go out to a paint store and look at colors. And then go to the mall and look for furniture or artwork or bedding. We can go to…"

He couldn't concentrate for a moment because all he could think of, all he could see in his mind, was Gabriella sprawled out on his bed. Maybe he hadn't thought this plan through far enough. Having her help redo his bedroom meant she'd be spending a lot of time…in his bedroom.

Dammit.

"So what do you think?"

Think? *Think?* Hell, Zach had no idea what she had even suggested because his mind had wandered down Dirty Lane. "Um…why don't we talk about it tomorrow? What time can you get here?"

"What time do you want me there?" she asked, and Zach had to wonder if she realized how sexy her innocent question sounded.

"How about right now?" he asked silkily and heard her soft gasp.

"Zach…"

"What? You asked me a question and I answered it."

"Tomorrow. What time should I come over tomorrow?"

"Spoilsport. Um…how about noon? I've got some food here we can heat up for lunch and…"

"How about I pick up some groceries for you? I'll get some stuff to make sandwiches and then we can make our plan and figure out what you need and where we need to go. Maybe we'll grab dinner out someplace?"

For a moment, panic began to overwhelm him. Going to a movie and sitting in a dark theater wasn't so bad. Eating at an out-of-the-way diner wasn't so bad. Walking around a mall and eating someplace local and crowded on a Saturday night was definitely taking on more than he was ready for.

"What do you think?" she asked.

"We'll see," he forced himself to say. "Like you said, I don't want to get too far ahead of myself. I don't want to overdo it all in one day."

"Okay."

"You're not mad, are you?" he asked.

"Me? No, why?"

"You sound disappointed."

"I'm not. Not really."

"Gabs…" he prompted.

"It's like a weird balancing act," she said after a minute.

"On one hand we're talking about all the things we want to do and then when it comes time to actually implement them, reality sets in and it just…it makes me sad."

Well, damn. The last thing he wanted was her pity. He wasn't sure if he was angry or depressed at the thought of her feeling that way. Taking a deep breath, he tried to be optimistic. "It's not always going to be like this. I'm getting better. I really am. I'm just excited about the possibility of changing things up around here. It's a little frustrating that I can't do anything about it right now, but—"

"I guess I could come over."

Her words were said so quickly that Zach thought he might have imagined them. "What did you say?"

"It…it was nothing. Never mind. I'll just plan on seeing you tomorrow."

"You said you could come over. Like now."

"It's late," she said softly.

"Do you have a curfew?"

She giggled. "No."

"That's good. Neither do I."

"But…it's crazy, Zach. It's not like we can get anything done tonight."

He wasn't so sure about that. "So? We'll watch a movie, or we'll start our online research and make our plan for tomorrow."

"I'm…I'm kind of in my jammies already."

Was it too much to hope that it was scraps of silk and lace and she'd kept her stilettos on? "Me too."

Now she laughed a little harder. "Oh really?"

"Yup. Really. Flannel pants, a T-shirt. Very jammie-ish."

"I don't even think that's a word, Zach."

"It doesn't need to be. Come on. I'm not expecting you to come over in business attire, Gabs. I've seen you in jeans and dressed casually. It's not a big deal."

"I don't normally drive around a whole lot at night."

As much as he wanted to see her and spend time with her, he certainly wasn't going to be selfish and endanger her by making her drive around late at night. If he were ready to drive on his own, he'd suggest going over to her place, but he hadn't gotten the clearance from his doctor yet.

"It's okay, Gabriella. We'll leave things as we originally planned and I'll see you tomorrow for lunch." He sighed quietly and got comfortable on the couch. "I don't want you driving around by yourself late at night."

"You're very sweet."

He laughed darkly. "I bet it hurt to say that."

"Oh, stop. We agreed we weren't looking back, right?"

He nodded. "Right." God, he wanted to keep talking to her but he could hear in her voice that she was tired. "Why don't I let you get some sleep and I'll see you tomorrow?"

"Mmm," she sighed. "I'm sorry. If it wasn't quite so late…"

"It's all right, Gabs. Really."

"Okay. I don't want you to be mad."

"Not mad. Disappointed. I'm finding I really like spending time with you."

"I like it too."

She was killing him.

"Go," he forced himself to say. "Good night, Gabriella."

She made that purring sound again and everything in Zach hardened. "Good night, Zach."

Zach sat there for a long time after they disconnected. He was turned on. Confused. Energized. Tired. All rolled in one. There were at least a dozen things he wanted to do—most of them to Gabriella—but being that he was alone, he did his best to push those thoughts aside.

Slowly rising from the couch, he stood and waited for the feeling of instability to come.

It didn't.

"Well, all right," he said and made his way to his bedroom. There wasn't much he could do on his own to start implementing his plan, but there was at least one thing he could do. Walking over to the wheelchair, he grabbed it and pushed it out of the room and across the house to the mud room. When Alex came to get him on Monday, he'd give it to him, but until then, he didn't want to see it. Didn't want it sitting there in plain sight, mocking him.

As he walked through the house, he began turning off lights and thinking of things he'd like to change. Artwork. Wall colors. Stopping in the kitchen, he grabbed a bottle of water before turning off the light but not before coming to the decision he was going to get some new granite countertops. Why? He couldn't quite say. The kitchen was possibly his least favorite room to be in—he didn't cook—but for all of the high-end appliances and cabinets, the color of the countertops never sat well with him. He'd have to start thinking about it tomorrow.

He was halfway to his room when he heard a knock at the front door. A smile crept across his lips right before he pinched himself to make sure he wasn't dreaming. He counted to ten so he wouldn't seem too anxious and then walked over and pulled the door open.

"I came over," Gabriella said, looking absolutely adorable in a pair of yoga pants, an oversize T-shirt, and her hair down loose.

"Yeah, you did," he said softly and pulled her through the door and into his arms.

Chapter 9

FOR A BRIEF MOMENT, GABRIELLA SERIOUSLY second-guessed her decision to get in the car and drive over to Zach's. But the look on his face when he opened the door pretty much confirmed she'd made the right choice. No sooner had she announced her presence than he had her in his arms, his lips on hers, kissing her senseless.

It was madness. It was almost frightening how much she wanted him, and if the way he just slammed the front door and backed her up against it was any indication, Zach felt the same exact way. How was it possible they'd both had this much—desire? passion?—for each other locked up for so long and neither had been aware of it? She knew how he liked his coffee, what he liked to eat, and even at what temperature he preferred his office to be set. She even knew ridiculous facts, like how many times he tapped his pen when he was thinking or how many times he'd pace back and forth in his office when he was dictating something to her, and yet she'd had no idea he had these feelings for her?

"You're thinking," he murmured against her lips. "No thinking." His lips traveled along her jaw—lightly nipping and kissing.

Wrapping her arms around his shoulders, she pressed herself fully against him and sought his lips with her own.

She was done overthinking. She wanted to feel. And

oh, did the man know how to make her feel. Zach's hands roamed slowly up and down her back before settling on her waist and gently squeezing. Dressed the way she was, without her heels, he towered over her, and Gabriella found she enjoyed their difference in size. Normally they seemed to be on more even ground, but locked together like this, Zach made her feel petite and feminine.

It was a really good feeling.

Slowly Zach lifted his head and looked down at her, his eyes a little dazed. "I thought you didn't like driving at night?" His words were whisper-soft as he scanned her face.

"I guess I never really had someplace I wanted to be," she replied honestly. Gabriella always made sure she did the right thing—chose the right options. Going out late at night seemed like something she should avoid.

Until now.

Zach Montgomery—well, this new Zach Montgomery—was quickly turning her carefully organized world upside down. Gabriella couldn't remember the last time a man—or anyone, for that matter—made her want to be reckless. But as his hands began to roam again and his lips seemed intent on driving her crazy, it was exactly what she wanted to be. She whispered his name and then made a slightly needy sound when he lifted his head again.

"I'll probably hate myself for asking this," he said a little breathlessly, "but what changed your mind?"

Her lips twitched. "Aw, does someone need their ego stroked?" As soon as the words were out of her mouth, she wanted to die. Gabriella considered herself one of the least sexy or flirtatious people who ever lived. She certainly never said things that could be misconstrued…sexually.

Zach groaned. "Baby, if you're offering, then yes."

For a minute, she actually considered doing just that—stroking him, touching him—everywhere. But she needed a minute. Getting in the car and driving over here was a big step. But actually reaching out and running her hands all over Zach's body? Well, that was something else completely.

For the last month they had done this—kissing, some touching—but it was mostly Zach's hands doing all the work. For her part, she was content to hold on to his strong shoulders or biceps and just feel his strength. She was still shy when it came to them getting physical.

As if sensing her thoughts, Zach took a step back and then took one of Gabriella's hands in his and led her into the living room, where he turned on one small lamp before leading them over to the sofa. When they were both seated and he had his arm around her and her head on his shoulder, she let out a small sigh of contentment and relaxed.

"I'm glad you're here," he finally said, placing a kiss on her forehead.

"Me too."

"Are you sure? Because it seems to me like you're second-guessing yourself."

Get out of my brain, she wanted to say, but kept it to herself. "Honestly, I don't know what I'm doing here."

Zach was silent for so long she thought maybe he hadn't heard her. "I know what you mean," he finally said. "We've been…friends…sometimes not even that, for so long that this feels weird and yet right all at the same time. Does that make sense?"

She nodded.

"We've seen one another almost every day for years, and now? I'm still seeing you but I'm seeing you differently, and I"—he paused and shifted so he could tuck a finger under her chin and coax her to look at him—"I really like what I'm seeing. I like this new… us." He studied her face for a long time. "Tell me what you're thinking."

"I feel the same way and yet…I'm a little scared, Zach."

"Of what?"

"Of the way you make me feel. I'm normally very in control of my thoughts, my words, my actions, and in the last month you've made me…"

"Lose control?" he prompted and smiled when she nodded. She tucked her head down so he couldn't see her blush, but Zach simply held his finger under her chin until she looked up at him again. "Don't you think I feel the same way? I'm struggling with this just as much as you are."

"Really?"

He nodded. "I knew how I felt about you when I hired you. For years I did everything humanly possible to keep those feelings under control, and now that they've started to come out, and I see you feel the same way too…" He sighed and rested his forehead against hers. "Sweetheart, it's making me kick myself for all the time I wasted."

She let his admission wrap around her. Now it was her turn to scan his face. She reached up and traced the strong line of his jaw and then gently raked a hand through his hair. "Shouldn't this feel more…awkward?"

He chuckled. "I know. I thought so too at first. But this?" He captured her roaming hand and brought it to his lips and kissed her wrist. "It just feels right."

Words escaped her, so all she could do was nod.

They settled back into their earlier position and were temporarily content to stay like that, but she knew it wouldn't be long before Zach grew restless. She knew he wouldn't push her into doing something she wasn't ready for, but she also knew he wasn't the type to just be content sitting still for too long.

She almost laughed when he shifted and started to speak. "So I've been walking around the house," he began, "and I think I want to put some furniture in storage." For the next twenty minutes, he shared his thoughts and plans with her, and Gabriella was happy to just listen to him speak. For so long his words to her had been dripping with sarcasm and anger, she couldn't help but revel in his joy and enthusiasm. It was good to finally have the old Zach coming back.

"So what do you think?" he asked after he finished laying out his vision.

"I think it's a little ambitious," she said.

"A team of movers can get all of the heavy stuff done in a couple of hours. There are dozens of temperature-controlled storage places in the area so it won't be hard to find one of those. I'm just not sure what I really want to do in the master. All I know is I need it to change. Soon. Like now if it was possible."

She laughed at his impatience. Yes, the old Zach was definitely coming back, and she loved it.

—✳—

It was after midnight when Zach heard the soft snore coming from beside him. They were still on the sofa, his laptop in front of them. Together they had searched what seemed like hundreds of home decorating sites for inspiration. He enjoyed listening to her ideas and getting her input when he found something that appealed to him.

Doing his best not to disturb her, Zach closed the computer and put it on the end table. Next he maneuvered his arm out from around her so he could get up and allow her to fully lie down on the sofa. Once he was standing, he cursed himself. Gabriella should be home sleeping in her own bed, but instead he had called her, disrupted her evening, all for his own selfish intentions. Although, if he were honest, looking at decorating websites was not what he'd had in mind when he invited her over.

Or did she invite herself?

He chuckled for a minute while he studied her. Her makeup was long gone, her hair was loose and draped over her shoulder, her breathing even. She looked nothing like the ever-efficient assistant he knew, and yet she had never looked more beautiful to him. There was no way he could wake her up and make her drive home, but Zach wasn't foolish enough to think he was able to pick her up and carry her to one of the guest rooms. He was going to have to grab a pillow and some blankets and try to make her more comfortable. It wasn't ideal, but it would have to do.

Walking away, he shut off all the lights in the house except for one small table lamp by the sofa. Along the way he locked the front door, gathered a pillow and blanket from the linen closet, and returned to Gabriella's sleeping form.

This was new territory for him. He wasn't a nurturer. He was tough and independent and always felt that others should be the same. But with Gabriella, it was different. He wanted to take care of her, protect her.

Carefully, he slid the pillow under her head and she hummed softly in her sleep. Looking down, he saw she must have kicked her shoes off earlier. He draped the soft blanket over her and smiled when she snuggled into it.

Then he stood back and simply enjoyed watching her.

Zach knew he should move, go to his room, go to sleep. But he couldn't. What was it about her that made it impossible to be away from her? He eased himself down in front of her so they were eye level. His hand reached out and softly caressed her cheek and she whispered his name on a sigh.

He wasn't going to his room.

Doing his best not to disturb her, Zach eased back onto the couch, under the blanket, and gathered Gabriella into his arms. Maybe it was wishful thinking, but she seemed to sigh happily in her sleep. The sofa wasn't overly large, but tucked together the way they were, it was perfect. A bed would have been better, but he was more than happy with the current situation.

Reaching over his head, Zach fumbled blindly for the lamp to turn it off. Then, in the darkness, he felt himself relax. Really relax. If possible, it was the first time since he'd left for Denali that he felt at peace with the darkness.

Within minutes, he was asleep.

Sometime later, he had no idea when, Gabriella shifted beside him, moved closer. They were pressed together so intimately that he felt every curve, every dip of her body. A strangled moan rumbled in his throat, and Zach felt her stiffen in his arms.

"Zach?" she whispered.

His throat was completely dry, his tongue felt like it was the size of a fist as panic swamped him. Swallowing hard, he said, "Yeah?"

"What happened?"

All the blood in my body went south and I'm really, really sorry. Dammit. That wasn't going to go over well. "We fell asleep looking at room designs."

"Oh," she said sleepily and wiggled next to him a little more. "I don't remember us getting the blanket."

"Um…I grabbed one." *Well, duh*, he silently cursed himself.

"Mmm…good. It feels nice."

Baseball stats. Rebuilding a transmission. Four-wheeling in the mud. Zach forced all kinds of nonsexual thoughts and images into his mind, but Gabriella continued to move against him. Finally, unable to help himself, he tightened his arms around her. "Um…Gabs?"

"Hmm?"

"You need to stop doing that."

She craned her neck slightly so she was looking up at him. "Doing what?"

The wiggling and moving had stopped for a minute. With only moonlight bathing the room, Zach couldn't think of anything but her. Then she moved her leg so it was almost draped over his. "The moving," he said, though it came out sounding raw and gravelly. "I need…" He cleared his throat. "I need you to not…you know…move around so much."

Now she went completely still. A minute later she placed a hand on his chest and gently pushed as she sat up. "What time is it?"

Zach cursed himself. Now he'd done it—he'd woken her up and now she was going to want to leave. They'd argue because he'd ask her to stay and it was going to ruin everything. "Late."

Gabriella looked around the room. "Why…why didn't you just go to bed? I appreciate the blanket," she looked down, "and the pillow, but you should have just gone to bed. I would have been fine out here."

Sitting up, Zach caressed her cheek. "If things were different, I would have carried you to bed with me." He didn't bother to explain; he knew she'd understand.

"Oh."

"If I couldn't bring you in there with me, then I wanted to stay out here with you."

"Oh."

Then she became silent again, and Zach had to wonder what was going on in her mind. Was she angry with him for staying with her? Would she feel like he'd taken advantage of the situation? It was too dark to fully read her expression, and the silence was starting to kill him. He was just about to question her, when she spoke.

"I'm too sleepy to drive all the way home."

"No one's telling you to leave." Even in the dimness of the room, he could see her shy smile. His hand continued to cup the soft skin of her face. "I want you to stay."

Gabriella stared at him for what seemed like an eternity. "This couch isn't very big."

And there went all the blood again. "There are four beds here for you to choose from." Zach stood carefully and held out a hand to her. She looked up at him with those big blue eyes and he was lost. It was everything he wanted and everything he was afraid of.

If there was one thing he prided himself on, it was his honesty. Well, at least recently. He'd been honest with Gabriella in a way he'd never been with anyone else before. He stepped in close, so they were touching. "There's nothing I want more than to take you to my bed and make love to you."

Her eyes went a little wide. "But…?" she whispered.

"I… I'm not…" He cleared his throat again. "I'm not sure…I can. Not yet." He waited for a look or a word or a sound of pity to come out of her. But it didn't.

Gently, Gabriella squeezed his hand and turned to lead him from the room. At the door to his bedroom she stopped. "I hope you like to sleep in a little on the weekends." It was all she said before releasing his hand and walking into the darkness of his bedroom.

Zach heard the rustling of the comforter and sheets being pulled back. Heard the soft sounds the mattress made when someone climbed on. Hell, he even heard the whisper of fabric slipping from skin to floor.

And then he heard her sigh. "Zach?"

Slowly, he stepped into the room and shut the door. When he was standing beside the bed, he pulled his T-shirt over his head. And hesitated.

"Will you hold me like you were doing out on the couch?"

"Yes."

She let out a sleepy purr, and Zach climbed in and

pulled the blankets over him. Reaching over, he guided her into his arms. It felt…right. Gabriella's lips gently grazed his chest before she relaxed against him with a whispered "good night."

Indeed.

———

Gabriella was afraid to open her eyes.

She knew exactly where she was and exactly whom she was with.

And how she had pretty much invited herself into his bed.

There was no way she was going to be able to look Zach in the eye, not now, and possibly not ever again. For most of her life she had mastered the art of self-control, and in the last month she had pretty much thrown it right out the window. At first it had felt pretty good, liberating even, but now? Now she was mortified by her behavior. What must Zach think of her?

She almost laughed out loud at her own question. He was a man. She had crawled into his bed and wrapped herself around him. Of course he wasn't going to complain. She cursed her own stupidity.

Peeking out under her lashes, Gabriella saw the sun was up and filtering in through the blinds. Getting any glimpse of the time would require her to move and lift her head, and she wasn't ready to do that just quite yet. Unfortunately, she had no idea if Zach was a light sleeper or a heavy one. For all she knew, she could jump off the bed and slam doors without it bothering him one bit. Could she possibly be that lucky?

Carefully, she started to untangle herself from him.

Good Lord, she thought to herself, they were completely wrapped around one another. She had never been one for sleeping so closely with anyone—she enjoyed her personal space—and yet she had slept deeply and peacefully all night long with Zach's arms secured around her and her legs tangled together with his. It was almost hard to tell where one ended and the other began.

It actually felt really nice. Maybe, just maybe, she could stay put for a little while longer. With a quiet sigh, she relaxed against him and simply enjoyed the feel of her cheek against his bare chest and his arms holding her close.

"Did you work it all out?"

A small squeak escaped Gabriella's lips at Zach's sleepy question. "What…? How…? Work what out?"

"I figure you've been awake for a few minutes worrying about how you were going to sneak out of here."

"Now I know how Summer feels," she mumbled.

"What does my sister have to do with this?" He chuckled.

"She's always telling me to get out of her head and now I totally get it. It's freaky."

"What? That I can read your mind?" He didn't wait for her to respond. "Because you do it to me too, all the time. Turnabout's fair play and all."

"I wasn't thinking of sneaking out," she said with a pout.

Zach laughed. "Sweetheart, you are many things but a liar isn't one of them. I think you woke up and felt awkward about…this." He gestured to their position. "It's all right. I mean, I was hoping you'd be okay and comfortable with it, but I completely understand if you're not. This is new territory for us. It seems like every day is something new for us."

Sitting up, Gabriella looked over at him. "And doesn't it bother you or make you uncomfortable? Ever?"

He studied her for a long moment as if choosing his words carefully. "No," he said simply. "That's the strangest part of all of this—every time we…cross a line…no, that's not the right phrase." He cursed. "Every time we…evolve or try something new and move forward, I keep waiting for it to feel awkward or weird or uncomfortable, and it doesn't."

Gabriella's eyes went wide at his admission. She knew he was telling her the truth, knew he wasn't just saying what he thought she wanted him to say. Ducking her head, she combed her hair behind her ear. "I…I don't normally…do this kind of thing." Her words were spoken so softly she wasn't even sure Zach heard her until she felt him sit up and put his lips on her shoulder.

"Good," he whispered. "I like the fact you were comfortable enough with me to do this." Then he chuckled. "Not that we've done anything."

"Don't say it like that. It was very nice. I think snuggling is an underrated activity that gets a bum rap. Personally, I enjoyed it."

Zach eased them back against the pillows. "Sweetheart, I am all for snuggling with you." He wrapped an arm around her while his other hand began to roam casually up and down her body. "Particularly when you're half naked."

She blushed furiously. "I can't sleep with anything on my legs. I kicked my yoga pants off when I climbed into bed."

"And I, for one, appreciate it," he said and kissed the tip of her nose.

It was still a bit amazing she was able to relax so easily with him. One minute she was shy and apprehensive, and the next Zach managed to put her completely at ease. Gabriella wasn't sure if it meant he was sincere or she was gullible.

No. That didn't sit right with her. She'd learned her lesson a long time ago where being gullible was concerned. She knew Zach well enough, and long enough, to know that part of what made her feel the way she did was because she knew him. But even though she knew it and it made perfect sense, there was still a niggling sense of doubt about what they were doing, sharing.

"You're doing it again," he said quietly.

She chuckled. "Sorry. I can't seem to help it."

Zach gently released her and rose from the bed. "Come on. Let's scrounge up some breakfast and make our plan of attack for shopping."

Gabriella warred with feelings of relief and disappointment. Zach had been completely honest with her about why they weren't…advancing their relationship. There was no doubt in her mind it had been painful for him to admit his struggles to her—especially ones that were personal. It made her feel special—that he trusted her enough to say it. But there was another part of her that was curious to test the waters, so to speak. Had the doctors told him he shouldn't try to have sex yet? Had Alex? Or was this something Zach was feeling and thinking on his own?

Looking up, she found him standing in the doorway. "You coming?" he asked.

"I'll be there in a minute," she said, still feeling a little shy about climbing from the bed in nothing but a T-shirt and a pair of panties.

"I'll meet you in the kitchen. I'll get the coffee started."

"Okay." As Zach walked from the room, Gabriella noticed he was using only one crutch. His movements were still slow and stiff, but he was definitely making progress. She knew he had an appointment with his team of doctors on Monday and couldn't help but wonder what kind of news they were going to receive.

Or how it was going to affect where they went from here.

――⌇――

"So how was your weekend?"

Zach looked over at Alex as they drove to his appointment and grinned.

"That good, huh?" Alex asked with a chuckle. "Do tell."

"If I told you, I might have my man card revoked," Zach replied, unable to help the laughter that came with it.

"Now I have to know. Come on. Out with it."

With a roll of his eyes, Zach shifted uncomfortably in the seat. "Do you think the rehab facility will get some use out of the wheelchair?"

"Ah," Alex said, nodding his head. "Avoidance. Changing the subject. You must have really done something lame to go there." He looked over at Zach and laughed. "And now I'm even more curious."

"Okay, fine," Zach said, trying to sound angry but failing miserably. "I spent the weekend…redecorating."

At first Alex didn't respond. Then he held a hand to

his ear. "I'm sorry. What was that? You…redecorated? Do I have that right?"

"I told you. I'll have my man card out and ready to shred by the time we reach the hospital."

"I don't think we'll have to go that far. Yet." Now they both laughed. "So you started redecorating the house." He looked over his shoulder toward the wheelchair. "And getting rid of the chair was part of it?"

"Getting rid of the chair is what started it."

"Go on."

Zach explained his realization that he felt his surroundings were playing a large role in hindering his recovery. "Maybe I'm crazy," he finally said. "I don't know." He raked a hand through his hair. "I love my house. I fell in love with it the first time I walked through it. But after being confined to it? I feel like the walls are closing in on me. I don't want to move, but I need to change things up a bit."

"Plus it gave you a good excuse to hang with Gabriella all weekend."

While it was true, it still bothered Zach to hear the implication. He didn't want anyone thinking anything crude or disrespectful about his and Gabriella's relationship. As of now, the only ones who were even aware of their relationship included him, Gabriella, and…Alex. Somehow Zach had managed to keep his usually nosy family out of the loop on this one. As far as they were all concerned, he had simply seen the error of his ways and decided to get back to work with the help of his longtime assistant.

He crossed his fingers and hoped they could keep it to themselves for a little bit longer. There was no way he was going to be able to hide the way he really felt about Gabriella in front of his family. They'd call him out as soon as they got one look at him.

That's how out of control he felt.

And it was important to him that his family never see him out of control ever again. It had been hard enough dealing with their concern and pity while he had been in the hospital and recuperating from the fall. There was no doubt he'd be subject to a completely different kind of pity and concern and mocking if they were to watch him acting like an idiot over Gabriella.

Then he stopped and considered that. No one would really have to see him acting any different from how he always had. He'd hidden his feelings for Gabriella from everyone for years. Surely he could keep it up for just a little longer.

Crisis averted.

Zach looked up in time to see Alex had pulled into a parking spot at the hospital and was looking at him expectantly. "This is it," Zach said with a weary sigh.

"Don't go in there with that kind of attitude," Alex said, his own voice sounding encouraging. "You're making great progress, Zach. The doctors are going to be impressed."

"What if…what if they do the scans and see things aren't healing?"

"Why are you looking for trouble?"

"Habit," Zach said with a mirthless laugh. "Every time I seem to get my hopes up with this recovery, I end up being completely mistaken."

"That's because you weren't fully focusing before. We haven't been working together very long, but I can tell you're way more committed to the rehab than you were a week ago. These things take time." He paused and collected his thoughts. "I wish I could tell you you're going to wake up tomorrow and never have to use the crutches or a cane ever again. But I can't. Someday it's going to happen but it doesn't happen overnight. You need to be patient."

"Not my strong suit."

"No kidding." Alex chuckled. "Look, you're doing great. I'm really pleased and impressed with the progress we've made. I watched you come out of the house this morning and you had a much more confident walk. You're getting your strength back. But we have to take it slow and do this right or you'll end up hurting yourself. Trust me."

"I do. I really do. I'm just… I don't know if I'm ready to hear what the doctors are going to tell me."

Pulling the keys from the ignition, Alex turned and put a reassuring hand on Zach's shoulder. "Whatever it is, we'll deal with it. If we have to adjust your routine and your therapy, then we'll do it. Nothing they're going to tell you is going to stop the momentum. Okay?"

Zach eyed him warily. "Man, I wish I had your optimism."

Alex opened the car door and climbed out before turning back to Zach. "It's all right. I've got enough for the both of us right now."

—⁓—

"I cannot believe you and Zach!" Summer huffed as she walked over to Gabriella's desk and sat herself down on the corner.

Gabriella's eyes went wide with surprise. "*What?* Me and Zach? What are you talking about?"

Summer rolled her eyes. "What are you even doing here in the office? I thought the two of you were working from Zach's until he was ready to come back here. Did he throw you out again? Did you quit? Because honestly, I cannot take much more of this drama."

Gabriella almost slid to the floor with relief. Work. Summer was talking about work. *Whew!* "He had a doctor's appointment this morning, so I came into the office."

"Really? Why didn't he call me or Ethan to go with him?"

"His therapist took him."

"Oh," Summer said, her brows furrowed. "But... why?"

Crap. Gabriella didn't want to get in the middle of this, and she had just assumed Zach was keeping his family up to date. "I think Alex wanted to go with him so he could ask the doctors questions and do whatever he could to make sure the therapy is conducive to how Zach is healing."

"Oh. I guess that makes sense. Still, I wish one of us were with him. I hate to think of him being there alone."

"Summer, he's not alone. Alex is with him and he's a really great guy."

"Oh really," she purred, leaning in closer. "Do tell."

"Stop it. Aren't you a happily engaged woman?"

Summer waved her off. "Of course I am. I wasn't asking for me, I was asking for you. It's the first time I've heard you refer to any guy as a great guy. Is he cute?"

"I'll tell you all about him in study hall. Now shoo... I have a lot of work to do while I'm here. I know Carolyn is doing a great job but I hate all this paperwork piling up on my desk. I think my assistant needs an assistant just to do my filing."

"Please, you know you would hate that. You like to look at every piece of paper, commit it to memory, and then file it away yourself."

Gabriella frowned. "When you say it, you make it sound like a bad thing."

"It's not a bad thing. I'm just reminding you of your OCD."

"Thanks. Like I could have forgotten."

"What are friends for?"

Gabriella looked at her watch. "What's on your agenda today? Do you think we could grab some lunch later?"

"I'm sure I can do that. But are you sure you can?"

"Why wouldn't I?"

"What about Zach?"

"What about him? He knows I'm here and he doesn't mind us going out together."

Summer giggled. "I love how defensive you get where he's concerned. Honestly, I still can't believe you went back to work for him and you haven't killed him yet."

"It's a daily struggle."

"Well, I'm glad you haven't because even though he is a major pain in the butt, he's my brother and I love him."

"I'll try to remember that the next time he's being difficult."

"Thank you. Back to my original question—don't you want to be at Zach's when he gets home?"

It was an innocent enough question, and yet

Gabriella's heart was racing. Did she want to be there? Yes. Did it have anything to do with business? No. She had been mildly disappointed when Zach had told her Alex was taking him to his appointment. When he explained why, she completely understood, but part of her wanted to be there for him, to share in the news he got—good or bad.

What if he got bad news? What if he wasn't going to get any better? Gabriella would stay with Zach no matter what, so if he never went skydiving or climbed another mountain, it would be fine with her. She knew Zach would hate the loss, but together they'd find a way to keep forging a path forward with this new version of them.

And if the news was good?

What if Zach got the news that he was healing and getting better and he could…resume some of his normal activities? Like sex. Gabriella would be lying if she said it hadn't been on her mind—a lot!—but it was a line that, once crossed, couldn't be uncrossed. They'd been kissing and fooling around but that wasn't the same. Once you were intimate with someone, it had the potential to change everything.

Her stomach churned at the thought. Not the reaction she would have expected. While of course she wanted Zach to get better, it opened the door to a host of other issues—some she wasn't sure she wanted to deal with.

The little green monster on her shoulder made her wonder if Zach was simply killing time with her because she was safe. He knew her, they were comfortable with one another, but there wasn't a risk involved. Not really. Gabriella would be accepting of Zach and any limitations he had due to the accident, and that made her safe. Not like if he went out and pursued a woman he didn't know.

A nameless woman—whom she already hated—might not be as accepting. It would be a blow to Zach's ego if he were rejected because of his injuries.

Ugh. This was a nightmare.

"Wow. Whatever it is you're thinking, you're looking pretty fierce. You okay?" Summer asked.

"What? Oh, sorry." She fidgeted in her chair and made work of straightening some of the papers on her desk.

"Wait…what's going on with you? You're all… twitchy." Summer stood and circled Gabriella's desk. "You're never twitchy."

"I'm not twitchy. My mind wandered for a moment. It's no big deal." More paperwork shuffling and straightening.

"And you're fidgeting. You never fidget."

Gabriella felt her cheeks heat and wished Ethan would come and distract Summer. "I'm fidgeting because I feel like you've got me under the microscope for some reason. Ease up, Nancy Drew. I've got work I need to deal with. Are we doing lunch or not?"

"And now you're being snippy."

"It's a trifecta of suspicion."

Summer sat back down on the corner of the desk. "Fine. Keep your secrets. We'll talk more at lunch."

That's exactly what Gabriella was afraid of.

Chapter 10

"You're overreacting."

Silence.

"Seriously, you're missing the entire point. I thought you'd be happy."

Zach's head snapped to the left to glare at Alex. "You're joking, right?"

They had left the hospital almost thirty minutes ago, and Zach had been stewing the entire time. He had been examined, scanned, poked, and prodded every which way. Then he and Alex sat down with a team of specialists to get a better look at how he was doing and discuss his prognosis.

"Okay, look. We're just about at your house and I'm not leaving until we talk about this. Obviously you're upset but for the life of me, I don't understand why. And until I do, we're not going to get anywhere with the physical part of the therapy."

Zach snorted with disgust. "Nice how you added 'physical' to that. Up until a couple of hours ago, all we had to say was therapy. Now all of a sudden I'm some kind of head case."

"That's how you're choosing to look at it." They pulled into Zach's driveway and Alex kept his silence until they were out of the car and inside the house. As soon as Zach sat down on the sofa, Alex began. "You're focusing on the wrong thing here. Your scans were good, great even! The swelling is just about gone. Your muscles are getting stronger, and everyone was very pleased with what you've accomplished."

"Did you see the looks on their faces?" Zach interrupted. "They looked at me like I was crazy."

"No," Alex said adamantly. "No, they didn't. That's how *you* perceived it." He paced back and forth a couple of times. "Zach, you've said it dozens of times yourself, during the bulk of your recovery time, you spent a lot of time in your head. You had a hard time staying positive and believing you were going to get better. The doctors are simply…suggesting…some of the issues you're still experiencing with the temporary paralysis are brought on by anxiety. It's not unusual."

"Why would I *want* to be paralyzed? Huh? Answer me that one! I've wanted nothing more than to get better and now they're trying to tell me I'm *making* myself paralyzed? That sounds to me like they don't have an explanation and they're trying to blame it on me!"

Alex shook his head. "No. That's not it at all. I knew you weren't listening to them."

"I heard every damn word they said," Zach snarled, teeth clenched.

"There's a difference between hearing and listening," Alex said and then paused to calm himself. "I want you to take a deep breath and relax."

"Screw you."

"Dude, I have invested too much damn time with you to have you quit on me now because you're having a hissy fit. Man up and listen." He never raised his voice but his tone was firm enough that Zach knew he was serious. After a minute he repeated, "Take a deep breath and relax."

Zach did.

"I want you to think about some of the times—we'll deal with the most recent ones—when your leg went numb."

Zach threw his head back and closed his eyes. "Okay."

"How were you feeling right before it happened?"

"I don't know."

"Then think," Alex countered.

Zach glared at him. "Fine." He thought about the day Gabriella had come over and how he had felt anxious and had freaked out about her seeing him in this condition. "One of the last times I had one, I was having a mild anxiety attack about Gabriella being here at the house and seeing me like this. I was in the shower. By the time I started to feel that...tingling, I was in a full-blown panic."

"Okay. Now we're getting somewhere. Would you say that on other occasions, you were feeling similarly?"

"Not over Gabriella."

"No, but were you having anxiety about other things?"

Zach shrugged. "Some episodes happened during therapy treatments when I felt the therapist wasn't listening to me or pushing me harder than I thought I could handle. Then I'd get that feeling and my body would shut down."

"Like a defense mechanism."

"What?" Zach snapped.

"Think about it. And this time I want you to really listen. Every time you felt overwhelmed or challenged by a situation, your body would respond by this tingling in your leg and then the paralysis set in. You'd feel justified in your feelings of outrage or anxiety and then, once you felt better, more relaxed, you'd regain feeling. Am I right?"

Zach wanted to disagree, but Alex had a point. So he simply nodded before saying, "It wasn't like that all the time."

"I'm sure it wasn't. And the doctors know it wasn't. All we're saying is the mind is a strong thing. In the cases of the paralysis coming on in certain situations, it all starts to make sense. From what you've just shared, anxiety plays a huge role in this. Most people who are experiencing an anxiety attack—for any reason—tend to hyperventilate a bit. Hyperventilation is the act of breathing out too much carbon dioxide, so your body responds by slowing down blood flow to certain areas of your body. This is what causes it to feel as though certain body parts can't move. They may start to tingle or feel numb, causing you to feel as though your muscles aren't working." He paused. "Sound familiar?"

It did, but Zach stayed silent.

"You heard the word 'anxiety' and thought they were minimalizing your struggles. That's not it at all. Anxiety is very real, Zach. When someone suffers from anxiety, they can focus so heavily on the way their body feels that they actually make these movements consciously. That means your movements aren't automatic anymore, and you have to think about each and every muscle you need to move in order to get them active. That's considerably harder than it sounds, so in the end you may find that a particular muscle or area of your body isn't moving the way you expect it to."

"So what you're saying is, if I overcome my anxiety, I should be completely back to normal."

Alex chuckled and sat down on the opposite end of the sofa. "Don't oversimplify, buddy. Your body suffered a big trauma and still needs to rebuild itself and get your muscles working normally again. We're not going to sit around a campfire and sing 'Kumbaya' and then *bam!* You're going to get up and walk away and climb another mountain."

"Then what the hell am I supposed to do?"

"Exactly what we're doing. Be patient. We keep doing the physical therapy. You keep building up your strength while maintaining a positive attitude. There are going to be setbacks. There are going to be times when your body isn't going to want to keep up this pace, but in the long run, it's going to be worth it."

Zach sighed loudly. "I just never thought... I knew my head was messing with me, but I never realized to what extent. I feel like a jackass."

"Why? Because you're human?"

"I should've known better."

"How would you have known that this—your emotional state having such an impact on your physical state—was even possible? Were you an expert on the human psyche before the climb?"

"Well, no..."

"Then give yourself a break. I mean, damn it, Zach. Ease up on yourself a bit. You fell off a freaking mountain. You're lucky to be alive. You can't control everything and you can't know everything."

"My family's been trying to tell me that for years."

"Maybe it's time you listened."

Zach's mind was spinning in a dozen different directions. Where did this leave him? Where did he go from here? "Can I ask you something?"

"Anything."

"About a month ago, Gabriella was here and we were arguing." He stopped and shifted his position. "We used to do that a lot. Anyway, she was walking out, walking away, and I stopped her and…I kissed her for the first time."

"And that was only a month ago?" Alex asked, his expression showing his disbelief.

"It's a long story," Zach said. "But…while I was kissing her, I felt the tingling in my leg and thought it was going to give out. But she stayed with me. Helped me over to the couch."

"How long was the feeling gone?"

"That's just it. I didn't go numb. The tingling just sort of went away."

Alex smiled. "Because you didn't freak out. You didn't panic. There was no anxiety. Are you seeing it now? Can you understand it? I know you're going to beat yourself up over this and there's nothing I can do to change your mind about it, but you need to see how no one is making light of your situation. What you're dealing with is very real. Personally, I'm glad we realized what it was."

"How could they not?"

"Well, if they had found something that suggested something else was causing these episodes. But since you were pissed when they suggested the possibility of it being anxiety related, that made it easier for them to come to that conclusion without having to do more tests. Which, ironically, is fortunate for you, because I would imagine you're over being poked and jabbed by a medical team by now."

"You've got that right."

"So? Are you up for a session today?"

Zach looked over at him. "I don't think it's a question we should be asking. I think ready or not, willing or not, I need to be doing it."

Alex chuckled. "Do you want to call anyone first? Let them know how the appointment went? I'm sure your family and Gabriella are anxious for news."

Zach hadn't thought about it. "Maybe."

"Tell you what. I think you had enough of a workout today between all of the walking at the hospital and the tests. Take the rest of the day and wrap your brain around what you learned. Talk to your family. Talk to Gabriella. We'll pick up again in the morning."

"Are you sure?" Zach asked, confused. "I thought it was important for us to keep going forward."

"We are. Not all of our sessions have to look the same."

"I guess."

Alex stood and shook Zach's hand before walking toward the front door. "Oh, and Zach?"

"Yeah?"

"You may have been too busy stewing over the word 'anxiety,' but the doctors pretty much gave you the green light to go ahead and resume your sex life." He gave an exaggerated wink and a thumbs-up. "Just thought I'd throw it out there." And then he was gone.

And Zach was stuck sitting on the couch wondering what he was going to do with that information.

—⁓—

"So basically this is great news, right?" Summer asked excitedly as she held the phone to her ear and gave Gabriella the thumbs-up.

"I'm trying not to get my hopes up," Zach said, but there was a smile in his voice.

"Such a guy."

"Is Ethan nearby? I'd like to talk to him."

"Actually, he's back at the office. I'm having lunch with Gabriella right now. Do you want to talk to her?"

"Um…no. That's okay. I'll talk to her when she comes to work tomorrow."

"It's only lunchtime, Zach. And really, she's so efficient I think she's done with everything at the office that she can't do at your house. Do you want her to come over and finish out her day there?"

Gabriella rolled her eyes at Summer's desperation. She was ready to snatch the phone out of her friend's hand and throw it. It didn't take a rocket scientist to realize Zach hadn't deemed her important enough to call and share the news about his doctor's appointment. All she could tell from listening to Summer's end was that it was good.

Lot of good that did her.

She was surprised and yet she wasn't. This was typical Zach behavior—come on strong and then back off. Maybe he had gotten cold feet about where they were heading. Or maybe it was just as she had predicted: he had gotten his good news from the doctor and didn't feel the need to tie himself to the safe bet after all. He was free to go back to dating the socialites he always seemed to favor.

Summer said good-bye and put the phone back in her purse. "Hey, you're strangling that breadstick," she said with a laugh. "What gives?"

"Nothing. So he got good news, huh?"

Summer's smile was huge. "I'm sure he's going to tell you everything tomorrow, but the swelling is almost gone and the doctors feel pretty confident he's going to make a full recovery." She sat back in her chair and sighed happily. "I've been praying for this for so long and I know Zach's got to be relieved."

"But…" Gabriella prompted.

"But…he just didn't sound as happy as I thought he would."

"How do you even know what Zach sounds like when he's happy?" Gabriella said sarcastically and then cringed.

Summer could only laugh. "Ain't that the truth! It's been so long since I've seen or heard him laugh or make a joke that I probably wouldn't know it when I saw it." She shrugged. "I guess I just expected a little more enthusiasm."

Gabriella made a noncommittal sound and pushed her salad around on her plate.

"This has to be good news for you, though," Summer said.

"Why?" Gabriella asked with a frown.

"If Zach's getting better, then that means you'll be back to working in the office with everyone. No more going to his house and being cooped up with him while he growls and grunts and basically acts like a jerk."

"Yeah, now I get to come back to the office and deal with him while he growls and grunts and acts like a jerk with a bigger audience."

"Not that you're bitter or anything."

Gabriella made another small sound and forced a forkful of salad into her mouth.

Summer gave a dramatic sigh. "All right. Out with it. What's happened now?"

Daintily finishing her forkful of salad, Gabriella wiped the corners of her mouth and placed the napkin back in her lap. "What are you talking about?"

"Clearly Zach has done something. Honestly, I don't get it. I mean, you were all set to work with Ethan. I thought it was a done deal. Then you call and say you and Zach talked and you're going to stay on and help him. Why? If he's this much of a jerk to you, why do you keep putting up with it? Uncle William will find you a position anywhere in the company. Take my advice— take him up on it. I hate seeing you so upset."

Gabriella was completely torn. On one hand, she needed to talk to someone about what was going on and her feelings for Zach. On the other hand, that person should probably *not* be Zach's sister.

"Gabs? Come on. Talk to me."

"Things have gotten a lot better this last week."

"That's great!"

Shaking her head, Gabriella felt tears threaten to form in her eyes. "I thought it was. We were back to being the way we were in the beginning. Only better."

If Summer was even remotely suspicious of anything, she chose to keep it to herself.

"You weren't completely off base back in Alaska," Gabriella began slowly, refusing to meet Summer's gaze. "I did have feelings for Zach." Then she looked up. "Turns out he had them too."

"No. Freaking. Way!" Summer almost jumped up from her seat but managed to refrain. "This is amazing! You and Zach! Oh my God! How could you keep this from me?"

"Summer, it's not… It's not like that. Zach is dealing with a lot of stuff. And even though we admitted to having…feelings, we work together. Neither of us is willing to risk our business relationship right now. He has too much riding on him getting better and getting back to his position in the company to waste it fooling around with me."

Summer arched a brow at her. "Seriously? Fooling around? If there's one thing I know about the both of you, it's that you're excellent multitaskers. I don't think either of you is the type to get so distracted with 'fooling around' that it's going to hamper your working relationship." She paused and studied Gabriella for a minute when realization hit. "You're upset because he didn't call you about what the doctors told him. I'm right, aren't I?"

Gabriella had had enough. "So? What do you want? A medal?"

"Okay, no need to get snippy."

Unable to help herself, Gabriella slammed a hand down on the table. "You know what? I think I'm entitled to be a little snippy! Your brother has jerked me around for years—blaming me for something he misunderstood—and then I had to deal with his verbal abuse and now he begs and grovels and convinces me to stay on and I stupidly agree. And on top of it, I foolishly agree to fooling around but at the end of the day, you know where I am? In the dark! I don't mean enough to him." She took a deep breath. "I don't think I really mean anything to him."

"Gabs, I'm sure that's not true."

Gabriella shared her theory on her being the "safe bet" for Zach to ease back into dating.

"I think it's the most ridiculous theory I've ever heard," Summer said flatly. "I'm kind of disappointed in you. For someone who usually has all the answers— you're like Yoda or Obi-Wan to most of us—you've suddenly turned into some sort of...I don't know... amateur. I'll be honest, I'm a little concerned."

"Okay, dramatic much?" Gabriella asked, crossing her arms over her chest.

"Look, I don't think Zach's that kind of person. He doesn't just...use people like that."

"Summer, I love your loyalty to your family, but you weren't around here the last couple of years. Your brother had a revolving door of women he never went out with more than a handful of times. I even had to break up with some of them for him!"

"I promise to not break up with you—even if Zach asks me," Summer said seriously, right before her lips began to twitch.

"You are so not funny right now."

"Yeah, but you love me anyway."

"Damn you," Gabriella said. "So what do I do? Am I crazy? Am I wrong to be offended that he not only didn't call but clearly didn't want me around this afternoon?"

"Honestly, Gabs, I think Zach's trying to come to grips with it all. Let him have today. Then go to the house tomorrow and see how it goes. I think you're overreacting. I don't think Zach's just playing with you. He wouldn't do that. Especially not to you."

Gabriella suddenly wasn't so sure anymore.

—∿—

Zach paced the living room the next morning, doing his best to ignore the muscle cramp from his morning session with Alex. Gabriella was late. Gabriella was never late.

Another glance at the clock showed it was almost eight thirty. Their day normally started at eight, but she was always ready to go by seven forty-five. It was a little unnerving. Had something happened to her?

He cursed the fact he hadn't called her the day before. When Summer had mentioned they were having lunch together, he panicked. There was no way he could have the conversation with Gabriella he wanted to, knowing his sister was sitting right there. It was a lame excuse, but it also allowed him the time to just wrap his brain around everything he had learned yesterday.

He was going to be okay.

This morning during his session with Alex he had asked if by being okay, it meant that there'd be no outward signs of his accident. The answer wasn't quite what he had hoped for. Due to the complexity of the breaks in his leg, there was a good chance he'd have a limp for the rest of his life. Not the worst-case scenario, but it did mess with Zach's head a little.

He wanted to be perfect. He wanted to be exactly like the man he was before the climb. A limp might not seem like much to most people, but to Zach it was the equivalent of a giant neon sign saying he was flawed.

Should he ever go on any adventure trips again, people

were going to look at him differently—simply because of
the limp. They were going to be concerned, or wonder if
he were up to the task, no matter how small it was. That
wasn't something he was looking forward to.

He looked at the clock again and cursed. "This is ridiculous," he muttered as he picked up his phone and called
Gabriella. It went directly to voice mail. "Dammit." He
called the office next and asked for Summer.

"Wow! Twice in two days!" she said cheerily. "You
really are getting better."

He wanted to laugh and smile with her, but he was
too concerned. "Do you know where Gabriella is?"

"What? No. Why?"

"She hasn't arrived yet and…"

"She's never late," Summer finished for him. "Have
you called her?"

"Of course!" he snapped and then reeled it in. "It
went directly to voice mail. I don't know what else
to do. You had lunch with her yesterday, was she
feeling okay?"

"Other than being annoyed with you, she was fine."

"Annoyed? Why?"

"Really? You're going to play the dumb card?"

"Okay, fine. That's our usual MO, but I thought I was
doing better. I can't think of anything I could've done
to upset her."

Summer sighed. "You didn't call her," she said.
"You. The guy who normally calls her even when she's
in the next room just so you can report that you're almost
out of paper clips. But this time you didn't call to share
actual news with her. I totally agreed with her that it was
a crappy thing for you to do."

"I'll tell you what, when something like this happens to you, then you can judge. I know I don't make the greatest decisions—"

"You got that right," she interrupted.

"But," he said loudly to stop her from talking again, "I didn't do it to be mean." He sighed wearily. "So do you think she's just…pissed? Do you think she's just being a little spiteful and coming in late to prove some kind of point?"

"The two of you are exhausting," she muttered.

"What's that supposed to mean?"

"It means I wish you'd stop tiptoeing around one another. She's clearly into you and you are so totally into her and yeah, we all get it, you work together, but could you please just *communicate* with one another? Honestly."

Zach was stunned speechless. It wasn't really surprising that Summer knew about his feelings for Gabriella. He was certain Ethan had ratted him out. But the fact that Summer was in the know about Gabriella's feelings meant the two of them had talked about it.

"So she's into me, huh?"

"Oh, good Lord. Don't even go there. Keep calling her and let me know when she gets there. I'll look around and ask if maybe she stopped in here this morning and I just didn't see her."

"Thanks, Summer. You're the best."

"Yeah, sure. You say that now. I'll be sure to remind you of it when you're back to working in the office and I do something to annoy you."

"I'm sure you will, brat. I love you."

"Love you too."

———

For the first time in over five years, Gabriella considered calling in sick to work. She felt fine if you didn't count the fact her heart ached every time she thought about all the amazing things Zach had said to her in the last week and then didn't bother to call her when he received the good news from his doctor. Didn't that pretty much tell her how he really felt?

Unfortunately, her work ethic got the better of her. She'd go to his house and she'd get to work.

On her own terms.

Deciding to stop by the office first, she grabbed up a box of files she had started working on yesterday. They weren't overly important, but they were clients who could use a little follow-up and it would be the perfect kind of busywork that would keep Zach on the phone and out of her hair.

Next she decided to stop for her morning coffee. Normally she grabbed a cup for herself and Zach and brought them to his house, but today she only purchased one for herself—along with a muffin—and sat and ate it in the café. Looking at her watch, she smirked. Yeah, Zach would be having a fit by now, but she didn't care. Let him stew. She had to wait to hear about his doctor's visit; he'd have to wait for her.

Um…rubber? Meet glue.

This was so not the person she wanted to be. Petty. Childish.

Heartbroken.

With a sigh of resignation, Gabriella stood and threw her trash away, then walked out to her car and drove over to Zach's. Once there, she pulled the box from her car and balanced it under one arm while she used her key to let herself in.

"Where the hell have you been?" Zach yelled as she walked through the door. "I've been trying to call you for over an hour!"

"I had some stops to make. I didn't think it was a big deal." Shrugging, she walked across the living room and placed the box on the coffee table, and then back to the front door to hang up her jacket and purse.

"What stops? You didn't mention needing to make any stops."

"Contrary to popular belief, I don't have to report my every move to you," she said coolly as she sat and began pulling files from the box. "I went through my files at the office yesterday. We have about fifty clients we haven't had direct contact with in over a year. I thought it would be a good time to go through the list and reach out to them." Systematically, she grouped the files into piles on the table. She gasped loudly when he grabbed the bunch she was holding in her hands and tossed them aside.

"What's going on here?" he demanded.

She looked at him defiantly. "I'm working. Isn't that the purpose of my being here?"

Zach scrubbed a hand over his face and looked down at where she was sitting, his voice softening. "Is this about me not calling you yesterday? Summer said that upset you for some reason."

She looked away and shrugged before resuming her task. "Not that I expect you to report your every move to me, but you called everyone and let them know how it all went. Except me." When all the files were laid out in an order she was satisfied with, Gabriella went to the kitchen, poured herself a glass of water, and then leaned against the counter to look at Zach.

"It wasn't like that," he said quietly as he stepped into the room. "You have no idea how hard yesterday was for me. I called my parents, and then I tried to call Ethan. When I couldn't get him on the phone, I reached out to Summer. I didn't go through my contacts and call everyone but you. Honestly."

"You know what, Zach? It's fine, really. Like I said, we don't have to report our every move to one another. Things got a little…confusing…between us. It's okay. I think it's better for us if we just leave it at that and get back to where we belong. We work together and we're trying to get you caught up so when you return to the office, everything will be in place. Okay?"

"No, it's not okay!" he snapped. "There was nothing confusing about last week. We were moving forward in our relationship! We both admitted we had feelings for one another, and I don't understand why you're suddenly pulling back!"

Words died in her throat. She had no idea how to have this conversation with him. It was bad enough just thinking she was wrong about what was going on between the two of them. Admitting out loud that she knew she wasn't enough for someone like him just might kill her.

"Gabs? Come on," he said, taking a deep breath and letting it out, his eyes never leaving hers. "Talk to me."

If she ever wanted to be done with this awkward conversation, Gabriella knew she was just going to have to spit it out and be done with it. She wasn't a coward—no matter how badly she wanted to be one at the moment.

"You want to know?" she huffed and slammed her glass down on the counter. "Fine. I think it was all fine and well to cozy up to me so I'd come back to work for you and make your life more convenient. I think you even thought it was a good thing for us to get involved because I was safe—someone you knew would understand your injuries and recovery. But as soon as you got the good news from the doctor, you realized you didn't need someone safe. You could go back to your old ways and your revolving door of women and didn't need me. So I'm giving you an out, Zach. Do us both a favor, just take it and don't make this any more awkward than it already is. Please."

She was nearly out of breath and wished to God Zach would say…something. Anything. He continued to stare at her—hard. It was almost too much to bear. It was enough to make her squirm. Then, without a word, he reached out and banded an arm around her waist and hauled her roughly against him. Her eyes went wide and she gasped right before his lips came crashing down on hers.

It was pointless to fight it or pretend she wasn't interested. Her arms went around him, her hands raking into his hair. It was hard to say who was in control because they were both so out of control.

Zach pushed her back up against the kitchen counter, his entire body pressed intimately against hers. Gabriella slowly rubbed against him and smiled at the feel of his hardened length against her belly. Of course it didn't matter what part of him was pressed against her. Zach Montgomery was solid muscle from head to toe and she wanted every inch of him whether she was pissed at him or not.

Gabriella purred as Zach's hands began to wander and reached down to the hem of her skirt and began to lift it. He had it up around her thighs when he finally raised his head. They were both breathing hard as he looked down into her glazed eyes. "Damn, I'm ready to take you right here," he growled. "Tell me you don't want me. Or this. And I'll stop. But if you do, say something now so we can take this further and I can finally do all of the things I've been fantasizing about for five damn years."

Slowly, Gabriella licked her lips as she lowered her hands and smoothed her skirt back into place. Keeping her expression neutral, she almost felt bad when she saw the hint of vulnerability in Zach's eyes. Then she reached for his hand and led him from the room. With a knowing smile she said, "I guess it's a good thing we have all day then. I'd imagine we'll need it to cover those five years."

Zach groaned with relief. "Sweetheart, one day won't be nearly enough."

As soon as they were in Zach's room, he closed the door and leaned against it and simply stared at her. She felt the urge to squirm again. "Zach," she sighed softly, hoping to encourage him.

He stalked toward her like a predator stalked its prey. When he was right in front of her, his hand cupped her cheek and then raked slowly into her hair. "I don't know if there'll ever be enough time," he said thickly before kissing her again.

This time there was no urgency. He gently explored as Gabriella sighed against him. Her hands reached up to cup his cheeks and then stayed there, enjoying the rough feel of his stubbled jaw against her palms. As if it were the most natural thing in the world, Zach began to unbutton her blouse. Gabriella couldn't stop the trembling she felt as he parted the material and then stepped back to look at her.

She had never been more thankful for her Victoria's Secret obsession as she was right now. The hungry look on Zach's face made all of her overindulging completely worth it.

"You are so beautiful," he murmured as he skimmed a hand along the swell of her breast before completely covering it. "So damn beautiful."

There was no way to respond to that. Saying thank you seemed way too formal, and the way he was looking at her, touching her, pretty much robbed Gabriella of the ability to form words. Her head fell back as she sighed. That's when she felt Zach's warm breath on her throat right before the slight scratch of his tongue as it traveled back up to her lips.

Zach kissed her lightly and then pulled back. "Don't ever think I don't want you or that I'm settling for anything. You're all I've wanted for as long as I can remember and I am humbled to have you here with me."

And then he was done talking.

Carefully, he peeled her blouse off and let it fall to the floor. With his eyes on hers the entire time, he reached down and unzipped her skirt and let it fall to the floor. His hands trailed from Gabriella's waist to her breasts to her face where he stopped. "You're all I need," he said solemnly as he led her to the bed.

Gabriella started to kick off her heels but Zach stopped her. "Leave them. Please." Then he smiled sheepishly and she couldn't help but blush. "I mean…if you really want to you can, but…"

"Zach?"

"Hmm?"

"They're staying on," she said quietly with a sexy grin of her own.

Chuckling, he looked up and sighed. "Thank God."

Chapter 11

IT HAD BEEN SO LONG SINCE GABRIELLA HAD ALLOWED herself to fantasize about being intimate with Zach that it was hard to tell if the reality was better. No, that wasn't right, because there was nothing better than what was happening right now. The feel of Zach's hands, his mouth, his breath on her was setting her on fire. She was on sensory overload and wanted to touch him everywhere at once.

She both wanted to rush him and beg him to never stop what he was doing. They were still standing next to his bed and Gabriella wanted to pull him down onto it with her, but that would require moving and she wasn't ready for that yet either.

Over and over Zach kissed her while his hands seemed to keep moving, exploring. His skin was rough against hers—something she hadn't completely appreciated while she'd been fully clothed. Every inch of her was sensitive, every touch made her gasp and purr with pleasure. And while her own hands anchored themselves in his silky hair—a favorite place, she was finding—she couldn't help but smile when Zach momentarily lifted his lips from hers and whispered, "Touch me."

It was all the encouragement she needed. Slowly, shyly, her hands began their own slow journey downward—over the stubbled skin of his strong jaw, to the broad shoulders that bunched under her touch.

Carefully she made her way down his arms, loving the play of muscles under her hands.

Zach's mouth was back on hers, and suddenly Gabriella wasn't content with her slow exploration— she wanted to feel more of Zach. More skin. More heat. More…everything. Reaching up, she played with the top button on his shirt. Slowly she undid it and then the next. Her knuckles gently grazed his chest and she was rewarded with a deep growl from him.

It was like waving a red flag at a bull. It had to be now. She wanted—needed—to touch him now. Having never been the aggressor in a relationship, Gabriella wasn't sure if what she was doing was allowed but she couldn't help herself. In a flash, she yanked Zach's shirt open, scattering buttons all over the floor before spreading her hands across his chest.

"God, yes," he growled, raising his head as he cupped her face in his hands. "Do you have any idea how many times I imagined you doing that to me?"

Gabriella couldn't speak—she could only manage to shake her head.

"I've lost count of the times I thought of you coming into my office, locking the door behind you, and walking over to me and taking what you wanted. It's a fantasy that nearly drove me insane."

Her hands continued to roam over his chest, her nails gently raking down and over his nipples. "Was it everything you hoped for?" she whispered, uncertainty lacing her voice.

Zach swallowed hard. "It was more," he said before kissing her again.

Wow. It was all Gabriella could keep saying in her

mind. *Wow* to his words, *wow* to his touch…just *wow* to the entire situation. The only problem she had was that her legs were getting weak. Zach was slowly making her crazy, and the need to feel him stretched out beside her, on top of her—everywhere—was getting hard to ignore.

Raking her nails down his chest one last time, she locked her hands for a moment on his belt buckle and tugged slightly before going to work on ridding him of the belt. When it hit the floor, she took care of unbuttoning and unzipping his trousers before breaking their kiss and taking a step back.

No words were needed. Her eyes said it all.

Gabriella took another step back and then another until the mattress was pressing against the back of her legs. Then, slowly, she sank down and stretched out until her head was on the pillows and her entire body was on display on top of his dark comforter.

"So damn beautiful," he said, letting his trousers hit the floor. He braced one hand on the bed to get rid of the pants and socks before standing and simply looking his fill. "I know I keep saying it and it doesn't seem like enough. I've wanted to say it to you for so long and now that I can, I don't want to stop."

"But you have to," she said softly and smiled at the confused look on Zach's face.

"Why?"

"Because there are other things I'd rather have you doing right now," she said saucily.

Zach lifted one knee onto the bed and slowly crawled up her body until he was stretched out on top of her. Gabriella noticed a slight pained look on his face and reached up to smooth a hand across his temple.

"Are you okay?" She spoke quietly and was afraid she was going to ruin the moment, but Zach turned his head and kissed her palm.

"I'm not as confident as I'd like to be," he replied honestly. "It's been a long time. I don't want to disappoint you."

And in that instant, Gabriella grew bold. Slowly, carefully, she reversed their positions until Zach was the one on his back and she was straddling his thighs. "You could never disappoint me," she said, her hands quickly streaking across his chest before reaching up and releasing her hair from its punishing updo.

Zach's eyes blazed at the sight of her in white lace as her long black hair cascaded down over her shoulders. He reached up and cupped her breasts in his hands, and Gabriella's head fell back as she sighed. The moment was perfect.

"Gabriella," he said softly, "I meant what I said. I'm not sure how—"

"Shh," she said, placing one perfectly manicured figure over his lips. "Why don't you relax and stop thinking so hard." She smiled sexily and made herself more comfortable against his growing arousal. "Better yet, why don't you lie back…and enjoy the ride."

Zach's eyes grew wide right before he clasped his hands on her hips. "You've got yourself a deal."

~~~

What seemed like a lifetime later, Zach opened his eyes and looked at the woman sprawled across his chest.

Mind. Blown.

To Zach, Gabriella was normally very reserved. She

never showed a lot of emotion and seemed cool, calm, and completely in control at all times.

Until now.

A slow smile played across his face. He'd made his cool and calm assistant completely lose control and it was glorious. The image of her naked and glowing and crying out his name would forever be burned into his brain. Never had a woman made him feel more alive than Gabriella just had.

She was everything.

The thought should be scaring the crap out of him, but it wasn't. Actually, it was rather comforting to actually be able to say it—even if only in his own head—and to accept it and believe it. For so long he wanted to believe it, wanted to know it was true, but now there wasn't a doubt in his mind.

He was in love with Gabriella Martine.

And it wasn't about sex and it wasn't about his getting better. It was about her—the woman—and him. They fit. In every way possible, they were compatible.

Zach had learned from watching his family how a relationship should be. Even though he did his best to deny it, Zach always knew he was the kind of man who wanted to get married and have a family.

He just needed to have his adventures first.

But now that he had, he was ready for the next phase of life. After years of watching his parents and his Uncle William and Aunt Monica, Zach knew they were exactly the kind of role models he wanted to emulate. And there wasn't a doubt in his mind he and Gabriella would have the same lasting relationship as his relatives.

They even had the potential to be stronger.

His smile grew.

Reaching a hand up, he stroked it up and down Gabriella's spine and then up into her glorious mane of hair. It was like silk wrapping around his fingers. Gently he massaged her scalp—unsure if she was awake or asleep—but perfectly content for them to just stay like this. He felt like a new man.

And a complete one.

Something he hadn't been sure he'd ever feel again.

If anyone asked him right now, Zach would tell them he was strong enough to climb any mountain or compete in any marathon. And then it hit him—neither of those things held any real appeal to him. In the past, just the thought of an athletic challenge was enough to get his heart racing and his mind swirling with possibilities. But right now, all he felt was contentment in the knowledge that he *could* do those things again.

Gabriella began to stir and move off him, but Zach placed his hand firmly at the base of her spine and held her to him. She raised her head and sleepily looked at him. Her beauty was simply staggering.

"I should probably move," she said softly. "I don't want to hurt you."

And that was Gabriella right there—always concerned about everyone else, particularly him, first. "Sweetheart, after everything we just did, you don't have to worry. I'm feeling no pain."

She rose slightly, clearly misunderstanding what he said. Zach read her mind and immediately reached up to stroke her cheek and calm her.

"I meant that in a good way, Gabs," he said. "Having you here like this feels really good. Incredible, actually."

"Oh. Okay." She combed her hair behind her ear, and Zach could see the wheels in her head already beginning to turn. She looked shy, vulnerable…unsure of what exactly to do right now. That made him feel even better—knowing she was maybe just as blown away by what they'd shared as he was.

"Hey," he said softly and waited until her eyes met his. "Are you okay?"

Gabriella blushed slightly and ducked her head to avoid his gaze.

Zach tucked her in against his side and was pleased when she seemed to relax. Her hand rested over his heart, her head on his shoulder. There were at least a dozen things he wanted to say, that he wanted to share, but he was afraid to break the spell and scare her off. So he held her. Kissed the top of her head. And simply enjoyed the moment.

While Zach was comfortable with everything he was feeling—emotionally—he wasn't sure where exactly Gabriella was. He'd hidden his feelings for her for so long, he didn't want to keep it to himself any longer. This wasn't exactly a new relationship to him—it was just one that had taken a really long time to kick into gear.

But how did Gabriella view it?

"I can hear you thinking from here," she teased, using the familiar phrase.

Zach chuckled. "Sorry." He pulled her closer. "I'm just wondering why we didn't do this sooner."

Now it was her turn to chuckle. "Probably because you spent too much time barking orders at me."

She had him there. He felt a pang of guilt. "I'm so

sorry, Gabriella. You have no idea how much. I can't believe the time I cost us."

Raising herself up, she looked at him, her expression soft. "We're not going there. No more looking back. No good can come of it. I think there are too many bad memories—for both of us—to waste time harping on them. There's so much to look forward to. Why ruin it?"

Hmm…it was a good opening, he thought, and couldn't help but touch her. His fingers skimmed the side of her face, and he loved how her eyes drifted shut with the movement. "You're right. We do have a lot to look forward to."

"Mmm…" she purred.

"I want you to know," he began cautiously, "this isn't a one-time, temporary thing."

Gabriella opened her eyes and pulled back slightly but remained silent.

"I've wanted you for a long time. More than I've ever wanted any other woman. And now that we've finally talked and we're on the same page, I want more. I want to move forward—with you. With us." He waited for her to say something but Gabriella remained quiet. "Please tell me you want the same thing." It cost him everything—his pride—to voice the request. Zach wasn't used to being the vulnerable one in a relationship—any relationship. And now that he had put it all out there for her, he had a moment of panic she wasn't looking for something more.

"Please say something," he finally said, hating the plea.

"This is all happening so fast," she said.

"No. It's not," he assured her. "It's been five years in the making. I don't want to waste any more time, Gabriella. I want to see where this can go."

She shook her head slowly and pulled back. "I...I don't know if I can do that, Zach."

"Why? Why not?"

"There's a lot at stake."

"Like what?"

"Well...there's your family," she said as she fully sat up and adjusted the sheet to cover herself.

"My family loves you," he said firmly. "Next."

She made a face at him. "Okay, then there's the office. I don't want to be the subject of office gossip. I don't like it. I'm a private person, Zach, and I...I don't like the thought of people saying crude things about me behind my back. And you remember how you..."

"I'll fire anyone who does." Zach stacked his pillows behind him so he was sitting up beside her.

"You can't go firing everyone. That's ridiculous."

"Everyone's not going to be talking about us behind our backs."

"Zach, you can't know that. All those years ago, you caught some of the guys talking and there wasn't even anything going on between us then."

"Yeah, they were a bunch of gossipy jerks who were letting their imaginations run wild. We're not going to be hiding anything from anyone and we're not going to be sneaking around. So really, there won't be anything to talk about. There'll be no reason for any speculation because it will all be out there for the world to see."

She glared at him for a moment before slouching down on her pillows. "It's...inappropriate," she finally said quietly.

Leaning over, Zach ran a reassuring hand up and down her arm. "Sweetheart, there is nothing inappropriate about this. We've known each other for years and we've had feelings for one another for years. I think, if anything, the masses are going to be relieved we've stopped dancing around one another and snipping at one another and finally gotten ourselves together." He smiled. "Seriously, they may throw a parade in your honor because I'll be a much happier man around the office."

Gabriella rolled her eyes.

"There'll be cake," he said in a singsong voice. "And you know you like cake."

"Well, now you're just being ridiculous."

In a flash, Zach had her pinned beneath him. "I don't see it that way. Everything about us makes sense and everyone knows it. I'm telling you, there is going to be a collective sigh of relief when we're not arguing at work anymore."

The laugh came out before she could even stop it.

"What? What's so funny?"

"Zach, it is in your nature to argue," she said when the giggles stopped. "Things may be a lot more pleasant, but you're never going to stop arguing with me—or anyone for that matter."

"I guess we'll just have to wait and see, won't we?" Lowering himself down so he could nuzzle her neck, Zach felt Gabriella soften and sigh beneath him. He nipped and kissed his way up the slender column of her throat and when his lips finally covered hers, he felt as if he was coming home.

Slowly, her arms came around him and were soon followed by the silky glide of those long legs.

Perfect.

"Zach." She whispered his name on a sigh, arching up to press more firmly against him. He knew they should be tired. He knew he should probably let them both rest. But his need for her was too great. He'd been denied the pleasure of touching her and kissing her for far too long, and he was anxious to make up for lost time. So he silenced her words with another kiss.

This time there was no uncertainty. This time, Zach had all the confidence a man could have. The thought of possibly not being able to follow through never entered his mind. The only thing on his mind was the woman moving restlessly beneath him, and pleasing her, loving her.

Keeping her.

Forever.

———

"For the tenth time, I don't mind."

"It's not a big deal. I can totally cancel the session."

"Zach, you've come so far with your therapy," Gabriella said. "Now is not the time to start slacking off. Besides, I really wasn't…prepared for what happened here today. I've got things I have to do."

"You're going to come back though, right?"

It wasn't that she didn't want to come back; she did. But having some time and space between them to digest the events of the day appealed. "Why don't we just play it by ear? You know, see how you feel after your session." Walking over to him, she placed a kiss on his cheek and then finished buttoning her blouse. "Besides, you may be too tired. You've had quite the workout already."

She hoped her teasing tone would lighten the mood.

It didn't.

"Do you think I'm still too weak to handle sex and a therapy session?" Zach snapped.

Rather than argue, Gabriella turned and leveled him with a glare. "I rest my earlier case on the arguing theory."

Zach raked a hand through his hair. "You're right. I'm sorry. I just…" He stopped and sighed loudly. "I just don't want you pitying me or thinking less of me."

And that took a bit of the fight out of Gabriella too. Walking over to him, she wrapped him in her arms and kissed him again. "Believe me when I tell you I certainly don't feel any pity for you, Zach Montgomery. You're the strongest man I know."

He kissed her fiercely. It was hot and deep and ended just as quickly as it started. "Come back later." ·

She chuckled softly. "We'll see."

Knowing Alex was going to be arriving shortly, Gabriella went to work putting Zach's room back in order—making the bed, fixing the pillows, and making sure it looked as if they hadn't spent the entire day making love in it. When she was satisfied everything looked all right, she walked out to the living room and found Zach sitting on the sofa looking over one of the files she had brought earlier.

"I'm hoping we can start going through those tomorrow," she said, doing her best to get back into her "assistant" mode before Alex showed up. "There's a lot of them, but I think together we can get through them and really have a leg up on some new business for when you get back to the office."

She stopped. She wanted to ask him if he had a plan

or a specific time frame in mind for when he'd feel ready to make that step, but so much had already happened for him, she figured she should just let it rest for now. When he was ready, he'd let her know.

"How did we let so many customers go without contact for so long?"

She shrugged. "We were getting new clients all the time and some of them were big accounts. These are all relatively small—not all of them, but the bulk of them. I think we were just focusing more on expansion and working with the clients who really needed us. When I was looking through the files the other day, it seemed like some of these were just consultations or one-time investors. But enough time has gone by that I think it might be nice to simply touch base with them and see if there's anything we can do to help them and their businesses."

"Won't it sound a little bit like we're trolling for business?"

"Absolutely not. We're not cold-calling anyone and—" She stopped when her cell phone rang out with an incoming text. "Sorry. Excuse me for a minute."

Zach sat back and watched her brow furrow as she read the text before sending off a quick reply and putting the phone back in her bag.

"Problem?"

"Hmm? What? Uh…no. It was nothing."

"Gabs, come on. I know you better than that."

Sighing, she turned and faced him. "Honestly? It was from your uncle."

His brows rose. "My uncle? William?"

Gabriella nodded.

"What did he want?"

She really didn't want to get into this with him. Especially not today. Not after their wonderful, wonderful day. "It's nothing."

"Gabs?" he prompted.

"Okay, fine. He was letting me know about a position that just opened up in the San Diego office. You know, the one your cousin Christian is running since Ryder went back to North Carolina."

With his mouth firmly shut, Zach studied her for a moment as if trying to read her mind.

"I'm not interested in going to San Diego, Zach," she finally said after letting him sweat it out for a minute. "I'm not going to lie to you, a couple of weeks ago I would have jumped at the opportunity, but now? I'm not looking to go anywhere. I'm exactly where I want to be."

Rising from his seat on the sofa, Zach walked over and stopped right in front of her. "Are you sure?" he asked softly, his eyes scanning her face. "I know I didn't play fair. I pulled out all the stops to keep you here with me."

"Was seduction part of it?" she asked as her heart beat wildly in her chest.

"No. I begged and groveled and apologized, and I played on your sympathy. I know that. But seduction had nothing to do with business. How I feel about you is another matter entirely."

Gabriella swallowed hard. "How *do* you feel about me?" Her words were spoken so softly, she wasn't sure he even heard her.

Zach closed the distance between them. "I'm in love with you."

She gasped. It wasn't possible. "You...you can't be. It's too soon. It's—"

He placed a finger against her lips. "We've been there already today. I didn't plan on saying it like this but...there it is. I'm in love with you." He removed his finger with an unexpected feeling of relief. And then he laughed with joy. "There. I've said it. I finally said it out loud. I'm in love with you, Gabriella Martine."

"But..."

"I'm not pressuring you to say it back to me." And then he kissed her, and Gabriella felt all the emotion, all the love he had for her in it.

When they broke apart, she skimmed her hands down his cheeks until they rested on his shoulders. "Wow."

"Yeah. Wow," he replied with a knowing smile.

While she wasn't ready to profess her love to him— yet—she couldn't deny how strongly she did feel about him. If only to herself. Before she could say anything else, the doorbell rang. "That'll be Alex." She couldn't hide the slight disappointment in her voice even though she knew she needed to go. Even though just a few minutes ago she actually wanted to go, the kiss had her reconsidering.

"I know." Zach didn't even try to hide his disappointment. "It's not too late for me to cancel our session. He'll understand."

She playfully swatted him away. "Stop. This is important for you, and like I said before, I have things to do too." Stepping away from him, she walked over to the door and let Alex in. Then she made quick work of getting her things together before Zach could change his—or her—mind.

Zach caught up with her at the door and kissed her hard. "Come back later."

Dazzled by the intensity in his gaze, in his touch, she replied, "I'll be here later."

———

Honestly, Gabriella didn't have anything to do. She needed to make sure Zach continued to commit to his therapy sessions, and if she hadn't left, he would have canceled. The last thing in the world she wanted was to be responsible for any kind of setback with Zach's recovery.

Driving around aimlessly, she chuckled. Heck, even if she hadn't known the extent of his injuries, his performance today would have been spectacular in and of itself. But knowing how hurt he'd been—how, up until a few weeks ago, he could barely walk—she was even more impressed.

She'd never had a doubt in her mind that Zach Montgomery was going to be phenomenal in the bedroom. Besides being incredibly athletic and physically fit, he was sex on a stick personified. Gabriella had lost count of the number of fantasies she'd had over the years about what it would be like to make love with Zach.

The reality was enough to make her blush.

It was hard enough to wrap her brain around the fact she and Zach were lovers. Hell, it was still a bit mind-boggling that they were working civilly with one another. But having Zach tell her he loved her? She was at a complete loss for words.

A panic attack was beginning to make her twitch and she knew she needed to talk to somebody. Calling

Summer was her immediate thought but, as usual where Zach was concerned, it seemed a bit awkward. Unfortunately, Summer was the only one who could possibly understand what Gabriella was going through.

Ten minutes later, she kicked her shoes off and collapsed on her sofa at home. She closed her eyes and began to imagine the conversation with Summer. She'd explain how things had progressed with Zach, without too many intimate details because…well…gross. Then Summer would get all excited about Zach's profession of love. She'd ask how Gabriella felt about it and if she was in love with Zach.

Was she?

Could she possibly be? For real? After all this time?

It didn't seem possible. She could handle being Zach's assistant and even being his friend. But his lover? His… She stopped. That was what she couldn't let herself believe. If Zach was truly in love with her— and why should she even doubt it?—the next logical step would be to become his…wife.

She groaned.

"I so need to talk to Summer," she muttered as she sat back up and reached for her phone. She nearly screamed when it rang as soon as she put her hand on it.

William Montgomery's name and number came up on the screen. She had texted him back earlier that she appreciated the offer for the position in San Diego but things were fine for her with Zach. Either he didn't believe her or he was making sure she really meant it.

"Good evening, Mr. Montgomery," she said as she answered the phone.

"Gabriella! Come now, I thought we had moved on from all that formality. I insist that you call me William."

She couldn't help but smile. The man simply had a knack for making her smile no matter what was going on. Maybe it was his voice or just his infectious enthusiasm for just about everything. Either way, tension seemed to release from her body as she sat back and relaxed.

"Okay…William," she said, but it still felt like she was being a little disrespectful. "What can I do for you?"

"Well, I'm calling to check on you. Last we spoke, you were pretty much all fired up to quit on Zach and seemed open to a move and even a promotion within the company. Are things really better between the two of you?"

You have no idea, she wanted to say. "Actually, Zach and I finally had an intense heart-to-heart a couple of weeks ago. We got to the root of our problem with one another and decided we make a good team."

"Really? Well, that's wonderful! Although I have to admit, I'm a little sorry you won't be going to San Diego."

"Oh? How come?"

He sighed. "I don't think you've ever met my nephew Christian. He's my brother Joseph's son. He's been running our European division for the last six years. We didn't think anything would ever bring him back to the States but for some reason, when Ryder needed a break and wanted to take a leave of absence, Christian volunteered to come home."

Gabriella had heard some of this before but wasn't sure where William was going with all of it. "I don't understand what this has to do with me, William.

Last I heard, he was doing fine with the San Diego office. I've talked with his assistant many times—particularly after Zach's accident. What could I possibly do over there?"

"Actually, as I'm sure you're aware, his assistant Beth is pregnant."

"I know," Gabriella said with a smile. "It's her first child and she's been telling everyone how excited she is."

William chuckled. "It's an exciting time, for sure. However, when she first found out about the pregnancy, she planned on taking maternity leave and then coming back to work." He paused. "But she's changed her mind. She wants to be a stay-at-home mom now, and honestly, I think it's great."

"I do too." And Gabriella truly felt that way. She couldn't imagine not staying at home with her own baby—if and when she had one—no matter how much it would inconvenience Zach or whomever she was working for at that point in time. "So Christian is going to need an assistant."

"Exactly. I think he's doing a good job in California but…I'm concerned. He's not really…engaging. Does that make sense?"

"Kind of. Beth hasn't said he's having any issues. As a matter of fact, she's kind of gushed about how smooth the whole transition went."

"Well, Ryder ran a tight ship and he worked closely with Christian to make sure it went smoothly. But it's more than just business, Gabriella. All he's doing is working! He's not getting out and meeting people. I guess I just hoped you'd take the position and you'd hit it off with him and…"

"Wait a minute, wait a minute, wait a minute," she said, swiftly interrupting him. "Are you trying to set me up with your nephew?"

He chuckled again. "I don't know if I'd say *that*…"

"Don't even try that with me, William," she said good-naturedly. "You know darn well that's exactly what you're doing. It's your thing! It's what you do! What I don't understand is why?"

"Why?" he repeated. "You just said so yourself. It's what I do!"

She laughed at his ability to poke fun at himself. "Yes, but what I meant was…why Christian? I mean, I would have thought you'd be playing matchmaker for me and Zach."

"Would you, now?" he asked slyly. "Interesting."

"William?" she asked cautiously, suddenly suspicious as she wracked her brain for any proof she'd been set up.

"What? What did I do?"

Gabriella thought over the last few months and her interactions with William, dating back to their time in Alaska while they were waiting to hear about what had happened to Zach. All she could remember was William trying to convince her to leave Zach. "Don't you think I'm good enough for Zach?"

Now he laughed heartily. "Maybe I don't believe Zach is good enough for you!"

She was beginning to feel like they were talking in circles. "William, I'm being serious. Why have you been doing your best to convince me to leave Zach?"

"Maybe I'm just curious to see how committed you are to staying."

Gabriella rolled her eyes. The conversation was going nowhere and starting to make her a little crazy. "Things are going very well right now," she said vaguely. "I hope you find someone to take Beth's place, but it's not going to be me. I hope you understand."

"There's a big raise and a bonus involved if you change your mind. Plus, Montgomerys would pay all of your moving expenses and your housing for the first year. Think about it, Gabriella. Zach's a little contrite right now; he's still healing. How is he going to be when he's better and ready to take on the world again? Are you sure you want to deal with his moods?"

There was a time when she would have questioned it, or when William's offer would have really turned her head. But now? After today? Gabriella knew exactly where she wanted to be and whom she wanted to be with. And why.

"Thank you for thinking of me and for the opportunity, William. I really am happy with my decision to stay on with Zach. We're a good team, and when he makes his full recovery," she said for emphasis, "I'm still going to be happy to be here."

"Are you certain?" he asked. But Gabriella could tell he was pleased with what she had just shared with him.

"Yes. I'm certain."

They hung up and Gabriella looked at the phone in her hand. She contemplated calling Summer. Only… it wasn't necessary now. Somehow her conversation with William Montgomery had gone a long way toward clearing her head and giving her the insight she was looking for.

The man was beyond crafty. He was downright spooky.

Putting her feet up on her coffee table, she sat back and let out a deep breath. She was certain about her decision now more than ever. This was where she was meant to be, where she wanted to be.

Because she was in love with Zach Montgomery.

Chapter 12

FOR TWO WEEKS GABRIELLA FELT LIKE SHE WAS living in a dream.

A really sexy dream.

At first she did her best to keep her work time and personal time with Zach separate. It wasn't easy because Zach always wanted her to spend the night, but she felt it was important for them to have some time apart. But eventually, he wore her down—in a good way—and she had all but moved in with him.

While he had his sessions with Alex, she did her own thing. They had moved the rooms around as Zach had wanted, so while he did his therapy in the home gym in the morning, she would be in the master bedroom getting ready for the day. She still wanted to maintain her professionalism, after all. During his evening sessions, she would make dinner or run errands.

It was hard to even remember what their relationship had been like before because Gabriella felt like a new woman and this was their new life. They were blissfully happy. Zach was getting stronger every day, only using a single crutch and even that only if he overexerted himself during the day.

That's not to say he was fully recovered. Sometimes he would lose his balance, and he still had a fairly pronounced limp. Although he never mentioned it, Gabriella had a sneaking suspicion it was the limp keeping him from returning to the office. She knew him well enough to know he wanted to be absolutely perfect before he'd be comfortable working around other people again. She wished he didn't feel that way—she knew no one was going to think any less of him—but it was his own demon he had to defeat.

Not that she was particularly anxious for them to return to the office yet either. While they were actually working from home and getting a lot accomplished, there was something to be said for the way they could simply stop what they were doing and make love whenever the mood struck.

With a final notation in a client folder, Gabriella looked up and caught the familiar look in Zach's eyes.

She loved that look.

"Did you finish with that file?" he asked, slowly rising from his seat across from her.

Gabriella chose not to answer right away. Instead, she closed the folder and added it to the stack on the coffee table. Then she straightened it. Looking up at him, she gave him a knowing smile. "I did."

"I was thinking I'd like to take an early lunch," he said, his voice deep and sexy as hell. "Care to join me?"

She pretended to consider it. "That depends."

"On?"

"Where are we eating today?" She could barely keep the excitement out of her voice.

Slowly, Zach dropped to his knees in front of her. His hands immediately found their way to her knees and began a slow journey up her thighs under her skirt. "I was thinking right here."

Gabriella blushed clear to her roots. No man had ever

been so…vocal…about sex the way Zach was. At first she was a little shocked by it, but now she found it really exciting. Her pencil skirt didn't allow for too much freedom of movement, so she did her best to accommodate Zach's large hands as they slid the garment up her thighs.

"Hmm…right here?" she purred. "That sounds very…decadent."

Zach inhaled deeply at the sight of the dark red thong she was wearing. "Believe me," he growled right before he began to lower his head to kiss her thighs, "it is."

She couldn't help the low moan that escaped at the feel of his hot breath and his lips on her sensitive skin. It was always like this—Zach Montgomery was a skilled lover and it didn't matter how he touched her or how many times he made love to her, he made sure she completely lost her mind in the sensations he created.

Gabriella thought at first it was because they were new lovers and eventually things would slow down or get a little less…intense. But if anything, it kept getting better. Never before had she lost control and been such an active participant in the bedroom.

With the few previous lovers she'd had, Gabriella had been relatively reserved. She didn't like the feeling of letting go or letting anyone else have control. But Zach left her no choice—she gave everything she had to him willingly and begged for more.

Something she was on the verge of doing right now as he peeled her panties down her legs and tossed them over his shoulder with a wicked smile on his face. She returned it with a smile of her own. "You know, this really isn't proper office protocol."

One strong finger stroked her inner thigh as he intently watched her face. "It's a good thing I'm the boss. I can change the policies."

She chuckled. "Mmm…that is a good thing. But it makes me wonder…how are we ever going to get any work done if you keep me here like this?" The last was said with a throaty moan as his fingers went to work doing more than just teasing.

"I guess we'll just have to work late," he said, returning to placing kisses on her leg, starting at her knees and working his way up. "Probably long into the night." And then it wasn't his fingers making her cry out but his mouth, and all thoughts of work were forgotten for a very long time.

"I think you've corrupted me," Gabriella said much later as they sat down for dinner.

Zach arched a brow at her. "How so?"

"I'm a very regimented person. I have a routine, a schedule. You've completely ruined that for me. I barely know what day it is because I've lost track of my schedule."

"And this bothers you?" he asked with a smirk.

"I don't know if bothers is the right word, but…I don't know. I kind of feel out of sorts."

Zach looked at her and realized she was serious. If he were honest, he knew this subject had been bound to come up. He'd known Gabriella for too long to think she would just be able to change her life around without any complications. Reaching out, he placed a hand over hers.

"It's not a bad feeling though, is it?"

"No, it's not bad," she began slowly, "but it is a bit unnerving. You know me, Zach. I like order. I like things to be neat and tidy, and right now I kind of feel like a kid running with scissors."

"I'm not following you, Gabs."

She sighed. "I spend a lot of my time here now—even my nights—but I still have my apartment. Some of my things are here, some of my things are there. I'm living out of a weekender bag and things are wrinkled and messy and…" She threw up her hands. "It just makes me a little cranky when things are out of order."

"I have an iron," he said half-jokingly, but the sour look on Gabriella's face made him realize this was a little more complex than wrinkled clothing.

"Things are wonderful right now for us. I know that. It's new and exciting and I love being with you."

"But…" he prompted.

"But…I feel like I'm losing a bit of myself. I went home the other night and there was nothing to eat in my refrigerator. I had laundry piled up and a huge stack of mail to go through."

"So what are you saying?"

"I think we need to…I don't know…get a little back to normal."

Zach did not like the sound of this. He had a feeling Gabriella's version of normal would include more work and less play, and he was not ready for that. He was enjoying the way things were going between them. There was an amazing sense of freedom to being here all alone and being able to reach out and touch her without prying eyes looking on. Their modified work schedule meant they were able to take time to go for a walk or a drive or make love on the living room floor. All of that was going to go away—quickly—if they tried to go back to "normal."

But he wanted to be fair to her. It wasn't only about him and his wants. "And what does 'normal' include?" he asked, hoping he didn't sound nearly as nervous as he felt.

"Well…" she began as she pushed her food around on her plate, "I think I need to spend a little more time at home. I need to go grocery shopping and do laundry, pay bills, clean… It's important to me that my life not spin out of control because I'm spending all my time here."

Unease began to wrap itself around him. "I didn't realize you were unhappy spending time here," he said quietly. "I didn't mean to monopolize your time."

Now it was her turn to comfort him. "No, I don't think of it like that, Zach. Really. It's just…you know me. I thrive on keeping things orderly. I'm not used to this. It feels weird."

"Weird isn't always a bad thing, Gabs." He squeezed her hand. "I like having you here. I kind of like the chaos having you here has brought."

She smiled. "I do like being here with you, Zach, but I can't just change who I am." She gently disengaged her hand and went back to her dinner and Zach did the same. They finished their meal in companionable silence, then together went about clearing the table.

"You could move in here."

The fork in Gabriella's hand clattered to the floor, unheeded. "What?"

Zach picked the fork up from the floor, put it back on the table, and pulled Gabriella to him. "Live here. With me. All the time."

"I…I don't know. I think—"

"Don't think, Gabs," he said softly. "We could share all the responsibilities—food shopping, laundry, mail sorting. No messes. No wrinkles. Just…you and me."

Her eyes went wide. "I don't know what to say."

He squeezed her hands and positioned them until they were touching from head to toe. "Say yes. Say you'll move in with me."

Zach watched as her eyes scanned his face and her mouth moved but no words came out. "Just think about it, okay? You don't have to answer right now." He placed a gentle kiss on her forehead. "Promise me you'll at least consider it."

She nodded before taking a step back. "Let me get this cleaned up."

"It's not a big deal." But he watched her, noticed the nervous energy coming off her. "What's going on, Gabs? Something's on your mind. I can tell."

Gabriella turned and faced Zach, her expression serious. "I think it's time for you to start getting out more."

It was the last thing he was expecting her to say. He figured he'd freaked her out by asking her to move in. He never even considered her wanting to talk about this. "I get out. We went to a movie the other night, and we had a picnic in the park just the other day."

Gabriella sighed as her expression softened. "Your therapy sessions are going great. You're moving around wonderfully and it's pretty rare that you rely on the cane Alex gave you."

Zach smiled. "I like it more than the crutch but I still hate to use it."

"And that's the thing—you hardly need to use it and yet you're still hiding out here at home. Your family has been dying to see you and yet you turn down all of their invitations to get together. You don't want them all here but you don't want to go to anyone's house."

"We talk on the phone all the time. I don't see what the big deal is about getting together."

"Zach," she said with a hint of exasperation, "they're your family. They love you. Most of them haven't even seen you since you started working with Alex. Your brothers are curious about your recovery and how far you've come. The only reason Summer's seen you is because she decided to just drive over and see you for herself. She was tired of waiting for an invitation."

"That's not true. She had some contracts for me to sign. It was about business."

"You don't really believe that, do you?"

Zach frowned. "What? She brought contracts here. I signed them."

She smiled and shook her head. "She could have emailed or faxed the contracts. She came here herself because she wanted to see you. It's not always about business, Zach." She paused. "And that's another thing."

He was almost sorry he'd brought any of this up. "What?" He sighed loudly.

"It's time."

Confusion marked his features. "Time for what?"

"It's time for you to go back to the office. There's no reason why you can't. You can still do your sessions with Alex here at the house, but there is nothing stopping you from working out of the actual office. Even if it's only part time."

Panic nearly choked him. He hadn't felt it in a while. Gabriella was right, he *was* better and there wasn't any reason for him to not go back to work, but…doubt and insecurity grabbed him by the throat. "I'm not ready," he said.

"Seriously? You're going to use that excuse? On me? Zach, this morning we had rather…energetic sex in the shower. You held me up. You're stronger than you're giving yourself credit for. What are you afraid of?"

Everything. "I…I haven't even driven yet. I'll need to drive if I'm going to go to the office. I don't want anyone to see you driving me around like I'm some sort of invalid."

"So what's stopping you from driving? The doctors gave you clearance for that a week ago. You haven't had any signs of the temporary paralysis in a while now. Why haven't you gotten in the car and tried? I would think by now you'd be anxious to."

"It's not that easy," he snapped, raking a hand through his hair.

Zach started pacing back and forth, and Gabriella walked out of the room briefly, then came back in.

"Catch," she said and tossed a set of keys at him. He caught them instinctively, and Gabriella turned and walked back out. "Let's go."

Zach stalked after her. "Go? Go where?"

She was already at the door, pulling her jacket on. "Wherever you take us," she said.

Zach stared at the keys in his hands like they were explosives. "I…I can't, Gabriella. I'm not ready for this."

"Yes, you are," she said and stepped closer to him. Softly, she skimmed a hand across his cheek. "Tonight you asked me to move in with you. That scares me to death. In the last couple of weeks I've left my comfort zone for you in a dozen different ways. I'm asking you to do this one thing. For me."

If it were anyone else, Zach would have argued and told them to go to hell. But the look on her face and the sincerity in her tone told him she was doing this because it was something he needed to do. "What if…what if something happens?"

"Nothing's going to happen. We're going to go for a short drive. Let's go get ice cream and we'll come right home."

"What if…what if my leg cramps up and I can't feel the brake pedal?"

"Your leg hasn't cramped up in weeks and it's not going to happen now. We'll take the Lexus because it's an automatic. You won't have to worry about the clutch so it will be easier. We'll work our way up to the Porsche, okay?"

Zach hated his lack of confidence. Reluctantly he nodded. Gabriella held the front door open while he put on his jacket, and they walked together out to the car. Zach didn't look at her as he unlocked the doors and climbed in. He didn't say a word as he buckled his seat belt and started the car. His white-knuckle grip on the steering wheel said enough.

"Relax," she said softly from beside him, her hand gentle on top of his. "We're just going for ice cream. It's only a ten-minute drive to the store. If you feel like it's too much by the time we get there, I'll drive us home, okay?"

He nodded, put the car in gear, and pulled out of the driveway.

"Zach, it's almost midnight. Can we please go home?" She laughed as she said it but it was quickly followed by a yawn. Their ten-minute trek to the store for ice cream had turned into a three-hour drive around Portland.

"This was your idea, sweetheart," he said with a wink and a smile. "God! I cannot believe I had forgotten just how good it feels to be out on the road! Seriously, Gabriella, thank you. I had no idea how much I had missed this. I feel like…I feel like I've gotten my freedom back!"

Zach relaxed in the driver's seat, and took the exit off the highway that would take them home. This was a piece of his life he'd been missing—his independence, his freedom. Now that he knew he could, in fact, get in the car and drive without incident, he knew he was back.

Physically, he'd admit to being about ninety-five percent. It didn't seem like the limp was going away any time soon, and his doctors and Alex had warned him that might be the case. He didn't like it—as a matter of fact he hated it. Hated the reminder of a time in his life when he was at his lowest and most vulnerable. But the rest of him was fine.

He'd just have to deal with the fact he was no longer the athlete he once was.

Quickly he shoved the thought away. Tonight was a revelation. Gabriella had put her trust in him and convinced him to take a risk—something he used to do without blinking an eye. And thanks to her he'd hit a turning point. There was no more looking back. He was done with that. From now on he was only looking forward— and learning to accept the things he couldn't change.

Once they were back at home, they climbed from the car. Gabriella walked around it and went to open the front door. Zach's movements were a little stiff. He didn't realize how much tension he'd carried during the drive. He stopped and stretched and turned to see her standing in the doorway, waiting for him.

He liked the sight of her standing there.

Swinging the car door shut, he walked slowly toward her, his eyes never leaving her face. He stepped up and stood in front of her. "Thank you," he said, his voice like gravel.

Gabriella smiled a little sleepily. "You're welcome."

Taking her by the hand, Zach pulled her from the doorway and shut the door. Then he led her to the bedroom and closed that door as well. Turning her toward him, he wrapped her in his arms and then…words simply eluded him.

She was perfect.

She was everything.

She had given him his life back in a million different ways, and he had no idea how he could ever even begin to thank her. There was only one thing he could do, and that was love her. Slowly, thoroughly, and completely.

He caressed her face and smiled when her head fell back and the small purr escaped from her lips. He gently lowered his hands to her waist and simply held them there for a moment before reaching up and slipping his hands under her sweater to take it off.

"Mmm…Zach," she whispered, her head still back, her eyes closed.

The sweater hit the floor as Zach began to rain kisses along Gabriella's jawline, her throat, her shoulders. His hands anchored her hips as he took his time exploring her with his lips. When he felt her trying to move against him and get closer, his hands moved around and cupped her bottom before reaching for the zipper on her skirt and slowly lowering it.

"You're killing me," she moaned but let him keep doing what he was doing. When her skirt pooled around her feet, she kicked it aside without stepping out of Zach's grasp.

It was a sight Zach knew he'd never tire of—Gabriella in nothing but lace and high heels. There wasn't a pinup model alive who could hold a candle to her. He finally allowed his hands to wander—to skim up and down her back, her bottom, to reach up and gently knead her breasts—all while his mouth, his lips, his tongue did their own exploration.

Up until now—until Gabriella—Zach didn't understand all the fuss about foreplay. He loved sex, but it was about the end goal. Right here and now, watching how Gabriella reacted to his touch, seeing how her skin flushed, hearing her purr and moan, and having her breath quicken—well, that was quickly becoming addictive. He released her abruptly and swung her up into his arms—a move he wouldn't have considered a few weeks ago—and carried her over to the bed.

And then stood back and marveled at how glorious she looked sprawled across the king-size mattress. Her eyes were glazed and she reached out a hand to him.

She may have whispered his name, but the blood was pounding in his ears and he couldn't be sure. Swiftly he kicked off his shoes, undressed, and stretched out beside her to resume his explorations.

Gabriella cried out his name again and again, and each time it filled Zach with pleasure to know he could do this for her. And when she cried out that she couldn't wait any longer and she needed him—all of him—he happily obliged.

And later, with nothing but moonlight shining through the window, Zach realized he finally had what he'd always wanted. For years he'd done extreme sports and kept challenging himself in search of the elusive something that would make him feel complete.

Kissing the top of Gabriella's head as she slept curled up beside him, Zach knew he'd actually had everything he could ever want all along—Gabriella.

―∾∾―

"I feel ridiculous."

"You're fine."

"I don't want to be on display like some freak in a sideshow."

"Okay, dramatic much?"

Zach huffed loudly. "Easy for you to say, no one's going to be watching you to make sure you're walking, talking, and moving like a normal person."

"Oh please. You watch me walk and move all the time."

He chuckled. "Yeah, but not because I think you're a freak. I just like watching you." He waggled his eyebrows until she laughed with him.

"Okay, you win. You're ridiculous."

They were driving to Ethan and Summer's place for dinner. After their conversation a week earlier, Zach had finally agreed to a get-together. Once Summer got the A-OK, she ran full force with it and organized a total Montgomery family dinner—including their parents and brothers who were all flying in from the East Coast.

"It just seems like overkill for Ryder and James to be coming all the way here for a dinner. That's all I'm saying."

"They've wanted to see you for weeks and weeks, Zach. It should make you feel good that your family loves you so much that they want to be with you on a moment's notice."

"But they have babies at home. They have more important things to do with their time than to come and see if I can walk."

She rolled her eyes. "If you think that's why they're flying across the country, then maybe we should cancel because clearly you're still suffering from some sort of head injury the doctors missed."

"Ha, ha, very funny," he said dryly. "I just think they should be home with their families."

"Their families are coming with them," Gabriella said. They had been going on and on and on about this dinner all week. She knew Zach was feeling apprehensive about the entire thing. "Casey and Selena are coming along and bringing the kids so no one is missing out on anything."

"Lucky me."

"Don't be like that."

"I'm not the kind of guy who gets really excited for big family gatherings."

"It's going to be fun."

"Says the one who's not going to be on display."

"Oh, you don't think I'm going to be on display as much as you?"

"Sweetheart, I know it."

Twisting in her seat, she faced him. "Do you realize this is the first gathering of any kind that we're going to as a couple?"

"So? It's not like they don't know you," he said.

"Yes, they know me, but they know me in a business capacity—as your assistant. There's a whole new dynamic now and you can be sure we're *both* going to be observed together. It's not just your show today, buddy. I'm going to be right there with you."

"Now I really don't want to go."

Now that she'd voiced it, Gabriella wasn't so sure she wanted to go anymore either. They had been so wrapped up in the fact that Zach had finally relented and agreed to get together with people that she had completely overlooked the whole new relationship angle. Reaching over to him, she grasped his hand and then drove the remainder of the way in silence.

When they pulled up and parked in the driveway, there seemed to be more cars than either of them were expecting. "How many people did Summer invite?" Zach asked.

"Your parents, Ryder and Casey, James and Selena, and us. At least, that's all I know of," she replied as they climbed from the car.

"Remind me to strangle my sister. This is not the way I wanted this day to go," Zach grumbled as he reached for Gabriella's hand and began to walk toward the house.

His mother emerged from the front door first and was quickly followed by Summer, Casey, and Selena. The excitement level coming off the three women was enough to make Zach cringe, but he good-naturedly accepted their hugs and kisses and praise of how good he looked and how happy they all were to see him. He looked up toward the house and saw his brothers and Ethan filling the doorway with grins on their faces that clearly said, *Better you than me, bro.*

He'd get even with them later.

When he finally got a little space around him, Zach immediately reached for Gabriella's hand like a lifeline and she couldn't help but smile. He needed her. This strong man needed her. It made her feel good. It wasn't just about business or about sex; he well and truly needed *her*. Gabriella. It made her feel all warm and gooey inside.

"Thank you for convincing my brother to finally do this," Summer said as they all walked into the house.

"You owe me one," Gabriella said with a laugh. Beside her, Zach was walking with his mom, her arm hooked through his. *So this is what it feels like to be part of a normal family*, she thought to herself.

"Well, I'd like to say I did this all for him, but I kind of had ulterior motives," Summer said.

"Do tell," Gabriella said slyly.

"Well, you know Ethan and I wanted to have an engagement party and all, but we wanted to wait until Zach was better." They climbed the front steps to the house and did another round of greetings with all of the guys before Summer continued. "So we decided to make this an engagement party!"

"Summer! Why didn't you tell me? We didn't get you anything!"

"You got my brother here," Summer said, a huge grin on her face. "And that's really all Ethan and I wanted." She reached out and hugged Gabriella. "I knew you'd be good for him. I just knew you were the one."

Gabriella had no idea how to respond to that. Fortunately, she was saved from having to when Zach's mother, Janice, came over and hugged her. "I have to agree with my daughter. We're all so thankful and happy for you. For a while there I didn't think Zach would ever get out of his funk and want to leave his house. But you managed to get him to do it!" She kissed Gabriella on the cheek. "I seriously can't thank you enough!"

"Okay, Mom," Zach said, overhearing the entire conversation, "that's enough. Believe it or not, I do have a mind of my own and Gabriella doesn't make all of my decisions for me." He turned and winked at Gabriella. "Only most of them."

Relief washed over Gabriella when she realized Zach wasn't upset with what everyone was saying, and was even able to laugh at himself a bit. They worked the room for a little while and eventually he let go of her hand long enough for her to go to the kitchen with the girls and help with the food. "I can't believe how fast you threw all of this together, Summer. I really wish you would have let me help."

"Like I said, you getting Zach here is what we wanted most."

Gabriella looked around the room and did a quick head count. "How many are we?" she asked. "There seemed to be more cars than people outside."

"Oh! That's because Uncle William and Aunt Monica just got here. They're down the hall in the guest room, freshening up. Their flight just landed about an hour ago."

A twinge of nerves fluttered in Gabriella's belly. It was one thing to talk to William on the phone about her work relationship with Zach; it was quite another for him to witness that they were more than work associates now. "What a nice surprise," she managed to say before grabbing a bottle of water for herself.

For a few minutes she talked with Casey and Selena and had the chance to really get acquainted with them. Both babies were down for naps, but Gabriella couldn't wait to actually see them and hold them herself. Gabriella never thought of herself as the maternal type—certainly not with the example she was raised with—but something in her softened at the thought of snuggling with the two babies when they woke up.

"Zach! It's good to see you looking like your old self again!" William's voice boomed from the next room.

Gabriella walked toward the living room and stopped to watch the scene unfolding before her. She wasn't sure how much William knew about her and Zach, and she kind of wanted to get a handle on it before calling attention to herself.

"It's good to see you, Uncle William. I didn't think you were flying in too," Zach said with a genuine smile on his face.

"Well, we weren't quite sure if we were going to make it. Lucas and Emma's little girl's birthday was yesterday and we didn't want to miss her party. But we were able to get a flight out this morning and decided to take it. Your aunt here wanted to see for herself that you were doing better."

Monica walked over and hugged Zach. She reached up and cupped his face in her hands. "You have no idea how much I've been worried about you," she said, kissing him hard on the cheek before pulling back and staring at him. She was all of five feet four compared to his six-foot frame, and yet at that moment it seemed the other way around.

"You were our first nephew. You were the first baby I ever held. I watched you take your first steps. You're as much a son to me as my own three boys. When you're hurt, we're hurt." She pulled his face in close. "Don't ever scare me like that again."

And then she hugged him again and Zach wrapped her in his embrace and simply held on.

Silence filled the room for a long moment before Ryder broke the spell. "Geez, Aunt Monica, way to make the rest of us feel special." Everyone laughed.

"Oh hush, Ryder," she said playfully before returning her attention to Zach. "I had just found out I was pregnant with Mackenzie when Zach was born. I knew nothing about babies or being a mom and you, my sweet Zachary, were a complete wonder to me and your uncle. You still are." She squeezed him again. "I'm thrilled to see you looking so happy. Nothing is more important to me than you being happy and settled. I never cared about your adventures. I want you safe and healthy."

"So, just to be clear…you're *still* saying Zach's the favorite," Ryder deadpanned, and everyone laughed and then began talking all at once.

Zach released his aunt after kissing her on the cheek

and went to stand by Gabriella. His arm easily found its way around her waist to keep her close. They both groaned a little when William spotted them and made his way over.

"It's good to see the two of you finally got it together," he said when he stood before them. "I was beginning to think I'd really have to send Gabriella to San Diego with Christian!"

Zach looked at his uncle with confusion. "What are you talking about?"

Before William could answer, James sauntered over. "Zach, Zach, Zach," he said with a knowing smirk. "You weren't paying much attention to the activities of our dear uncle here before your accident, were you?"

Zach looked at his brother, then his uncle and Gabriella before he finally admitted he had no idea what James was talking about.

"Seems Uncle William has fashioned himself as some sort of matchmaker. He thinks he's responsible for Lucas, Jason, and Mac finding wives, and when that wasn't enough, he went on to take credit for Ryder and Casey, *and* me and Selena. It was only a matter of time before he honed in on you and Gabriella."

"Oh, and don't forget about me and Summer," Ethan said, joining the group.

"So…wait a minute. Are you trying to say you're taking responsibility for me and Gabriella getting together?" Zach asked with a chuckle.

"Guilty as charged!" William said, giving Zach a friendly pat on the back. "Oh, I knew the two of you were already well on your way, but you just needed a little…nudge. It's what I do. I don't claim to fully find the right person for you young men, but I do pay attention to the women around you and get *you* to start paying attention. It's really quite simple."

"He's taking credit again, isn't he?" Ryder asked as he sauntered over.

Zach and Gabriella stood there and chuckled at all of the good-natured ribbing going on between William and his nephews. Actually, Gabriella's was more of a nervous chuckle because she was afraid Zach was going to get upset by the things being said. She knew how much he hated family interference in any capacity, and there was a good chance he'd be offended by William stating that he had orchestrated anything between them.

"Don't get me wrong," William was saying, "I may not have been as hands-on as I was with my boys, but you were all still challenging!"

"Well, I, for one, am thankful," Zach said as he raised his glass. "And I'd like to propose a toast to my uncle." He looked at his brothers and Ethan and everyone else in the room until they all had a glass in their hand. "Thank you for giving us all the nudges we needed."

"Hear, hear!" was the chant throughout the room, and Gabriella noticed tears shining in William's eyes. Unable to help herself, she stepped forward and pressed a gentle kiss to his cheek. "Thank you," she whispered.

The rest of the day was spent celebrating—primarily the engagement of Summer and Ethan, but Zach was clearly the star of the day. Gabriella was amazed at the transformation. In all the years she'd known Zach, she didn't think she'd ever seen him look so happy or so relaxed. He was laughing and joking with his brothers,

and it filled her with pride to know she had a little something to do with it.

But she also was a little more skilled at noticing when
something was wrong. It wasn't anything major, but
after a couple of hours she did notice that he was sitting
more, and every once in a while, she'd see his smile slip
slightly. He wasn't exerting himself in any capacity, but
this was a lot more activity and interaction than he'd had
in a while. The thing she feared most was that he was in
pain—and feeling discouraged that something as minor
as a family get-together could cause him pain—and he'd
use it as an excuse to hide away again for a while.

Excusing herself from her conversation with Summer
and Casey, Gabriella walked over and sat beside him,
taking his hand in hers and squeezing. Zach looked at
her and she knew he could tell she was concerned for
him. Gratitude shone in his eyes.

"Hey, look who's finally awake," Selena said with
her baby in her arms. "I promised you a snuggle once
he was awake." She placed the baby in Gabriella's arms
and then stood back and smiled. "If you wouldn't mind
holding him while I get a bottle ready, I'd really appreciate it."

Gabriella looked down at the tiny baby in her arms
and felt oddly emotional. "That's fine," she whispered
softly, her eyes never leaving the infant's face. Her
finger skimmed the soft skin of his cheek as she looked
at him with wonder. So small. So precious. Her heart
squeezed hard and it startled her a bit.

"That's a good look on you, Gabs," Zach whispered
in her ear.

She couldn't look at him. Not now. He'd see too

much. It would be so easy to get caught up in the moment and start planning a scene like this of her own—with a baby and Zach.

Having a family had never been part of her plan. Gabriella learned a long time ago that marriage and children were not always all they were cracked up to be. She was from the ultimate dysfunctional family, and the thought of turning out like them was terrifying. But sitting here right now, surrounded by the Montgomerys while holding this precious baby in her arms, her plan started to crumble.

"You okay?" he asked quietly, as if sensing her sudden unease.

She nodded. "Mmm-hmm." Taking a steadying breath, she said, "He's just so small. It's hard to believe something this tiny and fragile is the same person who was crying so fiercely a little while ago."

Zach chuckled. "Yeah, James mentioned he's got some set of lungs. I told him it served him right. James was a brat as a kid and I'm hoping this little guy gives him just as much hell—if not more—for everything he put all of us through."

Just then Selena reappeared. "Hey! Why do I have to suffer along with that too?" she asked with a chuckle.

"Goes with the territory," Zach said, still laughing. "Sorry."

"Yeah, yeah, yeah," Selena said, pulling up a chair beside them and testing the bottle before handing it to Gabriella. "Would you like to feed him?"

Gabriella's eyes went wide. "Me?" she squeaked. "Really? Won't he…won't he be upset if his mom isn't the one doing it?"

Selena laughed softly. "Are you kidding? He's comfortable there in your arms and you're about to feed him. Right now, you're his new best friend."

Gingerly, Gabriella took the bottle from Selena's hand and offered it to the baby. She gasped with surprise when he immediately latched on and began to drink. "Oh! He's doing it! He's really letting me feed him!" Her words were said softly enough, but the excitement was palpable.

Selena squeezed Gabriella's arm reassuringly. "If you'll excuse me for a minute, I think I'm going to snag a few more of those mini quiches before they're all gone. Can I get you guys anything?"

"We're good," Zach answered for them, placing an arm around Gabriella's shoulders.

Neither of them noticed the knowing smiles around the room that were directed at them. Neither of them had eyes for anyone but each other and the baby in Gabriella's arms. And they certainly didn't notice when William walked by his brother Robert—strutting like a peacock—as he murmured a cheeky, "I told you so."

Chapter 13

ZACH MONTGOMERY WAS NOT KNOWN FOR HIS patience. But if there was one thing everyone kept telling him throughout this whole experience, it was to be patient. So for the last few weeks, he had been the most patient man he could be. There should be a damn award for him. Gabriella still hadn't given him an answer about moving in with him, but was he going to mention it? No. Was he going to push the way he wanted to? No. Was he slowly losing his mind?

Hell yes.

She still slept at her place at least twice a week, and for Zach, that was two nights too many. He was trying very hard to respect her boundaries, but it really would make her life easier to just have everything at his place. For a woman who was all about efficiency, she certainly wasn't being very efficient about how they were living and working.

He liked the setup they had at home and he felt comfortable without prying eyes watching him. Plus, he knew now that physical exertion wasn't the only enemy. He had been trying so hard to present the look of a totally healed man on their outing to Summer and Ethan's party that he had tensed up more than he should have and paid the price for it for days afterward.

Lesson learned.

Today was the first day he was returning to the

office. He and Alex had been working on getting to a point where Zach was confident that he would be able to relax enough at work that he wouldn't cause himself discomfort, even with an audience. Still, he hated not having a guarantee.

Gabriella sat in the car beside him. If she had picked up on any hint of the things racing through his mind, she wasn't letting on. He couldn't quite put his finger on it, but something had changed Gabriella that day at Summer's house. Maybe it was the fact that they'd finally outed themselves to his family, or maybe she was just overwhelmed by his family in general. The Montgomerys were a fairly rowdy and intimidating bunch, but by now he would have thought she'd be used to it.

Or maybe it was James and Selena's son, Jamie. Zach could still hear the wonder in Gabriella's voice as she'd fed the baby his bottle, and see the serene look on her face as she'd held him. He hadn't realized before then that he had no idea if she was a "kid" kind of person; in all the years they'd known each other, the subject had never come up. But something about her reaction to Jamie told Zach the wonder she'd had was a new feeling for her.

It was just one of several things he wanted discuss with her. Maybe she knew it, too, because lately, every time he wanted to have a serious personal conversation, she distracted him with sex. Not that he was complaining. Not really. The woman had a way of bringing him to his knees with just a look. She'd blown his mind and completely exhausted him more times than he cared to admit.

But Zach needed answers and he needed them soon.

He was tired of living in limbo. He'd finally figured out what he wanted in life, and he didn't want to waste any more time. It was all fine and good that he was learning to be more patient than he used to be, but if his close scrape with death had taught him anything, it was that time was precious. He was ready to have what his brothers had—love, marriage, wives, children. None of those things had mattered to him before, but now Zach was anxious to start a life with Gabriella.

If only she'd sit still and stop being sexy long enough for him to talk to her about it. He snorted with mock disgust—primarily at himself for being so weak.

"Are you okay?" she asked, turning to face him.

"Yeah. Why?"

"You just sort of sounded like you were annoyed at something."

Here was his opening. It was a potential segue into the conversation he wanted to have, but he didn't want to start it on an annoyed note. Plus, now was not the time. They were just about to pull into the corporate parking lot and he needed to focus on getting through the door and past all of the welcome-back greetings without getting tense.

Dammit.

Rotten timing.

"I'm fine. Really." He parked the car and took a minute to take a deep breath and get his head in the right place. Finally, he reached over and took one of Gabriella's hands in his. "Ready?"

Her smile was positively dazzling. "Absolutely," she said. "How about you? This is a big day."

Zach nodded. "Just promise you'll be ready to

turn some people away so we can actually get some work done."

Playfully, she pulled her hand from his and reached for the door handle. "I've been doing it for years. It'll be a piece of cake."

———

By five o'clock, Gabriella's head was pounding. The day seemed to have gone on forever. As much as she loved the fact that just about every employee at Montgomerys had stopped by to welcome Zach back, she was a little tired of smiling and answering the same questions about how it felt to have him back.

"You look like you could use a drink," Summer said as she walked toward Gabriella's desk.

"I think I need a bottle of aspirin more. And maybe a massage."

"Ooo…that does sound good. Think we can sneak out of here and arrange it? I can totally get Ethan to take Zach home."

It was tempting. "I don't know. We drove in together—his car. You'd have to drive me home." And then it hit her. This would be the perfect excuse to have a night at her own place. Gabriella wasn't stupid. She knew Zach was waiting on her answer about moving in together, but she just couldn't find the time alone to really think it through.

It wasn't that she didn't love Zach—she did—but they had spent so many years at odds with one another that she was afraid to trust this…honeymoon phase they were currently in. It was important for them to get back to a normal routine, to see how they'd function as a couple at this stage. Now that Zach had taken the first step and come back to the office, they were on their way. Of course, if she mentioned it to him, he'd probably argue with her how it didn't matter where they worked. He'd tell her if she really wanted to live with him, it shouldn't matter where they were working from. Maybe he was right. Maybe it shouldn't matter. But the fact was, it did.

"I can totally drive you home," Summer said, interrupting Gabriella's wayward thoughts.

"Do you think you can convince Ethan to take Zach out for a celebratory drink so it doesn't look quite so much like…?"

"Like you need some time away from him?" Summer asked with a smirk. "There's nothing to be ashamed of. It's completely normal."

Gabriella smiled with relief. "I feel kind of guilty. This was a big day for him and I should want to be with him and celebrate."

Summer waved her off. "Nah. He should want to celebrate and talk shop with Ethan. It's the final piece of the puzzle. Now they can make plans for the future of the company—hopefully ones to include me and Ethan getting some time off to head back to North Carolina for more than two days to look at our house and plan the wedding."

"Now we definitely have to go out. I've been so wrapped up in your brother that I've completely forgotten there's a wedding to plan! I want to hear all about it!"

Summer dashed off toward Ethan's office, and five minutes later he strode across the reception area and saluted Gabriella with a big smile on his face. "Go have fun. I've got this," he said, and knocked on Zach's door and went inside.

There was no way she was just going to slink out the door without saying good-bye, so Gabriella took a few minutes to straighten up her desk. Summer sashayed back over with a huge smile on her face.

"I called the spa and we have appointments in thirty minutes." She looked over toward Zach's office. "Has Ethan come out yet?"

"Not yet."

"Hmm… Let's go in and say our good-byes together. Less of a chance for Zach to throw any guilt your way."

Gabriella grabbed her purse and chuckled. "You are a scary woman sometimes, Summer."

Big blue eyes and a dazzling smile at the ready, Summer looked over her shoulder. "Trust me, I've learned from the masters." She opened Zach's door immediately after knocking and walked over to Ethan and wrapped her arms around him. "Gabs and I are going out for a little girl time. Massages and then maybe some sushi." She kissed him soundly on the lips. "I'll call you when I'm on my way home."

Zach sat at his desk and eyed his sister and Ethan for a moment before his gaze darted over to Gabriella. "Massages?"

She nodded. "After the day we've had, I think I need it."

He smiled and stood, walking around his desk to her. "Well then, go enjoy yourself. Summer's gonna bring you back to my place, right?"

"Actually, it's easier for me to stay at my place tonight. It's closer for her. Can you pick me up in the morning on the way here? My car is at your place."

"You know there's a solution to that," he whispered in her ear, and the feel of his warm breath gave her chills.

She knew exactly what he was getting at, but she was definitely not in the right frame of mind to get into it right now. Plus, they had massages to get to. She kissed him on the lips. "I'll see you in the morning."

Summer grabbed her hand and tugged her along. "Let's go, girlie! Our spa time awaits!"

—⁓—

"Okay, now that I've got you like putty, why don't you tell me about how things are going with you and my brother?" They were at their favorite sushi bar after getting hour-long massages when Summer decided to get to the good stuff.

"He wants us to move in together."

"Okay," Summer said as if waiting for something more.

"What?"

She sighed. "Gabs, you're practically living together already. Why haven't you sold your condo? It's a total drag spending time in two different places and having your stuff scattered in between. Blech! I hated that part of my relationship."

"Um, I hate to remind you of this, but you never really dealt with it. You had about two minutes of living separate from Ethan before he literally hijacked your moving truck, kidnapped you from the airport, and moved you in with him, so save it."

"Okay, okay. Let's just say...blech, I hate even the *thought* of doing that. There. Is that better?"

"You're so cute when you're sarcastic," Gabriella

said as she reached for some salmon. And then she sighed. "So…okay. Okay." Another sigh. "I'm scared."

Summer looked at her blandly. "You're going to have to do better than that. You're not afraid of anything."

"Says you."

"Look, it's always scary taking a relationship to the next level," Summer said comfortingly. "I was nervous about moving in with Ethan, and I've known him my whole life. We went from ignoring each other to being all over each other to ignoring each other again to living together in a matter of weeks. It was like a roller-coaster ride I couldn't get off. But once we settled in…oh, Gabs. It's just the best. I can't stand it when he has to travel and he's not sleeping beside me."

"I know what you're saying. Going back to my place and having a night to myself is okay, but…I really do miss Zach when I'm there."

"Then why do it?"

"Because we are together all the time. All. The. Time. There's no break. There's no escape. It's not healthy for a relationship of any kind. When we were working from home it was like we almost never had to leave. We were shut off from the rest of the world. While Zach was more than happy to have it that way, the walls were starting to close in on me. I can't live like that."

"Yeah, but it was a temporary thing. Now that he's driving and working in the office again, it's going to be better. It won't be just the two of you." She gently placed her hand on top of Gabriella's. "You guys have been dancing around one another for so long, and now things are finally going your way. It's only natural that some things change as you move forward. Do you *want* to live with him?"

"I think so," she said, but the hesitation was there.

"Okay," Summer began diplomatically. "Do you want to continue your relationship with him?"

"Of course I do! But continuing the relationship should not be contingent on whether or not I move in with him."

"Of course it shouldn't, but it's a subject that's going to keep coming up whether you like it or not. Think about it from a practical angle; you're paying rent for a closet. That's what your apartment is at this point. Your stuff is there but you're primarily with him."

"But that was because of his homebound recovery. I had no choice but to be at his place. Now that we're back at the office, we can take a step back and have our separate spaces for a little while."

Summer leaned back in her seat. "It's your family, isn't it? You don't have any idea what it's like to be in a normal, healthy relationship because you've never seen one."

Gabriella moved on to a California roll. Pointing her chopsticks at Summer, she said, "I hate when you're in my head."

"Well, you've done it to me enough times, so deal with it," she replied with a smile. "Gabs, I'm serious here. Don't think about your family. Break the cycle. Zach's always been around good, healthy relationships. Our parents, our aunts and uncles…they're all success stories. He'll be right there with you and…I'm not just saying this because he's my brother, but…he's totally worth it. You really should give this a chance."

"What if…what if things don't work out? Then I'm homeless, probably out of a job, and have the whole Montgomery family after me… It's a big risk to take."

"If you're concerned about your job hinging on whether or not you're sleeping with him, there's a solution to that too. Find another job. You can't tell me you want to be Zach's assistant for the rest of your life."

Gabriella shrugged but didn't meet Summer's gaze.

"You already have something in mind, don't you?" she asked excitedly. "Does Zach know? Have you talked to him about how you'd feel better if the two of you weren't working together? How you'd feel more comfortable moving in with him if you weren't his assistant?"

"Okay, you're getting way ahead of yourself here. No, I haven't talked to him about it and I don't have another job in mind. Not really. Well…kind of."

"Tell me," Summer demanded, bouncing in her seat with excitement.

Gabriella gave her a brief summary of her executive assistant agency. "I'm really good with training people, and I know I'm good at my job. I've gotten dozens of offers over the years from other companies and from headhunters trying to lure me away from Montgomerys, but I never wanted to leave."

"You would train the most kick-ass assistants ever! And you know if you got the word out—through Montgomerys—how you were doing this, you'd have a pretty impressive client list. They might even hire you to come in and train their existing staff."

"Wow. I hadn't even thought about that," Gabriella said as the wheels in her head began to turn. "But it would…" She stopped and shook her head. "It doesn't matter. I'm not prepared to take something like that on right now. I mean, if I were forced to…if things didn't work out with Zach, then maybe…"

"What if things *do* work out? What if things work out so great that you're actually happy? Why are you looking for trouble?"

"Trust me, I don't look for it, but it usually finds me."

"Well, it's time to stop thinking like that. It's time to have a positive outlook. I've seen such a transformation in Zach, Gabs, and it's because of you! If you give him a chance, he could possibly do the same thing for you."

Summer latched her big, sad blue eyes on Gabriella.

"Does that whole act work with Ethan?" Gabriella asked with a smirk.

"What? The sad eyes? Batting of the lashes?"

"Yeah, that."

"Most of the time. Sometimes I do it while I'm in my underwear. It usually tips the scales in my favor."

"Well, keep your pants—and your shirt—on. You've given me a lot to think about."

"And…?"

"All right. I'll give it a try. I'll give my notice to my landlord tomorrow."

Summer jumped up and came around the table to hug her. "Yeah! I knew you'd do it! And just think, soon we could be related!"

Gabriella nearly choked on her roll. "One thing at a time, blue eyes. One thing at a time."

"Oh, you're no fun."

"Sit your butt back down. Enough about me. I want

to hear all about the wedding plans and how the house is coming along."

Luckily, Summer didn't argue with the change of subject. Gabriella's mind was spinning with the thought of taking this leap with Zach. She knew he'd be thrilled, but she still struggled with the thought of losing herself. Zach was larger than life and he liked things a certain way. They had a great balance now in their work relationship, but they were just starting to find it in their personal one. Being lovers who worked together was bound to bring up issues.

And, like it or not, she was going to find out what they were—probably sooner rather than later.

———

"I can't believe I let you talk me into this. All that massaging and relaxing…gone. I'm going to need another massage tomorrow."

"Hey, lighten up. This was all your idea," Gabriella reminded Summer.

"What? No, no, no. I said you should move in with Zach, I didn't mean we should pack up your whole apartment and move it all over there *tonight*."

"And the award for biggest overexaggerator goes to…!"

"Okay, fine. We're not packing up your entire apartment, but there's enough luggage here to make it feel that way. I hope it all fits in my car."

Gabriella stopped and took inventory. "You may have a point there. I didn't think about that. Okay, let's start with the big pieces and see how far we get."

They worked together for another thirty minutes until there was barely enough room for the two of them in the car. "Just so you know," Summer said when she closed her car door, "when Ethan and I move into our new house, you're in charge of loading the truck."

"It wasn't so bad."

"Oh, I don't mean it like that. I mean I cannot believe we fit fourteen suitcases in my car. You're like a packing wizard."

"It wasn't that hard, and besides, some of them are really small. They're not all suitcases."

"It was a thing of beauty. Seriously. You've got a gift."

"Please, I'm blushing…" Gabriella teased, and they both broke into fits of laughter. "Come on. I know it's late and Ethan's probably going to be mad at me because you're not at home and Zach's already called three times and I let them all go to voice mail. He's probably having a fit."

"It will be worth it when we get there. I'm just glad I get to see the look of surprise on his face. Can I take a picture?"

"Don't poke the bear," Gabriella said with a chuckle. "He's not big on surprises, and I'm sure he's going to need a minute to digest all of this. After all, I haven't talked to him about it or brought it up in weeks."

"I'm definitely taking a picture. I may make it my screensaver."

"Do you think he's going to freak out? Like in a bad way?"

Summer laughed. "I think he's going to be very happy. *That's* why I want the picture. It's been a rarity to catch Zach laughing and smiling. It'll practically be like a Bigfoot sighting."

They made the short drive to Zach's house and pulled

into the driveway. When Summer shut the car off, she turned toward Gabriella. "Are you ready for this?" she asked excitedly.

"I think I am."

Summer shook her head. "No, no, no. *Are you ready for this?*" she asked, sounding more and more like a motivational speaker revving up a crowd.

"Okay, I am," Gabriella said with a little more enthusiasm.

"I can't hear you!"

"Oh for the love of it," Gabriella muttered before turning and facing Summer. "Ma'am, yes ma'am, I am ready for this!"

Summer broke out in a fit of giggles. "That's more like it. Now, go knock on the door—don't use your key!—and let me get into position."

"You're not really going to take his picture, are you?"

"It's my right as the little sister. I'm just getting even for all of the times he teased me when we were kids. I haven't had too many opportunities to catch him like this. Humor me."

"Yeah, well, the joke may be on you when he gets mad and tells us both to leave. Then you'll have to help me lug all this luggage back to my apartment!"

"I highly doubt it. Now go!"

Climbing from the car, Gabriella had a bit of pep in her step as she walked toward the front door. This was a good thing. She really did want to be with Zach, and if she could just stay out of her head for a while, everything would be fine.

Taking a steadying breath, she stood up straight and rang the doorbell. And waited.

And waited.

And waited.

Zach pulled the door open looking a bit frazzled. "Gabriella?" he asked, sounding concerned. "Are you all right? Did something happen? I've been calling you for hours!"

"Actually…everything's…great. Better than great."

Now his expression was pure confusion. "What's going on?" He looked over her shoulder and saw Summer's car. "Did you borrow Summer's car to get here? Is she all right?"

"Zach Montgomery," Gabriella began seriously, "I was wondering if you were still looking for a roommate."

A slow smile played across his lips. "A roommate? No."

"No?"

He shook his head. "What I had in mind was a lot more…intimate."

"Ooo…I like the sound of that," she purred as she stepped closer. "I like the sound of that a lot. If you're still looking for someone to fill that…*position*, I'd really like to be considered."

"You would, huh? It would mean moving all of your things here."

"Well then, it's your lucky night because I happen to have a ton of my stuff over there in the car, just waiting to be moved in here."

Zach's eyes went wide. "Are you serious? You really have your stuff in Summer's car?"

"I do. And if we don't get everything out soon, her car may just explode."

Gabriella didn't have a chance to say more

because Zach lifted her up into his arms and swung her around.

"I take it this means you're happy?" she asked.

"You have no idea," he said. "So happy that I want to take you inside right now and have my way—"

"Stop it! Stop it! Stop it! La la la la la!" Summer sang out as she stepped from the bushes. "I don't want to hear any more of that. Sheesh!"

Zach looked at his sister and chuckled. "What, may I ask, were you doing in the bushes?"

"I was going to snap a picture of you to prove to the world you really do smile. But then you went and got gross with your sexy talk and now I may have to stab pointy things in my ears. *Blech*." She shuddered and walked over to her car. "C'mon. Give us a hand with all this luggage so I can go home and make Ethan give me a massage."

"Oh, so you can talk about you and Ethan but I'm not allowed to mention sexy stuff with me and—"

"You're doing it again!"

"I haven't said anything yet!"

"But you were going to!" Summer said, pointing a finger at him. "Just…no talking. Just get the luggage and go in the house and don't tell me about what happens after that!"

Zach did as she asked, for the most part. He took several pieces of luggage but muttered under his breath the entire time about this being *his* house and *he* should be able to talk no matter what his little sister thought. Both Gabriella and Summer stood there laughing for a solid minute before they each grabbed some of the luggage and hauled it into the house.

When they were done, Summer said her good-byes and drove away. Once the door was closed, Zach walked over and wrapped Gabriella in his arms. "Hey, roomie."

She giggled. "Hey, that's *intimate* roomie to you."

He reached up and stroked her cheek. "No, that won't do. I'd like to call you so much more."

She sighed and rested her forehead against his chest. "One thing at a time, Zach. This was a very big step for me. I…I need us to settle in a little bit before we talk about anything more." She looked up at him. "Is that all right?"

He nodded. "You know how I am, Gabs. I'm a man of action and I normally go after what I want full force. I'm not known for my patience but I'm trying to be—for your sake. We'll figure this out and what's right for us together. You'll just have to be patient with me, too."

"Deal." They stood there wrapped up in each other until Gabriella really got a look around. "I don't even know where we're going to fit all of this stuff. We may need to build an extension."

He chuckled. "It's not that bad."

She leaned back and looked up at his handsome face. "Baby, this isn't even half of it."

Zach paled slightly. "Okay then. What I think we need to realize is it's not all going to find a place tonight. There are two walk-in closets in the master bedroom and one of them is just my sporting equipment. I can move all that to the gym room tomorrow and have it ready for you. Then if that's not enough, there are closets in the guest rooms you can branch out into."

"Sounds like a plan. But like you said, it's too much for tonight. I have enough things here to get ready for work for the rest of the week. So let's just move these so they're not in the way and we'll make this our weekend project. What do you think?"

"That you're an amazing woman and I love you," he said, his tone deep and serious.

"Zach…"

"It's how I feel, Gabs, and I'm going to say it. Get used to it." He kissed the tip of her nose and went about tucking the suitcases out of the way. When that was all done, they walked arm in arm to the living room and sat down on the sofa. She rested her head on his shoulder. "Welcome home, Gabriella," he said softly.

"Mmm…I like the sound of that." And it was the truth. Ever since she'd moved out on her own, she'd been so focused on working and separating herself from her family that her condos and apartments were simply a place to sleep. But this? This house? This was going to be a home. A place where she was going to have a life—a life with Zach.

"Good. I want you to like it. Everything here is ours. There isn't going to be any 'that's mine and this is yours' crap. I won't live like that. This is *our* home, all right?"

She nodded her head but didn't look up at him. It was like the day at Summer's house when she'd held baby Jamie in her arms. Her emotions were too close to the surface. She wasn't ready to cry in front of Zach or to show her weaknesses. Maybe it was crazy or maybe it was pointless—he would see them eventually—but for now, she wanted it to be like this.

"I think we need to celebrate," he said softly.

"Do we have any champagne?"

"That wasn't what I had in mind."

"Oh really?" she said silkily, her hand coming up and stroking his chest. "What did you have in mind?"

"I think we need to do something to christen the place as ours."

She chuckled. "We've already made love all over this house. I believe it has been well and truly christened."

Zach tucked a finger under her chin and gently forced her to look up at him. "That was before. We're starting fresh right here, right now."

"And getting naked on the sofa will help us do that?"

His lips twitched. "It certainly couldn't hurt."

Gabriella straightened and put a little distance between them before standing up. Keeping her eyes on his, she unbuttoned her blouse and dropped it to the floor. Her skirt followed. Zach put his hands on her waist and pulled her between his spread legs and placed soft kisses on her belly.

"I know it's wrong, but if I could, I'd make this a work uniform for you."

She made a throaty sound. "Then we'd have to move the office back here full time."

Zach lifted his head. "You'd…you'd actually work in nothing but stilettos and a thong…if we worked from home?" he croaked.

She pretended to consider it. "Well, maybe not every day, but I could be on board for a once-a-week gig."

He groaned. "You're killing me. You just got me to go back to the office and now you throw this at me?"

"You never asked," she teased.

"Hell, had I known you'd consider it, I would've begged sooner. You have no idea how many times

I've fantasized about his. You and me, my office…my desk…" He groaned again and went back to letting his mouth roam over her belly.

Reaching down, Gabriella raked her hands through Zach's hair and tugged slightly to get him to look back up at her. "You have a desk here." She motioned over her shoulder. "We could…practice. It could be fun to get back into work mode for a little while and then christen the desk."

He quickly stood up and took her by the hand, leading her to the office. "If I wasn't in love with you before, you definitely sealed the deal now."

—–∾∾–—

By Friday afternoon, Zach was beat. It was hard to deal with the fact that he used to work twice as many hours as he had this week without giving it much thought. Now all he wanted to do was go home and have a quiet evening with Gabriella. He'd like to say it was only because he just wanted to be with her, but he also felt like he'd run a marathon this week.

Looking at the clock on the wall, he saw it was only four o'clock. Another hour to go before he would feel comfortable calling it a day. The newspaper was on his desk and he reached for it. Earlier in the week the local paper had sent someone over to interview him about his accident and comeback—it wasn't something Zach had particularly wanted to do, but it was good PR for the company so he reluctantly agreed.

Scanning the pages, he found the story and read it. Not bad. It didn't get too invasive and it didn't go into too much detail about his personal life, but there was a good picture of him with Ethan, Summer, and Gabriella. He smiled. They all looked good, happy. By now, Ethan and Summer were on their way to the airport—finally heading back to the East Coast for a weeklong vacation where they could oversee the construction of their house and start their wedding plans.

Zach was happy for them—even a little envious. He hoped he and Gabriella would be ready for that step soon. He didn't want to take away from his sister's big day, but he also didn't want to wait too long before asking Gabriella to be his wife. In his heart he knew that's what he wanted.

Raised voices out in the reception area made him jump to his feet. There weren't any appointments on the calendar, and at this hour on a Friday afternoon it seemed odd for anyone to be coming around. But when he opened the door, he saw Gabriella walking away with a man, heading into the conference room. More than a little concerned, he followed. He supposed she thought she'd slammed the door shut, but it hadn't latched. Zach stood outside the door and listened.

"What are you doing here, Alan?"

"What? Can't a guy come and visit his favorite sister-in-law? You know, there was a time when you and I were friends."

"Yeah, well, it was a long time ago," Gabriella muttered.

"It doesn't have to be like this, Gabby. You don't visit near enough."

Zach heard Gabriella's huff of frustration. "And we all know why I don't. Why don't you get to the point about why you're even here? Somehow I doubt it's to talk about how much everyone misses me."

"See, that's where you're wrong," Alan said. The tone of his voice set Zach's teeth on edge, but he waited the guy out to see where this was going.

"Seriously, Alan…"

"I made a mistake, Gabby. Chose the wrong sister. I never should have married her."

"You're joking, right?" Gabriella spat. "There was never a choice. I was never attracted to you. We were friends. That's it."

"No," Alan said dismissively. "You wanted me. I know you wanted me. You were just so damn uptight back then and didn't know how to relax and have fun." He made some sort of sound deep in his throat before saying, "But you're different now. I saw that picture of you in the paper and just…knew. I knew you were finally ready for me."

Zach had heard enough. "Excuse me," he said smoothly, walking into the room. "Is everything all right? You okay, Gabriella?" he asked as he took his place beside her and wrapped his arm protectively around her waist.

Alan looked at the two of them. "Found yourself another one, did you?" he directed at Gabriella. "Couldn't land one boss so you moved on to another." Then he turned toward Zach. "I read about your accident and your remarkable recovery in the paper. That's awesome. Of course, you had our girl Gabriella there." He took a deep breath and almost seemed to take pride in Gabriella's role in Zach's rehabilitation.

Zach just glared at him.

"You know," Alan continued unaware, as if hearing him reminisce were the most important thing they could be doing right now, "when my wife left me, I was a broken man. But luckily I had Gabriella right there to…help me up." His gaze lingered on Gabriella's body before looking back at Zach. "I'm sure she was very *helpful* to you too. She's a great…motivation."

"I think it's time you left, Alan," Zach said, feeling how stiff Gabriella had gone beside him.

"Nonsense," the man countered. "Gabriella and I are family. You know the importance of that, don't you, Zach? I mean, you work with yours. Certainly you wouldn't throw any of them out." It was a challenge, and Alan met Zach's steely gaze to see how far he could push.

"Here's the funny thing about family," Zach began, his hold on Gabriella never relenting. "Family should be there to build one another up, support each other. From what I've seen of your family, you only come around to tear Gabriella down. I don't know why you're here, I don't want to know why you're here, but I will tell you this, you're not welcome. Not here in this office, not even in this state. If I were you, I would turn around and walk out the door and not look back." His words and his tone left little room for argument. A smart man would simply admit defeat and go.

"I don't think you realize who I am to Gabriella," Alan said. "I could easily walk out of here now, but like I said, we're family. Next time I come back, her sister and parents will be with me. I'm sure they'll just *gush* with pride to see how far Gabriella's come."

Gabriella broke free of Zach's arm. "What is wrong with you? What could I have possibly done to make you ruin my life like this?"

He stepped in close. "You always thought you were better than everyone else even though your own family didn't want anything to do with you. You thought I wasn't good enough for you, or your sister. Even though she was the one who pursued me," Alan said, pointing at his chest. "And then you had to rat me out."

"You were cheating on her!" Gabriella cried.

"So what? She was too desperate for me anyway. It will be very different for you and me, Gabby."

"You make me sick, Alan. Get out."

"Come on. You're not serious," Alan said, taking a step back and looking between her and Zach. "I'm offering to leave your sister. We were a good team once. We can be again."

When Gabriella made no move away from Zach, Alan raised his eyebrows skeptically. He nudged his head in Zach's direction. "How long do you think he'll keep you happy? He's never going to be man enough for you. You saw the way he walked in here and—"

In an instant, Zach lunged and went to grab Alan by the throat—a feral growl coming from his very soul— but his leg gave out and he lost his balance. "*Zach!*" Gabriella cried as she reached out to steady him.

Alan resumed his arrogant stance, fixing his coat. "See, Gabby? You need a man like me. He needs a woman to catch him when he falls." He smiled at her in a self-satisfied way. "Give me a call when you come to your senses." And he turned and strode from the room.

Gabriella did her best to steady Zach but he jerked from her grasp. "*Don't!*" he snapped. "Just…just don't."

"Are you okay?"

"You mean for a guy who isn't man enough to defend a woman?" he sneered.

"I didn't say that, Zach! I wouldn't even think it!"

"Yeah, well…it's the truth, isn't it?" He turned and walked a few feet away and stretched before pacing back toward her. "What the hell was that guy even doing here?"

"I don't know!" she said, leaning against the conference table. "I was typing up the last of today's contracts and I looked up and there he was."

"So you didn't invite him here?"

She looked at him incredulously. "Invite *him* here? Are you out of your mind? Zach, I haven't invited my family anywhere near me since that day at my apartment years ago. I have no idea why Alan chose now to show up."

Zach thought about it for a moment. "The article. That damn article." He cursed again. "He mentioned he read it."

"I'm so sorry, Zach. I…I don't even know what to say. I'm so embarrassed."

"Why?" he asked, taking a seat and flexing his leg to work out the cramp.

"Why? Didn't you hear all the ugly things he said? And you know he's going to go to my family and twist everything so that I look like the crazy person!" She began to pace. "He'll say I'm the one who contacted him and I'm looking to get out of this relationship and—"

"Are you?"

She stopped pacing and looked at him. "Am I what?"

"Looking to get out of this relationship. Does it bother you that I'm not the same man I was before the accident? That I have a limp? That I'll probably always have this limp?"

"Zach," she said softly, going to stand in front of him. "I think you're a better man now than you were before the accident. A *better* man. I'm not looking for an out."

Zach wasn't so sure. Everything about the last few minutes was twisting things he thought he knew and suddenly old insecurities and doubts began to surface. She might say she was fine with the way he was, but the mere fact that he couldn't defend her when she needed him to all but killed him. He wasn't a better man. At the moment, he didn't feel like a man at all. "Maybe he has a point."

"What are you talking about?"

"Maybe this is your…thing. Maybe you like the idea of chasing the boss. Back then, maybe it bothered you that he chose your sister over you and you created all this drama for sympathy."

She recoiled as if he'd slapped her. "How can you even say that? Think that? I've always been honest with you, Zach. I never lied."

He shrugged. "Maybe. But now that he's come sniffing around and you can finally have what you obviously once wanted, you should go for it."

Her eyes went wide before welling with tears. "What are you saying?"

"I think it would probably be best if we…if we were honest with each other. It turns out I don't like being second best."

"But you're not! Zach, I don't want Alan! I *never* wanted Alan! That was a story he concocted to cover his own ass! You know me better than that!"

He couldn't look at her. He focused on his hands that were clasped in his lap as he spoke. "I didn't like it when the guys in the office were gossiping, and I didn't like coming in here and listening to Alan either."

"You're not making any sense," she sobbed as the tears began to fall freely. "This was just the act of a pathetic, spiteful man. He means nothing to me. You know that. It's you I want, Zach. It's you I love!"

He shook his head. "I thought I was ready for all of this, Gabs, but I'm not. I don't like drama, and I certainly don't want to go around wondering if it's me you really want or if you're staying with me out of pity or… you'll be eyeing the next executive who comes along."

"Stop it!" she cried. "Please! Let's go home. Let's talk about this. Don't let him ruin this relationship too!"

"So now you're going to blame him for ruining your relationship with your family? I thought that was strained long before he came along."

"It…it was," she stammered, wiping away the tears. "He just made everything that much worse." She reached out for his hand but he pulled away. "You're not being fair, Zach. You're listening to the rantings of a sociopath over me! I thought you said you loved me!"

She was killing him. In that instant he wanted nothing more than to quiet the demons inside of him that were making him second-guess everything he had come to believe, but they were too loud, too demanding.

"I was wrong," he said flatly and then forced himself to look up at her as his heart ripped in two.

The look of utter devastation on her face made him curse his very existence. He thought for certain she'd curse him to hell and fight back as she always had.

But she didn't.

Gabriella transformed right before his eyes. She wiped the last of her tears away and straightened her spine enough that she could have given a soldier a run for his money. And with nothing more than a nod of her head, she turned and walked from the room.

And out of his life.

Chapter 14

"BUT...YOU HAVE TO BE AT MY WEDDING, GABS. YOU just have to!"

They'd had this conversation on the phone at least a dozen times in the last three months, but no matter how much Summer tried, Gabriella stuck to her guns. "Believe me, I would love to see you and Ethan say 'I do,' I really would. But unfortunately, I can't get the time off."

"I still don't see why you didn't take Uncle William up on his offer. If you were working for any other branch of Montgomerys, your attendance at my wedding would be mandatory." She paused before whining, "Come on, Gabriella! You're supposed to be my maid of honor! We talked about it. Remember? The night with the massages and the sushi? You promised!"

Gabriella was normally a fairly patient person with Summer, but right now she just wasn't feeling it. In the three months since she'd last walked through the doors of the Montgomerys office in Portland, she'd pretty much cut herself off from everything and everybody. It was for the best—apparently she couldn't trust anyone.

Even the person who claimed to love her.

"I promise we'll get together when you get back from your honeymoon. I'm really sorry, sweetie, but I have to go. My lunch break is over and I have to get back."

Summer was silent for a long moment. "Won't you

at least tell me where you are? It's been months, Gabs. I'm worried about you. I hate that you're somewhere out there all alone."

So did she. Being independent had been fun and invigorating when she was younger, but this version— coupled with self-imposed isolation—really sucked. "It's not important, Summer. I don't want you to worry about me. I'm okay. Really. I want you to marry that handsome man of yours and be happy." She choked back a sob and took a moment to compose herself. "Okay?"

"You know he's a mess too, right?" Summer said quietly. "Zach. He's worse now than he was after the accident."

It shouldn't have made Gabriella feel better, but it did. A little.

"Has…has he asked about me?" As soon as she asked the question she wanted to take it back. She'd been able to control herself in all of her previous conversations with Summer but for some reason today, she just needed to know.

"Not directly. But whenever your name comes up, I tell him how you've probably started the agency you always dreamed of—you know, the one you never told him about."

"There was a reason I never told him, Summer," Gabriella hedged.

"Yeah, yeah, yeah…whatever. The look on his face when I told him what you really wanted to be when you grew up was pretty priceless."

"Did you get a picture? You know, for your screensaver?"

Summer laughed. "I love you, you know that, right? And I miss you like crazy."

"Text me some pictures from Hawaii," Gabriella said. "And try not to do anything crazy like skydive into a volcano."

"Please. I think Ethan might have been up for that about a year ago but we're both just looking forward to being away from everything and finally being married." She sighed. "I feel like I've waited my whole life for this."

"You have," Gabriella said sadly. "You've been in love with him your whole life, remember? Go have that happily ever after, blue eyes. No one deserves it more than you." She hung up quickly, before Summer could say anything more.

Slipping her phone into her purse, Gabriella made the two-block walk back to her office. The weather was beautiful and people smiled and waved—it was something that should have made her smile. But she just didn't have the energy to do it.

Her position at the small insurance company was well beneath her skills. It was mind-numbingly boring. But after her years in the corporate world and all she'd endured there, this was the perfect fix. Zach had shipped her luggage back to her apartment the day after their fallout and Gabriella had essentially been on a plane east the day after that. There was no way she was going back to Seattle, and staying in Portland was out of the question.

There had been no calls to William Montgomery. She didn't want to have anything to do with the company— there was too much of a chance of seeing or hearing about Zach. A clean cut was what she needed most.

South Carolina wasn't really a conscious decision. But she'd heard Summer talk so much about the home she and Ethan were building in North Carolina that she knew she'd at least be close enough to get to see her friend once in a while if she wanted to. Like when her heart was healed.

So maybe never.

North Myrtle Beach was close enough to the coast if she wanted to go to the beach, and it was easy enough to blend in and not draw attention to herself. She learned to tone down her wardrobe and went from what Zach used to call her sexy librarian look to just librarian. She missed her shoes. She missed her makeup. But in order to stay under the radar, it was better to be as plain Jane as she possibly could. It wasn't the way she had ever envisioned her life, but it certainly cut back on the drama.

So she worked a boring job.

Lived in a tourist town where nobody knew her name.

And essentially relegated herself to a life of complete and utter boredom.

"Yeah, I'm living the dream," she sighed as she put her purse away in her desk and went back to filing claims. It was a Thursday. Summer's wedding was Saturday. She hated not being there. Hated that she was going to miss out on something she had really been looking forward to because…of what? Cowardice, or self-preservation? It was a coin toss.

Her plan was to drive up the coast to Wilmington and park a bit away in hopes she'd at least get to see Summer and Ethan as they left the church. Summer had given her enough details about the wedding that Gabriella knew the itinerary inside and out. She sighed as she thought about the gown she had hoped to wear.

Strapless.

Midnight blue.

Killer heels.

All going to waste in the back of her closet. Why she had even bought the dress she had no idea. Gabriella was a practical woman and when she spotted the dress in a little boutique a month earlier, she already knew she wasn't ever going to wear it. It wasn't even a bridesmaid dress, but she knew it would be perfect for Summer's wedding. But she was feeling sorry for herself and for a few minutes, it felt really good to just have it on.

She was losing her mind.

Slowly and painfully.

Maybe someday she'd have somewhere to wear it to. Of course that would mean doing more than eating alone in her little apartment, but that was a depressing saga for another time.

The day wore on and when she was finally ready to leave at five o'clock, she stopped at her boss's desk. "Mr. Anderson?"

"Yes?" He was an older man, happily married and a grandfather of five. The agency had been started by *his* grandfather.

"I was wondering if I might have tomorrow off. I know it's short notice. But I've completed all of the claims that were piled up and did the software update we talked about, and the new website will be up and running by Monday. I'm actually a little ahead of myself."

He took his glasses off his round face and smiled at her. "I don't think it should be a problem, Miss Martine. If anything comes up, you know my Norma wouldn't mind coming in to lend a hand. Go and have yourself a good weekend."

"Thank you, sir," she said with a shy smile. "You too." As soon as she was outside, Gabriella let out a huge sigh of relief. That office, that job were slowly sucking her will to live. Slinging her purse strap over her shoulder, she breathed in the night air and vowed she would try to have a better outlook by Monday.

Her apartment was only four blocks away—a happy coincidence—and she enjoyed the walk. It was amazing what sensible shoes allowed you to do! Once home, she thought about her conversation with Summer. She hated keeping her friend in the dark but she wasn't ready to face anyone—or more specifically, any Montgomery—just yet. Summer had given her hell for leaving Portland without telling her, but Gabriella had simply said she hadn't wanted to interrupt Summer and Ethan's week off.

That, and she didn't want anyone talking her out of what she was doing.

In the back of her mind, she kept thinking Zach would call her, reach out to her, even if it was only to remind her of her job. But he didn't. Even when he'd arranged for all her belongings to be delivered back to her apartment, there was no communication. She'd simply opened her door to a team of movers and thanked them for their time.

Bastard.

She knew him. Or at least she'd thought she knew him. She knew his moods and how he thought, and for the life of her she couldn't understand how things had spiraled out of control so quickly. Alan's appearance—while awful and annoying—should not have had the effect it did. For weeks Gabriella had refused to believe Zach had lied about loving her. But after so much time had gone by without a word from him, she had no choice but to accept that he had.

Even thinking about it now had her heart clenching. *Stupid heart*, she thought. *Lesson learned.*

It wasn't so much that Zach Montgomery hated everyone, but at the moment, he kind of did. It was like the entire world had just forgotten how to do any work and do their jobs because they were too busy laughing and smiling and joking around. Or getting married.

"Dude, come on," Ethan said as he popped his head into Zach's office. "You're all packed, right?"

"I said I was," Zach huffed and pinched the bridge of his nose.

"Well, the car's going to be here in fifteen minutes, and do me a favor, lose the attitude. If your sister is on the receiving end of one of your snarky comments, I'll seriously have to kick your ass."

"Isn't she already in North Carolina?"

"Why? Is the plane ride going to be the magic touch that takes the stick out of your ass?"

"Screw you," Zach muttered as he rose from his chair and shut down his computer. By the time he looked up, Ethan was standing right in front of him. "What?" he snapped.

"I asked you this once before—aren't you tired of this nonsense?"

"What the hell are you talking about? Don't we have a flight to catch?"

"Yeah, we do, as a matter of fact. But I'm tired of this. This last year has been a real bitch and it's mainly because of you. I'm done, man. You screwed up. You blew the greatest thing in your life and you won't tell anyone why. Fine. I get it. But it was *your* decision and you need to move on. Stop punishing everyone else for having a life!"

Zach raked a hand through his hair and paced away and then back again. "You know what, Ethan? You're tired of me? Well, let me tell you, buddy, I'm a little tired of you and everyone else trying to tell me how to live my life! I've been to hell and back and I'm here, doing the work, just like everyone wanted and expected. No one said I had to do it with a smile on my damn face!"

"I don't even care about a smile, Zach. Not being a complete jackass for even five minutes would be a great start!"

"You know what? I'm done. Go. Catch your plane. Get married. Live happily freaking ever after. If I'm such a damn nuisance to everyone, I'll do you all a favor and stay home."

Ethan sighed loudly and then clapped theatrically. "That's just wonderful. Seriously. Bravo. If I had a sword handy, I'd set it up for you to throw yourself on."

"I'm serious, Ethan. I'm not going."

"Um…yeah. You are."

"Why? If I'm such a pain in the ass, why would you even want me to?"

"Maybe because I'm marrying your sister! Or maybe it's because we've been best friends since forever and you're like a brother to me. Take your pick, man. You're getting on the plane. I don't care what the hell you do after I leave on my honeymoon, but for the wedding? You're going to be there for your family."

Zach glared at him. Hard. "I…I can't. I can't do it,

man. Everyone keeps asking and wanting to know what happened." His voice cracked. "I…I just can't."

Ethan sat down in one of the chairs and looked up at his best friend. "So tell me. Tell me what happened and I'll make sure no one brings it up."

"It's not that easy."

"So make it that easy. You have my word, Zach, right here, right now. You tell me what happened and I'll make sure everyone knows the topic is off limits for the weekend. Work with me here."

Collapsing on the leather sofa in the corner of the office, Zach finally let it all out. Everything he'd felt, everything he'd said. And then he just let his head fall back against the cushions and closed his eyes. Neither spoke for a long time.

"You know none of that ever mattered to her, right?" Ethan asked.

"Now I do. At the time, I couldn't see it. I didn't *want* to see it."

"When you were on the climb and we were all waiting for news about you, she was a mess. Honestly, there were times she was more distraught than Summer was. Neither of them were fans of you taking risks on those trips, but Gabriella? Man, she just… she just hated the thought of you getting hurt. And whenever someone tried to blow us off or didn't get us sufficient information, she was like a tigress. I had a lot of respect for her."

"Is there a point to this story?"

"She stayed, Zach. She stayed even after you treated her like crap, she put up with all your foul moods, and she fought for you when the rest of us were feeling too overwhelmed to even know what to do. And even after you essentially kicked her out of the state of Alaska—not your finest moment, by the way—she still stayed. She could have come and worked for me and things would have been easier for her. But Gabriella doesn't take the easy way out."

"She left."

Ethan nodded. "Everyone has their limits, Zach. She trusted you. She trusted that you loved her and when she really needed you, you chose a really crappy time to go back to being a jackass."

"It wasn't about her, it was about me!"

"That's the problem! She needed your support, but you were too focused on yourself and the fact that you couldn't throttle the guy. And how did you deal with that? You said to her face exactly what you threatened those guys for saying behind her back. Did it make you feel better? Did that make you a bigger man, putting her down?"

He couldn't speak even if he wanted to. He simply shook his head.

"Personally, I can't believe she stayed as long as she did. It's a good thing she didn't say 'I love you,' because—"

"She did." Zach looked up, his expression bleak. "She told me, that day, that she loved me."

"And you didn't believe her?"

"I didn't. I was so out of my mind and just couldn't hear what she was saying."

"Wow."

"I know."

Ethan looked at his watch. "Come on. The car's probably downstairs. Let's go."

"I don't want to ruin your wedding, Ethan. I wouldn't be able to live with myself if I did that."

"It doesn't seem like you're really living right now anyway. Might as well come along and at least go through the motions for a little longer."

Zach knew going was the right thing to do. He owed it to Ethan. And to Summer. They had put up with him almost as much as Gabriella had. With a weary sigh, he walked over to his closet and took out his suitcase and jacket and walked out of his office. The reception area was quiet. It had been quiet for three months. He hadn't hired a replacement. Gabriella's assistant had been dealing with everything and keeping a wide berth between them while doing it.

The elevator doors opened and Ethan stood there waiting. "You coming?"

A quick nod was Zach's only response.

She hadn't really set out to do it, but it just so happened her all-day movie marathon to take her mind off her crappy life was all about female empowerment—*The Hunger Games*, *A League of Their Own*, *Brave*... By the time *Erin Brockovich* was starting, Gabriella noticed the pattern.

"Why am I hiding out?" she asked herself out loud. "Why am I the one sacrificing my life because of the small-minded thinking of others?" Clicking off the TV, she went in search of her phone and immediately dialed the first number that came to mind.

Her sister's.

"Hey, Mel," she said when her sister answered the phone. "How are you?"

"Gabby? Oh my gosh. Fine. How…how are you? Wait…why are you calling me? You never call me."

"I know. I normally try to stay out of your life, but I have some things to say and you're going to listen for once."

"Well, really, Gabriella, why would I do that if you're just calling to nag me? I'm just saying—"

"No, actually, *I'm* just saying. And I want you to just be quiet for once, and listen."

"Fine. Whatever."

For the next hour Gabriella went on to tell Melissa just how she felt—from how she wasn't the older sister she'd wanted to be to Mel, to how Alan had come to proposition her in Portland.

"But…but he said he was in San Francisco. Why would he lie to me?"

Gabriella gave a long-suffering sigh. "*He is a liar. He is a cheat.* I have been telling you the truth for years. Despite the fact that you continually choose to believe him over me, you're my sister and believe it or not, I do love you. You deserve better than him. You deserve to be with a man who loves you and respects you. That's not Alan. It's never been Alan. Aren't you tired of putting up with a man who thinks so little of you that he's still out trolling for women?"

"Of course I am, but why would he keep after you specifically unless…there was something going on between you."

"That was never the case, Mel. I *never* had feelings for Alan as anything more than a friend. Believe me, I was shocked he turned out to be such a dog. But haven't you had enough?"

Melissa was silent for a long moment. "I...I thought you were just, you know, jealous. At first... I admit that at first I really only wanted to date him to piss you off. And then you went away and I kind of felt victorious." She paused. "And then I realized what a complete moron he was, but at least I had someone. And Mom and Dad love him, which made me feel like I made the right choice, too. They think he's amazing."

"Tell Dad how his amazing son-in-law has been spending the family money and cheating on you and see how amazing they still think he is."

"Gabby...I...I don't know what to say. I mean, why are you even doing this? Why now?"

"I'm tired of living like this. I'm tired of being a victim to other people's closed minds. I never wanted to hurt you, but I'm also tired of getting hurt."

Melissa was silent for a moment. "What now, Gabby? What do we do from here?"

"That's completely up to you. If it were me, I'd kick Alan's sorry ass out. But first, make sure you have enough ammunition to take him to the cleaners in the divorce."

Mel and Gabriella both laughed at that.

They talked for a few more minutes and by the time they hung up, they both promised to put in an effort to make their relationship better. Gabriella was just relieved they were both willing to try.

It was the first of three phone calls Gabriella made. The second one was to her boss, Mr. Anderson, to give him a heads-up that she would be giving her two weeks' notice. He didn't seem surprised by her announcement.

"Thank you for being willing to stay on for the

standard two weeks, but it won't be necessary. My beloved wife of forty years is here to help out," Mr. Anderson said with such tenderness in his voice it made Gabriella want to throw up, or cry. Or both. "May I ask what you're going to be doing now? I assume you found a better job." There was no condemnation in his tone, just general curiosity.

"Actually, I haven't found another job yet. But I think it's time I went after something I'm passionate about. Something of my own."

"Well, whatever it is, Miss Martine, I know you're going to be successful at it. Good luck to you."

"Thank you, sir. Thank you for everything."

The third call had been to her parents. She made sure they were each available to talk and then blasted them for picking favorites in their children and for not backing her when she needed them the most. They didn't put up as much of a fight as she'd expected—it was almost as if they'd known for a long time they'd done something wrong but didn't know how to go about making it right. She told them about her conversation with Melissa so they could be prepared for whatever was going to happen there.

By the time she hung up with her parents, she felt like she could conquer the world. No one had taken too kindly to her harsh words—at first—but by the end of each conversation she had gotten all her years of hurt and resentment off her chest, and their acknowledgment of their part in causing it.

Sitting back on her oversize sofa, she was feeling pretty darn good. She had faced her demons and the sky didn't fall. She couldn't say she was ready to move back to Seattle, but things were going to be all right. They no longer had any control over her.

That only left one final call.

Taking a deep breath, she picked up the phone and scrolled through her contacts and hit Call. And waited.

"Hello?"

"Hey, it's me," she said. "I think it's time we talked."

—∿∿∼—

Zach's tie was choking him and the smile he'd kept plastered on his face for the last twenty-four hours was painful. Just a few more hours and he could hop a plane back to Portland and be done with all this wedding nonsense. The only good thing about the whole weekend was that Ethan was true to his word—no one had mentioned Gabriella to him at all. There were some sad and pitying looks, but those were easy enough to ignore.

The wedding was in less than an hour, and as he stood in the corner and watched the flutter of activity going on around him, his thoughts strayed to Gabriella. How could they not? She should be here with him. They should be looking at all the choices Ethan and Summer made for their wedding and talking about how they would do it for theirs.

He sighed.

"You're looking mighty dapper today, Zach," William said as he strode over, a glass of champagne in his hands. "Can you believe your baby sister is getting married?"

Safe topic, Zach thought. "It certainly seems weird."

"Hmm…I imagine it does. I'm glad she's marrying a good man like Ethan. He's been like family for years. They're going to be good for one another."

Zach nodded and reached for his own glass.

"I think they're going to have a hard time finding the balance between the two coasts. Are you prepared for the possibility of Ethan moving here?"

It wasn't something Zach had thought about too much. He shrugged. "I wouldn't hold him back, if that's what you mean. I want him and Summer to be happy." He took a sip of his champagne. "It might take a while to get used to working with someone new—after all, Ethan and I have known one another our entire lives. We can communicate practically without uttering a word. We have plenty of potential to hire from within the company, but still, it won't be easy to find a replacement."

William chuckled. "Certainly not. It's not easy to find the right people, period." He paused. "Can I let you in on a little secret?"

Zach stifled a groan. He really didn't want to socialize and he'd had all the family banter he could stand for the moment, but he wasn't going to be rude. "Sure."

"Your aunt Monica and I are like that. That woman is in my head and knows what I'm thinking almost before I do. It's downright freaky sometimes."

Zach chuckled. "Well, you've been married for a long time. I suppose that's a contributing factor."

William shook his head. "It was like that from the get-go. Monica worked for Montgomerys when my father was at the helm. She was a secretary—back when you could still use that word—and she worked in the human resources department." He smiled at the memory. "I was smitten with her right away and was always looking for reasons to go down to see her. Of course she saw right through me. She seemed to know what I was bringing and then would follow it up with what she thought I should be doing rather than roaming around the office."

"I can hear her lecturing you," Zach said, the fondness in his voice very clear.

"Finally, one day, I asked her out. I was so nervous I could barely get the question out, and you know what she said to me?"

"What?"

William laughed softly. "From her seat at her desk she looked up at me and said, 'William Montgomery, if you hadn't wasted so much time bringing me silly nonsense paperwork, we could have been dating properly for over a month now!' I fell in love with her right then and there." He sighed happily. "Of course, that was just the beginning. She was just so in tune with my thoughts, my dreams. We were friends before we were anything else. We still are."

He reached over and gave Zach a friendly pat on the back. "What I'm getting at is when you look for someone to replace Ethan—if you have to replace him—make sure you genuinely like them. Don't just look at who they are on paper. Take the time to really get to know them." William took another sip of his champagne. "And that's just good advice no matter what the relationship is, right?" He gave Zach's shoulder a gentle squeeze before walking away and blending into the crowd.

"Well, if I wasn't mildly depressed before, now I have to worry about Ethan leaving me too," Zach murmured. The only difference was, Zach knew if Ethan left, it was so Summer would be happy. And that's really what Zach wanted, too. He looked at his watch. Forty minutes to go. He didn't want to chance any more chit-chat with the relatives, but other than hiding in a closet he couldn't think of what he could do.

Call her.

He shook his head. He couldn't do it. Not right now. There was too much potential for them to argue again. He'd call her when he got home and try to make some sense out of…everything. Ethan was right; Zach was tired of being a jackass and he was tired of being miserable. He just wasn't sure how to correct those things without making matters worse.

The wedding coordinator—his sister-in-law Casey—walked into the room. "Okay, gentlemen, we are getting ready. In a few minutes, you're going to line up and walk out to the sanctuary and line up in front of the altar like we rehearsed last night. The photographer will get some pictures and then the ushers will continue escorting guests up the aisle until I give you the cue to get back in line." She looked around the room and took a head count.

"At that point, the bridesmaids will begin their walk and then Summer and Robert will come up the aisle to you, Ethan. Then the ceremony. After Ethan and Summer are pronounced husband and wife, you will couple up with your assigned bridesmaid and follow them. We'll take pictures in front of the church after we go through the receiving line and then the remainder of the pictures will be taken at the reception venue." She looked over the list in her hands.

"Please finish your drinks now, use the men's room, and be picture perfect when I come back for you!" And then she was gone.

Zach looked over at his brother Ryder and walked over to him. "She runs a tight ship."

"It's not her first rodeo," Ryder said with a smile. "It still amazes me how she gets it all done."

"She looked completely in business mode. Is she going to change into her bridesmaid dress after she's done issuing orders?"

"Oh no. She's strictly here in coordinator-slash-guest mode. Her assistant's daughter got sick and couldn't be here to work the event, so Casey had to bail as a bridesmaid."

"Oh, man. Summer must be disappointed."

"She was, but she completely understood. Plus, I think it was comforting for her to know Casey will be taking care of everything."

"So what does that mean, we're down a bridesmaid?"

"Actually, no. One of Summer's college roommates is stepping in. She was already invited as a guest and she and Casey are similar dress sizes so it just worked out." Ryder chuckled. "Please, my wife would not be able to handle uneven members of the bridal party. It would ruin the photos!"

They both laughed. "I take it you've heard this sort of thing before."

"I've learned more about weddings in the last two years than I ever wanted to know. I blame Mac for making me help with his and Gina's wedding." He smiled. "But really, it was the best thing that ever happened to me. I might not have had the opportunity to win Casey back if I hadn't had that excuse to see her."

Lucky bastard, Zach thought. "Yeah, well, just as long as you stay on at the company and don't leave to set up food stations or take the groomsmen for tuxes, we'll all be fine."

"Are you kidding me? What my wife does is ten times more stressful than anything we do. More power to her. My job is practically a vacation compared to hers. Brides can be a nightmare."

"I'm sure Summer was no different."

"Nah. Summer just wanted to be married. Casey said she was one of the easiest brides to work with."

"That's surprising. Normally Summer is a handful."

"Ethan's really calmed her down. Helped her find her focus." Ryder smiled at his future brother-in-law across the room. "He's been good for her."

They stood in silence for a moment, each finishing their drinks before Ryder put his glass down. "Now, if you'll excuse me, I'm going to see if I can snag my wife away for a few minutes before the circus begins. I'll see you later."

"Yeah. Later." And then he was alone again. Wasn't that what he'd wanted just a few minutes ago?

Yeah, and didn't you want to spend your life with Gabriella just a few months ago? If he could punch his subconscious self in the face, he would. Now was not the time to start harping on that subject.

So he wandered the perimeter of the room, refusing to stop and really talk to anyone. He smiled. He nodded. He pretended to drink. It was almost a relief when Casey strode back into the room with a big smile on her face, Ryder right behind her.

"Okay, fellas! It's showtime!"

Chapter 15

"YOU KNOW YOU'RE TOTALLY STEALING MY THUNDER, right?"

"Only for a brief second. Once everyone sees you, I'll be all but forgotten."

"Not likely. You're going to be the talk of the night."

"I could totally back out. I'm serious. The last thing I want to do is take the spotlight from you. That wasn't why I came here."

"Oh, shut up," Summer said and smacked Gabriella playfully on the arm. "You're doing me a huge favor! My dad is a nervous wreck and on the verge of crying and I feel like I'm going to throw up, so really, as you walk down the aisle, if you want to tap dance or sing show tunes, feel free. Anything to keep those five hundred sets of eyes off me until I get to Ethan's side."

"You're going to be fine. This is the day you've been waiting for. You finally get to marry your knight in shining armor. How lucky are you?" Emotion clogged her throat as she said the words. Gabriella meant every one of them even as she envied her friend for finding such a perfect love.

"I know," Summer said softly. "But you have no idea how much it means to me that you're here. I know it wasn't an easy decision for you to make and—"

"Please, we both know I wasn't going to miss at least

seeing you get married. I was all set to perch up in a tree with a pair of binoculars if I needed to."

"This is way more dignified," Summer said. "Your gown is perfect. You look positively stunning."

"You have no idea how much I am loving my shoes right now." During their long phone conversation the other day, Gabriella had shared the transformation she'd undergone in an attempt to lay low for a while, so Summer completely got the heel relief.

"You are far too beautiful to live like that. Are you going to sleep in them tonight?"

"I just might."

"Okay, ladies!" Casey called out as she entered the bridal suite. "The guys are all lined up and waiting. Let's get you to the lobby and ready to go." She made a bee-line toward Gabriella. "I am so glad you're here. It was so hard to scramble around through the rehearsal last night without giving it away how you were part of the wedding party."

"So no one knows I'm here?"

"Oh, please. Everyone knows—except Zach. It's actually been kind of funny."

"I'm sure he won't look at it like that," Gabriella muttered.

"Well, that's his problem then, isn't it?" Casey looked around the room. "If everyone will follow me, we'll get you all lined up. Robert, you and Summer need to stay back a bit. When the doors to the sanctuary open, I don't want anyone to even get a glimpse of Summer. She needs to have her moment all to herself, okay?"

Robert Montgomery nodded, clutching his only daughter's arm like a lifeline. "Ease up, Dad," Summer said. "If you don't loosen your grip, I may spend my reception getting a cast on my arm."

"Sorry, sweetheart," he whispered. "I just... I just can't believe your wedding day is here. And by the end of the day, all of my kids are going to be settled."

Summer looked at him oddly. "Um...Dad? Zach's not settled."

"Not yet. But one look at Gabriella in that gown and he will be."

Summer squeezed his arm and smiled. "Let's hope so."

Gabriella's heart beat wildly in her chest. This was it. This was the last of her demons. She'd always stood up for herself with Zach—until the end. Then she'd simply been too broken to fight back. Now was her moment to get her self-respect back. She'd walk down that aisle with her head held high and not even spare him a glance. Then she'd stand there, less than ten feet apart, with a serene smile on her face.

She'd smile for pictures.

She'd dance with a dozen different Montgomerys.

And then she'd leave and pray he followed. It was a risk, but in her mind, it would all be worth it. She was done letting other people's thoughts and attitudes control her life. Gabriella knew what she wanted and she wanted Zach Montgomery—bad moods and foul tempers and everything about him.

She just wanted him to work for it a little bit.

"And now you, Gabriella," Casey whispered and directed her to the door.

Putting a dazzling smile on her face—one she actually felt—she began her slow walk up the aisle. Her heart rate had slowed down a bit and she couldn't believe the love she felt in the room. Not just for Summer and Ethan, but for her. As she walked, she got several thumbs-up from various Montgomery family members, but the biggest smile and "go get 'em" look came from William. She winked slyly at him as she passed by.

As she approached the front of the church, she looked at Ethan, who gave her a conspiratorial wink before looking beyond her for his first glance at Summer. Gabriella took her position next to the other bridesmaids and watched in wonder as Summer seemed to float elegantly down the aisle. Her blue eyes shone with happy tears as she kept her gaze on Ethan, and in that moment Gabriella knew she wanted that for herself—she wanted to know that moment of walking toward the man you wanted to spend the rest of your life with.

Unfortunately, hers was glaring at her right now. She didn't have to look at Zach to confirm it. She could feel it. That's how well she knew him.

For the entire ceremony, Gabriella kept her focus on Summer, fixing her train, holding her flowers... to the point that her eyes actually hurt from *not* looking at Zach. When the pastor finally pronounced them man and wife, Gabriella almost sagged with relief. She handed the bouquet of flowers back to Summer and then watched her and Ethan make their way up the aisle.

Now it was go time.

Stepping forward, she linked arms with Zach without even acknowledging him. She smiled all the way up the aisle and then took her place in the receiving line. But

Zach stayed close. He'd released her arm but he kept himself pressed to her side. Maybe it was because of the large bridal party and the size of the lobby, but Gabriella felt like maybe he could have put a little space between them—just to be proper.

But then again, when had Zach Montgomery ever been concerned with propriety?

Everything in Zach had stilled the moment Gabriella first stepped into the sanctuary. He wasn't the type of man who enjoyed making a scene, but he had been damn near tempted to stalk up the aisle and drag her out of the church.

And beg for forgiveness.

But he'd held himself in check and did everything he could to catch her eye, but she had been determined to not look at him.

And he knew she was doing it on purpose.

As the guests began to file out of the sanctuary and walk down the receiving line, Zach moved as close to Gabriella as he could get. He felt her stiffen beside him and almost smiled. They greeted the wedding guests and smiled and chatted. By the time Casey called them all to line up outside the church for photos, Zach was sorry they had to move. His hands were itching to reach out and touch Gabriella, to put his arms around her, to whisper to her how beautiful she looked.

"Zach, I want you standing behind Gabriella, just a little to the right so that we can see you over her shoulder," Casey directed and then the photographer took over.

"Place your hand on her waist and hold it there," he said and then went on to position the rest of the bridal party.

Zach was more than happy to oblige. After all, wasn't this exactly what he'd been after? Unable to help himself, he leaned in and inhaled deeply. Her scent had always driven him wild, and with her bare shoulders, her hair loose, and…god help him, those heels, she was too much of a temptation. "You look beautiful," he murmured in her ear.

She didn't respond. For a minute Zach thought she was being coy or spiteful, but the photographer was coming back over and made some minor adjustments before he began snapping photos.

It was the longest hour of his life—one of several that day alone, he realized. After the pictures in front of the church was the limo ride to the reception venue. Somehow Gabriella had managed to sit on the opposite side of the car from him, and he found this little game of cat and mouse kind of exciting. She might escape him now, but she couldn't forever.

The next round of pictures had him with his hand on her waist, her hip, her arm—hey, he was only following the photographer's directions—and he was loving every minute of it. She still had yet to speak to him, but once the reception began, Zach vowed to get her to.

When Casey finally directed them into the lobby to be introduced into the reception, Zach linked his arm with Gabriella's as he listened to what he hoped were their final instructions of the night.

"Okay, each couple will be introduced into the room. Ladies to one side when you get near the DJ, gentlemen to the other. Summer and Ethan, you'll be introduced and walk through the path your attendants have made for you and then the DJ will play your song for your first dance." She smiled at Summer. "Your first dance as husband and wife. The DJ will cue the rest of you when to join in, then the guests, and then…we're good until the cake cutting. But that's just for the bride and groom. Once the first dance is over, attendants, you're free to enjoy your evening!"

Relief washed over Zach. *Finally!* He waited until they were called into the room. He waited until Summer and Ethan began their dance. But as soon as the DJ invited the bridal party to join in, he immediately whisked Gabriella into his arms and pulled her close. He knew the exact moment she decided to try to pull back and the exact moment she simply gave up and relaxed against him.

It was the best feeling in the world.

"I've missed you," he said softly against her ear and almost immediately regretted it when he felt her stiffen in his arms. He soothed a hand up and down her back as the dance floor filled with friends and family. "I know you probably don't believe me but it's true."

He felt her take a shaky breath, and he tilted his head to hear her response. "I don't know how to believe you anymore, Zach. But this is not the place or the time to get into this. Please. I'm here for Summer and Ethan. Just…let it be for right now."

"For now," he whispered back and pulled her closer, simply relieved to feel her against him once again.

When the music ended, however, she became nearly impossible to find. Between all of his relatives and the dancing and even more picture taking, Zach couldn't find the opportunity to get close to Gabriella. Even at dinner, they were seated too far apart and he was growing more and more frustrated.

As soon as he saw the cake being wheeled out, he knew he had to make his move. The reception was coming to an end and if he didn't do something now, there was a very real chance Gabriella would leave and he'd have no idea how to find her. He should have done it sooner and cursed himself a thousand times over for being so stubborn.

He stood with his brothers as Summer and Ethan fed one another cake. "So," James said from his left side. "Quite a day, huh?"

"Oh yeah. Gotta love a wedding."

"I paid the photographer extra to get a shot of your face when Gabriella walked into the church," Ryder said from his right. "I've seen deer in the headlights with a less shocked look." He chuckled. "I may make that my new contact picture for you."

"What is it with this family's fascination with getting awkward pictures of me all of a sudden?" Zach snapped. "First Summer, now you."

"We just like catching you acting human once in a while," James interjected. "Plus, it's just fun."

"Yeah, well…find another way to have your fun. I'm not here for your entertainment."

His brothers both chuckled. "Are you sure?" Ryder asked. "Because you've been very entertaining tonight. Why don't you just go over and talk to her already? Please! Do us all a favor and get it over with. I've got a hundred bucks riding on her slapping your face and storming out."

Zach's head snapped around to look at Ryder. "*What?!* You're betting on me?"

"And Gabriella," James said. "I put money on

Gabriella throwing a drink in your face." He put his hands in his pockets and nodded approvingly before adding, "And then storming out."

"And I'm the jackass of the family," Zach muttered. "It's nice to know I have the support of my family right now when I need it most."

"Hard to support someone who is clearly going to blow it again because he's willing to sit back and let the woman he loves walk out of his life *again* without fighting for her," Ryder said and then patted Zach on the back. "Think about it, bro." And then he and James walked away.

Zach realized the cake cutting was complete and people were dancing again and he'd lost sight of Gabriella. "Dammit," he muttered. He stalked the entire room in search of her before Summer and Ethan stopped him.

"Okay, enough," Summer said. "No more scaring the guests, no more scowling. I'm done. I'll admit you played nice and smiled for the pictures but…please… just go after her already!"

"I would if I knew where she went!" Zach yelled and immediately apologized. "Honestly, I've been trying to talk to her all night but she's been kind of elusive."

"Do you blame her?" Summer asked.

He sighed with frustration. "Do you know where she is, Summer? I promise I'll leave and stop…scowling or whatever it is you say I'm doing, but I have to know where she is!"

Summer seemed playfully hesitant but luckily Ethan took pity on him. "She's up in the bridal suite with Casey. She's helping her get everything wrapped up." He placed a hand on Zach's shoulder. "Don't screw this up."

Zach was already sprinting from the room by the time Ethan's hand was back at his side.

Racing out into the lobby, he took the winding staircase that led up to the second floor bridal suite two steps at a time. It wasn't until he was up there that he realized he did that sprint without any pain. It was enough to stop him in his tracks. He actually stopped and flexed his leg and felt completely invincible.

He strode down the hall to the suite, more determined than ever to convince Gabriella to give them another chance. He knew he didn't deserve it. Hell, he knew he shouldn't even ask her to consider it after the way he'd behaved.

But damn if he wasn't going to do it anyway.

Because at the end of the day, no matter how he looked at it, Zach knew his life wasn't worth a thing if he didn't have Gabriella at his side. He stopped in the doorway to the suite and Casey spotted him first. She didn't alert Gabriella to his presence and quickly excused herself. As she walked out the door, she whispered to Zach, "Don't mess this up!"

He chuckled at his family's faith—or lack thereof—in him.

Slowly, he stepped into the room and stopped a few feet away from Gabriella. She had been placing gifts into large bags for transport and she suddenly stopped and straightened before turning—as if sensing his presence.

"Zach? What are you doing up here?"

"I told you I wanted to talk. I left you alone during the reception, but the party's dying down and I didn't want to take a chance on you leaving before I could talk to you."

"I honestly don't know what you could possibly have to say. I think you said it all back in Portland."

He sighed. "Yeah, I know. I said a lot of stuff without really thinking and I know I can't take it back, I can't make you un-hear it, but you have to know, it…it didn't have a lot to do with you."

"It felt like it had to do with me," she countered.

Zach took a hesitant step forward. "You know me, Gabs. You know me better than anyone. In that moment, I felt completely emasculated. I wanted nothing more than to take that bastard by the throat and pound him into the pavement for the things he said and—"

"Oh really?" she interrupted. "Because I seem to remember you agreeing with him after he left."

"Only the things he said about me! I couldn't defend you! I couldn't…I couldn't even defend you against that weaselly bastard! Do you have any idea how that made me feel?"

Her eyes went wide, flashing fire. "Do you have any idea how that made *me* feel? I mean, honestly, Zach. Your leg gave out. I get it. But you were still recovering. It couldn't be helped! But what you did to me? That completely could have been helped!"

"Gabriella, let me—"

"No. I'm done listening to you explain. I've been listening to it for months…years. And you know what? Your words mean very little to me anymore." She crossed her arms over her chest, cocked a hip that allowed the high slit in her gown to show a long expanse of leg. "I've listened to you and I believed in you. You told me you loved me and at the moment when I really needed you, you bailed." She stepped closer and poked a finger into his chest. "I was there when you needed me and you weren't willing to do the same for me. That's not love, Zach. That's selfishness."

Zach hung his head in defeat. "Gabriella, I've worked so hard my entire life. When I fell off the mountain, I wanted to die. When you came to the house and agreed to work with me again, you gave me something to work toward. You made me want to live again, and not like I had before. I wanted to be better. And for a time, I thought I'd accomplished it. But I had a setback. I made a mistake."

"A big one."

"Okay, yes. It was a big one, but…honestly, I didn't want you to be stuck with a man who wasn't…who wasn't a complete man."

"So you think I'm so shallow I wouldn't want to be with you, I wouldn't love you, because of a limp? Or because you couldn't punch my stupid brother-in-law in the face? Zach, in that moment I would have gladly punched Alan in the face myself, but I don't believe violence solves anything. And if you bothered to think about someone other than yourself, you would know that."

"I made a mistake. I know that. I've apologized. I swear it won't happen again. Please, Gabriella, please give me another chance," he pleaded, stepping forward and taking her hands in his.

"They're just words, Zach. I think you've proven you'll say whatever you need to to get your way. I'm done falling for it." Spinning away, she picked up one of the large bags and strode from the room.

"Gabs, wait! Tell me! Tell me what you want.

Anything…and it's yours. Please. I don't want to go home without you. I need you!"

She gave him a bland look. "Really? Do you need me as your assistant or as your girlfriend? Or are they supposed to be one and the same?" She paused. "I can't do it anymore, Zach. I'm tired of having to wear so many hats with you and yet never being enough. It's exhausting and I deserve better."

"You do. I know you do. You deserve only the best. But I love you and I want to be everything you want. Everything you need. Tell me what you want, Gabs. Please." He hated groveling, he hated begging, but right now he'd get down on his knees for another chance.

"For years we knew each other's every thought. We finished one another's sentences. I shouldn't have to tell you what I want, Zach. I left you and Portland because I knew what you needed right then and there." Her expression saddened. "It would be nice to know you paid as much attention to me as I did to you." She paused. "Good-bye, Zach."

This time, he couldn't bear to watch her walk away.

Sitting down on one of the plush sofas, he slouched down, his head resting on the back cushions.

"So you blew it?" Casey said as she came back into the room and began cleaning up.

"It looks like it."

"Hmm…that's a shame. Can you hand me those glasses please?"

Zach sat up and eyed her curiously. "That's it? That's all you're going to say about it? No lecture? No 'I'm really disappointed in you' speech?"

She shrugged. "What's the point? I figure you're

beating yourself up pretty good already. To just jump on the bandwagon would be overkill…and mean."

"Try telling that to the rest of the family before I go back down there."

She chuckled. "Sorry, Zach. You're on your own there. I'm on the job here and I don't have time to get involved with family drama."

"But it's a family wedding," he said.

Casey stopped bagging up gifts as her hands dropped to her sides. "Well, yes and no. Today, I was Casey Montgomery, wedding coordinator. I didn't ask for special treatment, and if you noticed, I didn't slack off on any of my responsibilities. I ate dinner with the family but as soon as I was done, it was back to work. My role as coordinator didn't hinge on my being married to Ryder. Work and family are separate. They have to be. Lines get blurred far too easily. Summer didn't ask for special favors and I didn't provide any."

Zach relaxed as Casey started up her task again. Soon he stood and began helping her clean the room. "So you'd never hire Ryder to work with you?" he asked.

Casey burst out laughing. "Hell no! We need the time apart. I love your brother more than I ever thought it was possible to love another person, but I love our time apart too. I like knowing that when he sees me, he sees his wife, his life partner. Not his business partner. I've seen it happen too many times to couples. It rarely is a good thing to work and live together. Eventually somebody's dream gets pushed to the side." She shook her head. "I definitely wouldn't want to see that happen."

They worked together in silence until the room was completely cleaned up. Then he carried all of the boxes and bags down the stairs and out to the car that would take everything back to his parents' home where it would all stay until Ethan and Summer got back from their honeymoon.

And then he was alone.

Standing outside looking up at the stars, he thought about all the conversations he'd had today—with his uncle, his brothers, and Gabriella. But it was his conversation with his sister-in-law that finally opened his eyes. Running back inside, he did a quick sweep of the room to say good night to his family. When he got to his sister, she hugged him close and shoved a piece of paper in his hands.

"Go get her," was all she said before kissing him soundly on the cheek and then shoving him away.

Gabriella rode the elevator up to her hotel room and sighed wearily. She was so happy for her friends and for the fact she had been able to be a part of their wedding, but it left her feeling even emptier than she had before.

Why did some people get to find their soulmates while others didn't? "It doesn't seem fair," she murmured as she pulled her key card from her small beaded purse. The elevator doors opened and she walked to the end of the hall. It was an indulgence—this night at such a swanky hotel. Her home was an hour away and she didn't drink so it wouldn't have been a hardship to drive, but it had been a while since she'd pampered herself and this seemed like the perfect way to do it.

Once in her room she lit only one of the small bedside

lamps and went out on her balcony. The hotel was right
on the beach, the sky was clear, and there was a slight
breeze that felt wonderful. Seeing a star off in the distance, she decided to do something she hadn't done
since she was a child.

She wished upon it.

Closing her eyes, she breathed in the night air. "I wish
for…happiness. I wish to find direction in my life so I
can discover what I need to finally be happy." Opening
her eyes, Gabriella wrapped her arms around her middle
and let the cool breeze wrap around her.

She had no idea how long she'd been standing out
there when she heard a knock on her door. She *had*
stopped at the front desk on her way in and asked for
more pillows. The king-size bed was fabulous but the
pillows were lacking a little so she wanted a few more.

Stepping back into the room, she slid the balcony
doors closed and walked to the door. "Who is it?"

"Housekeeping."

Without looking through the peephole, she opened
the door.

And almost fell over.

"Zach," she whispered. "How…? What…?"

"Can I come in?" he asked quietly and smiled when
she stepped aside to let him in. He immediately walked
across the room and looked out the balcony doors.
"Great view."

"How did you know I was staying here?"

He turned and looked at her. "Really? Did you think
no one was going to point me in the right direction?"

Gabriella couldn't help but chuckle. No, she wasn't
surprised but she wasn't sure what else there was for

them to say. "What are you doing here, Zach? It's very late and it's been a long day and—"

"I came here to fire you. Officially," he said.

"Excuse me?"

"It occurred to me that I never really fired you. Not formally. And you didn't tender a resignation either. I'm here to clear that up. So…you're fired."

She stared at him as if he were insane. "Is this some kind of sick joke?" she asked incredulously. "Because if it's not, then it's just mean, Zach. Even for you."

A slow smile crossed his face as he took first one step and then another toward her until they were standing toe to toe. "It's not a joke and I'm not here to be mean. I'm here to officially terminate your position as my assistant—"

Gabriella stepped away from him with disgust. "You are unbelievable, you know that?"

Zach smiled patiently. "May I finish?"

She glared at him. "If I let you finish, will you leave?"

Rather than answering her, he simply went on with what he wanted to say. "As I was saying, I'm here to terminate your position as my assistant so I can hire your firm to help train the new staff I'm going to be hiring for our expansion."

Her expression changed from hostile to wary. "I… what do you mean?"

"I understand you're considering starting up an agency that specializes in executive assistants. I'd like for you to take Montgomerys on as a client."

"A client?"

He nodded, shoving his hands in his pants pockets. "Carolyn's fine as an assistant but she could be better, and now she's going to need her own assistant. Ethan's going to be moving here to North Carolina within the year and chances are his assistant won't stay, so my new VP is also going to require a well-trained assistant. Speaking from personal experience, finding the right assistant is very difficult."

Her lips began to twitch with the urge to smile. "It can be. Especially if the executive is difficult."

He took a step toward her. "Oh, I'm very difficult."

"And close-minded. It's another familiar trait."

"I'm working on it." Another step.

"But the worst trait in you executive types is how you take your assistants for granted. I'll need some proof that prospective clients are fully committed to being the type of bosses my trainees deserve."

"I'd be more than willing to…demonstrate how committed I am to anything you want." He kept walking forward until Gabriella's back was against the wall. Reaching out, he gently stroked a hand across her cheek.

"Anything?" she whispered breathlessly.

Zach nodded. "Anything." Their breathing was ragged and Zach knew she was just as aroused as he was. "Gabriella?" he murmured, leaning his head toward hers.

"Kiss me." It was said so softly, so quietly she wasn't sure he even heard her but suddenly he was kissing her, his hands seemingly everywhere at once. Thanks to the slit in her gown, Gabriella pulled Zach close and wrapped her leg around him.

Zach's hand was on her thigh, holding her to him as he feasted on her. She sighed as his mouth wandered over her bare shoulders, her throat. She sighed his name as she raked her hands through his hair and pulled his lips back to hers.

It was madness and she knew she should be thinking with a little more clarity, but right now she couldn't. She'd been without the man she loved for too long. Zach shifted and lifted her until both of her legs wrapped around his waist. He raised his head and looked at her. "Gabs?"

"Yes. Please," she panted and almost groaned with relief when he turned them toward the bed. He'd placed her down on the bed when there was a knock on the door. "Oh…damn."

Zach looked down at her. "Were you expecting someone?" he teased.

"It's housekeeping. More pillows," she groaned.

"Stay there. I'll be right back." He walked out of the room and she heard him open the door, thank whoever was standing there, and then close the door.

And bolt it.

He came back into the room and tossed the pillows on the floor. "We'll deal with them later. Right now, all I can think about is you."

She smiled shyly and held out a hand to him to pull him down beside her. "That's good," she said. "Because I want to be all you can think about."

His hand roamed from her ankle to her thigh and back again. His expression hot, his hand exciting her as he continued the journey back and forth.

"Don't worry," she said after a minute. "The shoes are staying on."

He smiled and placed a knee on the bed before reaching for her ankle and unhooking the rhinestone-studded stiletto.

"Zach?"

He smiled at her. Sexily. Tenderly. "I think tonight we should take them off."

It was possibly the sweetest thing he'd ever said to her.

—∿∿—

The sun was starting to come up and Gabriella was sprawled across Zach's chest, watching the sunrise through the balcony doors. "So you really thought firing me was the way to get me to forgive you?" she asked sleepily.

They'd spent hours making love with short bouts of sleep in between. This was the first opportunity they actually took to talk.

"In my defense, I thought it would be a good conversation starter."

"Maybe someone needs to come in and train you," she teased.

He chuckled. "Maybe. But I wanted you to know I'm in love with you, Gabriella, as a woman. It isn't because of the job you did for me or anything work related. I want you—the woman. I don't want us to get settled into a routine where you're the only one sacrificing for me. I need to do a better job of paying attention to your wants and needs and dreams. You don't have to take me on as a client but I'd like to help you get your dream business off the ground."

She snuggled closer. "I appreciate that, Zach. I really do. It means a lot to me that you'd trust me to do that."

"How could I not? There's no one better than you.

And if you can't be my assistant anymore, then I'd like knowing you trained your replacement."

"Well…just know this. My replacement is going to be old. Like, in her sixties and happily married and a grandmother to at least eight."

"What?" He chuckled. "What are you talking about?"

"If you think for one minute I'm going to hire anyone young and single who wears high heels to work for you, then you're crazy. You're mine, Zach Montgomery. All mine."

He kissed the top of her head. "Sweetheart, that's all I ever wanted to be."

Epilogue

Six months later

"UM...YEAH. I'M NOT DOING THAT."

"Oh, come on. Don't be such a baby. It's not so bad."

"Easy for you to say. Uh-uh. I can't. Let's just go back to the hotel and forget about the whole thing."

"Not gonna happen."

Zach tried for a distraction. "Did you ever figure out that text earlier? What it meant?"

She looked at him quizzically for a moment. "Oh, you mean the one from your uncle?"

"Yeah. It seemed a little weird. Even for him."

She shrugged. "Something about our favorite college. I don't know. I told him we'd think about it."

"Maybe we should. I mean, how do you feel about the Ivy League schools?"

Gabriella stared at Zach for a solid minute before breaking off in a fit of laughter.

"What?" he demanded. "What's so funny?"

"You are! Nice try with the distraction! You do realize this is relatively tame by your standards and you're refusing to do it!"

They were on their honeymoon, standing at the top of a nine-story-high waterslide the resort was famous for. "It's crazy! Why would anyone want to freefall for nine stories? It's insane!"

"This from the man who used to jump out of airplanes. You know those leaps were higher than this, right?"

"Sure, but there were parachutes and guides… It was completely different."

Gabriella stretched, the fabric of the tiny white bikini practically transparent. Zach groaned and she smiled. "I'll tell you what—you follow me down and then we'll spend the rest of the day doing whatever it is you want."

"Anything?"

She nodded. "Anything."

He studied his wife. It was a tempting offer. Very tempting. It had been a long time since he'd felt the pull of any extreme activity, and although she was right and this was fairly tame in comparison to the adventures he used to take, Zach no longer felt the need to push the limits.

"Okay. Fine. One time, and then…we're going back to the room and you're losing the bikini."

"Ooo…I like the way you think."

"And we'll swim in our own private pool."

"I like that even more," she purred, then pressed up against him and kissed him thoroughly on the lips before turning and sitting down at the top of the slide. The attendant explained the proper position to hold for the fall. Gabriella looked over her shoulder at him. "See you at the bottom."

He nodded. "See you at the bottom." He loved the look of pure joy on her face as she took off and knew he'd finally found his greatest adventure of all in Gabriella. Feeling anxious and excited, he assumed the spot at the top of the slide and waited for the thumbs-up from the attendant before taking his own leap.

It was fast-paced and blindingly terrifying. But just knowing his wife was down there waiting for him made it all worthwhile.

*Read on for a sneak peek at the next book in the
Shaughnessy Brothers series*

Love Walks In

STEPPING INTO THE EVENING AIR, HUGH SHAUGHNESSY looked around and couldn't help but feel a sense of pride. It never got old. This was his. All of it. He'd worked hard, invested well, ran a tight ship, and knew his limitations. Sure, he could have expanded on most of his properties, but Hugh liked a more intimate atmosphere—a place where couples could come and relax. Let the bigger names compete for acreage and the most amenities. What he had accomplished with his resorts was in a class by itself.

The walk to his suite normally would have had him turning to the left, but Hugh took the path to the right, toward the gardens. He was restless. Within the hour he'd have dinner brought to his suite and he'd be alone with his thoughts. Not that it was an unusual scenario, but tonight it felt a little more…lonely.

Luckily he had a trip home coming up. It had been almost six months since he'd been back. The last time had been for Darcy's birthday and even that had been nothing more than a quick weekend.

Or maybe he needed a date.

It had been about three months since he'd last spent a weekend with a woman and while it certainly wasn't a record for him, it was amazing how fast the time had gone and how it hadn't occurred to him until right then. As he strolled around toward the back of the main building, Hugh tried to picture his date's face in his mind and couldn't.

That couldn't be good a good sign. No matter. It was what it was. Note to self—after closing this deal with Bellows and finding a replacement for Heather, he needed to relax with the family. Then it hit him—maybe he should call Riley. Hell, his little brother was one of the biggest rock stars in the world. If anyone could hook him up with someone for a weekend fling, it would be him.

Problem solved. With a renewed pep in his step, he turned the corner and saw some movement up ahead. Guests didn't usually come around to this part of the resort. It was the back of the main building—there weren't any signs to stop them or warn them away, but it was mainly parking spaces, a couple of small storage buildings, and trees. Nothing to see.

Slowing his pace, he saw someone peeking into one of the windows. Odd. Doing his best to stay out of sight without losing sight of what was going on, he heard some rustling in the bushes lining the back of the building. Some were taller than others and now, from where he was standing, he couldn't tell what was going on.

With no other choice, he stepped back out into the open and walked toward this potential…what? Peeper? Perpetrator? Seriously, he had no idea what it was he was about to confront.

"Dammit," came a muttered voice and Hugh decided it was definitely female. *That* piqued his interest. He stopped just on the other side of the tall bush shielding her from his view and realized the woman was looking in *his* window! The window to his office! What in the world?

Not a minute later, he was appalled to see she was sliding the window open! How had he managed to lock the door of his office and not the window? Damn it, he'd opened it earlier in the day because the temperatures had been so mild and sometimes he just needed to smell the fresh air when he was cooped up in his office.

It wasn't likely to happen again after what he was currently witnessing.

The window squeaked and it snapped him back to the present. Great, he was so busy obsessing about fresh air he had forgotten about the person trying to break into his office! Stepping around the shrub and ready to haul off and give this person a piece of mind, Hugh immediately stopped short, his jaw hitting the ground.

There, right in front of him, were two of the longest legs he'd ever seen and quite possibly the world's most perfect female bottom.

In nothing but a hot-pink thong.

His throat instantly dried and his heart rate kicked up. He stood—mesmerized—as her sexy bottom wiggled back and forth. He couldn't tear his eyes away.

Or move.

In that instant, it didn't matter that she was trespassing. It didn't matter that she was clearly breaking and entering. All that mattered was watching the movement of her body.

Then she disappeared through the window and into his office.

It took a full minute for Hugh to realize he was staring at nothing but his window before he shook his head to clear it and made his move. In a flash, he was silently through the window, and his sexy intruder hadn't noticed. She was looking around the dimly lit room and unfortunately, he couldn't get a good look at her.

Standing in the corner, he continued to observe. If she was going to try and steal something, he wanted to be certain to catch her in the act. In a perfect world, he'd hit the lights as soon as she took something that clearly didn't belong to her so he could press charges. He hated people touching his belongings—especially when they so blatantly held such little regard for his privacy.

But who was she? Why was she here in his office?

"Finally," he heard her mutter. Stepping closer to his desk, he reached for the small lamp there and turned it on. A small scream escaped her at the intrusion of light.

"Is there something I can help you with?" Hugh asked with a calmness he didn't feel. As soon as his eyes adjusted to the light, he felt as poleaxed at the sight of her face as he had at the sight of her climbing through the window.

The first thing to register was the fact that she was wearing more than the hot-pink thong. She had on a strapless white dress. It hit mid-thigh and showcased a curvy body and tanned limbs. Her hair was long and blond and she looked like some sort of beach goddess.

Huge blue eyes stared back at him. One hand covered her heart as the other covered her belly. "Who…? What are you…?"

"Doing in my own office?" he supplied. "I believe that's what I should be asking you. How about explaining why it is you're in here and why you decided to climb in through the window? Some call it breaking and entering." Hugh watched the play of emotion on her face as she lowered her hands to her sides. He expected tears. He expected apologies. He certainly didn't expect attitude.

"You stole my suitcase," she snapped at him.

"*Excuse me?*"

"You heard me," she said, crossing her arms over her chest and cocking a hip. "That suitcase right there? It's mine. You had no right to take it."

Hugh was stunned speechless. He owned the damn resort—didn't this woman realize that? "You left it out in the middle of the property. I brought it here to keep it safe. Anyone could have grabbed it and taken off with it. I was simply making sure nothing happened to it."

She rolled her eyes. "Yeah, yeah, yeah. Whatever. It wasn't your responsibility. I left it there for a reason."

He cocked a brow at her. "Oh really? And what was it?"

"None of your business," she said evenly, then looked at the watch on her slim wrist. "Look, are we cool here? Obviously the luggage is mine so…can I go?"

Was this woman for real? "Actually, it's not obvious the luggage is yours. There's no tag on it, no identification. And if you knew it was in here, why didn't you go to the front desk and ask for it?"

A little of her bravado seemed to fade. "They were busy and…and…I needed to get it so I can go."

"Leaving already? Were you even a guest here?"

She nodded. "I really need to go. What's it gonna take to prove to you this suitcase is mine?"

The resort was small enough that Hugh normally recognized his guests. He didn't recognize this woman and God knew she was attractive enough that had he seen her before, he definitely would have remembered. "I don't believe you."

"About what?" she asked incredulously.

"About being a guest. I know all of our guests. I've never seen you before."

She rolled her eyes again. "We just checked in this morning. What are you, resort security?"

"No," he said smugly. "The resort owner."

Those blue eyes went wide again. Slowly she composed herself. "Okay, Mister Resort Owner. What happens now?"

"You said 'we just checked in.' Who's 'we'?"

"It doesn't matter. I checked in with someone and now I'm leaving. It's not a crime."

"No…but breaking and entering is."

"You stole my suitcase!" she cried.

"Okay, we're going around in circles here, Miss…?"

"Burke. Aubrey Burke."

"Do you have ID?"

"In my purse."

Hugh looked at her expectantly.

"It's outside in the bushes."

About the Author

New York Times and *USA Today* bestseller Samantha Chase released her debut novel, *Jordan's Return*, in November 2011. Although she waited until she was in her forties to publish for the first time, writing has been a lifelong passion. Her motivation was her students; teaching creative writing to elementary age students all the way up through high school and encouraging those students to follow their writing dreams gave Samantha the confidence to take that step as well. When she's not working on a new story, she spends her time reading contemporary romances, blogging, playing Scrabble on Facebook, and spending time with her husband of twenty-five years and their two sons in North Carolina.